THE CAYMAN HUSTLE

THE CAYMAN HUSTLE

DEVI DI GUIDA

Om-7 Press   Montreal

FOR MY HUSBAND JOSEPH,
MY CHILDREN ROBIN, NODIN AND SONJALI
AND IN MEMORY OF WESLEY BAUER

PART ONE

The mind is its own place, and in itself
Can make a heav'n of hell, a hell of heav'n

John Milton,
Paradise Lost

PREAMBLE

THERE ARE an estimated seventy million deaf people in the world and no clear statistics to show how many have jobs and how many are unemployed. My name is Kaman Colioni. I am deaf and currently unemployed. I have set my sights on the beautiful Cayman Islands with all intentions to hustle and find a job.

1   Grand Cayman Island

"PARADISE," Emma Wedgewood whispered as she lifted her face toward the bright, late afternoon sun. She felt sweat on her brows and turned to look at the expanse of blue sea that touched the sky. Taking a long sip of the local rum cocktail, *a Hurricane*, she instantly felt the brain freeze from the icy cold drink. The sun's glare forced her to close her eyes. She shook out her shoulder length, dyed black hair with its tinted brown streaks, inhaled the salty air and sighed in contentment. "Now that's a Category 5."

She tugged at the shoulder straps of the one piece bathing suit that hugged her full figure as she settled herself on a lilo. Sucking in her stomach, she looked at her legs. At least her long legs and her oval face had not given in fully to the aging process. Throwing aside those thoughts, she drifted off idly into the shallow waters of Seven Mile Beach behind her new residence, The Government House. At fifty-seven years old, a widow with no interest in relationships, she was honored to be elected as the next governor of the Cayman Islands. Slowly she mouthed out the title that would be hers once she took office in two weeks, "Her Excellency, Governor Emma Wedgewood." Too formal and too stiff, she decided. She didn't get to where she was by being one for formalities, she reflected. Yes, she was tough as nails, but it was mostly her people skills that had contributed to her illustrious career within the global financial market.

Although she had an analytical mind, Emma was not one who was afraid to take chances professionally. This was what had propelled her upward and now, onward, to this paradise. The timing was right, given it was now August 2009, supposedly the end of the recession and three years to her retirement. Who in their right mind would pass up an opportunity to retire in the world's second tax haven?

"Not bad for a girl from a little Yorkshire village in England." she mused.

It wasn't going to be a staycation, she knew. Last week, she had met with her boss, Nigel Moore, head of MI7, a new secret test unit recently set up to oversee the Representatives of British Overseas Territories, or ROBOT as referenced in communications. The meeting was to bring her up to date on The Cayman Islands' role as a British Overseas Territory, or BOT, her duties as governor and a ROBOT, and other matters of interest in the Caribbean.

"It is estimated that Britain loses more than a billion pounds in revenue having the Cayman Islands as a BOT, but . . ." Nigel paused shaking his silver-grey head. "The motherland does need these BOTs. It gives us a super power feeling to have these jewels in the crown."

At sixty, Nigel was a tall and handsome man with a commanding presence. With thirty years of experience in the secret service, his name had been up against hers for this appointment. Although he didn't show resentment toward her, Emma sensed he was disillusioned. Being her boss was a one-upper for him.

Emma's protocol had been clearly outlined. She was a political voyeur for the Motherland. An observer and a watchdog with a glorified title. Nothing more, nothing less.

Of primary importance to MI7, is that she keeps a watchful eye on the super yachts. Some of the billionaire owners are misusing the island for activities other than tax evasion. Recently there had been a gold heist which MI7 thinks may surface on the black market. There were also other problems bubbling under the surface. The opening of a casino also had to be watched. The local contact had passed on news that the locals were going to picket. Drug trafficking was becoming the biggest issue as it made its way from South America through Central America to the Caribbean and then rerouted to North America.

"Pornography is a small worry. Don't preoccupy yourself with it though. I see it as quite a lucrative business that boosts employment globally, especially for women." Nigel had said with a straight face.

"An upper class Dick," Emma muttered as she remembered that conversation. She was still weighing and sizing up the capabilities of MI7. What was that dodgy something about this test unit that she could not quite put her finger on?

She was advised that the CIA, the Caribbean Intel Agency, not to be confused with the other guys, have offered the services of two undercover agents who will work with the local contact. Updates will be forwarded to her.

Emma was given a special mobile which must be in her possession at all times. She knew what that meant. They will be keeping an eye on her.

As a single parent, Emma had her own personal agenda in accepting this appointment; a chance to make up for lost time with her daughter, Kara. At twenty-five, Kara was vivacious and friendly except her numbers weren't quite aligned. She had a mind of her own, sometimes two minds. In her heart of hearts, Emma wished her only child was not so star-crossed with her sixes and sevens, a worry she hoped this paradise island will counterbalance. She was pleased that Kara had found a job at the Tortuga Cake Shop.

Since Emma's arrival three weeks ago, she had been busy overseeing the renovations of the house while they stayed at a hotel close to Georgetown. How good it was touring the Cayman Islands in full with Kara; they hopped from the touristy Grand Cayman to the sister islands – Little Cayman and Cayman Brac. It had been a bonding period for both of them.

On a late night outing alone, Emma stopped at the ice cream store in Camana Bay and saw a naked woman dancing in the water fountains. Emma's chest tightened at this sight. In due course, she learnt that people had nicknamed her the water nymph who wasn't quite right in the head. Emma understood mental illness firsthand. Since Kara had been diagnosed with bipolar disorder at an early age, she had devoted much of her spare time as a volunteer in mental health institutions. She was saddened when she found out there was no care, social services or treatment center on the island for Caymanians. She was told that efforts had been made to acquire funding for such a facility but very little had been collected. This, she found, was a real 'piss off.' So many billionaires raping the island and not one had put up a farthing for this? She vowed that before her term was up, by hook or crook, there would be such a facility.

Emma heard a splash, and smiled a welcome to Kara as she settled on a lilo beside her. "How was your day, darling?" she asked, admiring Kara's svelte tanned figure in a white bikini.

"Busy. Five cruise ships in port. I sold 103 boxes of Tortuga cakes," Kara answered as she tossed her red curls backwards and dabbed suntan lotion on her face. "Oh, Mother, I saw the most beautiful thing today. A double rainbow. It was right after that spot of rain at lunch time. Did you see it?"

"No, I didn't. A double rainbow? Now, that's rare."

"Yes, it is. I also met a deaf man who was quite charming and funny."

"Did you now?" Emma was surprised to see her daughter in such a good mood after work. Kara had never been able to hold down a job for more than a day. This was day five.

"And hungry and funny. He kept gobbling up the sample pieces and, when I took the tray away and reproached him, he apologized and said that his palate is having a hard time deciding whether Tortuga Cake tastes better than Bakewell Tart." Kara's blue eyes twinkled in mirth.

"Was he British?" Emma asked with a smile.

"Not at all. His name is Kaman which he jokingly said rhymes with Cayman. He's Canadian but visits his UK family in York and Derbyshire. He wore a T-shirt with the Yorkshire slang *Eeh Bah Gum* in the front, with the translation *Oh my God* in the back."

"He only had one name, this deaf man?"

"Oh, no, Mother. His full name is Kaman Colioni." Kara swished the water around her, cupped a handful, closed her eyes and let it drip slowly on her forehead. As it streamed downwards, her face broadened into a full smile. It had been a long time since Emma saw her daughter with a smile on her face.

"Now that's a happy smile darling. What are you thinking?"

"Happy thoughts."

Emma made a mental note that she *must* meet this deaf man.

Kara sat up gingerly. "I forgot to tell you, mother, the renovation foreman said there are wood ants in the house and they will be here for another month. This morning, I saw a snake in the driveway. It was disgusting."

"Bollocks." Emma swore under her breath. "A snake? Are you sure?"

"Yes. The foreman caught it in a bag, but then it slipped out. Gone in a blink." She paused and trickled water through her fingers. "Maybe we should get a place in The Nexx Complex. It's close to the government house. This way, you get to see the renovations at the house on a daily basis and we still have the beach at our disposal." Kara's face mirrored her excitement. "What do you think, Mother?"

Emma's body broke out in a cold sweat in the heat. She bit her lips in revulsion as she imagined a snake in her personal space.

Paradise can be hell at times.

2 Camana Bay

IN ESSENCE, love makes no sense. In fact, there is more nonsense than sense in love.

Great philosophers – Socrates, Plato and Aristotle alike, could only ponder on this delicate and mystifying subject, and that was way before I graced this planet with my own messed up resonance of *amour*. Perhaps in an effort to make sense out of nonsense, the meaning of love was lost in translation over time, or by the mere fact that, to this day, there has been no valid interpretation.

How then, could I, Kaman Colioni, having lived a quarter of a century, get love right?

You see, getting things right has never been my strong suit. Now, as I sit on a shaded terrace in Camana Bay, where love was once so passionately declared, I started to question other aspects of my time in this not-so-forgiving world. I am indifferent to the world around me as I dwell on my sad state of affairs. For starters, the hard-on-the-butt wooden chair was too small for my six-foot-three, 220-pound muscled frame. I had thought a college degree in marketing with years of work experience in the world-renowned franchise *Montreal Pizza* would be interesting enough to invite job interviews. But in the end, none of it mattered. To date, I have not had a single interview.

Maybe I was just a glutton for punishment because, of all the places to sit and enjoy a coffee, I had chosen Café-del-Sol, the one that harbored the most memories with my ex-girlfriend, India Weinberger. It was she who insisted that I mention the small detail that I am deaf on my curriculum vitae. She had even made me do the unthinkable: attach a headshot of what she called, 'my friendly rugged face.'

India and I had some things in common: we were of visible mixed ethnicities, recent college grads and loved diving. Like me, she was twenty-five years old. She was not an ethereal beauty, but heads turned to admire her shapely figure topped with long, glossy jet-black corkscrew curls that framed a heart shaped face. Many turned for a second look at her unusual topaz-gold eyes that were as mystifying as the colors of the Cayman sunset.

My self-pitying reverie was disturbed by a commotion. I turned my head toward the sound and concentrated as Om-7, my hearing device, did his work.

A female security guard in front of Books & Books appeared to be under attack by a huge, weird-looking dog tied to a fire hydrant, or so it seemed, but at a closer glance, it wagged its tail, which meant it was being playful. People stood around at a safe distance watching as it jumped around the guard. A well-dressed lady rushed out of the bookstore and quickly took control, using hand gestures and leash maneuvers. The animal immediately went on all fours, blue-black tongue hanging out. Words were exchanged in a friendly manner as the crowd dispersed and the mollified guard moved on. The owner with the canine in tow headed toward the terrace.

The dog, the lady and I recognized each other at the same time; but it was the dog that rushed toward me, barely able to control his excitement. On reaching my table, he jumped up, clumsily knocking over the café au lait on my shirt and slobbered my face with wet, slimy saliva.

"Chewy, down boy! Down!" I said, forgetting he was deaf like me. I spoiled him with love until he calmed down and tucked his head on my lap.

"Kaman." Dr. Olga O'Ligue greeted me, her voice tinged with surprise. She was easy on the eyes, dressed in an executive-style, tight-fitting beige suit, with open-toed, high-heel sandals and an oversized handbag. She was a tag hag – loving everything that screamed designer.

Our acquaintanceship ran back to my teenage years when I spent time in her company professionally, thanks to my parents, and for reasons I am not totally comfortable rehashing now. My face broke into a half-hearted smile. I had always addressed her as "Dr. O" though she preferred that I call her Olga. Still, my upbringing did not allow me to address someone who may be twice my age by their first name. India had a special name for her – Double O.

She dropped a copy of the *Caribbean Express* with a bold red headline on the table and extended a hand in greeting. As I stood up to take her hand, I read the headline: 12 MILLION $US GOLD STILL NOT FOUND.

I think, *now there's a job with a good payout.*

"I am so sorry for your shirt and your drink. May I join you?" Dr. O asked as she reached into her handbag and gave Chewy half a coconut shell, filled with the white, nutty flesh that he attacked as though he had not eaten in weeks. Although she had lived in Canada for decades, she hung on to a crisp British-English accent. "Let me replace your drink. I could use one myself."

"Sure," I answered half-heartedly, pulling out a chair for her, as the waitress arrived to take our order. At the waitress' departure, Dr. O turned to me with a genuinely warm smile.

"So," she began, "can't say I am not happy to see you, but it does surprise me. What brings you to the island?"

I shifted uncomfortably in my chair. She was the last person I had bargained on meeting. Maybe she had forgotten that day when I had rushed out of her office during a therapy session.

"I'm doing what all unemployed college grads do." I answered in a tight tone. "You know, hanging loose, wasting time, heart-broken at the moment, and drowning my sorrows over a woman who may have been the love of my life, but who turned out to be the one who got away."

"India?"

"Yep."

Dr. O was India's aunt, by adoption. A well-respected psy-chologist and a radio-television host at one time, she had written a trilogy of best-selling books on love and sex, with very juicy, over-the-top graphic scenes that, ironically, appealed to housewives and perverts alike. Though meant for baby boomers, she had a huge following of young adults. After the first book's release, she had become an overnight sensation, sometimes referred to as the "Queen of Orgasm."

"I am so sorry, Kaman. I really thought you were both in it for the long haul."

"That makes two of us."

"Did you try and do anything about it?" she asked, sounding soothing and sincere.

"Nada. Zilch. I tried once and, when that didn't work, I decided to cut my losses. Call me old fashioned, but I'd rather deal with my depression than yield to my desperation."

"Nothing?" She raised an eyebrow. "Who broke it off?"

"She did."

"Did she give you a reason?"

"Verbatim, 'I need space and time apart from you. I have to find who my biological parents are. It has always been a question mark in my mind. There are so many secrets in my life that haunt me. Until I can free myself from it, I can't do this love thing. It wouldn't be fair to you or to us.'" I paused a minute, not for effect or anything, but because I realized that talking to my ex's aunt and venting my frustrations to her might be about as useful as trying to milk a bull.

"Wow. I am sorry to hear that. I knew India wanted to find out about her past, I never thought she would go to this length. I really didn't think she would make you feel like you were being abandoned. You know, you might want to . . ."

"Doc," I raised my hands up, palms out, to stop her, "you're doing it again."

"Doing what?"

"You're psychoanalyzing me. I am not your patient."

"I guess I am. Habit. Bad habit, I have to admit." She checked on Chewy.

Dr. O had a way of getting into your head and turning things around so that, one minute you were pissed off with the world, and the next you were a gifted soul, ready to take the universe into your hands and spin it in any direction. I had been more than content to sit here drowning in my sorrow and advancing through the grieving process.

I had no desire to tell her that, besides being heart-broken, I was almost broke and was only on the island thanks to the generosity of a mysterious fan named Zingaro who followed my deaf blog. He had sent me a plane ticket to the Cayman Islands as a thank you for the jokes I often posted, which he found funny. I still have yet to meet him. I entertained thoughts that some miracle might happen, whereby a decent looking guy with a slight handicap, such as yours truly, could manipulate his way into employment. But then, that was the humorous side of me striving for equilibrium, while I continued to host a serious pity party.

I picked up the empty cup, swirled the dregs, while thinking of a response that would not reveal too much. Being in a conversation with Dr. O was almost like being in a mental chess game. From my time in therapy with her I had learned it was best to take early control of the game. All it took was one, small verbal disclosure, and she was off to the psyche races. I was too frail to go through that bullshit.

"Let's put love aside. What's the real story behind your visit? Are you working here? Tell me."

"No, not working, but currently seeking employment."

"So, you've been interviewing?"

"Yes. Struck out twice today," I lied. "Looks like the sympathy card doesn't play in the corporate world, when my only work experience is rolling out pizza dough."

I patted Om-7, as he buzzed in annoyance. I am well attuned to the peculiar sounds that he emits that are indicators that he is in an erratic behavior mode. As weird as it is, these special sounds, while seemingly random in nature, are directly related to my own behavior, and although he is a thing that sits on my ear, I am sometimes awed by his apparent self-awareness. A buzzing sound is his reaction to any outrageous lies that pass through my lips.

"How about you? By the way, congratulations on the success of your books."

"You read them? That's so nice of you."

"No actually, I haven't had a chance to." I had always been an avid reader, but I intentionally avoided reading her novels for fear that I may find a character with my profile. I opted to change conversations. "Do you still live on Paradise Beach?"

"No. I live over there in The Nexx Complex, by the water." She pointed to a block of condos known for its upscale tenants. "What am I doing?" She took a deep breath before answering her own question. "Busy. Tired. The whirlwind life of being a best-selling novelist is exhausting. I'm supposed to be working on my next book to meet my contract deadlines. Since my husband Baron passed on . . ." She wavered, took some more deep breaths, "It's almost a year . . .," she stopped in mid-sentence, and exhaled. "Things change when you lose someone close to you. I have no desire to live in the condo on Paradise Beach."

"So you have two homes?" I asked.

"Yes, I like living in The Nexx Complex. I keep the beach condo vacant. Too many memories of my life with Baron. I have to say, writing has been a way of subduing the pain of losing someone I loved dearly."

I can relate to the 'too many memories' part, for it was in that same beach condo India had proclaimed her love forever and ever on our past visits to the island.

I wondered if she was hurting like I was.

"Are you staying on the island for long?"

"Depends if my status changes soon." I answered. Not quite the truth, as Jalebi, my lil' sister who works for the FBI, that is, the Food Bank International, had texted she would be delayed for an uncertain amount of time in Africa. Since my stay depended on her pocket book and the uncertainty of finding employment, going home any time soon was a definite question mark.

"Then, why not have dinner with me? The hardest thing, I find, since Baron died, is eating alone." She removed her sunglasses. Her eyes were still that amazing ice blue, appearing warm and intense and, at an unspecified baby-boomer age, she remained a lovely sight, as she sipped her drink.

Sensing my reluctance, she added, "I am alone, you are alone. Please, be by guest." She said.

I agreed, as the thought of a free dinner, and maybe some booze, held lots of appeal.

 Dr. Olga O'Ligue

DR. O HAD reserved at the French Fusion located along the waterway. The waiter, his name tag read "Ernesto," was friendly, average height and good looking. With book-style menus in hand, he led us to a table in a secluded corner. He apologized when he pulled out the chair for Dr. O and found it was wet with coffee stains. Frazzled, he left to find a replacement.

As we stood waiting for his return, Dr. O, leaned into the mirror that covered the upper half of the walls, positioned in such a way that diners had their privacy once seated. She scanned the room before her eyes focused on the right side of the mirror. I noticed that her facial expression changed. I turned my head slightly to follow her line of vision. There were two tables against the opposite wall. One was occupied by a stocky, middle-aged Japanese man with a double chin who was dressed in a black shirt with white hibiscus flowers. His companion was a beautiful blond woman who appeared to be in her late twenties. The other table was occupied by a lone man who I estimated to be in his mid-thirties. He had a shaved head, pumped-up muscles and tattoos along both arms.

I assisted Ernesto with the chair on his return. He bowed a thank you, and for seconds, his brows furrowed as he stared at Om-7. I am used to this scrutiny of my hearing device and so as not to make people uncomfortable, I usually point to Om-7, smile and make light of it, with, "I am not deaf." Ernesto smiled in return and said, "I-I believe you aren't."

Truth be told, I was not feeling adventurous, and being a recent college grad, I was only good at distinguishing between fast food burgers and strong alcohols. Dr. O seemed to know the ins and outs of the menu so I allowed her the liberty of ordering the hors d'oeuvres. As I perused the beverages section, *El Dorado 15-Year Special Reserve* rum jumped out at me. "You seem indecisive. I am having wine. Have whatever you wish." With such an open invitation, I ordered a bottle of my favorite rum and downed three stiff ones in between small talk about her writing career, forgetting my worries as she explained the basics of book publishing and the work involved in finishing a manuscript.

"You look pitiful. Sort of down and out." She gazed at me intently, as I fiddled with the foie gras feuiletté. I have to admit I was feeling somewhat uncomfortable at the way she did this. "You know, Kaman, you should give serious thought to writing. You'd be good at it."

"Why would you think that?"

"Your blog about being deaf is quite quirky and interesting."

"You follow it?" I was surprised.

"Oh yes. That's why I think you can easily cross over to a career in writing. Wasn't this your dream?"

I rubbed my hands through my hair. She remembered I had a secret wish to be a novelist. What else did she remember? It has been years since we last spoke. I thought my streak of bad luck had run its course when my wallet, passport, and cell phone were stolen earlier in the day. It was all India's fault. I had been reading a muddled text message that ended with a sad-faced emoji that was actually the very first communication from her since we parted ways. I deleted it as it didn't make sense.

What bugged me more is that I didn't walk away from this rendezvous.

She waved both her hands in front of my face. "You didn't hear a word I said."

"Yeah, I did. Blogging is for fun, Doc. Other than that, I'm an unemployed marketing graduate with barely any work experience. And it took me longer than the average student to finish a degree. Other than gaming consoles and, maybe, my ability to expertly maneuver myself through a good bottle of rum, my life hasn't been full of interesting things or people to write about." My tongue was getting looser with my liquor intake, so was Dr. O's, judging from the way the tip of hers circled the glass.

"Besides, what can I write about? My breakup? Millions have had similar breakups. Shakespeare had fun with Antony and Cleopatra and Romeo and Juliet" I tipped another shot of rum, savored the aroma, my palate loving the melange of fruit, tobacco and chocolate. I swallowed it slowly. "All dead. Such tragedies. Hey, though I'm drinking and pissing my sorrows away, I am alive and kicking."

"Aha!" She exuded delight as she raised the balloon glass. "Now you're onto something. You may just have said the most sensible thing tonight. Heartbreak sells. So does sex."

"What is sensible about writing on a topic that has been done a million times? Besides, when you look at me, Don Juan isn't the first thing that comes to mind." I touched Om-7 who was dangerously quiet.

"Look at it this way. You are a multiracial, multilingual kid, who grew up in a proclaimed multicultural city. Throw in your need to succeed, the different friends, the different schools, the so-very-different parents. You've had a romance that has seen its fair share of ups and downs. And to top it off, there is your handicap of being deaf."

Her reference to my being deaf is a reminder of Om-7's role in my life. He's my buddy most of the time, though he switches from being my nemesis to my mimesis depending on the sounds he hears. His worst characteristic is picking up irrelevant stuff which he regurgitates at the most unexpected time, like now. *"Three multi's and three differents."* He tweets into my head. I tapped him gently in response.

"Yeah, I know this," I answered Dr. O. "I've been ridiculed most of my life for being a mute, a mutt, or a geek. All roads pretty much lead to what may be a boring read."

"You're a marketing grad. You know sex sells. Throw in a lot of your sexual relationship with India. The more, the better." She smiled and for the first time, I noticed that her cuspids were quite pointed. Maybe it was all the vampire books I had been reading lately, but at a second glance, they looked like fangs.

I exhaled and attempted to cover my rising uneasiness. Ernesto returned to ask if the meal was to our liking and engaged her in a discussion about the varietal of the Cabernet Sauvignon she drank, a bit thirstily, I might add. He did extend a courteous smile and indulged in small talk while he served the meal. I couldn't figure why he looked at me oddly, then at my hearing device in a strange way.

Not that this bothered me. I used to be very self-conscious about wearing a hearing device. As far back as I can remember, the first models had antennae. People stared at me and the antennae sticking out of my head as if I were an alien. Over the years, Om-7's DNA evolved with science and the model I now wear hooks over the top of my ear and is connected to a moulded clump of plastic stuck in the outer ear's orifice. It's a nice looking piece except it has a few kinks; the major one being sound amplification. Earlier, when I went to change in the public facilities at Camana Bay, the guy in the next cubicle did an anal salute to the toilet bowl. The acoustics that reached my ear was like a volcano erupting.

There've been several Om-7's in my life. My very first one was the best. Remembering him always brings a smile to my face.

"You're smiling. It must be a good memory." Dr. O remarked.

From her smile, I gathered that she thought I was remembering my intimate and very personal togetherness with India.

"It is." I said. "I'm reminiscing about the Russian audiologist who fitted me with my first hearing device in exchange for a demijohn of bush rum. He was a friend of Uncle the Drunk."

"Blimey." She giggled. "Here I am thinking that it was some nice memory of you and India in coitus."

It crossed my mind that I should have studied psychology instead of marketing. It pays good money and it doesn't matter if you're deaf. So far, I'm getting Dr. O's numbers right on cue.

"For the record, that's one area of my life that I don't share."
I answered.

"So you're nostalgic about your first hearing aid? Wasn't this
done in Cuba? If memory serves me correctly, you were very
young then. How can you remember? The first memory only goes
back to the age of three-and-half to four years."

"I *was* three-and-a-half years old. I remembered the scientist.
He called me 'comrade' during my stay in the hospital. I specifically remember this trip to Cuba, because Fidel Castro visited
me on one occasion to check out this new technology. *Nueva
tecnología*, he called it. He brought me a pulled pork sandwich.
Because it was the first time I could hear clearly, I heard my
Uncle the Drunk, mention that the pork was from a swine caught
in the Bay of Pigs." I felt I was justifying myself because no one
has ever believed this story except my mother.

"See what I mean. You tell cute stories." Dr. O laughed, a
gurgle-y sound that Om-7 was impartial to.

Her cell phone beeped, interrupting this nice exchange. She
looked at the screen before she answered the call.

"Excuse me. I can't hear a thing with the noise in here." She
rose from her chair and briefly glanced into the mirror. With the
phone plastered to her ear, she headed outside. I turned to have
a look at the opposite table. The Japanese man had left. The man
with the tattooed arm took his seat and stared aggressively at the
blond woman who now was doubling up on cocktails.

I tripled up on the Special Reserve, long acknowledged as the
Caribbean's premier rum.

Dr. O had a dismal air about her when she returned a few
minutes later and sat down with a frown on her face.

"Are you okay?" I asked.

She guzzled down a quarter glass of wine before answering
me. "Nothing I can't handle."

4 Opportunity Knocks

SHE LOOKED at the cell phone once more, then placed it beside her handbag. I gathered that it had not been an entertaining phone call.

"What were we discussing? Ah yes. We were speaking about you writing your memoir."

"Doc. Face reality. I'm not a rock star. Or famous. Nor have I done anything monumental that will appeal to readers. Who would want to read about a deaf man and his struggles?"

"There are people out there who want to hear a deaf man's voice, about the trials and tribulations of growing up within a multi-state of identities, about your love life and how you came to be in this pathetic state of being so madly in love with a cocaine addict, especially the details of what took place in my beach condo." The soft blue eyes were now a cold, hard slate-gray.

I downed another glass of the 15-year rum that had won so many prizes worldwide, my tolerance juice at the moment and met her steady gaze. Boy, is she hot and cold. She was always an anomaly to me, with an intelligence that was captivating, but there was something frightening about her ability to dissect my inner thoughts. Her real intentions always eluded me. They seemed to occupy a gray area between being a talented and accomplished therapist and a conniving woman who wanted to guide me and watch as I self-mutilated my psychological well-being. I've loved figuring things and people out, so it is no wonder that I always wanted to know what Dr. O's motivation was, why she had to know, and for what reason she had to be, 'in the know.'

I concluded this demi-analysis that she needed a shrink.

"So, let me get this straight, just to see if the booze is affecting a little more than my speech. Here I am, totally messed up. The love of my life decided she has to find herself." I stared her down and grew ever more serious. "By the way, she no longer has an addiction. To continue, my ex-shrink, showed up and elected to psychoanalyze me. For what, old times' sake? I held onto the empty glass for some kind of support. "And now, you want me to write about how screwed up I am, have been, and will be, not for my benefit, but for yours." I placed the glass on the table. "So, to keep things honest, are you giving me an assignment?"

"You shouldn't think of it as such, but more as an indexing of your life's timeline. It could be a good thing for you, considering how, and I quote, 'screwed up' things are for you now. Maybe it will give you some perspective."

"You really think I need more perspective?"

"Yes, and it is a good thing. I am doing some work on psycholinguists and how the human brain is linked to languages. You are a deaf man. So you had to find what works for you and what you can do best. Once you can determine this, then it becomes your own survival tool. In your case, you used the deaf disadvantage to your advantage, and so well that your blog has aroused a whole lot of empathy. Still, there is that twist of how you can speak five languages so easily, including Mohawk. How many people do you know who can speak this language outside of the Mohawk community?"

"Correction Doc, I speak only three languages. Sign language is not a 'speak' lingo, and I only know about two hundred words in Mohawk. I am too inebriated to digest this scientific crap, and I still think you are playing me a little. Kinda like blackmail. To be honest, it may be a little unprofessional. Look, my concentration is all about finding a job, making some money and just hanging loose."

"Why are you so bitter? You think I'm blackmailing you?"

"Yeah. It's more of an emotional hijacking type thing. Sounds like you want to use me as basis for your next book or paper, or whatever that psycho-cunnilingus mumbo jumbo you spoke about."

"It's psycholinguists. What if I told you there was a paycheck involved? It's a standard fee, really," she said sweetly.

My eyes squinted at this information. "How much?"

She named a figure that had some interesting zeroes, but, in my intoxicated state, I had difficulty comprehending it. Om-7 whistled at the mention of money, he always does, followed by his tweeting as he once again regurgitates. "Salaries are negotiable," my Pa screams into my good ear. "Don't let anyone take advantage of you because you're deaf." My Ma calmly advises in the other. "Money, money, mo-ney. Chichink, chichink," Biig Baba, my older brother is singing. Jalebi, my lil' sis is enticing me with, "Hey, come down to the Cayman Islands. There's jobs aplenty here. We can have the annual bonfire on Paradise Beach."

This was my family. We were all born of a unique, blended, unconventional heritage that empowered us to be emotionally resilient. We did not expect our lives to be predictable, systematic and orderly. We were different, and once we understood this basic concept, we embraced our distinct identity. Life as we knew it became a cliché with a mantra: persistent optimism in the face of adversity is the best ultimate guarantee of success. We were so damn tight.

Where are you all now when I need you the most? I asked, not expecting an answer as I knew this already. Like God, they were always busy, on holiday or held up in something or the other. Ma and Pa were still on their world cruise, hopping from ship to shore and sending postcards to me at each port of call. Last I heard from Biig Baba, he had been hired as a private investigator and was now on a mission impossible to track the Mexicans and their trade routes for human trafficking in the Caribbean. Jalebi, my younger sister had been in constant contact and texted wherever her job with the Food Bank International took her.

I stilled my wandering mind as Dr. O continued texting away aggressively.

"Excuse me," she whispered. "Won't be long." The way she punched at the keys, I could tell that the person at the other end was on her case.

My inner ear buzzed to life, distracting me from the current monetary discussion and reminiscences of the people I held dearest in my heart. I guided Om-7 so that I could have better spatial hearing and sound localization. I sometimes liked, and at other times disliked, the discomfort that these auditory hallucinations caused, defined as *paracusia*, where within the absolute threshold of at least twenty feet, I can hear people whisper. Slight angle adjustments later, I am tuned in and listening to the conversation from a table some distance away, hearing things that the normal ear cannot pick up.

"Yoo, mon, the boat sailed from Venezuela with Guyana gold. Twelve million Yankee dollah in 24-karat gold bars. I tell yuh, its waiting fuh someone to grab it." Creole, from Jamaica. I know that lingo.

"*Ah oui*. Oh yes. *C'est big.* This is big." Franglais. Québécois dialect. I know this person, Toussaint les Patants, practicing his east-end Montreal accent. We played hockey together since we were in grade school.

"Yoo. What's with you and *ah-we,* ah-we? Speak English, mon." I was wrong. It was Creole from Guyana. I recognized the voice of MJ Rafiq, Trinidadian by choice, currently an expat Caymanian who always knew the latest shit that's going down around town. He was a very old friend from my childhood days. "So, where ez the drop off?"

I leaned my head at an angle so that Om-7's receivers could pick up and transmit the intonation to my brain.

"Paradise Beach." I couldn't place the speaker. However, I knew that Dr. O's beach condo was located there.

"I say we take it then. Small job. Big payout."

Om-7 sings in my ear. He too had recognized that voice, had heard it from the first time my ears started playing tricks with me – my brother, Biig Baba. Over the years, I had shortened his name to BB for simplicity.

"Holy f," I stifled the f-bomb out of respect for Dr. O. She reached for my hand on the table and entwined her fingers with mine as I fidgeted with Om-7.

"You need to exorcise and cleanse yourself. You must write this memoir. It will be like yoga for the mind," she chirped.

I removed my hand from her grip. Touchy-feely was not my modus operandi. I didn't want to send out vibes that she might misinterpret. "I would like to re-negotiate the salary." I chirped back at her.

"How can we re-negotiate? We haven't even negotiated."

"Well then, let's start the process. I am looking for . . ." I name an amount much higher than her offer.

"Ah. You like to play the numbers game. Let's take that sum and divide it in two. I will even throw in the beach condo."

I cannot get my head off the conversation I had just overheard. Twelve million Yankee dollars in gold bars close to the Doc's beach condo.

I came back in time to hear Dr. O say, "on condition that you keep Chewy. I am leaving for Europe very soon. Be warned, because I want you to know exactly what you are getting into." Her tone was businesswoman bossy. "Sex sells. A memoir of a deaf boy's sex life with a cocaine addict will sell even more. The deliverable is five chapters as soon as possible with a finished draft for review in three months."

"So I am writing your book? You are devious, Dr. O."

"Not really, you are providing the research subject and material. It will keep your brain busy. And take your mind off India."

I sighed. Dr. O was the only link to India. I had a momentary flashback of India's text message I had deleted.

Please cooperate with Double O. ☹

It is the emoji of a sad face that bothers me.

I slumped in my chair, not because I felt defeated, but mostly because whomever designed the chair didn't really have orthopedics in mind. I was not thinking of the ordeal of writing. I was ruminating over $12 million in 24 karat gold, waiting to be grabbed, within the vicinity of her beach condo. And the emoji of a sad face.

"I need to sleep on this, Dr. O. Does the offer of the beach condo still stand?"

"Oh yes. The code key is still the same as when you visited the last time with India. Take Chewy with you just in case. We'll pick him up on the way out."

"Just in case what?" I slurred.

"He might just save your drunken butt." She quipped.

Very funny, I think. That's like a pot calling its bottom black.

 ## 5 William Churchill Stuttered

ERNESTO came to wish us a good night. His shift had ended. He was replaced by Bjorn, a blond waiter who spoke German to Dr. O. From the cordiality he extended to her, I surmised they knew each other very well.

Since the Cayman was a last-minute decision, I had travelled with a backpack stuffed with only the basics. I had lived with less, but the funding of this little expedition was troubling, as I currently had enough money to last me five days if I lived frugally, now that the rest had been stolen.

There was something about drinking rum straight or on the rocks. It took a short time to reach the brain cells and a longer time to make its way through the system before sending messages you had to go. Another notable about rum, which I forgot at this time, was never drink too much, too fast, or you become a messed-up ass. This lesson was taught to me by Uncle the Drunk at a very tender age, which involved a machete, a rope, a coconut tree and a donkey. But that is a story for another time.

Since Dr. O and Bjorn were still in conversation, I excused myself to search for the public facilities. When I got up, I felt dizzy and held on to the chair until I was steady. Not one to waste time, I seized the opportunity to check out my buddies whose intriguing conversation I had overheard earlier.

They were seated in a semi-circular booth, only their heads visible in the candlelit decor of the restaurant. Toussaint wore a baseball cap over his blond crew cut with his signature sunglasses perched atop. MJ Rafiq's dreadlocks looked real, but I knew it was fake hair imported from India and weaved into his 150,000 real hair follicles that had sprouted to a three-inch growth and refused to grow a millimeter more. BB wore his hair long and scraggly. The fourth person in the booth was a man with salt-and-pepper hair who wore dark-framed glasses.

Although I was not desperate to go, I still felt a tickle around the corner, which meant I should probably pre-emptively strike it. I headed toward the open air with the intention of having a smoke and finding a suitable spot to take a leak.

The terrace was loud with Friday night, white-collar revelry. Someone bumped into me in the narrow aisle.

"S-sorry. Excuse me." I turned around. It was Ernesto. He was now dressed in a parking valet's uniform. It was understandable, as quite a number of expats held two jobs.

"No worries." I spared him a smile, feeling sorry he had no social life. Yet, he was better off than I, at least he had a job.

I walked to the stairs that led to the waterway. A bridge passageway led to a man-made island. It was bordered by a few palm trees illuminated with lights that danced on the water. I was on the first stair when I realized Ernesto was behind me.

"You following me?"

"N-no," he tapped a cigarette in his palm. "S-smoke."

I had noticed that Ernesto had a distinguished way of speaking when he served us. He took deep breaths before he said what he had to say. As he walked down the stairs, he spoke Spanish into his cell phone. I heard it – long pauses before he started a sentence. At the bottom of the stairs, he walked over to a grassy patch and sat in the dark. Om-7 picked up a tune he hummed. I was transfixed as I listened. Shit, I am drunk. I had to be. My parents sang that song to Biig Baba, Jalebi and me when we were younger. My Pa sang one line in Italian and my Ma followed with a line in Hindi. Together they sang the last verse in English.

I fumbled in my pockets for a cigarette, walked over, plopped myself beside Ernesto and asked for a light.

"So where do you valet?" I tried for small talk.

"I-in the parking lot of this complex. W-we can't all be lucky like you." Yup, it was there – long pause, deep breath, hesitation before he spoke.

"What do you mean by that?"

"Y-you sir, the doctor. Things got pretty intense in there. Y-your sugar mama takes care of you."

"Oh, no. You got that way wrong, brother."

He looked confused. "S-so. So what was that? I know when a woman is in heat and that doctor was on fire!"

"It was just a job offer brother. The most intense grilling I ever had. But I think I nailed her. I mean, it. Can I ask you a question?"

Ernesto lifted his shoulders and shrugged off a quick, "S-sure."

"Why do you think I'm her boy toy? You think I'm knocking boots with her?"

"I-it's nothing personal. It's just August according to the other waiters. I've only been on the island two weeks."

"So you're saying it's like a new moon type of thing that makes people assume that a man and woman hanging out are automatically intimate?"

"N-no man. My fellow waiters explained it to me like this. During the summer months, men bring the kids and wife-ys to the island for a good time, and leave at the end of August. Within a week, those same men return with their mistress, girlfriend, boyfriend, hooker or whatever they are into. It's the cheat month. Tips are usually bigger at this time. They call them guilt tippers."

"So basically, she bought me diner, offered me a job, her beach condo to stay in, and for me to babysit her dog. What do you think that means?"

"Y-you, my friend, have gotten yourself a sugar mama. Enjoy it!" He lifted his hand up in the air expecting a high five, but I was a little too drunk and too shocked to process it.

He looked around in a sneaky manner, which had me puzzled, as he seemed a nice sort. Walking closer to the water, he unzipped his pants, and let a stream into the canal.

I joined him. He started to laugh. I chuckled.

"Y-you know," he paused, shaking off the last drops. "Winston Churchill is known to have taken a piss in the Great Thames before a meeting with heads of state and royalty. He didn't even have time to wash his hands. So, we are only following the footsteps of a great and eloquent statesman. It's hard to believe he stuttered."

He zipped up his pants, in a macho man manner, lifting up his heels, pulling the zipper up and, if you are a guy, you would understand what I mean. But in the event you do not know; this is how it works. If you are pissing in the company of the same sex, how you zipper up your pants is an indication of your sexual preference.

Ernesto was straight, so I really wasn't worried that he would be rubbing one out later thinking of me. I followed him as he made his way to the water fountain under a dimmed light. From the corner of my eye, I saw the Japanese man smoking a cigar approach from another direction. I checked him out as he went past. His double chin appeared to be triple-layered in the dim light. On his neck, he had a small snake tattoo. Probably a businessman, I think, as snakes bring good luck in Japanese superstition.

"Hey, my brother. I am embarrassed. Ever happen to you that you know someone and can't remember the name that goes with the face?" I whispered to Ernesto.

"N-never," he chuckled. "You've been hitting the bottle pretty hard during dinner."

"I know. The girlfriend broke things off. I'm pretty messed up right now. I feel such a fool because I'm still trying to remember that guy's name. You served him earlier."

"I-I am surprised you don't remember. Your sugar mama met up with him half an hour ago. They were having a pretty heated discussion."

"That's why I feel so foolish. I can't remember his name."

"I-I-zanagi Yoshio. There was a story about him in the papers today. He and his wife Shizu are making a huge investment in casinos on the island."

"Aw yes, that's it. Thanks my brother."

'A-and what's your name?" He asked.

"Kaman." I squinted my eyes to read his name tag. "Ernesto, I think, I am pissed drunk."

"Y-you are. G-go easy on the booze. It damages the brain." He waved a goodbye.

On my return, Dr. O was absent. I ordered some iced water from Bjorn and questioned him about the doctor's whereabouts.

"Oh, she left a message for you. You can go over to the condo to get the dog." From his stilted English. I could tell he was a newcomer to the island.

A brain fart struck me. Had she left without paying the bill? Now, this will be embarrassing if I have to pay for that extravagant bottle of rum. When Bjorn returned with my latest order, I had worked up the courage to ask about the tab.

"Oh no, no. Olga always looks after her guests. She has a running tab. It's the shits, because I have to wait till the end of month to get my tip." I breathed a sigh of relief. His change of manner indicated he was not happy with the doctor.

When he left to attend another table, I focused Om-7 to the conversation at the circular booth. Boring, as they spoke about the iguanas that basked in the sun in the middle of the road and how difficult it was for motorists to avoid running over them. Not as exciting as hearing about the gold heist they were planning. I tuned out.

Bjorn returned as I was getting ready to leave.

"What, no dessert. Oh, I see." He winked at me, in that, 'oh, I know' manner with a smart ass smile. "Dessert is served at Madam O's boudoir. I did hear she was into coloreds these days."

I got off my chair, ready to punch the smile into his head. But then, hands and a forceful bodyweight pushed me against the table. I turned to look Biig Baba straight in the eyes. It was like looking into my own eyes in a mirror: brown, almond shaped, long lashed with a steady gaze over a sizable nose that our mother jokingly said looked like a distorted Italian tomato. The only difference was that his eyes rested on a face covered with white skin whereas mine was set in bronze.

"Sorry. I didn't expect you to get up," BB apologized. "Here, let me help you." I was so thrown off balance that, like a child, I allowed him to straighten the chair and watched as he pushed it to a neat, square position. He turned to Bjorn. "Give this dude a tall glass of coconut water on the rocks. No more booze. From the looks of his face, he is ready to puke. You don't want that, do you? Put it on my tab."

When Bjorn left in a hurry, BB whispered. "Make yourself scarce. I am onto something big. And check your pockets." He swaggered off leaving me stupefied.

I had plenty of time to recuperate when Bjorn returned with the coconut water. I noticed the Japanese man, the man with the snake tattoos and the pretty blond woman were leaving.

"I am sorry for saying those things." I knew then that BB had spoken to him. It lifted my spirits up a notch to know my brother was still looking out for me.

"No worries." I reassured him. "See, I am only the dog watcher while she's on her book tour. As a matter of fact, I probably will come have dinner here more often while she's away. She did say I can put it on her tab." Om-7 buzzed at this lie.

He walked me to the exit when I left the restaurant. "Come again. I usually keep the bones for Chewy." I actually liked the guy. I asked him for directions to Dr. O's condo.

"Be careful," he said. His voice sounded a warning but it was the added emphasis of his furrowed brows that convinced me he was serious.

6 The Ketchup Kid

CAMANA BAY had a decent amount of people for an August weeknight as I exited French Fusion. With designer boutiques, restaurants, cinemas and outdoor cafes, it attracted tourists and locals alike. I did a detour to the Observation Tower and held onto the rails for steady support as I climbed the four sets of stairs to the top. India and I had always liked this view at night. To the far right, lights blinked back at me from Rum Point and, though some buildings blocked the view of Seven Mile Beach, the hotels that dotted the edge were lit to illuminate sections of the beach. Below, the shops and stores had sprinkles of customers. The water fountains, the main attraction to the urban complex, spewed up and dropped down while a few teenagers in their bathing suits enjoyed the coolness of the spray.

I descended, my stomach a bit queasy as I reached street level. The teenagers had moved on from the fountain and now stood making faces and monkey antics into the live webcam, something I had learned about first-hand when India and I decided to take a small dip in the pool sans the proper attire, or more accurately, without any attire at all. In my head, I repeated the directions Bjorn had given me: walk to the end of Market Street, cross the canal over to The Nexx Complex, follow the walkway that leads to the courtyard, go past this to the last block of condos, climb the stairs, take a quick left, go down the corridor to the last unit.

As I rang the doorbell, a pimple-faced adolescent opened the neighboring condo door. He held a laptop and looked away as soon as I made eye contact, then slammed the door shut. My stomach was now in a ridiculous uproar, a sign that I knew denoted discomfort. Bjorn's snarky remark resurfaced. I rang the doorbell a few times, before Dr. O, with Chewy in tow, opened it. As usual, he greeted me with a slobber bath.

"Sorry, I had to leave. I think I had a bit too much wine. Come in for a bit. I will get the dog's stuff ready." She closed the door, leading the way in to an open concept affair, each room overlooking the other with large windows that allowed a view of the waterway. Sliding doors opened to a balcony. From what I observed, the condo was two-storied as there were steps leading to another floor. As I turned to admire, she busied herself placing toys and dog treats in a bag.

It had no shortcomings in terms of decoration as the divan and the accessory chairs were black and white, with tropical plants and brightly colored vases to offset the starkness. The few steps that led to the second story were carpeted. Altogether, it fitted well with her persona: elegant.

She offered me a drink, which I declined and asked if I could have water with ice instead.

"Come," she invited when she returned with water and wine from the kitchen. "There's a gorgeous view from the balcony upstairs."

"Would love to see it, Doc," I said, as flat, dopey and vacuous as a delivery guy in a second-rate porn scene.

She held onto to the rails to steady herself as she climbed the carpeted stairs, her body swaying. She was visibly very drunk, as was I. My stomach calmed down and I felt relieved as I followed her. There wasn't much damage she could do with a bottle of wine under her belt.

She showed me the marble washroom attached to the laundry room, then pointed to the closed door of a bedroom that faced the master suite which we now entered. "The balcony is this way." She handed me her glass, clapped her hands and when nothing happened, she thumbed a switch on the wall. The bedside lamps came to life and she reclaimed her glass.

The suite was dominated by a king-size bed on which rested an opened suitcase filled with clothes. She was obviously packing for a trip as she had neat piles of documents, a laptop and other electronics, as well as copies of her books. The nightstand had a framed picture of Dr. O and her husband Baron, who I had never met, and another of India with her adopted mother, Mrs. Weinberger. There were mirror strips on the walls and over the bed.

"Hey, you go on out. I must charge my phones." She fished out two cell phones from her handbag and plugged them in, then took a long sip of wine.

"When are you leaving?"

"Midday tomorrow. I have to meet my agent in Miami for dinner."

I stepped out into the night, cool with a gentle breeze and

sucked in several lungfuls of fresh air and felt refreshed. Wicker furniture with plump cushions made for a cozy seating area. A bar-type table with four high stools occupied a corner, surrounded by plants, attractively placed against the barrier wall of the neighboring balcony. I made myself comfortable in the stool at the farthest corner. There were binoculars on the table. I picked them up and inspected the view. They were night vision. I focused on a small yacht that was advancing to the dock and, as it turned to the boat booth, it disappeared from my view. My attention turned to a helicopter, its noisy twirling blades disturbing the patrons below. I watched it land on the helipad. Shadowy figures emerged and made their way across the bridge over the waterway.

Two things happened simultaneously and so quickly that I was riveted to the stool. The adolescent, still with his laptop, stealthily came out onto the balcony next door. As I sat in the dark, he could not see me. He perched himself on a chair, his back facing me and close enough that I could see as he scrolled on his laptop. My eyes widened as I watched screens change with his quick hand movements. He had a live view of The Nexx Complex – the restaurants below, the corridor, the helipad, the indoor and outdoor parking areas. Then, suddenly, he changed screens to Hot Babes.

Teenager. I looked away with a smile, and caught a movement reflected in the mirror strips of the master bedroom. Dr. O stood in front of the closed door of the bedroom opposite the master suite. She opened it and switched on lights: red, changing to blue then to green then to yellow. I couldn't see clearly inside the room, but there seemed to be a bed with what appeared to be a mosquito-net canopy, but the lights changed so quickly that it was just a blur of kaleidoscopic colors.

The nerdy adolescent made a sound and I guided the binoculars to him. His pimples, ten times their size, came into view, taking over the circumference of the lens. I played with the settings until I had a more favorable view of him and his laptop, and a live view of Dr. O's movements in the other bedroom.

She pulled back the covers, and plumped the pillows. The teenager zoomed in on the screen to what I thought was a canopy. It wasn't. It was something that made me very uncomfortable.

I got up to have a better look and the movement alerted him. He scuttled back inside, tripping over his pants.

I have to get out of here.

I was a bit slow recovering from the shock of what I had just seen so that by the time I had made my way out the master suite, she came out from the opposite door, closing it behind her.

"Oh, hi," I greeted, not able to look her in the eyes. "I think I am ready to leave."

"So soon?" She asked as if all was well in her world.

"I am beginning to feel very drowsy and bed's calling."

"You can sleep here if you wish." She invited.

My stomach went topsy turvy again.

"Oh, no, I will pass. I will take the dog, if you still want me to." I knew the dog and the condo went hand in hand. "But if you don't, that's okay, too."

"But where will you stay?"

"I can stay at Jalebi's place. I have the keys." I lied, as, one, I didn't have the keys, and two, I couldn't, as my sister's roommate was a total psycho, who had repeatedly threatened to have her way with me. Om-7 buzzed to remind me that I shouldn't tell tall tales.

"Oh, no. Chewy gets anxious and the only place he totally comes to life is on the beach. Come help me with his bed. It's on the balcony." I was slow to follow her, but once there, I looked over. The lights were on and there was the adolescent again, laptop-less. He was squeezing ketchup onto bread from a Cost-U-Less-size bottle. On the table was a full bag of sliced bread.

"Hola, Dr. Oligue." He greeted her, ignoring me completely.

She returned the greeting warmly. "Didn't Ernesto bring you food from the restaurant, Carlos? You're eating ketchup sandwiches again?"

"No, I don't like the restaurant food. I like Mexican food, and I loo-ove ketchup." He held the bottle two inches away from his mouth and squeezed, the thick red liquid spurting out, some dripping on his chin.

"Ah, well, don't eat too much of it or your tongue will stick together. Buenas noches. Good night."

She turned back to me. "Look at this view. I always enjoy it. As much as I love the beach condo, this is so a-la-mode. It's Caribbean with a flair of European." She pulled out the dog's bed which was tucked under the wicker chair *"Ah voilà.* Here it is."

"What do you think?" she asked amicably.

Just for something to do, I picked up the binoculars, did a panoramic sweep and then turned to a short focal point at street level. Right below was Mr. Izanagi Yoshio in the company of a very tall, thin man dressed in a loud pink shirt and a black cowboy hat and boots. They both smoked cigars and were in a deep discussion as they walked. Behind them was a petite woman dressed in a short length kimono over shorts and a midriff shirt. I figured she was Mrs. Shizu Yoshio. She was accompanied by a man dressed in a sleeveless undershirt. I zoomed to max vision and did a double take. There were snake tattoos that ran the length of his arm. He was the man I had seen earlier at the French Fusion.

"I like the set up. The logistics are monumental and attractive." I answered as I led the way inside, just desperately wanting to be out of there.

7 Paradise Beach

IT WAS half past ten on the taxi's clock when I arrived at the beach condo's parking lot. I was grateful for Chewy's company, as I stumbled up the stairs to the pathway that led to Dr. O's unit. Forgetting that he was deaf, I mumbled, "Here boy, let's go," and pulled his leash gently which he resisted. Instead, he sat down, lifted his legs and took to licking his testicles. I could see his actions from the tiny decorative lights strategically placed in the small shrubs of the grounds. I let him have his way as I took stock of the surroundings in the semi-darkness.

The condo was in the center block of three buildings fronted by Paradise Beach with sugar-white sand washed up over millions of years from the Caribbean Sea. The "oh wow" beauty was best in daylight when the immediate view of layers of blue greeted you on reaching the last stair. It was a backdrop to the swimming pool. As a matter of fact, twenty steps from the condo brought you to the pool; another twenty steps from the pool and you were on the beach with palm fronds swaying to the tune of the trade winds and, with twenty more steps, you were at the water's edge where waves meet, greet and massage your feet.

A hundred-foot wooden pier extended out from the beach with stairs that brought you into the underwater reef inhabited by every color of fish and coral life imaginable. It had been declared a Heritage Park some years ago to protect the lobsters that spawned, the stingrays that fed, and the octopuses that hid behind the three dark grey rocks that jutted above the sea. Less than one kilometer from the sandy shore, Ghost Mountain, a popular diving site, dropped into the sea. Nature had built an opening, which allowed for exit and entry from the sea into the reef. The most complaints from environmentalists were about the jet skiers and baby sharks that sometimes lost their sense of direction and arrived to stir things up.

Now, with barely a moon in the sky and only artificial lights around the pool, it appeared as a shadowy tableau with the sound of bull frogs and crickets.

Chewy finally got up, on-the-ready-to-go, when a police car, red lights blazing, drove past on its way to Barkers National Park. Had he not tugged and shoved me to the correct door. I would have key-coded the neighbor's unit as the doors were side-by-side. On my last visit with India, it had been rumored that a retired ex-Russian spy, by the name Rooslahn, had moved in. The word was he kept a cricket bat by his door and was prepared to use it first and ask questions later. I had never met him and had no desire to, not in my rum-infused drunken condition. I was not

to be spared. As I entered the condo and searched in the darkness for the light switch, he poked his head into the doorway. In
the shadows, I saw that he was a big man who looked to be about
sixty years. He held a cat that meowed in an ugly tone. I turned
on the lights in the stairway and did a double take. Rooslahn was
built like a refrigerator, a very big one.

"Keep the mutt quiet," he said in a threatening voice. I don't
know how he could say this, as the dog could not bark, but not
in a mood to argue with his kind, I said, "OK." He nodded and
closed his door.

"Don't worry, my faithful friend," I said as I patted Chewy's
head. "That's probably the only pussy he gets to fondle these
days." I swear that, although Chewy couldn't bark, he was
smiling.

I made my way upstairs and checked out each room in the
condo. It was as I remembered it, clean and cozy. In the guest
room's closet, I noticed there was diving gear and equipment
from Baron, Dr. O's deceased husband. I bypassed the luxury of
the master bedroom, not wanting to remember the coupledom
I had shared with India on past visits to the Cayman Islands.

Ω   Ω   Ω

Arranging Chewy's toys around his bed, I indulged him with
a surplus of hugs as I tucked him in. Satisfied he was asleep,
I grabbed a bottle of water from the fridge with intentions of
heading for some alone time on the beach. My foot was barely
out the door, when he jumped up and was at my heels. I patted
him with a 'dumb dog' affectionately and remembered, because
he was deaf, he had never learned how to bark even though India
and I had tried to teach him.

I closed my eyes tightly and commanded my brain to delete
thoughts of India from my memory bank. It proved to be difficult,
as my central processing unit taunted me with flashbacks – many
of them on this beach. She loved diving and snorkeling in the
night and, together, we had accumulated books, watched videos

and spent hours in the reef and around Ghost Mountain. On each occasion, we had practiced static apnea and had become quite disciplined in holding our breath underwater for as long as possible. I had discovered then that there was something unique about my ears and that my deafness was, in a weird way, a blessing in disguise more than a handicap. Many divers had pressure problems if they didn't equalize before submerging. I had no such problem as my ears loved the water; a gift India said, as she had to engage in a whole series of breathing exercises before she dived.

We knew all the nooks and crannies as we followed and observed the varied aquatic life of the underwater world. On a full moon night, it was the most fascinating experience as the colors had different hues from that of a bright, sunny day. She made it a goal that we venture out farther each day and revisit the same area in the night for at least two kilometers from the pier in all directions. When we returned to the beach, exhausted, but on a high, we would rid ourselves of the wetsuits, frolic in the sand, and, like an octopus, the memories wrapped its arms around me and sucked into my skin, squeezing the breath out of my body. I struggled to release them and eventually won the battle.

Overhead, the waning moon was a very small left-side crescent, allowing little visibility of the Caribbean Sea, which now appeared as an ink-black sheet beyond, except for the lights of a lone vessel in the far distance. My squinting, drunken eyes adjusted to the darkness as I followed Chewy to the deserted beach and located a chaise lounge under the palm trees. Without much thought, I slumped down into it. Chewy dropped his heavy body beside me, slurped my face a few times before he folded his legs and slept. Before long, he started snoring and I dozed off.

My slumber was disturbed by his tail brushing against me as he rose quickly, ready to jump, but stopped just as quickly, his tail wagging, his nose sniffing. Following his head movements, I strained to see in the darkness, finally locating the silhouette of Netts, the old fisherman, readying his twelve-footer. He was a friendly, likable soul who had a penchant for telling funny, verbose fish tales. I had slept on this beach in the past so I became

familiar with his habits. At midnight when the world around him
is asleep, he went out in his boat, sunk his lines and returned with
his catch before dawn casts its orange-red light in the water. His
basic grievance had to do with recent laws that declared his fishing ground, rich in seafood, to be a no-fishing zone. The authorities now considered fishing in the area to be poaching, but that
did not deter him. "The authorities have to go to sleep sometime," he often joked.

In the old days, he only fished for Caribbean red-brown lobsters with no claws that fetched a good market price. What he
didn't say was, these days, he fished only for white lobster and
that the Colombian pure white packaged tightly in plastic bags,
fetched an even better market price.

Ω   Ω   Ω

The automatic lights by the pool area blinked several times; a
warning they would be shut off in three minutes. Om-7's sudden
tick-tocking drew my attention to a steady vibration in my
pocket, which also reminded me that BB had whispered something about 'check your pockets.' I reached in and pulled out
Vibe, my computerized diving watch I recently won in a competition. This was another reminder of India's influence in my life,
as she had christened Vibe as a girl and referred to 'it' as she.

Biig Baba, a gadget freak, had borrowed Vibe when I told him
about all the cool gizmos that were integrated into the chronom-
eter. As a trade-off, he offered to reconfigure and fix the important things that would make night diving an awesome experience.
Now, as she vibrated and I looked at her, I read the message,
"Check the audio." I replaced her in my pocket.

All around, it was a still world with a still atmosphere and an
even stiller night. The usual trade winds were missing and the
coconut fronds above my head did not stir. I dozed off only to
be awakened by the sound of heavy hooves. My heart stopped.
Wild horses.

The pack was approaching at a speed that, in a one-minute

time frame, brought them into view as they headed to where I sat. I saw their outlines about four hundred yards away, and reckoned I would be a mangled body that Netts would find on his return. But strange things happen that can never be explained. Chewy jumped up and ran in front of them. He stood on all fours and started to dance in the sand. The pack stopped in their tracks, neighing, then nickering in a submissive manner. There were seven, in total, and they took a few minutes to re-organize, bumping into each other before veering back in the direction they had come from. Within minutes, they had picked up speed and their hooves were once again a heavy sound of thunder as they departed. It took quite a while for my heart rate to return to normal.

I still can't understand how the dog made the horses stop in mid-track, especially since he is deaf. Animals are weird and wonderful, with Chewy at the top of the list.

I settled back into the chaise lounge, Chewy once again beside me. I offered him some water, which he drank thirstily. Satisfied, he fell asleep, his tongue hanging out.

Nausea rose in my throat. I emptied my innards onto the sand, feeling the gritty part of the filet mignon on my palate as it expelled itself in a long, watery stream. Some landed on my clothes, but it was mostly the liquid part, perhaps the rum, as it smelled like urine. I wondered if it looked that way and then put this thought away, as another wave approached. It continued, intermittently, for a good hour. When I was done, I felt better, but dirty and longing for a shower.

My thoughts strayed to the conversation with Dr. O earlier. She was accurate on one count. I needed to cleanse myself, starting with the basic body hygiene. I discarded my clothes and shoes, and with the extra care required, I removed Om-7 from my ear and wrapped him carefully in my underwear. Vibe, strapped on my wrist, showed the time to be 00.49. Butt-naked, the moon behind me, and with stealthy footsteps so as not to disturb Chewy, I made my way down the pier. Usually all the lights were on, but only one was lit as I reached the end and faced the dark sea that lay before me. Earlier, it had rained lightly and I looked up to the sky to see the arc of a rainbow, a rare sighting in the night that had me mesmerized. It appeared that one end touched the three jutting rocks and the other dropped into the reef. When I looked down, the rainbow was reflected in the same arc on the water's surface.

It beckoned to me.

A Rainforest in the Sea

WILLINGLY, I slipped into the salty water as I gripped the last stair for balance. I sucked in a mouthful and rinsed out the acrid taste of after-vomit before immersing my entire body. Total blackness surrounded me. I could not see my arms in front, though I could feel my boys floating at liberty between my legs. I tapped a button on Vibe and she responded with a globe of light that brightened the area in front of me. I released my hold, closed my eyes, let my body go with the flow and gave in to the comfort of nothingness in *que sera sera*. Was this nirvana?

I welcomed it.

I felt the gentle brush against the soles of my feet. It travelled to my ankles, tickled me softly as it moved upwards and then stopped in between my inner thighs as if investigating. At its own pace it moved to my midsection, to my chest and when it reached my head, I re-opened my eyes. I was momentarily blinded by the school of orange, blue and green fish that swam above me. I blinked, in amazement, at their shapes which glowed in the darkness and lit up the water with their intense colors. Beneath them, coral swayed. I plunged deeper to have a better look. The shoal sloped down and surrounded me, giving me the feeling of being in the midst of a paranormal world. I swam lower so that I touched the sandy bottom and then came up higher to water level. They followed me still. I was able to observe how they could turn around, swim in one direction, and fleetingly reverse in the blink of an eye. Vibe had automatically shut off. I am puzzled. These were genetically engineered fish from Asia and were meant to be in artificial aquariums. I had seen similar types in the pet store. Were they released here as a testing ground to see how the species can survive in a salt water environment? I could not help thinking something fishy was going on.

I surfaced to exhale and refill my lungs. When I dived below, it was as if they waited for my arrival as they recommenced their wild darting movements, dipping deeper and deeper with me. There was even a social order to the school. The orange led the way, the blue skirted and the green were at the tail end. There were some weak ones in the lot, mostly green, who swam a short distance away from the others. In an upward glide, they were above me, their glow covering me from head to toe in an incandescent circle. When I looked below me, their fluorescent profiles were reflected in the sand as dancing dots of fireflies that surrounded an alien body. It was surreal.

They stayed with me, until I reached an area where a long piece of tubular pipe, about thirty inches in circumference, was half-buried in a sandbar. It had been there the first time India and I snorkeled to this very spot. This was an indication that I was in a depth of ten to eleven feet at the most, which meant that I was very close to the reef. The clumps of coral fern that had grown around the pipe were now taller, but at one end, they lay flat as if someone had trampled over them. The school dazzled as it dodged in and out of the fronds.

There was something attached to the pipe that floated loosely, and it definitely was not coral. On closer examination, I found it to be a yellow polypropylene rope, about an inch thick. I followed it and found that it was secured to a white, water-resistant jute-type bag that lay just above the sand. Nearby, something shiny glistened.

WTF! My suspicions were confirmed. Some careless person had been here and had dropped a knife, which now lay flat in the sand.

I re-surfaced for air and set Vibe to vibrate at three minute intervals to remind me when I had to come up for air. As I dived below, I discovered not only one rope, but two – the second being a thicker white rope attached to something buried beneath the sand and stuck into the pipe. The school made a sudden loop around me, blocking my view. Fearing it might be dynamite, I treaded underwater and concentrated on the glow loop that, in a measure of seconds, seemed to brighten with my movements. I wondered what in God's name was going on in this underworld haven. Who would want to destroy this beautiful rainforest of the sea?

I cannot say how many times I came up for air or how long I was underwater when the school's stronger members started to race away from me.

It was a frenzied departure that preceded the calm arrival of the predator.

The sleek, unfamiliar shape with its cryptic coloration glided above me, mouth opening and closing and from the departing light of the glow fish, I could see the sharp, serrated teeth.

A Shark! I froze, mesmerized by its beauty and with the terror that gripped me.

The weaker green fish lagged behind in a disarrayed group, emanating a greenish glow that reflected off the shark's seven-foot-or-so, body length. I estimated its weight to be approximately 700 pounds. It appeared to have bluish-green stripes, which, I suspect, might simply have been a reflection of the fluorescent fish. One thing was for sure, it had a yellow underbelly.

A tiger shark!

I surfaced and looked for land, swirled around several times in different directions before locating the single light on the pier that seemed to be miles away. I calculated I was about one and a half kilometers away – a good fifteen minute swim. I am an excellent swimmer, with good lung capacity and endurance. A tiger shark, however, swam from the day of its birth. With excellent eyesight and an acute sense of smell, it could locate me at all times. My only advantage was I knew this reef like the back of my hand.

Energetically, I dived below and swam toward the light, as I saw no logic in sticking around to become his supper or breakfast or, for that matter, its meal of the day. My ears were ringing, a gurgling sound of water flowing within, the hammer pounding like a carpenter beating nails into a wall. With every stroke, I grew more terrified.

I remembered what I had read about the man-eating tiger shark. It was aggressive and indiscriminate in its feeding style. Singularly, before it is born, it practices cannibalism, eating the embryos of its siblings in the womb so that it can stay alive. When it finally arrives in the world, it has already acquired experience as a hunter. The stripes on the body only last through the juvenile years, disappearing at maturity. Commercial fishermen have found everything from rubber tires to license plates, shoes and even baby bottles in the guts. Scientific research into its eating habits suggests it has no preferences. It eats everything in its path and is known to attack humans. There are cases where it has sunk those big teeth into people's heads. The only restriction on its hunting range is the depth of the water. Less than ten feet, it cannot play its mind-game of calmly circling and circling, creating a fear factor before attacking its prey.

Only minutes ago, I had a close-up of those big teeth, which can easily crack a turtle shell in the same way that a human's teeth can crack a peanut. With powerful strokes, I swam toward the light, and to an area that I knew was at a seven foot depth and a safe ground. The old adage, 'better to try and fail than fail to try' repeating itself in my mind with each stroke.

The glow fish returned. In their own way, they had figured that the shark no longer was a threat to them and were now reunited with the weaker, green-colored ones. I saw clearly now the outline of the shark's big body. It circled around me, its huge body movements, though composed, created v-like ripples in the water that was tranquil not so long ago. It seemed to be sizing me up in that sleepy, but deceitful, manner it is known for. Any second, it would make that powerful turn with its body and I would become shark meal. The only sensible thing to do was to go lower in the water and swim behind him. It had the same thought. With a single move, it lowered itself and was alongside me.

In doing so, it had disturbed the ropes, made them tangle and, with the water movement, had somehow entangled itself in them. As it tried to break free, it pulled up the white rope and an oblong shaped object wrapped in a grey covering which, at a quick glance, appeared quite heavy as it didn't float like the jute bag. Disoriented, it lashed out, swimming in big circles and this allowed me to reach down for the knife, which I used to cut the yellow rope. I pulled the jute bag, held it in front of me, on-the-ready to shove it down its throat, praying that the dynamite, as I assumed it to be, was not triggered by a mechanism attached to the oblong-shaped object.

It approached me as I had feared, with its big mouth open, showing off its humongous saw-blades. Was it laughing at me?

"Come on, let's party." My brain was now in full working gear. I stayed still, looked into its eyes as it made its powerful hunting maneuver for me just a body length away. My lungs screamed for air, my ears thumped away but, with all my strength, I fed him the bag.

"Good Night." I ducked immediately under its yellow belly, touched it and swam for safety like I was in an Olympic meet.

Once in the shallows, I tapped Vibe to life and turned around for a look. The glow fish had surrounded it, but seemed to light up more brightly with the movement of the jute bag. I watched as the powerful teeth ripped into the bag and then sucked it in. As it swallowed, another yellow rope attached to another jute bag appeared and this was attached to still another. I counted seven, before the water turned milky white with the small plastic packages dispersed around its head. White powdery stuff, expelled from broken packages floated into its mouth and eyes. It was blinded, I could tell as the eyes were shut as it flapped over and around several times. I filled my lungs in long gasps of air as I made it to a point where I could stand in the water. I watched, still amazed that even in blindness, it found a getaway through the opening into the Caribbean Sea.

Tiredly, I climbed up the stairs to the pier where Chewy awaited me. Inside me rested the sad awareness that it was now a coke-contaminated juvenile tiger shark, but I was also relieved. We were both alive.

Back on the chaise lounge, as I rolled out my underwear, Vibe reflected 02.05 a.m. I picked up my clothes, patted Chewy, and walked back to the condo in naked splendor.

I couldn't sleep. The unintentional workout had re-energized me. My close encounter with the shark and my near departure from planet Earth left me wound up. The second polypropylene rope attached to a heavy object that looked like a crate was also something that didn't seem right. The more I thought about it, the more I wanted to investigate.

For the second time that night, I headed out to the rainforest in the sea. I was fully dressed in a wetsuit, Vibe strapped to my wrist and equipped with all the necessary paraphernalia I needed for a few hours' dive. Included were two coils of twenty-foot rope I found in the closet. The last thing I did was place Om-7 on the nightstand with the few dollars I had emptied from my pockets.

I was not alone. Chewy tagged along for a dip.

Handcuffs

I AWOKE STRETCHED out on a chaise lounge in the bright morning sun, the distant cry of seagulls and a gun stuck into my ribcage. I am dressed only in shorts and a T-shirt.

Two sturdy men stood above me. One had his hand on his duty belt. The other pointed to two small plastic packets of white powder, one on my chest and the other beside me on the chaise lounge. He said something but the words bounced harshly in the center of my head. See, sounds entering from my deaf, right ear must pass through my head to get to my functioning left ear. This makes it hard to hear these sounds clearly coming from the direction of the deaf ear. In the world of deafness, this condition is called "head shadow." Om-7, my hearing device balances these sounds and makes them clearer.

My hand automatically moved to my right ear. Om-7 is missing.

I presumed that the men were plainclothes cops. The gun is pressed firmly into my sides once again and this time I can lip read the words.

"Rise and put your hands over your head."

Slowly, I rose.

"What's your name?" I lip read again. He was a tall, heavy-built man in his mid-thirties. His mannerisms swung between Jamaican and Barbadian; sometimes it is difficult to tell the difference, as there are many cross-island imports. His partner was equally tall and had the tanned coloring of a Caymanian.

"Kaman Colioni," I muttered, trying to recollect where I had last placed Om-7. There were some precautions involved with such a device; it was not very compatible in water. I remembered now I had left him on the night table at the condo before my second underwater outing, which turned out to be an insane adventure with Chewy.

"Where do you live?" I pointed to the condo complex.

"Show me some identification." It was difficult to understand him as my lip reading was a bit rusty and he spoke quickly.

"Repeat, please." It was the wrong thing to say as he went into a tirade where only the word deaf repeated several times registered in my head.

"I am deaf." I said, maybe looking for some slack or some sympathy.

He moved as close as possible to my right ear and barked. "I want to see some ID, deaf boy."

I explained that it was in the condo, not hearing my words clearly. This too was a small lie as the only identification I had, after being rolled over yesterday, was the stub of my boarding pass and this was not considered a real proof of identity.

"So, you a HOH?"

As far as I know, this is a slang word for a female or male who gives out easily.

"I am not a HO." I answered defensively.

"I mean HOH as in hard of hearing" The import replied. Something from behind me caught their attention and interrupted this exchange as both men forced me down into the chaise lounge. One handcuffed me to the beach chair. The other pocketed the two plastic packets. They left in a hurry, heading in the direction of the nature park as they spoke into their walkie-talkies.

Their departure allowed me to settle myself into the chair, wondering what was going on. Digging my feet into the sand, I managed to turn the chair and was able to watch their progress. Without Om-7, events appear as montages. Overall, the montage was of Netts swaying in the distance with his hands up in the air. The policemen arriving on the scene. Netts pointing to a big blob of something unclear in the sand. Other people arriving and surrounding the policeman, Netts and the blob. I figured someone very obese had probably died on the beach.

From this unplanned get-together, Dr. O and Chewy made their way toward me. She had obviously gone to the condo, as I knew for certain that I had left Chewy asleep after the tedious workout we both had when I took him for a dip on my second outing underwater. He had been so exhausted, he snored the minute his head touched the bed.

Unleashed, Chewy ran ahead to jump and lick me and, though my state of mind was unsettled at the moment, I managed to rub his back with my free hand.

I watched Dr. O, dressed in running gear and oversized sunglasses make her way to me. Usually, she walked in long strides, but this morning, she was slow. When she reached me and noticed that I was handcuffed, her mouth opened in a big, "Oh my God, what happened?" I indicated to her I did not have my device. She mouthed and signed the query a second time.

"Don't know. I decided to sleep on the beach and, when

I woke up, there were two cops questioning me about some plastic packets that contained white powder. They handcuffed me to this chair and took off to where you were. What happened there?"

"There's a big shark with its belly slit. I have never seen a shark close up but this one has a yellow belly and some stripes on its body. What a shame. Such a beautiful thing lying there with its guts cut up in pieces. Sadly, it is one of the sharks that had been tagged by the Department of Environment and Fisheries, so the crowd there is made up of officials doing a preliminary investigation of what might have happened." She stood in front of me, speaking slowly, enunciating each word and, though her eyes were hidden by the sunglasses, I can lip read her words.

"How big is it.?"

"In my estimate, I'd say seven to eight feet, and over 700 hundred pounds. How could someone haul that amount of weight through the reef onto the sand? I tell you, I can't wait to hear the details of this drama."

Me too. I can't believe that someone would be so heartless, especially since I had been so close to it. I actually touched its belly with my hands.

The desire to go to the washroom was becoming imminent and I voiced this to her.

"Stay here. I will get us some coffee and see what I can do."

More people had arrived on the beach and made their way to the center of activity. Some vehicles, including a truck with a Department of Environment logo drove past me. You would think a live shark would attract attention, but here, a dead one attracted more. The sun at the back of me when I woke up was now shrouded by clouds and, the day, which had started out sunny, was now overcast and grey. The Caribbean Sea was a blanket of grey ripples dotted with some white cruise ships heading toward the port in Georgetown.

Chewy ran off to chase seagulls on the pier as Dr. O arrived with two large mugs of coffee. "I have something for you. Be discreet about what you do next." She handed me a mug, dropped a small screwdriver in the sand and then departed in the direction where the crowd had gathered.

I stuck the cup in the sand and picked up the thin screwdriver. It was about three inches long; one that could be used to take apart very small screws or to pick a lock. In my situation, it would serve ideally to undo the handcuff.

Chewy returned and I made him sit beside me so that his body blocked the view as I tried to snap apart the ring-shaped metal. It took a lot of effort and persistence as the tiny tool would slip into the sand and then I had to waste time to locate it. After several tries, it finally opened, and I was a free man.

The crowd had gotten larger at the other end. I made a get-away to the condo, dog at my heels. The smell of coffee greeted me. On the counter beside the coffee pot were a bunch of keys. I opened the broom closet and hung them on the key rack. They were so heavy they fell behind the vacuum. I gave Chewy a bone and watched him settle himself on his bed.

I calculated I had at least an hour before the cops remembered they had a prisoner. Time management became my priority as I jumped into the shower and luxuriated in the warm spray. Fully dressed, I searched the entire condo for Om-7, retracing all my steps before and after my second outing. I was certain I had left him on the nightstand. The dollar bills were there, but were scattered loosely. I always fold my bills neatly. Maybe I had mistakenly taken him out with me. In frustration, I reprehended myself for being careless with something so necessary in my daily life.

In less than an hour, the cops arrived in the company of Dr. O. It seemed they had forgotten they had handcuffed me a short while back.

"Kaman, tell me it's not true," she said. "Tell me that these gentlemen are making a mistake and wrongfully accusing you of possession of illegal substances."

She looked straight at me when she spoke, her index finger painted blood red with tiny white decorations, pointed to the subject and object of her dialogue.

A non-comprehensive look must have crossed my face as she signed and repeated. I don't know if this was theater, done for the benefit of the cops or real stuff to make me understand my current predicament.

"I need some identification." The Cayman policeman said so loudly his words bounced off the wall. "Do you have a passport?" I lipread his question quite clearly but, just for the hell of it, I made him repeat.

"No, I lost them. I reported this to the immigration department yesterday morning."

"Where did you lose it?"

"I was in Georgetown, by the port, when tourists surrounded me and grabbed my fanny pack with all my stuff."

"What kind of tourists were they?"

I thought about this. It was not a clear question.

"They were from the gay cruise ship. All the passengers were gay. I don't know if they were male gay or female gay."

"Uh huh. Do you have the name of the person you spoke to at the immigration office?"

I wished the jerk-off would not scream. I couldn't remember the name.

"Yes, it was E-banks." There were at least one hundred E-banks listed on the island.

"All the same, we have to take you in and book you, because of these packets of illegal substances in your possession." He pulled out four packets from his pocket. *Something was not right. There were two packages when they woke me up.*

Chewy had finally crushed the bone to bits. Satisfied, he walked over to inspect the cops, sniffing their crotches. Dr. O apologetically pulled him away and with the effort required, she dropped her cell phone, which landed at my feet. I bent to pick it up and glimpsed India's name on the screen. Dr. O had made three outgoing calls to India.

I was handcuffed and escorted out of the condo.

10 Engine

I WAS LED to a sedan with POLICE emblazoned in bright blue decals on the two front doors. The coat of arms of the Cayman Island with a yellow-gold colored crown topped it off. At the bottom was the slogan: WE CARE, WE LISTEN, WE ACT. From past visits to the island, I had always found the Caymanian police to be courteous, helpful and they always did this with a smile. These guys were different.

The Caymanian had the air of a gentle person. He tried to open the back door but it was stuck so he assisted me into the front seat where I sat sandwiched between him and his partner who drove. The bullish voice of his partner suggested he wanted to keep me in the police car as they made their rounds, with the air conditioner off and make me sweat. The Caymanian pleaded on my behalf; that I was deaf and it was inhuman to punish me in that manner. Good cop, bad cop pairing. Though their words did not reach me clearly, I can now lip-read if I looked straight at their mouths. In general, I had a good idea of what was being said.

They had excellent cop habits, for without fail, they stopped at The Donut Shop. It wasn't a quick get in and get out. They took their sweet time about it, eating in air-conditioned comfort while I sat and boiled in the cruiser, sweat running down my face and armpits. When they returned, the Caymanian asked if I was all right and slipped me some gum.

At a turtle's pace, they drove along West Bay Road that paralleled Seven Mile Beach. It was fine until I saw the six cruise ships docked in the waters, which meant there could be at least fifteen thousand people in a three kilometer area in downtown Georgetown, and a painfully slow drive through. I slouched low into the seat as they stopped at the busiest corner by the port. I worried that people would see me through the tinted window. I closed my eyes and shut out the world.

A string of harsh cuss words from the driver and an abrupt braking of the vehicle jolted me upright. He turned on the flashing lights and the siren. As throngs of people dispersed in confusion, he advanced to a parking space, opened the door and ran out, the Caymanian following. Neither took the time to lock the doors. I could not see who or what they were chasing, but what I saw was the plastic statue of Big Black Dick, Cayman's most famous pirate, hoisted up in the air. I opened the sliding panel above the seats and climbed over to the back.

A bearded man with a knapsack, oversized straw hat and sunglasses that covered half his face, blocked my view through the windshield. When I refocused again, some street cops had joined the chase. The driver's door of the police car opened and the bearded man settled himself behind the steering wheel, dropped the knapsack on the passenger side, and took about setting the mirror to his liking. He lifted his hat in greeting and jet black hair, the sides shaved to the skull and the back, long to the waist, came into full view along with his muscled, hairy arms exposed in a cut-off T-shirt. The vehicle purred to life and as he placed his arms on the steering wheel, I saw the word *Kanien'kehá:ka*, tattooed on his upper right arm. On his left arm was inked the English translation, People of the Flint. He wore a ring with an unusual stone on his pinky.

He took off his sunglasses and looked at me through the sliding panel between the seats. My face widened into a smile despite my current predicament. "Engine? What are you doing here?"

He turned around to face me. "I can do two things. Drive like a crazed madman or we both get out and run. Choose your poison fast before tweedledum and tweedledee realize what's going on." It was easy to lip-read his words as I was used to hearing his voice.

"Speak slowly. I lost my device."

He switched to sign language. "Holy shit, now you are really deaf. I am here to see you, my sorrowing, sulking friend and right now, I am trying to save your ass. What are you doing breaking the law?"

Most of my close friends can communicate with me using minor sign language. Engine, however, was proficient. Perhaps because we knew each other since we were very young, and he had been a constant visitor at our house, he had picked it up from my family. He often joked and said it came naturally to him as his people had centuries of practice in sign language since it had been the only way they were able to communicate with the barbarians who stole their land.

His real name was Ten-squat-a-way Rarahkwenhá:wi Montour. His mother had explained to me that *Ten-squat-a-way* was the name of a great Native American Indian Prophet whose brother Tecumseh had fought with the pro-British forces during the war of 1812. His Mohawk middle name *Rarahkwenhá:wi* meant, he who carries the sun. My mother had accidentally nick-named him Engine and the name had stayed, though only within our family circle and some very close friends.

"I have handcuffs." I raised my hands to show him.

"And you're proud of that?" He shook his head in disbelief. "What do you know? I thought the Cayman Islands would be boring." He flicked on the siren. "Lay low in the seat."

People moved as he eased the car out of the parking space.

"Give me a short cut to get out of this zoo. My wheels are by The Donut Shop where your cop friends had breakfast."

"Go down past all the jewelry stores and take the first roundabout. Engine, you are crazy. You know how much more trouble I will get for this?"

"Hey, they have to find me, and then you. First, I have to find a barber. Need a shave and a haircut."

"What for?"

"Dude, you don't check out social media anymore. I posted it last Monday. I, Ten-squat-a-way Rarahkwenhá:wi, a seventh generation Mohawk, have officially passed my bar exams. I sent you an e-mail. And I am here for a job interview with the best known law firm that handle billions of dollars in hedge and trust funds. I cannot attend a job interview with a beard and a Mohawk. They sort of hinted at this."

Since he was half-signing and half speaking, I pretty much understood 'Engine got job,' which worried me, for all I know, job could have been preceded by hand or blow. "Congratulations. This is how you start your career? By becoming a criminal?"

He answered using the one finger salute, the one word in sign language which was known throughout the world, as he manoeuvred the car.

"This is not a good idea Ten-squat-a-way Rarahkwenhá:wi, the seventh. I hope your other six ancestors didn't have bad ideas like this," I complained.

We had come to an intersection and people seemed to be staring. I dug lower into the seat, almost lying down.

"Tell you what we will do. I drive. You enjoy the ride."

"How did you find me?" I asked.

He started to sign to me but then realized that he could not drive and do this at the same. "Later," he signalled.

He parked the police car in the rear parking lot of The Donut Shop. As he reached across to pick up his knapsack, he jingled some keys and did his Mohawk cry of joy as he passed them to me. The first one I tried opened the handcuff. I was once again free.

He led the way to his rental, a small imported Korean vehicle we both struggled to get into, being six-foot plus guys. As we buckled up, our knees almost to our chins, he told me how he had been out to Paradise Beach to see me in the morning, and had witnessed the cops taking me to their car.

"So where is the barber? Cops will be looking for someone with a beard. So let's do this." I detected that Engine was having some issues about getting a haircut. He had worn his hair the traditional way of his people as far back as I can remember, and had repeatedly said that it would be a big ritual on the day he had to change the Mohawk.

"You're sure about this haircut?"

He nodded.

I directed him to a little strip mall owned by MJ Rafiq which had several stores including a two-chair barber shop. MJ worked harder than any businessman I knew, as he had several side businesses: liquor, pirated movies and hot electronics inclusive. He was well known in the Cayman Islands for his restaurant Da Roti Shaq, which I had helped him to set up on one of my visits some years back. I had shown him the art of rolling out dough to make perfect shaped rotis, having accumulated years of experience working in my parent's restaurant, *Montreal Pizza*. He always felt indebted to me for this favor as he called it, although he was, in fact, the one I owed the biggest debt to.

MJ greeted me enthusiastically when I entered the restaurant. He hadn't finished high school and when he meets someone with higher schooling he gets all shy as he was now when I introduced Engine as my lawyer friend. I pointed to my ears to let him know that I could not hear. Once Engine was settled into the barber's chair next door to the restaurant, we went out the back entrance to have a smoke which turned out to be a grilling on Engine's background. He asked me if I was hungry and packed me some roti and goat curry sandwiches in a paper bag. When I told him I was low on cash and can only pay him later, he replied, "Yoo, No worries." He slipped a half bottle of rum with the food, then dug into his pocket and passed me two twenties with a packet of cigarettes.

On my return, Engine was shaved but still had his Mohawk. "I can't do it." He said. "I refuse to be manipulated this way."

He had his knapsack opened on the barber's chair. He rummaged through it until he found a plaid shirt and a Blackhawks cap. "We need to look different." He handed me a T-shirt that read "THE MOVEMENT."

"Where are you staying?"

"Someplace called The Nexx Complex. On the map it is close to Seven Mile Beach and Camana Bay. You know where it is?"

"Everyone who comes to The Cayman Islands knows where Seven Mile beach is. You're staying at The Nexx Complex? Mr. Big Shot, how can you afford these luxuries? Most students I know are broke. What are you into Engine? And don't mess with me," I warned.

Some years we were apart, some years we were tight. One thing I knew without a doubt was that he would watch my back and would always tell me the truth. If ever I got in trouble, he would be the first person I would go to without a thought.

"My people look after me well. How do you think I managed Oxford? See man, there is something to be said for being of The First Nations. No expense was spared. There were times when I hated being considered a visible minority within my own country but the flip side of the coin, there are people who acknowledge the injustice done and want to repair the damage. I am such a product."

Engine always had a history lesson about the conquest and rape of Native Indians and their land rights that was not taught in Canadian schools. I didn't encourage him now as he rendered this bit of information.

With my directions, he pulled into the parking lot and glided the car into a vacant spot.

"So how did you know where to find me in the Cayman Islands?"

"I got the beach condo's address from Jalebi. As I pulled into the parking lot, the cops came out with you. I followed the police car to The Donut Shop, parked my car and jumped into a taxi as they continued along West Bay Road. So what's the high and low of being in handcuffs?"

I related my last twenty four hours of being on the island as we walked back to the car.

"Do you notice a pattern? Whenever Dr. O'Ligue is around, you get into some kind of fiasco." He shook his head from side to side. "Where's India in all of this?"

"Finished."

"What?" His expression was one of surprise.

Someone knocked on the window on my side. It was Ernesto, the waiter from the restaurant, who had taken pride in taking a leak in the canal.

11 The Hybrid Vigor

ERNESTO was dressed casually in shorts and a T-shirt. He removed his sunglasses as I rolled down the window. "H-hey. M-my little brother found this." He held up Om-7.

My face scrunched up in puzzlement. "Where did you find him?"

"B-by Dr. O'Ligue's door. W-why do you call it, *him?*"

"Because he's part of me. You know, he's my buddy."

I inspected Om-7, caressed him as I wiped him clean before placing him on his regular spot. He was a bit off at the moment, picking up blurred lines and static, but this didn't matter as he hugged my ear tightly, as if he had missed me. Soon, he did what he was manufactured for – making me aware of the world around me.

"Thanks. I really appreciate you thought of me. And thank your little brother for me. What's his name?"

"Ca-Carlos."

I recognized it as the name of the ketchup kid who lived next door to Dr. O.

"I guess you are Dr. O'Ligue's neighbor."

"O-oh her." From the emphasis on "her," it was clear that he had some misgivings about Dr. O. "S-she is very amusing. Later." He replaced his sunglasses as he walked away.

"I . . . we know that guy from somewhere." Engine said.

"What makes you think that?"

"The way he speaks." Engine seemed puzzled. He had, in the meantime, opened the trunk of the car and took out his suitcase and other stuff. I helped him with his suit bag.

"Armani?" I lifted an eyebrow.

"Yes. Only the best. Got to dress to impress."

"Dude, you've been a lawyer for what, two weeks? It amazes me how fast you've become a name-dropping douche."

"Don't hate the player bro! And screw your Old Navy-wearing ass, too!"

As we made our way to find Engine's unit, Carlos stood idly by the stairs, laptop held in the crook of his arm. When he saw us, he looked the other way. I tapped him on the shoulder.

"Thanks for returning my . . ." I pointed to Om-7. He didn't give me a chance to finish.

"It's not me. It's my brother. Ernesto said ya whole world would be upside down if ya didn't have it." He looked about fourteen and uncared for. He was dressed in the same clothes he wore last night, his hair rumpled and bed-head messy. Now, up close, his face was covered with red pimples that looked like he had had a good scratch session with them. There were ketchup stains on his shirt. He started to walk away.

"Hey Carlos. Thanks anyway. Tell me, did you see the doctor?" The kid stopped in his tracks "How would I see the doctor?" "Your laptop."

"*Qué*?" He said and at my look of non-comprehension, he stepped back in a defensive stand. "Ya don't speak Spanish? *Qué* means what in English."

He seemed a bit thrown off balance that I mentioned his laptop. "Thanks for this." I touched Om-7.

"Ya not welcome." He said rudely. "Besides, Ernesto took it away from me. "

I reached into my pocket and held out a twenty, even though I wasn't rolling in dough, for I think he needed food. He looked at it, unsure of what to do.

"Take it, kid. It's free money." Engine reached into his pocket and passed him another twenty.

He grabbed it. "She left an hour ago on a flight to Miami. She said she will be back early Monday morning." He took off in a rush.

I felt relieved to know that Dr. O was away.

We finally located the condo only to find that it was next door to Carlos and Ernesto's unit, and two doors away from Dr. O's. The interior was of the same layout as Dr. O's, but while hers had an elegant female touch, this one was crisp. The walls had pictures by Mohawk and Inuit artists. On a dresser was a huge black irregular stone piece of an *Inukshuk*. Other pieces included a bear, a turtle and a clam, all shiny black and arranged prominently around the furniture. The sofas were made of totem poles with cushions covered in woven material with purple designs. A series of wampum belts hung loosely behind the sofa.

Engine busied himself arranging his stuff while I set out the meal and poured us some rum.

"Here's to you, my friend. Congratulations on being the first from Kahnawake to become an Oxford grad." I raised my glass. A deep admiration filled my heart in recognition of his success against all odds, for always being there whenever I am in a crisis, and for being a friend whenever I most needed one. I choked up and looked away.

"And to you, too, for being the deafest and almost the dearest friend I have, and I will put you to the friendship-test later. Look how far you have come." He lightened the moment. *"Skén:nen. Atenrò:sera."* He said in Mohawk.

"Yes. Peace and friendship." I said as we clinked glasses.

"I hate rum," he said after he took a swig.

"Got any other choice?"

"Yes." He walked over to the kitchen and opened a cupboard. From where I stood, I could see some cases stacked within. He opened one and took out an unlabelled bottle.

"Try this." He poured some into a shot glass.

I tasted it. Surprisingly, it is smooth.

"No name?"

"I guess you didn't know that besides internet gambling, we Mohawks have found a way to distill whisky." He swallowed a half glassful. "It makes sense, doesn't it? The white man introduced us to it. Now, four hundred years later, we can make it better than anyone else."

"What is it called?"

"No Name," he laughed. His laughter lifted me a bit. His persona always had that effect on me. I felt at ease.

The last time I saw him had been a year ago when the group of eleven had met in Danz Park, not far from where my parents lived. We all knew each other since we were kids in primary school and did this as a commemorative get together for my friend Wes Beier who had been murdered some years ago. We usually played catch-up, laughed at life, dissed each other amicably, repeated old stories, had a few drinks and remembered Wes. I realized now I had been so absorbed in my life the past year I had forgotten my friends, or maybe that is just the way things happen. A guy has a girl, they become a couple and things just move in another direction.

There were two things about Engine that defined the man he had become and that spurred him to become a lawyer.

The first was his pride of being a Native Canadian Indian. Even though he was a hybrid like me, being a mix of Mohawk, English and French; he wore proudly the heritage of his Mohawk ancestry. In his wallet, he carried a picture of the Pope blessing him. The occasion had been when the papacy apologized to the First Nations People for the Catholic Church's involvement in residential schools that separated many Native Indian children from their families and subjected them to horrific psychological, physical and sexual abuse. It had been this campaign "to kill the Indian in the child," which now fueled the fire in Engine. The second was he was very involved in 'The Movement" that linked all North American Indians with a common goal: to reclaim their culture and language, which had been eradicated. He was passionate on both fronts. As a friend, I never crossed the threshold of questioning his choices.

He settled himself into the comfort of a sofa, and before long he had fallen asleep from jet lag.

"Wake up, dude. Too nice to just sleep." He shook my shoulders.

I rubbed my eyes and yawned noisily before I sat up. "Here's a stupid but sensible thing. Have you ever woken up and realized you didn't know you had fallen asleep?"

His meeting was scheduled for the following morning, he said.

It was set up as a Sunday Brunch at the Ritz, with the law firm's three managing partners. I could tell he was nervous. It was his first interview.

Later that night, after he won the competition of who could drink the least – his excuse, a valid one, was that he wanted to be clearheaded for his meeting in the morning, I told him about Dr. O, and the memoir.

"Run," he advised, "as fast as you can. She's bad news." As an afterthought, he asked. "Are you broke? Do you need a loaner? I can lend you some moolah to tide you over." He reached for his wallet.

I lied that I wasn't broke and declined his offer. He couldn't sit still, I noticed. He went from the kitchen to the balcony, back to the sofa, got up, went to the washroom, picked up a book, put it down.

'Let's go out for a drive," I invited. "I want to show you something." As we walked to the car, I told him about the shark and the glow fish and the cocaine and how lucky I was to be alive.

"Pure bullshit," he said and let out a laugh.

"Look, I can't promise you the dead shark. The environment people probably removed its carcass by now, but I'm telling you, there are glow fish out there. C'mon, I'll show you."

"Let's go Jacques Cousteau," he joked.

I rode shotgun as he drove to Paradise Beach. Flashlight in hand, we scoured the beach. The shark was covered with a huge tarp.

"Now you believe me?" We re-tracked to the pier and from a flashlight on his keychain, concentrated the light in the water. Nothing. Fifteen minutes later, no signs of glow fish.

"You're screwing with me, aren't you?"

"I swear to you I saw them last night. You didn't believe me about the shark, did you?"

"It's a choppy story Kaman. You know anyone would have questioned a shark story. But now that I have seen it, gotta say, I can't doubt the actual proof." We sat down, our feet dangling over the water, comfortable in each other's company.

"What if I tell you another story that involves some solid gold hidden not far from here?"

"Ridiculous. What have you been smoking?"

"Clean Cayman air. See over there, where those three rocks jut out above the water. You have to remember that place Engine."

He laughed, really laughed. "You drank too much."

"Engine, I am talking about twelve million gold, bro. So you better remember this. I moved it there myself."

He shrugged it off. "How? Like superman, batman or ironman?"

"Do you recall in our younger years when all of us went roller blading in Caughnawaga and we went swimming off that place near the bridge?"

"Caughnawaga is the name given to the reservation by Europeans. In the Mohawk language, the name is Kahnawake." He corrected me. "Yes, that was a real cool-off after the sweating. So, what's the relation to twelve million dollars in gold?"

"Who was the strongest swimmer?"

"Ok, you were," he conceded after thinking about it.

"Who had the lung capacity to stay under water for the longest time?"

"Ok. So what do you want, a medal?"

"No, but yours truly, with the help of Chewy, moved twenty bags of solid gold from over there," I pointed in the direction of where over there was before I continued, "to where those three rocks jut out."

"I still don't believe you. How long did it take you?"

"God and nature were on my side that night, because I met Dr. O for dinner. I got very nervous so I drank too much. When I got here, some wild horses almost made me chopped liver but Chewy stood up like an animal god and stopped them, I got nervous again that I spilled out my gut." I stopped as I remembered. "Bro, it was awful, the barfing. I retched all over my clothes. It stunk like when my brother takes his famous fifteen-minute craps. But I felt rejuvenated afterward. I decided to take a dip to wash off."

I lost my train of thoughts as I remembered the glow fish. They followed me in the first outing but *were not there* in the second outing. Something was not right about their sudden appearance and disappearance.

"No one takes a dive after getting sloshed. That's a basic diving rule. What do you have? A death wish?"

"That's a rule for normal people. I'm deaf so I'm abnormal and that rule doesn't apply. Back to the gold. See, the tide was on my side. I dived like a male mermaid bro. You know what was the most interesting part? Whoever put the gold there made it easy for whomever finds it."

"How?"

"Left a utility knife behind. It was different. Not one you see very often. It was weird how the oblong shaped crates were attached to each other. They were strung together in units of five. Any good diver can pull it with ease through the water." I chuckled when I thought of the idiot's no-brainer.

"Ok. Oo-kay. Say, I believe this story. Why did you choose those rocks?"

"It's a chance. There's hundreds, if not thousands of octopuses' hatchlings at the front of the rock. At the back, the rocks are the same shape and grey color as the covering of the crates. It works well as a camouflage. Well now, what do I have to lose? Never was my gold in the first place, so nothing to worry about." I shrugged like he did before.

"How do you know it is gold?"

"Trust me, it is gold. I opened a crate."

"The dog helped you?"

"Surprised the hell out of me, his strength. It must be – you know, the hybrid vigor that brings out abnormal qualities with cross-breeding?"

Engine got up. "You tell the best stories. You should start writing them, not a memoir."

12 Æsa the Supermodel

IT WASN'T a bright sunny day as forecasted when Engine and I left the condo for his interview. He was dressed in his Armani suit, and I wore one of his Bermuda shorts and a T-shirt that read "THE MOVE IS ON." In the parking lot he asked me to drive. He looked like the rich guy and I, his chauffeur as we drove along West Bay Road. Noticing that his face was covered in beads of sweat, I stopped at a gas station and grabbed two cans of coconut water.

There wasn't much traffic as I turned the small car toward the Ritz, thinking that yesterday I was the passenger of a police car and today I am sitting in the driver's seat. Sundays are usually quiet days in Grand Cayman, as the locals are church-going people and worship services fill the mornings. In the afternoons, they sat on their porches breezing off, with their front doors open.

Once we parked, I walked with him to the pagoda style restaurant decorated in tropical colors with a full view of Seven Mile Beach. We had agreed that I would leave after he met up with the representatives from the law firm.

"I am so damn nervous," he confessed as we waited.

"You are not. You're just over-thinking. Here, drink up. Coconut water is a fixer-upper for queasy stomachs." After he had downed half a can, he seemed to be more in control.

"Do I look good?" He asked.

"You look awesome. C'mon, you are the guy who can talk a mile a minute, so to speak. You can do this."

Upon asking the maitre d' for his interviewers, he was told that they had not arrived yet and pointed him to a reserved table in case he wanted to wait for them. Engine was so edgy he asked me what he should do.

"Something's happening over on the beach. Let's go see," I said to distract him.

There was a low wall that separated the restaurant from the beach. A camera crew, equipment scattered around them, was setting up a photo shoot. A long legged blond woman sat on a chair near to the wall. She was surrounded by several helpers. I couldn't see her face and would not have recognized her, if not for Engine.

A smile broadened on his face as he boldly walked over. "Move aside ladies."

She was dressed in bikini thongs and wore a top that barely covered her breasts, I noted as she rose to greet Engine.

"Ten-sqúat-a-way." They hugged for minutes, excited conversation between them, not quite reaching Om-7 clearly. I half-turned, tapping him gently, still no clear sounds. I decided to leave. Engine would be fine, now that he had a half-dressed woman to take his mind away from the impending interview. I didn't get far as she pounced on me.

"Are you trying to ignore me Kaman?" The hug reminded me that the touch of a bare fleshed woman, well almost, could be flattering.

"Æsa." I said her name, rubbing the A and E together on my tongue to make it sound right. She was a photographer's dream. Her beautiful face framed with butter-yellow blond locks and her six foot Viking curvaceous 'bod' all fitted together with her unusual name, which had the two vowels fused together. Her face graced numerous magazines in many languages. As of date, she was the most famous person of my high school graduating class.

"I want a photo with you two." Æsa turned to a cameraman who appeared to be in his late twenties. "Stieg, can you please snap some pictures of us?"

"Certainly. Æsa, my love . . . this would make a nice center for the magazine. Your fair looks against the flesh of these two so well sun-tanned handsome men." Stieg batted his mascara darkened eyelashes as he moved effeminately to where we stood. He was of average height, well toned and wore flowered shorts. He didn't hide that he was gay as he openly gave Engine and me the look over.

"I can't. I have an interview." Engine protested. "And I am already nervous."

"Just for me guys. Come on." Æsa begged. "We don't have a picture together since the last bonfire."

Stieg seemed to be drawn to Engine. Much to my amusement, he took a step closer to him and sniffed his neck. "Nice aftershave. Later?" He winked coyly at Engine who had the most uncomfortable look on his face.

Some pictures later, a happy Æsa sat down with a tall glass of iced coffee. Engine complained about his balls sweating in the Armani, and Æsa responded with a, "oh show me Ten-sqúat-a-way."

"In public Aesa? You have no shame woman." Engine responded lightly.

"So tell me, what are you two fools doing on this island? And why did neither of you had the courtesy to contact me?" I felt a moment of guilt at this as Æsa and I had been friends for so long. I had been so busy job hunting that I had forgotten she had married Leif Torje, a Norwegian billionaire three months ago and had moved with him to The Cayman Islands.

"Well," Engine started, "I am going for an interview and Kaman is going to jail."

She laughed, as if it was a joke. But then the maitre d' came to get Engine and the moment was gone to tell her it really was the truth. She had taken the time to put on a wrap that covered her lower body but left her bare above the waist. I sat down at her invitation and Stieg came to snap more pictures.

"Can you tell that guy to go away? He makes me jittery."

"Are you still homophobic, Kaman? Why are you so close minded? I don't understand this part of you."

"I am accepting. I am just watching my backside."

"I can't believe you're so backward in your thinking." She shook her head from side to side in disbelief. "So, what have you been up to? Just like that, you committed internet suicide?" Æsa had a soft gentle voice, one that Om-7 loves. Suddenly he was back in business as he cooed in contentment. If he wasn't a thing, I would believe that he had a hard-on for her.

"Æsa, I hate when people start sentences with 'so' and I dislike that you, a good friend, is spying on me."

"Oh get over your ass-holish-ness and get to the point. What is really happening to you? It's just not like you to disconnect from everyone. You are the guy who held us together. When we were all messed up, you clinched us together." She paused to take a sip and offered her straw to me. We had a special relationship, Æsa and I. She had shared her biggest secret with me years ago and so far I had not shared it with anyone, dead or alive. It had nothing to do with the size 36 CC breast implants that photographed so well and about which she was extremely sensitive.

I turned around to see how it was going with Engine. He didn't seem to have a problem. He was being put to the test. His interviewers were dressed casually in Bermudas and short sleeves shirts.

I noticed Mr. Yoshio then. He was big into black and white as he wore a shirt that was solid white with black collar and pockets. He was dining with his companion of last night, who now wore a mint green shirt over chinos and black cowboy hat on his head. I estimated both men to be in their late fifties.

"Æsa. Do you know those guys seated at the table next to where Engine is currently being put through the dryer."

Sipping her drink, she discreetly looked. "Yes, I do. Leif knows them very well. The Japanese guy is Izanagi Yoshio, internet porn king. The American is Jeremy Richard. He is in electronic commerce – specifics credit card. They work together in X-rated entertainment. Their names are never attached directly to these businesses. They have front men who do their dirty jobs. The snake man sitting at the table beside them is the body guard. Very dangerous, I heard."

I changed topics as Æsa's assistant arrived to arrange a hat. "How's the billionaire?"

"You mean the man I married and who you guys call the' rich old fool?'"

"Yeah, that same man."

"He has a name, you know. You guys are idiots. He's a good man. As we speak, he's probably trying to make another billion a million miles away."

She always spoke kindly of the billionaire whom I had never met. She took another sip from her drink and passed the glass to me. "Lex Xi is in Hong Kong," she said matter-of-factly.

"What's she doing there?" I had met Æsa and Lex Xi when we were kids and introduced them. They had become best friends, inseparable over the years until a recent falling out – the details of which neither of them wanted to divulge.

"You know Lex Xi. She's always in some martial arts competition. Oh, did you know Lex Xi met up with your sister in Hong Kong? Here's a photo Jalebi sent me. They both went crazy and had triple ear piercings." She passed her cell phone to me. It was one of those funny photos where Lex Xi and Jalebi, their tongues stuck out, pointed at each other's ears. I chuckled as I looked at the oddities in their appearance. Lex Xi was very delicate looking with straight black hair and had the pretty, pale complexion of an Oriental doll whereas Jalebi was taller and tanned with a full head of unkempt brown frizzy curls.

"How's it going with Lex Xi?" I asked cautiously.

"Good," she said, looking away.

I caught on to her tone. All was still not well. "The truth."

"Okay. You'll find out sooner or later. It's my fault. Lex Xi and I had a big fight. I shared my secret with her, the same one I shared with you so long ago. She had to open her big mouth and tell Leif that I don't want children. And he wants a child. He wants an heir for his massive empire. I really love this man and was working up the courage to tell him. I will never, ever forgive Lex Xi."

"Æsa . . . What can I say? Why didn't you tell him yourself?" I took her hands and massaged them.

"You think it's easy to talk about lynch syndrome? Suddenly, by default you're damaged goods. I remember my mother struggling to tell me about it before she died. Every day I wake up and worry that Æsa, the supermodel's fake breasts will be plastered over the media. No one will care about the circumstances behind it. I don't want to bring a child into this world who might be carrying the same gene. Don't say anything. I am selfish. I know I'm whining and complaining and I'm half naked sitting in a tropical paradise, so at least there's that. Enough about me. What's with you and India?"

"*Passé composé*, past tense. She ended it."

"See what I mean? Love sucks. In my case, it's man who could have been my father. Look at you. Just pining away for India."

Ω   Ω   Ω

Engine had texted Æsa that the interview would run late and that he would take a taxi back to the condo. When she passed the message to me, she apologized as she too had to finish another photo shoot at Rum Point. I got up to leave with promises that I would stay in touch.

"Promise me, you won't break that promise." She held on tightly to my hands. I promised, for the tenth time.

She suddenly smiled. "I still remember how I grabbed you in the gym and kissed you. It was the first time I kissed a boy. Do you remember?"

I did and laughed at the memory. "Was it that bad?" I asked mischievously.

"No, not at all. I was so madly in love with you then. And you, my first crush, had eyes only for India. Goodbye, my friend. I am always here if you need me. Always." She said softly into my eyes. She squeezed something into my hands. "Take this," she whispered.

I looked at the wad of money in my hands. "Æsa. No. I don't work this way. I have a policy. I don't take other people's money."

"I'm not other people, Kaman. I'm the friend whose hand you held while I recovered from a double mastectomy. And when you couldn't, you organized for one of our other friends to take over. You know, I was so close to having a mental breakdown when

I found out that I had breast cancer and had to have my breasts removed. Any girl at twenty would. I'm so lucky that I had you in my life." There was a tear in the corner of her eye. "Now, look what you've done. I am screwing up my mascara. Take the money and go or I will scream out so loudly that you grabbed my famous breasts." She reached for my shirt and wiped her eyes.

Once I was nestled comfortably in the car, I counted the money ... one thousand dollars ... a nice amount to last me a few weeks. I whistled and Om-7 whistled along with me as we drove out the parking lot of The Ritz.

Within twenty four hours, two friends had surfaced and it felt good to be surrounded by them. A last glance at Engine confirmed he was doing all right. He was relaxed in his chair.

Things were beginning to look up.

13 A Big Puzzle

MONEY can make anyone happy. Such was my mood as I turned up the volume and rapped along with the radio. I slowed down as I drove past the governor's house, as it didn't make sense to wake up the security guards who slept on the sneak during the hours that the governor went to church. I had to be careful, too, since I was an escaped convict with no identification.

What a mess, half of the house was covered in tarp. The gardens and grounds were dug up and there was no order to what was once a beautiful house.

My happiness was short lived. I saw the red flashing lights of the police car before I heard the sirens. It was speeding up to catch me. I cruised along slowly with the expectation to be pulled over while I thought up excuses. Maybe I will just slip them a hundred dollars now that I can afford it. These cops down here, like everywhere else, can turn a blind eye if you grease their hands with cash.

It pulled alongside and the cop indicated that I should roll down my mirror. 'Yuh crazy or what? Yuh bin to this island so many times before. Yuh should know by now that yuh drive on the left hand side. Pull over anyway."

I recognized him and apologized. He was a friend of MJ Rafiq. Having a cop as a friend in the Cayman Island makes for fewer problems with the law especially if you are a businessman.

"Where yuh bin hiding? I bin looking for yuh since yuh made yur great escape yesterday. No, don't tell me. I never saw yuh. If I did, then yuh know I will be helping a lawbreaker. I have a message from Rafiq. Says, he must see yuh, ASAP."

I thanked him and drove back to The Nexx Complex, parked the car and walked to Da Roti Shaq. MJ had just returned from church.

"What's so urgent you had to have your cop friend following me?"

"Yoo. It's a long story. In a nutshell it's like this. I had a visit last night from your friend, the Lady Doc. She had a proposition for me. Blew my mind away."

"Lady Doc?'

Rafiq and I often spoke English-based Creole, a common native language in Caribbean colonies. He had a very unique way of speaking – very fast with short sentences, and over-enunciating words. Sometimes, he starts off in English and then runs off in Creole or vice versa, depending on his mood.

"I know it is Sunday," he snapped his fingers. "Wake up mon. A whole lotta nefarious bizness happening on this island. I speak of your friend, Dr. Olga Old League."

"It's Dr. O'Ligue and she is not my friend. Just an acquaintance. What's with her?"

She's supposed to be in Miami, I recollected, at least that's what she said. Or was it the ketchup kid? I could not remember.

"Well, yuh know, word gets around on dis island. The Doc Lady found out I diddle-daddle in pirated movies. So she asks me if I'm interested in distributing X-rated adult movies. Yoo, can yuh believe dis?"

"That's porn MJ. What did you say?"

"I know eez porn. Think I'm stoo-pid? She made me an offer that was very interesting. She said she will be back with her biz-ness partner at a later date for further discussions. Yoo, when yuh gonna tell me yuh jumped jail." He placed both his arms on my shoulders and looked at me squarely. "I had to find this out in church. I look bad that I am your friend and I can't answer for you, especially since everyone knows you're deaf."

"I didn't want you to be involved in this mess."

"I'm already in this. I'll see what I can do on Monday. For now, stay low."

He left to tend to his business as a slew of diners arrived. I remembered then it was the ketchup kid who had told me about Dr. O's departure to Miami. I guessed she had returned early.

Ω   Ω   Ω

I decided to go back to Engine's condo and hang out. I saw Carlos on his balcony, his eyes glued to his laptop. He was still in his pajamas. From the sounds that reached me, he was play-ing video games. When I greeted him, he responded with a smile. I enquired about Ernesto, his brother, and he said he had gone to work.

"So, you alone?" I asked.

"Yay."

"Do you want to go for a burger with me downstairs?"

He thought about it. "Ya sure?"

"Yes. I hate eating alone. I don't hear too well. I need some-one to help me out." His eyes lit up. "But you gotta go change, comb your hair, and brush your teeth. You know, these boring things we have to do every day."

"Do I need to shower too?" It was not the kind of question I had expected.

"Most definitely. It makes the burgers taste better." He didn't bother to get out of the game he played. With speed he banged the patio door behind him. "Take your time, but I warn you, I'll be leaving in ten minutes." I reached over, picked up the laptop, and shut off the noise that was irritating me. After several pings and gotcha, I closed the game completely and froze when I saw the screensaver.

India.

The photo had to be recent for she wore a pashmina shawl with a heart pin I had bought her a month earlier. Some days later, I received the break-up letter. Her gold-colored eyes and the expression on her face were solemn. India always smiled and clowned around in pictures. Breaking the rules of ethics, I thumbed through the programs until a folder listed as Montreal caught my eye.

The contents were a series of old pictures of a family. The lady sat in a chair and held a baby, the man had his hand on her shoulder, and a young boy stood beside the lady. No one smiled in the picture. There were some of India when she was younger.

In another folder, I found out why India was so somber. She was in the company of Dr. O. Clicking "Properties" on the thumbnails, I saw they were dated two weeks ago with the location listed as Cayman Islands. I heard Carlos coming out of the shower, quickly deleted browsing history and brought up the Hot Babes site.

He smiled when he saw this. "I caught ya." He had that devilish look of a teenager. "I can show you better sites." I let him amuse me with several before we went down to the hamburger joint. The kid had the appetite of a rhinoceros. He ordered two half pounders, fries and onion rings, smothered them in ketchup, gobbled them down, and then asked if he could have two more.

I looked at him sideways. "What will you do for me in return?"

"I don't know. Ya asked me because ya is bored. So what ya want me to do in return?"

"I want to beat you in video games. Any game you want."

"Okay. But ya won't win. I tell ya now. I'm the best." He jabbed his index finger to his chest.

I suck at video games but most of all, the noises irritate Om-7. The idea was to get more information on India and the pictures.

He really was a nice kid. He told me his parents had died in a car accident in Brazil. The reason they were in the Cayman Islands was because all their inheritance money was left in a trust. Because of this, Ernesto had to work two jobs just to pay their living expenses. He mentioned Dr. O'Ligue was very nice and she let them stay rent-free in the unit she owns until everything is settled.

"Where were you born?" I asked him.

"Guess."

"Mexico?" He shook his head to indicate no. "Puerto Rico." He shook his head again.

"I will buy you two more burgers if you stop making me guess."

"Montreal. Canada," he said.

"That's where I was born." If my voice sounded surprised, I was.

"I know. Ernesto told me."

"How does Ernesto know this?" I am more surprised than before.

"I don't know. Ask him"

He ate the third hamburger with the same energy as he did the others and wrapped the fourth to take home. When he was finished, there was ketchup and mustard on his face. I reminded him kindly that he always had to wipe his face after he finished a meal.

Back on his balcony, I feigned noise disturbance, by touching Om-7 and asked if we could sit inside. At the kitchen table, he powered up the laptop.

"Who's she?" I asked, pointing to the screensaver.

"She's beautiful. She is from Montreal, too. I love her."

So do I, I wanted to scream.

"What's her name?"

"India."

"How do you know her?"

"Who ya be? CIA? FBI? KGB? MI6? Ya ask too many questions?" He thumbed her face to enlarge.

"None of those, Carlos, I only wanted to know how you know her. She is very beautiful."

"What now? Ya making me sound like a loser. Ya think I can't score because she's very beautiful? I don't want to score with her. She's like my sister. I tell ya something. I am not a loser. I scored with the maid."

I blinked a few times at this news.

"Wow," I managed.

"Why ya so surprise? Hollywood stars do it and other famous people too. Nothing wrong with me doing the same."

"Enough," I chuckled. "The maid is always a good place to start. So, you gonna tell me how you know this beautiful girl?" I used a gentle tone to coerce him as I pointed to the screen.

"I know of her and her family for a long time. My parents told Ernesto and me about our life in Montreal before we went to Florida. They told us how some families helped us." His fast fingers scrolled around to find games. "They always cry when they talk about that night I came into the world. But, I never met India in person. Dr. O'Ligue doesn't like her." He confided.

"How do you know this?" The hair on the back of my neck rose.

"She's mean to her. I heard them screaming at each other on the first day we moved in."

"What?"

"I heard other things, too, but can't tell ya? Only thing I tell ya is never enter small room in Dr. O's condo." He emphasized this by nodding his head. "Yes. Never. Let's go back on the balcony. It's so hot in here. I forgot to tell ya. The AC is broken."

I lost all interest in video gaming. Everything surrounding India was becoming a big puzzle. I will have to wait for an opportune moment to steal the kid's laptop.

14 Coming Out

THE KID GAVE me an ass-whooping in video games and he enjoyed every minute of it. Engine's arrival saved me.

"I am in," he shouted across the balcony.

I promised Carlos I would take him up on another challenge soon, as I climbed over the balcony rails, excited to hear Engine's news.

He had stripped himself of the suit and was only in his underwear when I re-entered. He emptied his backpack on the sofa opposite me, found some clothes and took his time getting dressed, his mood of happiness obvious in the manner he moved his torso from side to side. He stopped and raised his arms toward the ceiling, shouting, "YES!" He switched to Mohawk, "*Wakatonhnháhere,*" and back to English, "I am so happy."

There were several cans of coconut water on the table. He passed one to me and opened one for himself.

"This shit really works. Thank you for introducing me to instant calm-the-nerves remedy."

"Will you tell me, or do I have to wait till same time next year?"

"Well, it's like this. I have officially been hired to join the team of the British firm Maple & Maple, world-renowned for hedge funds. Below the surface, there's a hint they are trying to get their tentacles into the internet gambling business. And you know who Numero Uno is in that? My people." He said proudly.

"They had no complaints about your hair then?"

"They actually liked it. I asked if I could keep it and they said, 'most certainly.' Mo-fo's made me sweat in my suit while they sat comfortably dressed."

"So, what's next?"

"They made me sign a contract on the spot. The training will be rigorous. First month is wills and estates. Second month is acquisitions. Third month hasn't been settled yet. There's travel involved, depending on the case. I have already been lined up to go to England with the guy who handles trustees. Dude, I thought law school was hard but an interview by a team of three managing partners is frigging tedious. Whew." He took a long, deep breath.

"You clinched it."

"These guys handle a lot of stuff. I have to tell you two things. One has to do with you and the other with me. Which one do you want to hear first?"

"You choose," I said off-hand.

"During a break in the interview this morning, one of the partners was discussing the case of an estate. They were name-dropping without using the real names. The deceased, a thirty-seven-year-old financial whiz, died in a boating accident a year ago and bequeathed his estate to his dearly beloved wife who is in her late fifties. For the conversation, the man was referred to as Mr. Wiz and the woman as The Cougar."

I laughed. Lawyers have a way with words.

"Since it's a case that's handled by the number one law firm in Cayman, it goes without saying there's big bucks involved. Who do you think has the money?"

"The Cougar, naturally."

"They both did until Mr. Wiz started gambling and dried himself out. He then convinced The Cougar he could invest and double her money within a short time. So they opened joint accounts and he handled everything. Mr. Wiz had two addictions, internet gambling and pornography. He did well in the beginning with the gambling, but then his luck changed. He lost all of their money. The Cougar was under suspicion when he died in a boating accident off Paradise Beach, but she had a bona fide alibi. Two undercover police officers came forward with statements they were with her at a garage in Bodden Town as she had car problems. The garage owner confirmed this. So she came out clean, but not from the debt he ran up. The bottom end of it is Mr. Wiz had a two million dollar life insurance policy which he left to his parents. Now The Cougar is laying claim to it. The Wiz also had several condos and some high-end food and beverage joints that she did not know about. This, he sold in a private deal to a couple who passed away recently, and that's when the case becomes a dead end. Guess who The Cougar was?"

"Not my mother, nor your mother. For sure. Give me some hints."

"They didn't say her name outright, but said she's a bestselling author who lives on island."

"You're kidding? You're not speaking about?" I pointed toward Dr. O's condo.

"Yes, yours truly, Dr. O'Ligue. She is in dire straits. The money from the sales of her novels is barely keeping her afloat."

I am stunned as I summed up this information. I lived in her beach condo. She has several key codes allowing her easy entry and exit. Her husband died in a boating accident off Paradise Beach, and she has been a suspect. I am just lucky the cops got me before she did.

I reached for a bottle of Caybrew and downed the contents.

Ω   Ω   Ω

Once the shock of Dr. O's current financial situation receded, Engine and I passed the late afternoon watching golf and discussing why Tiger Woods was the world's greatest golfer. We became golf critics trying to second guess who would win, although we both wanted Tiger to walk away with the pot of money. Without either of us noticing, it had turned to a dusky evening.

"See, this makes African-Americans proud to have one of their own be the best," Engine remarked. He was now on his second can of coconut water.

"Tiger Woods would dispute what you just said. He came out and refuted that idea of being dubbed African American. He made up a new ethnicity 'Cablinasian.'

"He came out, huh?" Engine's voice was strangely quiet.

Something was not right or maybe it was the way he said it. I touched Om-7.

"He didn't come out like he's gay. He came out with a new terminology for his ethnicity." I said quickly.

He looked at his hands, thumbed his middle finger nails before he picked up the remote and channel surfed.

"Go back. There's my favorite comedian."

He switched back to Ellen doing her stand-up *shtick*. I laughed at the jokes; but he didn't.

"What?" I looked at his serious expression. "You don't like her?"

He muted the television.

"I am like her."

He was silent. I waited. Om-7 perked up.

"I'm gay," he said quietly.

I process those two words. There was a weird look on his face. I felt a heatwave slowly creep through my body as I looked at him and suppressed it. Another of Engine's jokes, I smiled.

"I got it. This is payback for the gold story, which you didn't believe." I shook a pointed finger at him and chuckled. "You're shitting with me, right?"

He looked at me, his face at an angle covered in conflicting emotions. "I haven't told my parents yet. You are the first person I am telling."

I got up, rubbed my hands through my hair, sat down, got up again as I tried to deal with the shock. My emotions went into every direction, I opened my mouth to say something and no words would come out.

He, too, tried to say something and couldn't. He sat quietly, looking at his thumbs and index fingers which he had joined to form a tepee. I looked at him, really looked.

He was still Engine, my best friend.

But he's gay. My brain screamed.

"Answer me one thing, Engine. Did you ever have it – I mean – the gay feeling for me?" I had to know if our relationship was like that. A disturbing thought at the moment. I saw the hurt in his eyes.

"No. You were always a friend to me. My best friend. Your

family was like my second family." His voice was so clear, so distinct.

"I can't deal with this." I walked out the condo, down the corridor, ran down the stairs out into the courtyard. I ran all the way to Camana Bay.

The dusky evening had turned into night.

A dark night.

Ω   Ω   Ω

I walked around Camana Bay, replaying Engine's coming out. Still, I could not understand how he, so macho with his muscled and toned body, could be gay. He had been the captain of the lacrosse team for years in high school and a strong wrestler who had won championships for his club. I questioned how and when he had turned for he always had a girlfriend, sometimes two at the same time.

Distraught. I found a bench by the waterway, far away from the hub of activity and sat down, ignoring the world around me. I got up, walked around and redid the same route several times. Still my insides churned. From time to time, I wiped the moisture at the corners of my eyes.

Om-7 had a reaction to this terrible news. He went from tooting to tick-tocking to zinging – ugly sounds that irritate me and made me angry

"Stop it." I aggressively tapped him.

"*No. You stop.*"

"Whose side are you on anyway?"

"*The right side. It's wrong what you did.*"

"He's gay. And that's not right."

"*According to who, you?*"

"Yes, me."

"*You forgot this gay person was the first friend to ring your doorbell back in the day when you had no friends.*"

I took him off and shook him vigorously, before replacing him with a warning to 'behave.'

"Ever think about how snafu-ed you are?" He just had to have the last word.

I looked at Vibe, counted the hours since I had heard those fateful words that now echo-chambered in my head. The right side and the left side of my brain had an ongoing argument that didn't improve my overall understanding or make things better. Accept it, the holistic side argued, but the linear and, supposedly, rational side just would not cooperate. 'Never,' it shouted into Om-7's sensory circuit which, in turn, reverberated into my head. The discussion went on for hours as I walked aimlessly around Camana Bay.

Yet, I could not come to terms with my best friend's homosexuality.

15 Da Roti Shack

AT MIDNIGHT, I took a taxi to Da Roti Shack and found MJ, car keys in hand, ready to leave for the night. On seeing me, he quickly opened the door and pulled me inside.

"You're all over the TV."

"What do you mean?"

"Well, the poo-lice are looking for you. TV news story is like this. Yesterday, they had you in a poo-lice car and a tourist drove off with the vee-hicle. They are concerned you may be in danger. They mentioned you are deaf and handicapped. They showed a cari-cature of what they think you look like. One ugly looking face the artist drew." He wiped his forehead with a hand. "Yoo, I am glad you okay. So? What's your story?"

I told him a partial version, excluding Engine's connection.

"I thought you're camping out with your friend Ten-squat-a-way."

"No, He just got hired by Maples & Maples. Won't do his career any good if he's caught helping a criminal." Om-7 buzzed at my little lie and I looked away.

"Can I do anything to help? Need a place to sleep? Need to go anywhere? I can drive you. I can't take you to my place. I already have three Cubans who have no work permits. You can sleep here if you want. Put some chairs together. But, I gotta tell you, there's a cock-a-roach infestation at the moment." He opened the fridge. "Lemme pack you up some food." MJ was a mix of half East Indian and half West African. His mother, like mine, was from Guyana where I met him. His dad was from Trinidad. In his teenage years, he adopted his father's country of birth as his own. Uncle the Drunk helped him move to the Cayman Islands some years back when he had a small run-in with the law in Trinidad. When he decided to open a restaurant that served Caribbean food, he asked for my 'background knowledge,' as he had put it then.

I took up his offer, and asked for a lift to Paradise Beach. My mindset was that I would find a comfortable chair and sleep on the beach.

"So, what you gonna do? You gonna go back to Canada? Yes?"

"I dunno."

"You gonna stay and go to prison? Yes?" He didn't wait for me to answer. "I had one young Cuban guy who worked with me. Good looking guy, too. Only twenty-one years old. Went in for selling ganja on the side. When he came out, he couldn't walk straight. He said every night he had to bend over for someone's pleasure. His knees were busted every time he refused. That's why he couldn't walk straight."

"Gee, thanks, MJ." I answered, my voice ten decibels lower than usual. I had no feeling left after Engine's bombshell. Jail time didn't bother me at the moment, not even the possibility of being subjected to . . . I didn't want to think further about this.

"Yoo, listen up. When I was a kid, MJ was cool. I am a businessman now, so the name is Rafiq. I know you have fond memories of our younger days. Me too. But, a guy has to grow up sometime." He swished his dreds a few times. "Back to Cayman prison. I ain't joking man. It ain't like other prisons. You gotta be tough and always watch out. Naa-sty place. And you have the rights to make one phone call. You call me if you happen to be there. I know the judge. He's from Jamaica. Comes in all the time to eat roti and goat curry and have a few slugs of Appleton. You have my cell number? Yes?"

I answered no.

"Just dial Da Roti Shaq. It's easy to remember. Memorize it in your head. Don't forget now. You did me a big favor once. Now, it's my turn. I mean this my friend." He saw me mumbling the number. "Here, take the number straight off the phone," he said passing it to me as he swerved to avoid a cow.

I didn't remember what favor I had done, but I was ready to take any favors Rafiq offered. He was a good sport whose biggest laugh in life was to cheat the system, and whose big heart readily gave to those in need: Robin Hood in real life, outside of Sherwood Forest.

He came out of the car when we arrived in the parking lot, and shook my hands till they hurt. "Yuh sure yuh gonna be all right?"

"Yeah, Yeah." I saw the worry in his face.

"Yoo, Most important is that you keep your ear to the ground. More news in Cayman jail than outside. Don't forget."

Ω   Ω   Ω

It was shadowy dark as I made my way up the stairs at Paradise beach. I lit a cigarette. It was a bad habit I had worked hard to kick, but hadn't. Not that I was a total failure. I had lessened my intake by fifteen per day with India's constant harassment. The payout had been worth the trouble; good sex in return for quitting. Not just good sex, but great sex, the kind that, when it was over, you lie back and realize you may have just crossed the Milky Way without dying. A smile broadened on my face as I remembered, until I felt the pain pummel my chest intrusively. The ache of losing her did not lessen as everyone who knew about it advocated. "Time heals" was pure bullshit. My cranium hurt from thinking about her, thinking about doing time in Cayman prison and the possibility of having busted knees on coming out, if ever I came out.

A movement caught my eye as I scanned the area. I saw Rooslahn, leaving his unit with something heavy which made him move slowly. Stamping out the cigarette, I stepped behind some sea-grape trees and watch him move along the sidelines of the buildings until he reached the beach. I sidetracked to leave the bag with the food in the back stairs, when I felt something vibrate. Rafiq's phone had fallen in the bag when he swerved to avoid a collision. I turned it off.

I followed Rooslahn, keeping my distance and staying in the shadows. He walked down to the end of the pier and started to dress in scuba gear. I realized then the weight he carried was diving equipment. All of his movements indicated he was doing something on the sneak; the way he looked around and lying down flat on the boards when the Cayman Police helicopter did its nightly check. He flicked on his dive light when he was submerged, visible as a streak as he moved toward the reef. I made my way under the pier to a point where there was bare sand, wet from the receding tide which gave me a good view of the water.

He skirted the area, moving from section to section, and then backtracked. When he finally surfaced and climbed the stairs to the pier, he seemed disappointed. The stop watch on Vibe showed he had spent one hour and fifty minutes underwater.

The slow dragging sound of rubber boots on the wooden pier announced the arrival of another person. Through the cracks I saw the outline of Netts. He turned around as if he sensed a presence. I held my breath. He stopped again, seemed unsure, and then continued on to meet Rooslahn. I exhaled.

There was an exchange that Om-7 could not pick up. From the time we left Engine's condo, I just could not depend on him. He was in a bad mood or chose to act up.

The gold-digging opportunists sat down at the edge of the pier. I crawled slowly in the sand until I was below their dangling feet. Some baby crabs scampered off.

Om-7 jerked back to co-operation mode. Perhaps the proximity of water, which he doesn't like, or his on-off relationship with Vibe who had no such problem, incited this new behavior. What I heard was a discussion about the recently dead, or more-likely, murdered, tiger shark and the amount of cocaine retrieved from its belly

"I am telling you," Netts insisted. "The usual drop-off point is northeast to the pier, about thirty degrees to the right. It is always white gold. I'm telling you too, as a certainty, there is no yellow gold. They don't do yellow gold."

"How do you know this?" Rooslahn asked. "The boat that did the drop has been in port. It means that someone else knows about this. The question is who."

"I am here every night. Besides the kid, there was no one else. And you know the kid is deaf and just does not have the capabilities and smarts to handle that kind of stuff."

I tapped Om-7 lightly, and mouthed, "You heard that?"

"Maybe the kid will surprise you," Rooslahn added. "Who would move it so quickly? Damn good whoever it is. You must know, Netts."

"What I know is that I am disgusted at the way that shark was killed. As a fifth-generation fisherman, I never kill unnecessarily from the seas. There is no respect for nature when such a useless slaughter takes place."

I silently lauded Netts and his ancestors for such strong beliefs.

"We know that the tiger shark accidentally ate up the white gold. I felt bad what happened to him after, but it was a lot of money sitting in his gut. Besides, it was blinded from the few packages that broke and was already beached." Rooslahn's explanation sounded like an excuse to placate Netts. They sat silently smoking until Rooslahn broke the silence.

"Goddamn, Netts. We have to watch the reef closely to see who's playing around here. I will double up your price if you find out who. I will bring you a deposit tomorrow. You okay with this?"

I knew Netts was always okay with money. He had three wives, and between them, eleven children to feed.

"Are you going out tonight?" The Russian rose and rid himself of his wet suit.

"Nah. See the clouds over there. Fierce storm coming in."

I believed him as he had often predicted the weather within the tolerances set by meteorological bodies. I heard their footsteps as they trudged overhead towards the beach.

I felt the intrusion of something crawling on my hand. It crossed the strap of Vibe, and settled one-half of its body on the plastic face and the other on my skin. It stayed still, and as lightweight as it was, I felt its presence. Slowly, I raised my hand up to inspect. It was a tiny baby crab. It moved away awkwardly as if bothered by my warm breath. In doing so, it activated one of the little buttons on the watch. The face lit up.

I had forgotten that Vibe had so many gadgets, a very good thing and a very bad thing. The worst of bad things was every time a function is initiated, Om-7 starts an ugly tick-tocking. I don't know if he felt some competition, but it irritated the shit out of me when he got like this. I wanted to swat him but that would only hurt me. Instead, I tried gently to flick away the baby crab, but the little guy, sensing danger, had made off, but not before he managed to set off more functions on Vibe.

The vibrations varied from slow to fast. The face changed colors, blinked from green to blue to orange. When the beeper went off, I ducked my hand into the water. It stopped, but the lights still changed underwater.

Overhead, the footsteps came to an abrupt halt. "Glow fish are back. I didn't see them last night," Netts said matter-of-factly.

They went their separate ways. Fifteen minutes later, I belly crawled in the sand to the front of the buildings. The skies opened in a downpour and the sea disappeared from view. Totally drenched, I let myself into Dr. O's condo and climbed the stairs in total darkness. With only the light of Vibe, I took a shower, dried my clothes and re-counted the ten hundred dollar bills Æsa had given me. I stuffed the ten crispy bills into the center of the foam in the double-zippered mattress of Chewy's bed.

I relished the meal that Rafiq had packed. At intervals, I checked out the apps on his phone. He had a profitable side business of bringing in high-end electronics, mostly cell phones,

that 'fell off the truck' in Miami, and sold them 'under the table.'
I slept very soundly that night, awaking only when Rafiq telephoned at ten o'clock.

"Yoo. Lady Doc just accosted me in parking lot. She's asking
if I knew your where-a-bouts. I said last time I saw you, you were
on the TV news. She's looking for you, all kinds. It appears she's
in one big hurry to find you. I say, you better disappear. She gives
me ugly-bad vibes. I am sending a taxi to get you out of there, but
walk to Conch Point. Leave my cell with the driver."

It didn't take me long to clean up and leave the condo.
I walked along hidden pathways to Conch Point where the taxi
waited. I didn't leave with the woman driver. I gave her my back
pack, Rafiq's phone and a letter.

16 Imprisoned

AT EXACTLY 11:11 A.M., I surrendered myself to The West
Bay Police. An hour later, I was driven to the Cayman prison
for men. Half-an-hour later, I was incarcerated for possession of
illegal substances.

I looked across at the paper pusher, an unfriendly character
who had taken, and now taped, a black and white Polaroid picture of myself on a sheet of paper. Across from the picture, he
wrote in big, bold letters, 'DEAF.' When he was finished, he forc-
ibly stamped a seal at the bottom of the page.

At the top, the words 'Her Majesty' was visible under a crown.
His hand covered some other words, but at the end, 'Service'
stared clearly at me.

I could think of only one other man who gave himself so freely
to be under the auspices of 'Her Majesty's Service.'

James Bond.

Later, a guard in his mid-fifties introduced himself as Mr. Rory
McCabe. He was a Caymanian, tall, muscular man with impressive biceps and wore a cross on a chain around his neck. This

meant the proper way to address him, Cayman-style, would be Mr. Rory, which I did. He seemed sympathetic to my deafness as he tried to communicate via signs. I had to empty my pockets which had some Cayman coins, a few US dollars, a keychain with a sign that read, "In God We Trust," and a business card of Da Roti Shaq. He kept the card, looked at the keychain with such interest that I offered it to him. He smiled and held it to his heart in an appreciative manner. He indicated that I remove Om-7 and inspected him thoroughly, then placed him beside the money. He signed for me to take off Vibe, and I explained to him that the watch and the hearing device worked together. The blessing in being hearing impaired is I can tell tall tales. In other words, bullshit. And since I do not hear clearly the sounds of my words without Om-7, there is no guilt.

He wanted to test it. He placed Om-7 on his ear and wrapped Vibe around his wrist. I had pressed the function key on Vibe prior to handing him over. Mr. Rory shook his head in a disagreeable manner, covered his ears with both hands and removed both of them simultaneously. I am sure Om-7 showed off with his tick-tocking sounds. When he returned the gadgets, he asked how come a 'clean-cut young man' like me got involved in drugs.

I asked for my one phone call and dialed Rafiq's cell phone. No answer. I tried Da Roti Shaq business phone, still no response. I tried Æsa's mobile and got a voice message that she is away and will be back in ten days, and to call her manager in case of emergency. As a last resort, I tried Engine and I hung up when his answering machine greeted me with, 'This is Ten-squat-a-way. Please leave a message,'

Mr. Rory took a call on his cell phone. His face softened to an intimate smile as he turned away to read my prison report; an opportune moment for me as I had noticed that one of the U.S. dollars had a heart with two arrows penned in red ink. A keepsake. Without thinking, I grabbed it, along with a few more dollars and tucked it all under Vibe.

He led me down a dark, decrepit and dirty hallway which

intersected with another. It smelled of stale urine, body odor and marijuana. It was an intimidating and oppressive atmosphere as I walked by the cells and prisoners stood to attention to welcome me in a silent check-out. Some called out greetings to Mr. Rory.

I understood what the word "pen" as used to describe prison meant. The cells were like cages with barred metal doors complete with locks, each with two prisoners apiece.

Mr. Rory turned a corner, opened a door, stepped aside and indicated that I enter. Though it was bright and sunny outside, the lack of light and ventilation made the small area dark and morbid. I saw the figure of the big, burly man who appeared to be sleeping on a cot, his back to the entrance. Another cot rested on the opposite wall. A tea-colored stained toilet bowl separated the two beds.

"Sparky, you got company." Mr. Rory shouted out.

The only part of Sparky's body that moved in response, was his middle finger.

"You behave now." Mr. Rory said as he locked the door and departed.

I said a greeting to Sparky, but he ignored me. Cautiously, I laid down on the vacant cot and fiddled with Om-7, comfortable only when I heard his heavy breathing. I made a silent vow never to go to sleep and never to use the toilet that faced me. Later, I heard movements. Sparky arranged a blanket to make a screen around his cot. My view became one of a wall, a blanket and a dirty toilet with a ring around the collar.

I had a good look at Sparky at dinnertime in the cafeteria. He was huge, at least three hundred and fifty pounds, light on his feet, a head taller than all the prisoners and spoke to no one. He had a full mouth of gold teeth. I figure that's how he got the name Sparky. I followed him. The other prisoners moved away from the food line when he arrived. They all stared at me, some shook their heads in disbelief. The servers behind the food counter stepped back when they served him, but they gave him doubles of everything. Once he was comfortably seated, the other prisoners made for the food line in a hurried manner that reminded me of a high school cafeteria, except that there were no girls with legs exposed in short skirts.

I decided to take the bull by the horns. I followed Sparky with a plate full of glob and sat opposite him at his table as he gobbled down his food. When he was finished, he leaned back in his chair and stared me down. As uncomfortable as it was, I kept his gaze and, thinking that he wanted my food, I passed the plate to him. Still in a full stare, he took it, scooped half of the contents into his plate, forked it down quickly and followed with a horrible belch. Then he winked at me.

He got up slowly, made his way around the room, grabbed plates at random, and ate half of the contents before returning them. No complaints were voiced. I noticed that when he reached the table with the younger prisoners, he bypassed them, touched their heads playfully. Were they his 'bend over boys?' My stomach somersaulted. *God, help me, I share a cell with this individual who may be a pervert.*

I made sure I stayed awake. I started to play mind games with Om-7, who was made in the USA and Vibe, who was made in Russia. Vibe was a vibrating state-of-the art prototype computer watch, newly developed for scuba divers who were hearing impaired. I won it in an online writing contest where I had to write a 1,000-word essay to explain why I would be a good match for this one-of-a kind gadget. The truth is India had entered my name in the contest and forced me to write the essay. Surprisingly, I won. When Vibe arrived in a beautiful box a month ago, she felt it had to have a cool name like Om-7, and so had laughingly called it "Vibrator." I shortened it to Vibe, for obvious reasons.

India insisted that Vibe should also have a mental sex and made it a female, since Om-7 is a male. The problem was that Om-7's electronics sometimes reacted to Vibe's mechanical and untimely malfunctions. Sometimes, I think they feel a certain entitlement that they should not get along because of their respective countries' history. They had their own cold war going on. I decided to be their peacemaker.

Now, as I worked my way through the buttons, I was able to associate some that were aggressors to Om-7. There were still others that I couldn't figure out. I set her to go off at quarter-hour intervals, in case I fell asleep.

Sparky got up fifteen minutes after lights out. He held a mini-lite, the size of his pinky finger which he used to find his way to the toilet, right in my view. I turned my back to the wall and pulled the blanket tightly around me.

No one would want to be where I was at that moment. Sparky's bowels exploded with horrific thunder sounds. The smell that emanated surrounded the room, and replaced the stale air very quickly. I covered my nose with the blanket; could not block it out so I took to deep breathing. I now know you could taste the smell of shit if you open your mouth at the wrong time.

This abuse of my senses lasted for twenty minutes as Vibe reminded me with her pulsations. I prayed the toilet would flush. I wondered if anyone had died from stench and if I would be the first before the night was over.

"*Merde*. Shit. No paper." Those were the first words I heard Sparky utter. I mentally noted that he said shit in *French*.

"You got paper?" He called out to me.

"Call the guard." I advised.

"I can't." He responded.

"Why?"

"Because he will come into the cell. I cannot allow him to do that."

"Why?" I sounded like a four year old, I knew.

"Lingo. Three hundred dollars' worth. Under my cot. And if you squeal, you die." The threat registered.

"I only have dollar bills." I got up, holding my breath as if I was underwater, releasing at intervals and gave him five single bills.

He concentrated the mini lite on the bills. "All Yankee dollars. Ah-ah-ah. Here's one that's different, a heart with two arrows

crossed at the midpoint, 'India loves Kaman.' And 'Kaman loves
India.' He looked at me, his head tilted to one side. "You sure
I can wipe my ass with this?"

I shook my head. "Yup, that's what Yankee dollars with love
notes are worth. Ass wipes."

Luckily the toilet flushed.

Ω   Ω   Ω

I found out what lingo was the next night.

It started at breakfast, continued through lunch and progressed
to dinner time. It was an impressive combination of a tiered supply
chain with free trade and barter within less than two blocks of run-
down buildings surrounded with a barbed wire fence.

In the morning, I saw some of the inmates fill large bottles
with orange and pineapple juice from the jugs in the cafeteria. An
associate filled up on sugar at noon. Some packets of yeast traded
hands at the food counter in the evening. These ingredients were
delivered discreetly to my new quarters, picked up by Sparky and
hidden under his cot

As soon as lights out was announced, and after Sparky had
indulged in his midnight-to-morn shit, he set to work in his
brewery. He asked me to help him fill plastic bottles with juice,
sugar and yeast. I didn't argue as I had suspicions that it would
not be of any use. He capped each bottle that I filled and placed
it neatly aside. He explained it took five to seven days to ferment
before it would be passed on to the distributor, who would then
deliver to the sales unit. From under the cot he withdrew his in-
process inventory and loosened the cap a notch on each bottle.
He whispered in the darkness that this released the pressure
build-up so it doesn't explode and he kissed each bottle before
replacing it in his stockroom. He offered me a bottle, which
I refused.

"You want to hear what it sounds like?" He didn't wait for an
answer. He went to the cell bars with the bottle, knocked gently
on the walls and whispered, "Hey, Loco, special bottle for you."

The bottle changed hands and Sparky indicated I should get back in bed. He hurriedly tucked himself in and closed the blanket. The explosion sounded like a gunshot which brought the guard to investigate. When the racket was over, he whispered. "You heard that?"

"Incredible." I answered back, amused at his mischief. "*Incroyable.*"

He pulled his blanket quickly to the side. "*Vous parlez français?* You speak French?"

He kept me up all night speaking in his preferred language. He told me he was a *méli-mélo*, a mish-mash and that he was born in French Guiana – *Guyane Français*, which used to be a French penal colony in South America and he had been a seaman since he was a teenager. The reason he was in prison, he explained, was that he was in the wrong place at the wrong time. His container ship had landed in the Cayman Islands at lunch hour. He was so hungry he went to a Spaghetti House that advertised 'All You Can Eat,' but forgot a time frame. So he had indulged himself and would not leave as he thought he had all day. The restaurant's management, all Italians, threw him out, which he thought was unreasonable. This made him so h-angry, and, as he was still hungry, he did something that anyone in this situation would have done. He sneaked back into the restaurant and broke all the chair and table legs before he hurried off. The police grabbed him by the port and he missed his ship. That was a month ago. He still had another two months of jail time.

"*Les Italiens.*" He was still bitter from the experience. "Goddamn Italians. When I get out, I am going to break all their legs. Give them a taste of their own medicine."

I thought it was best not to tell him that my Pa was Italian.

Ω Ω Ω

MJ visited the following week with a package of goat curry and rotis. He apologized for not being there earlier. He had to fly out to Trinidad on some emergency business. Customs had seized a recent shipment of electronics en route from Miami. Upon his return, he made contact with the judge who informed him that bail for inmate Kaman Colioni had been posted at twenty thousand Cayman dollars. He was more apologetic as he didn't have that kind of money. He asked me what else he could do to help.

"You want me to call your parents? Your brother or your sister? Your ex-girlfriend? What about your indigenous Mohawk friend?" They were all on the list of people I was embarrassed to call. I turned down his offer.

When the guard went to the toilet, I asked him about the meeting he had with Toussaint and my brother at the French Fusion and he whispered some tidbits about the gold, but not enough to make me worry.

"Yoo. The Lady Doc. She never came back with the porn business. I think someone is hustling her?"

"How do you know?"

"People talk on this island. I listen when they do. Can't say more than that right now."

I gave the food to Sparky. He ate it slowly, which was a surprise, and licked his fingers before he belched. "*Absolument Délicieux.* Absolutely Delicious."

Every second day, MJ visited with food packages. He had business with the guard and inmates on the side. He offered me a cell phone, which I gave to Sparky. On one of the visits, he told me that my Mohawk friend, Ten-squat-a-way had dropped by Da Roti Shaq to pick up some food and they had enjoyed a few beers.

"Nice guy. I have a lot of respect for him," MJ shook his dreds. "A whole lotta respect."

17 My Soap Opera Life

THE NIGHTS passed quickly now that I had befriended Sparky. After our lingo business hours, he sat on his bed and we chatted. He wanted to know about the Yankee dollar with the heart. My ex-love-life, cum failed-romance, became a nightly soap opera as I told him everything about India: how she was searching for her real parents; her life with her foster parents, and her adopted parents; how she was sexually abused by her foster father; how I didn't like her when she was little, and then fell in love with her, and now I wish I could fall out of love.

After the first night of me talking about India, Sparky moved over to sit on the floor beside the bed. The first thing he did was shut off his phone, or so I thought. He listened intently as I lay down on the bed and spoke about India. When I told him she had given me the Yankee dollar as a token of her love, and that, if it is returned to her, then she will know for sure that I love her back, he actually cried. "L'amour, it is so sweet." He wiped his eyes. "I wish in the final episode that it will be returned to her."

On the night that I told the story of our favorite diving experience together on our last visit to the island, Sparky inched closer to me as I spoke.

India and I had just returned from a trip out to the reef and sat in the sand at the water's edge. She was ecstatic and tickled to the core from what we had seen underwater. A male octopus had mounted a female. She chattered non-stop about the whole reproductive process of the octopus' genre. I felt sad for the poor guys as I had read that the male octopus dies soon after mating, and the female dies soon after her eggs are hatched. Such a poetic tragedy. I dozed off with this sweet memory and dreamt.

I AM ASLEEP IN a chaise lounge on the beach. Arms tighten around me, I awake in a start. Was it an octopus? The warmth of legs straddle

me and I feel the soft and curvy body. A woman. Gently, she moves
my legs apart as she tries to find a comfortable spot before she pushes
herself into a desired position, as if she was made to be there.

Her hands move along the sides of my body to my shoulders
where they stop for seconds and then continue upward to tantalize my
senses. Fingertips gently circle my head, my forehead and my neck.
I close my eyes, lost in the feathery touches along my cheekbones.

I gasp out her name. "India."

Soft lips plant kisses in the path of her fingers. I lift my hands to
touch the Cupid's bow. It quivers in response. I caress them over and
over. She moans softly.

"Kaman." She responds into my mouth.

She tastes of savory and sweet. A mixture of salty sea and tira-
misu. Of a good shot of aged rum that rushes to the head.

With both arms I reach for her, pull her body closer into mine.
She sighs pure contentment. I brush some curls off her cheek and
place them behind her ear. Her body trembles when I prop the back
of her head with one hand. She reaches out, takes my other hand and
places it over her heart.

The rest of the world disappears. We are alone, two souls reaching
out to each other with racing hearts.

I am in trouble.

Slowly, she brings her lips to mine. I inhale her breath, suck it
into my lungs and feel the desire to have her flood my body.

Her hips gyrate into mine, pushing . . . pressing . . . alternating
between the two. My hardness responds to her softness. My hand on
her heart continues on a journey to her navel, stops and plays with
the belly button piercing. I search for the clasps of a bra but there is
none. Slowly I pull the top over her head. Her breasts spill free. She
giggles and covers them coyly.

I rise, lift her with care, as if she were a delicate porcelain doll,
and ease her down to the far end of the chaise lounge. It is a fight to
unzip the jeans she wears like a second skin, but I was on a mission
where failure was not an option.

I lift her hips up to my face, bury my head into the part of her
body now exposed by the zipper. Bits of lace are rough against my

skin as I overdose on the scent that is just hers. I drop kisses and watch the fire in her eyes. Come hither, they blaze.

I kneel into the sand and lift one leg. With my teeth, I pull and tug at the jeans, undaunted by the obstruction of her curvaceous hips. Moving to the other side, I continue an onslaught that has her wild. She rears with a frenzy and helps me push her jeans to her knees.

She tingles with excitement.

Rising to a sitting position on the chair, she wraps her legs around my head.

My manhood is ready to explode.

Danger, my brain screams.

Her breathing comes out in short, desperate gasps. Mine is ragged. I feel the fiery heat of her womanhood, the sensual smell of her wanting us to become one. She is lost in lust.

"Take me," She begs.

Om-7, my mimesis, spits out his version of some Scottish poetry.

No you lovely lass of wickedness,

Nae joy nor pleasure shall thou see;

For, evening to morn thou shalt cry, alas!

And aye the salt tear shall blin's thy eye.

I stop and extinguish the fire.

Lust, I can find anywhere. It's just plain, old sex with nothing attached.

Love, on the other hand, has to be two halves coming together, fusing in body and soul to make a whole.

With a self-control I didn't know I had, I let her go.

"You think I am that easy?" I turned and walked away.

I didn't make it very far. She jumps me from behind. We tumble into the sand.

"Well, if you're not that easy, fight, dammit. Fight for our love. Fight for me as I do for you."

I woke up in a cold sweat with Sparky holding his cell phone over my mouth. He shuts it off immediately.

"What's happening?" I asked in confusion.

"You spoke the whole episode out. Detail by detail. That's gonna cost each guy who's listening some more money for broadcast and air time."

What I found out was that the minute I started to tell a story each night, Sparky would dial Loco in the next cell who then dialed the contact list of the prisoners on his lingo business directory and they would all listen in.

Anything can happen in prison.

Ω   Ω   Ω

Because of my deafness, I was allowed some slack such as missing regular activities for inmates. To manage time effectively, I slept at intervals during the days, but woke up when meals were announced. I started to get comfortable with the other inmates and to tell jokes that made them laugh. Loco announced that I was as humorous as the Canadian comedian Russell Peters. Mr. Rory agreed. I took it as a compliment although I didn't know who he was. I figured he must be pretty good for them to know him.

I helped Sparky with his business in the night. While we worked, he told me seafaring stories that ran from amusing to horrific to intriguing. The most intriguing were about billionaires and their strange hobbies.

"Billionaires are the biggest crooks ever. They have their hands into everything. These days with the internet, money changes hands with a click on the computer. You know how I end up in the Cayman Island? I was on a Japanese ship that delivered containers of electronics to the Cayman Islands and other Caribbean countries. There were strict instructions that the boxes have to be moisture free at all times. One night we ran into a squall and the containers got wet. The captain instructed me to organize a team to dry each box that had electronics labels. One guy carelessly dropped a box and it split opened. Guess what dropped out?"

"Money," I said. To me it is the logical thing as Cayman Islands is a tax-free haven.

"*Non, Non.* No. No." Sparky responded in French and English. "It was full of porn movies."

"Whoa!" I said.

"That's nothing. Amongst us seamen, there's another story going around about billionaires. They have a betting game every year. They try to outsmart each other with high technology and hire the smartest brains to win the prize. It's a big game. Millions and millions of dollars." He bent closer to me and whispered, "This year, the rumor is that the game will be right here in The Cayman Islands and that the prize is a shitload of gold."

Om-7 perked up.

"Gold? A game?" I whispered back.

"*Oui, mon ami.* Yes, my friend. The gold was stolen in Curaçao last December. No one knows for sure where it went after. The day before you came to prison, I had a visit from the captain of a small vessel – a friend from Guyana who told me of another secret rumor. A very unusual stone is hidden in the lot of gold, and all the billionaires want it. Keep your ears open when you get out. If you hear about the gold. I want a piece of the action."

"I'm deaf." I said. "I will be the last person to hear about it." Om-7 cooed in agreement.

He had a certain respect for me, he said, as I had overcome unimaginable obstacles because of my willpower so that I can speak three languages fluently and have a college degree even though I am deaf. He loved the poetry in the love scene and made me repeat it several times. I told him that it was my take on a very beautiful poem written by a Scottish poet named Robert Burns.

"It's all mind over matter," and touched his head to emphasize his point.

Because he gave my ego a super-needed boost, I did something nice for him. I got involved in his business, to an extent. I showed him how to distill lingo through a white t-shirt for a clearer end-product. By the time I left prison, he could not supply enough of this new blend to meet the demand.

18 Challenges and Clichés

I WAS AWAKENED EARLY on a Sunday morning by Mr. Rory with news that bail money had been paid and I was now a free man. There were set conditions and restrictions that I had to follow; the most important was that I could not leave the Cayman Islands. He informed me that Doctor O'Ligue awaited me in the reception area. I presumed she had bailed me out.

Sparky woke up to say goodbye with a hug and a slap on the back. "We will meet again," he winked. I couldn't say goodbye to the new friends I had made as they were asleep, which made me sad. Mr. Rory and the other guards shook my hands and wished me well.

Dr. O was the only person I had not called, yet she was there, all welcoming with hugs and kisses, like an old aunt who had not seen me for a long time. I had to be grateful for her generosity, though there was this niggling thought that the payback would not be to my liking. She drove straight to Paradise Beach, and, as we entered the condo, I noticed she had a special code for the keypad lock. Like a puppy minus a leash, I followed her lead to the living room area.

"Sit." It had a command attached and her face no longer bore the friendliness that was extended at the prison, when she had an audience. She indicated a made-to-measure sofa fitted into an alcove. As I sat down and dragged my feet closer, I felt an unevenness in the floor and looked down only to find the carpet lay crumpled.

The immediacy of wanting to go to the washroom was suppressed by her let's get down to business air.

"You didn't have to do what you did." I spoke above the air conditioner that buzzed noisily overhead.

"I feel responsible," she answered, after a while.

Of course, she was, but I had no proof of that. I said nothing.

"Look, this is all a stupid, costly mess for you and for me." She rose and turned the air conditioner off. "There are strings attached to your release. You heard the guard explain you cannot leave the island until the court hearing, and this can run up to six months. That is a lot of time on your hands. It is the perfect time to write."

"I guess I don't have a choice but, just for the record, it still feels like I am getting screwed."

She didn't answer, as she kept her pissed-off-auntie/business-shark face on, and it may have been an odd time for an epiphany, but the magnitude of my situation finally hit me.

"I am screwed, aren't I?"

"Not really. As we discussed before and you didn't agree wholeheartedly, you can write." She crossed her legs and removed her sunglasses.

"I went to see my agent and publisher last weekend and they are very interested in a story of a deaf, multicultural man. You are a very unusual person and the love story that's on-off with India adds more zip. Of course, they want a lot of sexual details too. It always amuses me how publishers think sex differs from culture to culture."

I thought of how I will ask my next question and settled on: "Have you heard from India?"

"No. She just went off the radar." She had a straight face telling this lie. I changed the conversation.

"How will my writing a memoir, I mean, the set up of me writing and you publishing it – will you be the front person and I, the ghost writer?"

"I made an offer to pay you and I will. My promise still stands. It's a good deal. If you look at your current situation, it's a great deal."

Great, my ass. She had reneged on other deals with pie-crust promises. The distrust I had went up a notch.

"I see you're still hesitant." She opened her handbag, pulled out an envelope and took out some stapled sheets which she passed to me. "Here, read."

It was a signed contract for a book deal she had made. There were pages missing but on the last page, she had signed for receipt of a deposit.

"I will only write if we have a contract and, since you took a lump sum, then I want to have fifty percent of that as a deposit." I calculated it would take care of some of the bail money.

"No contract needed. A deposit is not a problem." She withdrew her pocket book and gave me a check. Too easy, I thought as I had expected some haggling.

"I leave for Europe tomorrow." This would explain her desperation to find me. She, herself was in a binding contract and she had a deadline to submit a manuscript.

"The dog's in the deal," she said after a while.

I graciously responded. "That's not a problem." I always felt Chewy was mine to begin with, since I found him.

"I can bring him by later," she offered.

"No. I can pick him up tomorrow." I had some reasons for wanting to go back to Camana Bay, the main one being that I wanted to see Engine and make peace with him.

She showed me the office, which had been set up in the guest room upstairs, repainted while I was in prison and fully equipped with impressive electronics. If I were in a better frame of mind, I would have appreciated the computer real estate and the state-of-the-art modular work station that faced the beach and the sea.

Ω   Ω   Ω

The following day, as I walked up the stairs to the condos at The Nexx Complex, I saw Ernesto and Carlos, overloaded with grocery bags and offered some help. They invited me for coffee and, when I refused, they both showed disappointment.

"I will come back another time." I promised.

"I saw ya on television. Ya looked uglier than me." Carlos playfully punched me in my stomach. "Ya know, I don't think ya is a criminal."

"Me, neither," Ernesto added. He asked if I was staying on the island and if he can help me in any way.

"Can I come visit ya?" Carlos wanted to know.

"Sure Carlos. I am only fifteen minutes away. You both come out and I will take you to snorkel in the reef. And you can teach me Spanish. Fair enough?" This was working out better than I thought.

"Here is first Spanish lesson." He stuck a finger in my chest, "Ya is Chico, and I, Hombre. I give ya my cell number. Call me. I got new sites to show ya."

"I don't have a phone. Just come out anytime Carlos."

"I take ya up on that." He grinned from ear to ear.

"My friend, is he still there?" I directed the question to Ernesto, but it was Carlos who quickly answered.

"No, Ten-squat-a-way went to England. In the beginning, he was really nice. After ya went to jail, he changed. He walked around with pissed-off-at-the-world face."

Carlos had all the updates on everyone, I thought as I left. I just felt drawn to him for some reason. Perhaps it was because I had a big brother and always wanted to have a little brother.

Ω   Ω   Ω

When Dr. O opened the door, Chewy was on his leash and ready to go. He was so excited, he whipped me a few times with his tail and topped off the visit by knocking me down on the floor.

"Sorry, I have to go. Taxi is waiting. I hate to say goodbye, but alas, I must go. Remember, I need constant updates all the time, chapter by chapter," she said pulling several suitcases to the door.

I decided to do the gentlemanly thing and help her with her suitcases to the taxi. This was a challenge as Chewy, on his leash, found his way into any obstacle he encountered. When she turned to say goodbye to me, she did the most fucked up thing imaginable. She reached up and snatched Om-7.

"This will allow you to use your inner sense." She jumped into the taxi and was gone. I was so surprised and shocked that, when I did react, the taxi had disappeared around the corner.

Ω   Ω   Ω

Distraught, I walked the two kilometers and some to Da Roti Shaq. I needed some ears to listen to my bitching about the bitch. The restaurant was at its busiest, with a line out the front door. I made Chewy a cozy bed in the shed. Tired out from his exercise, he folded his legs and went into snooze mode.

Rafiq was working the counter in the front. When he saw me, the first thing he signed was, "Where is yuh false ear? Wait, tell me later. It's a zoo in here." In the kitchen, the helpers were running back and forth and the cook was overwhelmed. I found an apron, washed my hands and helped to roll out roti dough into perfect rounds and toss them on the grill.

Hours later, the staff gone, Rafiq and I kicked off our shoes and sat down with two bottles of cold *Caybrew.*

"Here's to you. And to your knees for being sturdy. Cheers." He signed.

"Get serious, Rafiq. I have things to discuss with you."

"I don't see why you are so sensitive. I am just happy you came out of the pen in one piece." He cheered to that, too. "So what happened to your hearing aid?"

He was mad as hell when I told him Dr. O had snatched my hearing device and taken off.

"See that Doc Lady is some nasty bizness. That's the meanest thing somebody can do."

"She gave me a check." When I showed it to him, he was, at first, happy for me, then he made me unhappy with what he said next. "Can I borrow some to clear a shipment of high-end electronics coming in? I promise I will pay you back. I'll throw in the latest model of cell phone as interest."

"If you cash it for me and pay me back." I had no choice, since anything to identify who I am had been stolen, and I have not met anyone who could live without money.

His face broke into a smile that made him look like a little boy. "I will be the first customer at the bank on Monday morning." He downed half a bottle of beer. "Wait, why did she give you a check?"

I told him about the writing I had to do and my nervousness about it.

"Yoo, Bro. That's what you do best. Look at the ad you wrote for Da Roti Shaq. This business would have never been up-and-running so well without that ad. I am telling you, when it comes to writing, you got words." He shook his head, his dreadlocks swishing against his shoulders.

"Here's something to remember." He wrote on a napkin and passed it to me.

EVERY MICKLE MEK A MUCKLE.

"What does that mean?"

"A book of a thousand pages starts with the first sentence."

"That is so cliché." I rolled my eyes at this nonsense.

"Sez who? If yuh see, hear or know anyone who sezs so, then dat person, for sure, didn't write a good-read like *Huckleberry Finn.*" He signed excitedly in half Creole, half English.

"Come on Rafiq, that's so ancient. So out of date." I know he meant well, but sometimes he came up with the most ridiculous ideas.

"I see yuh don't like that one. Okay, try this one. How about *Tom Sawyer?*"

I wasn't gonna argue with him. I knew he was a *Mark Twain* fan.

"Now, that has some merit." I raised my Caybrew in honor of his suggestion.

"One favor I ask yuh. Yoo, one favor only. Yuh listening?"

I nodded.

"Yoo. This is important."

"What?"

"Look me in the eye."

"Okay. Spit it out."

"Please, I beg of you. Can you write in simple English? Not in highfalutin, formal Eng-lish. Write, so that any brother, or sister, no matter who, or where, can relate to it. Most important is that when me, MJ Rafiq, read it, I will laugh 'till my belly bust and cry tears that are as long as the Amazon. I mean the river, not the e-commerce place. And then I will laugh again." He had his palms together namaste-style. "Gimme your word."

I did.

It will be a challenge.

Another cliché, as every single day in my life is a challenge.

Ω   Ω   Ω

I left Rafiq's place in a better frame of mind. I remembered, as I put Chewy to bed, that I forgot to ask him if there had been updates on the gold and porn distribution.

In the comfort of the queen bed, I overdosed on sleep through the day to make up for the lack of it during my nights of confinement, until I was awakened by Vibe's consistent beeping at midnight. I did the same the following day and, once again Vibe commenced her irritating beeping. On checking out her dials, I found that she had been pre-programmed to go off at midnight in any country on the globe. "BB, you bastard." I cursed, forgetting that we shared the same parents. He always liked to mess up my sleep schedule.

Since I was wide awake, I walked over to the work station, turned on the computer, closed my eyes and shut out the present. My fingers lingered on the keyboard as I tried to find a happy hook for the beginning of the memoir. Many images of people, places and things shuttered back and forth, as if I were looking through the lens of a view finder. They changed, but one scene kept coming back to me.

I AM BACK IN Montreal. I walk slowly down the aisle of the jam-packed church. I am afraid I might drop the box. I hold it with both hands, pressed closely to my chest. I wonder how someone who was six feet, five inches in height could fit in such a little box. I am torn-up. I think of Danz Park, where we hung out, played guitar, smoked and talked about everything under the sun. I remembered the bonfire he initiated and which we still kept every year. I looked straight ahead as I followed Pastor Ignatius, who led the way to the hearse. As he walked, he read a verse from Corinthians 13.1, King James Bible.

> *When I was a child,*
> *I spake as a child,*
> *I understood as a child,*
> *I thought as a child.*

The rest was lost as I thought of what Wes's reaction would have been to his funeral. It came to me. He would have lifted his shoulders and shrugged, "Move on."

My fingers moved to the keyboard. I started to draft an outline of when I was a child as I remembered it. I titled it after a song that Wes composed for me which he called, "The Deaf Boy in the Mirror."

PART 2

No one can make you feel inferior without your consent

Eleanor Roosevelt

19 The Governor

DRESSED IN A TWO-PIECE bathing suit, Governor Emma Wedgewood lounged on a beach towel in the sand behind the mess that was her house and sipped a *Cayman Mama*. She wasn't a heavy drinker, but of late, she quite enjoyed a tipple of the rum-based tropical cocktails. She gazed at the sea in the midday sun and tried to count the many shades of blue.

Her mind wandered, as always, to assess the current affairs in her life.

She was discouraged with the renovations. The house was now covered in a white tarpaulin which gave it the appearance of being encased in a condom. The backyard was a mass of rubble and the front lawn was dug up for a sprinkler system. The move into the short-term rental condo in The Nexx Complex had gone smoothly thanks to Kara and her new friends, the Spanish-speaking Ibáñez boys. Daily, she took the five-minute drive to check on the renovation team's progress and enjoy the tranquility of the beach. Here, she found, she did her best thinking as she connected with nature.

She thought about the benefits of living close to Seven Mile Beach. It put her in contact with everyday life as she interacted with tourists and locals. Her ears were becoming attuned to the Caymanian way of speaking. Every Sunday, she attended a different congregation and she was connecting to people. She ate local fare, had developed a taste for goat curry and got hooked on a local colloquialism, "no hurries, no worries." She understood that when Caymanians asked, "How long you bin on island," they meant, "how long have you been in the Cayman Islands?" She visited the open air markets, started conversations with the peddlers and customers alike. Some asked her for a hug and she gladly obliged, enjoying the touch of their warmth. She always felt good. Every morning, she walked the beach for an hour and, every evening, she swam for half an hour at the pool in the complex. She was pleased with the results, her clothes were looser and she had tanned to a golden brown. She had a feel-good moment earlier as she walked toward the beach. She overheard the workmen speaking about her – nothing crass, just man talk about how much younger she looked than her real age and that she had a good figure in her two piece bathing suit. She was more tickled that they called her, 'The Gov.'

Feeling a need for something different, she had signed up for diving lessons. So far, she loved it. On her last dive, she descended fifteen feet and was enthralled by the beauty of the coral life.

Oh, how she loved this new life. She sank her toes into the hot, white sand and recapped her time as governor.

Meetings with politicians and government officials filled her days since she took office. MI7 made sure her weekly calendar was filled with social appearances. The last communication from Nigel Moore had been gratifying. He was pleased she was on track and following M17's directives. He wrote a personal note saying he cannot be reached for the next week, but she can leave messages with M17. He was off to a diving trip with his son in Australia. She had forgotten that Nigel had a thirty-five-year old son from one of his many liaisons who lived in kangaroo land, way Down Under.

She also had received the coordinates of the local informant, a Dr. Olga O'Ligue. Once again, she was sent a timetable and reminded that she was an observer.

Governor Wedgewood's personal phone beeped with a sound she knew to be the latest news bulletin. Her eyes bulged as she read the few lines. *Woman's body washed up in Cuba. Identified as actress in adult movies. Cause of death linked to poisonous snake bites.*

"Snake bites? This is serious." She reached into her carryall for her special mobile to call M17. It wasn't there. "Oh, bugger!" she swore.

Using her personal cell phone, she dialed the special mobile's number and a voice answered. "Hola."

"Who is this?"

"Oh, Señora Governor. It is I, Carlos. I found this phone in the corridor."

"Oh no." She was worried. Carlos is the not the person who should touch that phone. On meeting him, she had observed how quickly his fingers moved on his laptop.

"No worries Señora Governor. I am at ya front door. I was going to visit Kara and help her with her new laptop."

Relieved, Governor Wedgewood pulled out a notepad and wrote:

TO DO LIST

1. Check out landscapers/sprinkling system/fountain

2. Check out Casino Project

3. Hustle donations for mental facility

4. Costumes for Pirates Week – me and Kara

5. Buy cotton knickers

6. Check out Kara's new friends

She paused as she thought about Kara's new friends, Ernesto and Carlos, who lived in a condo on the opposite block. Nice kids, they were. Ernesto was quiet and very much a big brother. Carlos, the teenager, carried his laptop wherever he went and often sat at the coffee shop in Camana Bay. She smiled as she remembered the cute way he addressed her, 'Señora Governor.' She was quite taken with his knowledge of computers. That child was born with information technology on one side of his brain and electronics on the other side, she mused.

Ω   Ω   Ω

"Mother, you're drooling." Emma woke up with a start to see Kara spreading out a beach towel in the sand.

"Kara darling. How did it work out with the new laptop?"

"Great. Carlos is a genius. I met a Mohawk man today. He lives next door to Carlos. We had to borrow electrical plugs from him."

"A skinhead? Is he a racist? "

"No mother. He's a lawyer with Maple & Maple. He's a seventh generation Canadian Mohawk Native Indian and he has his own language. He showed me his ring. It's a tourmaline, a very unusual stone that belonged to his ancestors long before the British stormed North America."

"How can you identify the stone?"

"Mother, I am bipolar. Not dead to what's happening around me. I know about the tourmaline because I looked it up on the internet. A very big one was found in Brazil earlier this year and disappeared soon after. It is a very distinct stone. It has the seven colors of the rainbow. The Natives who found it believe it to be a chakra stone with each color representing the emotional and spiritual state of the human body."

Governor Wedgewood sighed and reached over for a copy of the *Cayman Weekly* from the previous week. Her brows furrowed as she read a quarter page column.

"Kara, the deaf man you met, is this him?" She passed the paper to her daughter.

"Oh yes, that's Kaman. Picked up with drugs? I don't believe this for one minute."

"He's been released."

"It's a good thing then. I think he's been set up. You know, he's deaf and when you have a handicap, people easily try to make you a victim." Kara said passionately.

 Montreal

Draft of *The Deaf Boy in the Mirror*

"Bienvenue à Montréal. Welcome to Montreal. On this beautiful day I will take you on a ride through the oldest city in North America that my ancestor, Jacques Cartier, from France, discovered centuries ago. But first, I want to introduce you to my horse. This handsome stud here is Tom Cruz. My name is René. I invite you to sit back, relax and enjoy the ride."

His voice sounded distant when it reached my ears. I arranged my *Canadiens* hat so that the peak is on the left side and my hearing device is fully exposed on the right.

René finished reading from a plastic-covered sheet which he placed on the seat beside him then turned around to smile at us. He picked up a whip and the reins that were attached to the horse's head. With a pull and a yank, the horse swatted his bushy tail and started to move through the throngs of people who zigzagged their way across the narrow street. I stared in fascination at everything around me.

About five minutes into this journey, Tom Cruz lifted his tail and let some rocks tumble down onto the street. They had the same size, shape and color as the charcoal rocks that Pa used on the barbecue. I am totally absorbed in the process, wondering if Ma would make René stop, so she could pick up the rocks to take home. Last week, on garbage day, she had made Pa go out early in the morning when it was still dark to pick up the barbeque from the curbside some blocks away from our house.

It was Jalebi's third birthday and she wanted to have a pony ride. Since she always got what she wanted, Pa packed us into the Lada, which he called the Russian tank, drove past Caughnawaga, where The Mohawk Indians lived, over the Mercier Bridge and across the St. Lawrence Seaway. He exited where the green signs read *"Vieux Montréal"* in French, and below, *"Old Montreal"* in English. He parked the Russian tank by the port where there were big ships docked, and huge cranes loaded and unloaded heavy containers. Here, Pa had negotiated for two carriages and that's how I came to be sitting between Biig Baba and Ma, and now watched the lava rocks fall onto the uneven cobblestones.

I remembered the above as Ma signed and pointed to places and things as we drove along. All members in our house knew how to speak with their hands. It had nothing to do with Pa being Italian.

Biig Baba giggled and elbowed me in the side. I started to giggle too, then Ma poked me on the other side to make me stop. But I couldn't and wouldn't because Biig Baba continued to whisper into my ear device.

"Look Kaman, here it comes, here it comes. There it goes . . . tt-th-ud." He did a play by play of how the horse excreted, just like the sports broadcaster on Channel 13 during Hockey Night in Canada. Biig Baba just wouldn't stop until René gave the horse a gentle tap on his rump, whereby he lowered his bushy tail, swished it a few times and reluctantly started to walk.

When Ma seated us in the carriage, René asked, *"Anglais ou Français?"* She did not understand, so Biig Baba had answered, *Anglais*, English. René had then reached into a box on the empty seat beside him, pulled out a plastic-covered sheet, and was now reading/speaking as Tom's hooves clickety-clacked.

"This is the City of Love, the city of English and French, the Paris of North America, and the city with the team that won the most Stanley Cups in the history of hockey."

Hockey. That got Biig Baba's and my attention. This was our sport, and we could not get enough of it. We didn't know how to skate, but Big Baba knew all the hockey teams, the names of the players and their jersey numbers.

"How many Stanley Cups did they win?" Biig Baba asked the tour guide.

I took some time off from horse-watching to check out the horseman's costume, so I would be able to remember every detail when I went to bed. He wore weird clothes from the old days with a pointy black hat on his head that covered his long white hair. He looked like a well-dressed pirate to me. Sometimes, he gently tapped the horse with the whip in a criss-cross hand movement.

"*Quinze* Stanley Cups. Fifteen Stanley Cups. That's how many cups the Montreal Canadiens have won," he answered proudly, just as the other carriage with Pa and Jalebi bumped into us.

It was driven by a woman who was also in a costume. She wore a big skirt with stripes; the same pattern as the curtains in our living room and a hat the size of the big enamel bowl that Ma used for washing salad greens.

"What's her name?" Biig Baba wanted to know.

"That beautiful *cheval* on the *calèche* is Angelique."

"Not the horse on the carriage. I am talking about the lady who's steering the horse."

'Oh, you mean Chantal. You got the eye for the ladies, Eh?"

I smiled when he said the word, 'Eh.' It sounded like the letter A. It didn't matter if you were French or English in Canada, as long as you were Canadian, it sounded the same way.

This had been my first visit to Montreal and my first time in a horse and buggy. I was only four years old on my last birthday, and I knew how to count to one hundred and say all the letters of the alphabet *in my head*. I would never say them out loud as they sounded funny. I also knew how to spell words, mostly words that Biig Baba taught me, *in my head too*. Biig Baba is six and had started school – French school, so he knew how to spell words in two languages. Every day, when he came home, he showed Ma his books and she, too, was learning French.

"Where you guys come from?" René asked Ma.

"New York." She replied. Biig Baba was going to say something, but she poked him before he got a word out.

"The Big Apple. The Rangers . . . not as good as Les Canadiens."

"They beat the Canadiens last game." Biig Baba corrected him.

"*C'est rien.* It's nothing. *Les Canadiens* will kill them next season." He laughed as he guided Tom Cruz into a very busy street. I had never seen so many people, as Chouguay, our town, was small and the most people I saw there were in the shopping mall.

"That's your husband and daughter?" René was trying to make conversation with Ma, but she was more engrossed in the old buildings and the street players.

"Yes," She replied.

"Ah, you're a haf-brid family. *C'est cute.* This is cute, very cute. I love mixed families." He smiled at us as he reached into the black box and gave us some lollipops. They were funny-colored, blue with a white flower in the center.

"That's the fleur-de-lys," Biig Baba explained to Ma. "It's the flower on the Quebec flag. I learned that in school."

"Oui, Oui, le fleur-de-lys. Today is the celebration of *La Fête Nationale* in Quebec, *mes amis.* My friends, it is the day of blue and white," René added with a grin.

Biig Baba started to giggle again. He poked me in the side, pointing to the horse. "Look at the size of his dong," he whispered. I started to giggle, too, as Biig Baba had learned this word in the schoolyard and explained to me that this is a certain part of my body.

The giggling brought Ma's attention away from the street entertainers and when she noticed what amused us, she started to giggle as well. René swatted the horse gently, saying words in French I was too young to understand. He was trying his best not to laugh.

Ω   Ω   Ω

Pa and Ma made that day a special one for us. We stopped for lunch at a French restaurant and ordered *poutine* from the menu. When the dish arrived, I was surprised to see French fries with hot gravy and cheese curds that melted like pizza cheese. Later on, Ma treated us to a dessert of pizza, except the pizza had chocolate and bananas and whipped cream and Biig Baba read the sign over the counter, "Beavers tail" in English, *"queue de castor"* in French. He was so smart, Biig Baba. I wish I could speak like him.

We sat down on a little table on a terrace. There were people with different colored hair, not yellow or brown like the girls next door, nor black like my hair, but red and blue and white. Some were carrying flags and shouting out *"Vive le Quebec."* And there were many cars. Biig Baba, his voice full of excitement, pointed them out to me, saying their names as they passed by, in the same way he taught me the names of the toy cars in the Matchbox® collection we shared.

Jalebi wanted to go to the washroom because she was sloppy and had chocolate all over her face. She did not want to go with Ma, so Pa had to take her inside to find the toilet. At the same time Biig Baba said he wanted to let loose some lava rocks like Tom Cruz. Ma pinched his cheek gently when he said that, but she smiled and shooed him off to follow Pa.

I sat across from Ma, enjoying my chocolate-covered pizza when the nice, red car pulled up next to the sidewalk. The engine made a lot of noise as the man driver moved it into a spot, blocking my view. I made sounds, trying to say words. Ma picked up a napkin and cleaned my hands. I pointed to the car as more sounds came out of my mouth, all the words stuck in my throat.

"Oh, you like the car," Ma said. "Come, we go look." She took my hand.

The driver opened the door and stepped out. He was a big man with long, black hair to his waist. Funny sounds escaped from my lips. He stopped and stared at me and the keys fell by my feet. I bent and picked them up, then raised my head again to look at him. He smiled at me. He had no teeth and this scared me so much that I moved back and held on to Ma's legs, the keys still in my hand.

"Hey, you are too young to steal cars." He reached out a hand for the keys, still smiling.

Ma looked down at me and signed. "Give the gentleman the keys. Give it."

I was too scared to move. So, she took the keys out of my hand. "I'm sorry, Mister. My son, he doesn't speak."

"Thank you, kid." He looked at my hearing device. "You want to see inside the car?"

I nodded my head excitedly and he opened the door.

"Go in. Don't touch anything."

I did. I looked and I took in all the details. I spelled out the word on the dashboard in my head F-e-r-r-a-r-i. Then the big man said he had to go, so I got out of the car. "Goodbye," he said and left.

I wished that Big Baba would hurry back from his lava rock business so he could see how beautiful this Ferrari was.

"You like that car Kaman?" Ma said to me as I ran my hand up and down the door. My mouth moved, but the sounds would not go past my lips. I pointed to the car.

She got down on her knees and held onto my shoulders. 'Say your words Kaman. Say your words. Ca-ar. Say it. Ca-ar."

I opened my mouth, closed it, and opened it again. The words were there, I can feel them.

"Come on." She coaxed. "Say your words, Kaman."

"Ka-ar. Ka-ar." I said and repeated it because I could hear my words and Ma didn't laugh.

"That's it, my little Baba. Say your words. "Car" is only your first word. There are so many more words. And before you know it, you will speak fluently." Big tears rolled down her face as she hugged me close to her body.

In a moment frozen in time, I can still hear her sing-song voice, see the tears of joy and remember my very first visit to Montreal on St. Jean Baptiste Day.

21 My Family

Draft of *The Deaf Boy in the Mirror*

On the return trip to Chouguay with my family, I witnessed a crying party.

It wasn't a sad affair. It was happy and funny.

As Pa drove along the Autoroute, Biig Baba pointed to the green signs, which I knew were directions. 'Pont Mercier/ Mercier Bridge,' he said loudly. I parroted his words. Half-way across, he pointed again to another sign, which showed the ramp to the Mohawk reservation. 'Caughnawaga,' he said proudly. I repeated after him even though it was a big word.

Pa clasped his hands together over the steering wheel. 'Oh Madonna. *Grazie. Grazie mille.*' He looked up to the skies, then at me in the rearview mirror. Tears rolled down his face.

I repeated all the words Pa said too. It wasn't difficult because he was always saying *grazie* to someone named Madonna. I suspected this was the lady in the music video who's singing about how she feels like a virgin.

"Oh, Dio, you heard my prayers." He turned to Ma. "See that Diwali. There is a God. This morning our son couldn't speak. Now within half an hour, he can say French, English, Mohawk and Italian words. *Non ci credo.* I don't believe it." His voice was one of disbelief as he wiped away the tears.

'Oh Giuseppe, this is wonderful,' Ma said. She started crying, too. Biig Baba felt he had to cry because Pa was crying and Jalebi started to bawl because Ma's whole body was shaking as she sobbed.

As we passed Caughnawaga, a big truck changed lanes without warning and cut off the Lada. Pa braked like crazy and honked at the driver. The rude man stuck his hand out the window and flipped him the bird.

"You gimme the finger? In front of my wife and kids? Well, take this." Pa let go of the steering wheel for a second, made a fist, swung his arm back, brought it to the front, cupped the elbow with his other hand and pumped it upwards. "Yes. That's right, the Italian salute for you. *Vaffanculo.*"

He turned to us kids in the back seat. "You never do that, or say that, *capisce?* Understand?"

I understood. It was only sign language and Pa was passionate about being Italian.

Ω   Ω   Ω

That night was special because that day I had officially said my first words, which meant I could now speak to Ma and Pa, talk to Biig Baba and tell Jalebi off, as sometimes she can be a pain in the butt. As a treat, Ma said I could sleep with my hearing device, but if I broke it, I would have to pay her for the rest of my life. She strapped a small cushion to the right side of my body to ensure that I did not sleep on that side.

Secretly, I had a name for my hearing device. I thought of sharing this with Biig Baba, but I didn't want him to laugh at me. I shared it with God, who probably knew about it before I did this, as I understood that He sat in the skies above and watched over everyone and knew everything that happened to everyone on Earth. I think he is a spy. I chose the name, Om-7, a good name I believe, because I heard the chanting of the sound Om repeated seven times, and soon after, I heard my laughter for the first time in my life. I also made Om-7 a boy so I could have a friend, as I really didn't care for girls.

Biig Baba made a tent between our beds with all the spare sheets he found in the linen cupboard after lights out.

It was story time.

I liked when Biig Baba told stories, because he got excited and showed the action of how the story unfolded. He started off by re-telling about Tom's Cruz's dong, stretched out his arms to show how big he thought it was. From downstairs, Ma shouted out, "You boys. Go to sleep. Now."

Biig Baba stayed quiet for a bit. Then, he started to make circles on the wall of the tent with the new flashlight he had sneaked out of Pa's toolbox. "Quiet, and look," he whispered in the dark. He opened the tent flap at the top, moved the circles from one wall to the other, then to the ceiling.

"Here's my spacecraft landing. Here's my spacecraft taking off into the Galactica. Here's my spacecraft crashing." He placed a blanket over his head, scrunched up his face like an alien, held the flashlight in front of him and zoomed in and out. "And here comes *ET* before he goes home."

He had done this before and it made me giggle. Sometimes, he sneaked into my bed, let out silent, stinky farts and pulled the covers tightly over my head. "Dutch oven," he called it, laughing at the funny way I squeezed my nose to block out the smell.

He signed to me now. "I wish you could speak more, Kaman. Then I can really, really talk to you."

"Biig Baba." I must have said his name at least twenty times since we came home.

"Yup."

"Teach me words," I begged.

"Okay. But if I teach you bad words like "bitch," you cannot tell Ma and Pa."

"Okay."

I knew many words. I understood many words. All members of my family knew sign language, as Ma had taped the alphabet in sign language on the fridge door along with the map of the world. Beside it, ten pages of proverbs held together with a magnetic clamp hung loosely. Next to all of this was a recent article from a Cuban newspaper. It had a side view photograph of my head with my hearing device attached to my right ear.

I didn't say words out loud because they sound funny to my ears. That's why everyone in the house treated me like a dumb kid and communicated with me through signing, and I responded in the same way. Until today, of course, I showed them.

I understood the difference in language as spoken by Ma and Pa as they came from different countries. Pa had pointed out and circled his country on the map of the world. He said it was called "Italy." He also showed Ma's country, a little dot named "Guyana" in South America.

When Pa called us for snacks, he would shout out, "*Vieni qua. Mangia sangwich.* Come here, eat your sangwich," or, "*vieni qua, mangia cake.* Come here, eat cake." Pa spoke half-and-half Italian-Inglish, a special dialect well-spoken Italians found humorous. In due course, these language snobs came up with a name, so now Pa is a *mangia cake I-talian.*

Ma, on the other hand, would screech out, "How many times do I have to call you? *Jaldi caro.* Hurry up. Food on the table. Come, eat." It was a different language. I think only omnipresent God understood her mixed up words.

Before I had officially spoken, I figured I would practice saying words to Jalebi because she is a year younger than me. I can still remember the words and her laughter. This is the main reason I didn't like her that much. The other reason is she is a girl.

Biig Baba was different from Jalebi. If I made a mistake, he didn't laugh and make fun of me. Every night, as he did his homework, he repeated words over and over from his books, pointing to the pictures. He said I was like a sponge, a "hard as rock" sponge that took a longer time to absorb, whatever that meant. I became confused as Biig Baba switched from English to French as he did his homework. How could a four-year-old know that the conjugation of the French word *aimer* in the present tense was not English? And that *aimer* meant to love.

"Tell me a story," I begged him another night after lights out. I was still allowed to keep my hearing device when I went to bed.

"Which one you want to hear? The village story in Italy, or the village story in Guyana?"

These were his favorites, his most action-packed. I chose the first one.

"You like that story, Kaman? You want me to tell you again?"

"Yup." I imitated his 'yes' word.

"See, it's like this. When you were two," he held up two fingers, "and I was four," he scooted over to my bed under the covers and pushed four fingers into my face, "you had ear infection. Yucky stuff oozing out of your ear. And you became deaf." He tapped his ears. "Deaf, deaf, deaf. The doctor said you deaf as a doorknob. Pa took us all to Italy. I was allowed to come because I had behaved for a whole week. Here, Nonna took us up to a church in the mountains where the priest prayed like this. Wait a minute. I'll show you. Don't look."

As Biig Baba moved around the room, I remembered Nonna who was Pa's Ma. She had a little restaurant called *Cucina Nonna* where she made pasta from scratch.

"Now look." Biig Baba covered himself with a sheet. He started to chant and speak like he had seen the preacher from the Sunday morning Christian show on TV, except he said some words in Italian. "Dio, Christo, spaghetti con poupette, pizza, lasagna, vino," and he finished in English. "Padre, removeth the excess wax and crap from his ears so this bambino boy can heareth the words of Biig Baba."

"What wuz his name?" I wanted to know.

"Padre Pio."

"Padre Pee-oh?" I asked. It didn't sound so nice a name for a priest.

"Well, that was his name. He is a Saint and, when you pray to him, he can make people do things they didn't do before."

That didn't make sense 'cos Ma said I was a good boy and, if a good boy like me goes to Padre Pee-oh and he made me do things I didn't do before, then I can do bad things, and then I wouldn't be good no more. I said this much to Biig Baba.

"No, it's not like that. See, Padre Pio is dead. When you are dead, and if you were a good person, you go to heaven. Then your spirit goes to Jesus and then Jesus talks to God and God sends your spirit to a place high up in the mountain and giveth you the power to healeth people."

This was too complicated for me. I stayed quiet and listened to the hamster climbing the wheel, pondering where God sent people who were no good.

"What happened after he prayed?"

"The prayers didn't work. You were still deaf."

I couldn't remember this, but I remembered Nonna, giving us our first cooking lesson. She had a wood oven under a shed. My mouth watered when I think of the delicious pizzas she made. Biig Baba and I helped her to roll out the dough, dab the top with tomato sauce, drop pepperoni slices over, sprinkle mozzarella cheese and drizzle with olive oil. Nonna would then slide it into the oven. We watched and waited until the cheese bubbled and specks of gold brown appeared. Then we sat at a table under a grape vine and ate pizzas until our stomachs were so fat we couldn't walk.

"Biig Baba, if Padre Pee-oh was dead, how come you said that a priest prayed for me?"

Now that I can speak, I can question Biig Baba's stories because he sometimes forgets.

"Well, see, Kaman, it was his spirit praying. But it didn't work, 'cos you were still deaf. We returned to Canada. Ma and Pa took you to the children's hospital and the doctor did an operation. When you came home, you were still deaf. That's when Nani, Ma's mother visited and brought us all to Guyana."

I remembered Nani. She had the same face like Ma and she loved to pray. She had many gods lined up on a shelf and every morning she did *puja* prayers with them.

"What happened in Guyana?"

"Nani had a small monkey. His name was SakiWinki. He loved you the best and he acted like you." I stopped to think if the monkey was handsome, 'cos Ma always said I was.

"Was he a handsome monkey?"

Biig Baba laughed so loudly that Ma shouted up the stairs. We mouthed with her, "Go to sleep, you boys," and giggled when she finished.

After a few minutes, I whispered, "What happened after?"

"Then, Nani took us to the clap-hand church in the tent. 'Mos everyone was African. They sing beautiful songs about my Lord and clap their hands. Every time they finished a song, they raised their hands in the air." Biig Baba got up, forgot that we wuz supposed to be sleeping, raised his hands in the air and shouted out, "Praise the Lawd."

I knew for sure that Biig Baba was not there at the clap-hand church, but he had heard Uncle the Drunk repeat this story to Ma and Pa and made it his own. Only thing I could think of was Biig Baba is the best big brother. I couldn't sleep as memories of the little village in Guyana twirled around in my head.

"Kaman," my hero said into my thoughts.

"Yup?"

"I am glad that you no longer deaf and you're not dum-dum."

But I was still deaf, not Mos' Def, but still deaf.

I remembered this, because I met Michael Jackson, and he told me so.

 Chewy

CHEWY LOOKED at me with such sad eyes that I took a break from writing. I was quite satisfied with the two chapters. I slept from dawn to dusk like a vampire and tapped away non-stop for four nights. Going down memory lane had brought back nice memories of Montreal and my family. I made a writing schedule and taped it on the wall. Since I had never attempted to write a book before, I found the process to be challenging and, at the same time, exciting. Also, writing stories of my childhood was, so far, reliving a time in my life that was happy.

Chewy was in dog heaven as I played catch with him on the beach, then later took him for a swim. As soon as we dipped into the water, he turned toward the three jutting rocks, thinking we were about to play the same game as the last time we swam together. I had to grab him quickly and steer him in another direction as I saw Rooslahn lurking on the beach. I found this humorous – my dog and me – we both think hiding $12 million in gold by those rocks was a fun game. It was a reminder I had not checked out the gold since my release from prison.

I found Chewy on the beach five years earlier, on what India had, at that time, suggested would be a 'deep weekend.' I misunderstood this as a potential 'dirty weekend.' It lasted a fortnight, filled with diving lessons. Many stray dogs wandered in and around the Barkers National Park. The puppy started to follow me on the first morning as I jogged along the beach. He was less than a year old, scraggly and with soulful, brown eyes. But it was his blue-black tongue that caught my attention. I started to bring him treats. One evening, India and I dove off the pier and he followed us. We were amazed at the way his powerful body glided in the water. She discovered he couldn't bark. Like me, he was hearing impaired. Like us, he was a half-breed. Unlike us, he had no home.

India named him Chewy. He is the only dog I met who could chew a bone to meal. After a week of tender, loving care, he could out-swim and out-run India and me. India wanted to bring him home with her to Montreal and proceeded to get all the necessary vaccinations and paperwork done. Because he was a mutt and a stray dog to boot, the authorities were not as helpful. In the end, India was disappointed. Chewy could not leave the island.

Dr. O returned from an overseas trip on the day of our departure. She came by to see India and fell in love with Chewy. She offered to adopt and care for him and, whenever India came to the island, she could have full access to him. I wasn't there when the agreement was made between them.

The adoption of Chewy got Dr. O started on a foundation which she called the Cayman Canine Society, CCS for short. Anyone from any part of the world could donate through the internet. It grabbed the attention of the CSI, the Church for Society's Improvement, who linked their ad page to the Cayman's site. Soon the rich and famous who hid their assets on the island were donating insane amounts to the foundation. Two billionaires had each dropped a million into the program. In the last three years, many dogs were adopted and shipped worldwide.

Ω   Ω   Ω

Carlos showed up unannounced. I welcomed his company even though it was daytime and it disturbed my sleeping pattern. He brought me coffee and a folded page which he had obviously torn out from this morning's newspapers.

"Look at this. I want to show ya some news." He unfolded the page to a photograph. "See her. Do you recognize her?"

"No. Who's she?"

"Come on." He had a look of mock disbelief on his face. "She's the girl from the Hot Babes site ya was glued to. Don't lie. I caught ya." He pointed to the headline which I read out loud. PORN STAR'S BODY FOUND ON BEACH.

"That's nasty stuff. How did she die?"

"Not mentioned. Her body was half buried in the sand in The Brac. I am just sad about it. Chico, that babe gave me many happy solo hours," he laughed.

I started to read the article, didn't get far.

"So let's get going already. I have to be back home at four o'clock on the dot or my brother goes a little bit crazy if I am late. Ya sure the water is not deep. Like, if I stand up, it will reach my neck?"

"I promise you. It won't go past your chest."

I took him out to the shallow waters to snorkel and introduced him to the underwater coral life. At the end of the session, he was converted from being scared of water to not wanting to leave. He enjoyed himself so much he invited himself back the following day. I think he was just happy not to be alone. Cayman immigration laws did not allow him, as a visitor, to go to school. He was bored.

I had to tell him I was on a project with a tight schedule and could only go the following week.

"What are ya doing? I help ya," he offered.

"I am writing a book."

"About what?"

"Growing up in Montreal."

"I wish I could visit that city, see where I was born. India promised that she will take me when she returns."

"When will she return?"

"She is in Europe with Dr. O'Ligue."

"How do you know this?" I am very intrigued at this bit of information.

"We e-mail every day. I show ya pictures she sent yesterday." He fished out his laptop from his carryall.

I recognized York, England's Medieval City. York Minster, the largest gothic cathedral in northern Europe loomed in the background. Several shots were taken on The Shambles and the Roman Walls where we had walked hand-in-hand when we did a European backpacking trip. Another was at Jorvik Centre where we had visited with Æsa and Lex Xi, to see the Viking digs where Æsa's father worked as an anthropologist.

I didn't expect Carlos to turn the laptop and click a picture of me.

Ω   Ω   Ω

I noticed that Rooslahn did laps in the pool every morning from 0600 to 0700. For a big guy, he moved effortlessly in the water. I peeped from behind the curtains with the patio door open, listening as he grumbled about the crabs that crawled into the pool. In between laps, he spoke to Koshka, his pet cat, a Russian Blue that sat patiently in a chair. They were my morning entertainment.

Some signs were posted on the beach that turtles had been nesting there in the last month. I actually saw their tire-like tracks in the sand as they searched for the perfect spot to lay their eggs on my morning jog with Chewy. There were six big signs that read, "TURTLE POACHERS WILL BE PROSECUTED."

That night before I started to write, I saw a strange yacht at the edge of the reef. It stayed there for an hour before it moved on. I thought, probably some idiot tourist fishing in the wrong place. Once it departed, Netts and Rooslahn emerged from the bushes and walked to the end of the pier.

Vibe reflected that it was 00.35 a.m. and the lights around the pool were still on, probably a malfunctioning switch. With Chewy on his leash, I went down to have a look-see and to spy on the duo on the pier. The switch was stuck. I let it be after several tries with no success. Chewy and I walked along the shadows of the trees that lined the beach close to the complex. Suddenly, he stopped and dug his paws deep in the sand, his tail erect and his nose flaring as he sniffed. Following his eye movements, I saw her. She was a big mother all right, at least 550 pounds.

Mrs. Green Turtle had arrived to lay her eggs.

She crawled slowly in the sand to find 'that' spot for her nest. I went down on all fours to watch her movements in the shadowy moonlight as she dug up sand.

"Poacher." The sound of Netts voice reached my ears distantly and locked itself within my hearing canals.

"Poacher, leave ninja alone." Rooslahn shouted.

Surprised, I turned around. They were heading towards me. Pulling Chewy along, I made for Barkers National Park, Netts and Rooslahn on the chase. I knew the park well, but Chewy knew it better as he pulled me deeper through the thick bushes and along rough pathways. My heartbeat escalates and, with it, the outside sounds bounced around halfway in my head like clothes in a dryer on a fast cycle. I could not think in the darkness and, unwittingly, let go of the leash. The next thing I know I am kissing ground, having stumbled over a fallen tree. I heard their footsteps swishing leaves as they search. It sounded far away, but I knew my ears, "far away" can mean just a few feet away. They were close, I could smell them. I held my breath.

The West Bay chickens came from all directions. Like angry birds, they swooped down from treetops, fluttered out of clumps of bushes, clucking and bwaking and squacking as they attacked Netts and Rooslahn. I heard Netts cursing in Caymanian and Rooslahn in Russian. Chewy tugged at my shorts. Grabbing his leash once again, I followed him in and out of the dark foliage until we reached a small bay. We slept on the beach undisturbed until the roosters woke us up at five o'clock.

On arriving at the complex, Chewy started to act strangely again. He walked to the pool and I followed to see what scent had tickled his nose. And there she was again. Mrs. Green Turtle had lost her sense of direction and landed in the swimming pool. The bright pool lights had disoriented her. Soon, Rooslahn would be out for his morning swim.

This had to be tended to. Opening my front door, I went upstairs and wrote on a carton box, NINJA IN POOL, and left it by Rooslahn's door and rang his doorbell. Back in the condo, I kept watch behind the curtains. I saw Rooslahn walk to the pool and drop Koshka onto a chair. I strained my ears, waiting for his mutterings in Russian. Nothing. I opened the door and went out to the patio with Chewy behind me. I couldn't believe my eyes. He held the turtle over his head. I watched in awe as he walked the distance and gently dropped it at the water's edge.

I turned to Chewy. "Did you see that? He just lifted 550 pounds like it was nothing."

My four-footed friend just nodded.

Tired out from my high-octane night, I slept through the day and picked up on my writing the following night.

23 Michael Jackson

Draft of *The Deaf Boy in the Mirror*

Every night, Ma read the ABC book to me, in sign language. The first picture I recognized was coconut, because I was surrounded by it.

Nani lived on a coconut plantation with palm trees that reached up to the sky. Once a month, a climber came by, tied a noose around both ankles and mounted the trees with a cutlass stuck in his waist belt. With one slash of the cutlass's sharp blade, the brown nuts fell down in bunches. The next day, women came and sat around in a circle, gossiping as they removed the husks, cracked open the nuts into halves, and caught the water. The grating followed and then the shredded meat is thrown into a big, three-legged cauldron with some lime juice to boil for hours. The white meat turned brown and sunk to the bottom of the cauldron and the coconut oil floated to the top. Nothing was wasted as the dry coconut husks were used to scrub pots with the ashes from the fire and the shells were placed in a tiled fashion to make pathways from the house to the vegetable garden.

There were no toilets in the house, so if you had to go in the night, there was a big enamel bowl with a handle that was called a *posey* because it had a picture of a posey of flowers on the outside. We did our business in this and, the next morning, Ma or Nani took it out and dumped it in the latrine. From the louvered windows, I spied the neighbor emptying hers on her aubergine plants. They were the biggest aubergines I have ever seen.

After Pa and Biig Baba returned to Canada, I was not allowed to go alone beyond the sandy area in front of the house. I spent my time in the hammock strung up between two mango trees and played games with SakiWinki, a squirrel monkey. His face was a white mask with black patches around his eyes and mouth, grey fur and bright yellow feet. He was about three pounds and he liked fruits. His favorites were bananas, guavas, and monkey apples. He had a long tail and enjoyed twirling it around my arms. I often had competitions with him to see who would win at copying each other. We were both losers, but we were besties.

Nani had a best friend who came to visit often. Her name was Miss Hilda. She was not like the other ladies in the village who wore flowery frocks and walked around bare-footed. She always wore nice skirts and blouses, a hat with flowers around the front brim and peep-toed shoes. They sat on the stoop in the front of the house and gossiped as they drank a bitter juice called *mauby,* which was made from a tree bark.

Miss Hilda brought her grandson one day. I checked him out, hiding behind the passion fruit vine that ran along the fence. He was older than me, taller and a big show-off with his brand new bicycle, which came from a place called America. He didn't let anyone touch it. While his grandma visited, he passed his time making designs in the sand. His hair was different, kinda like a black mushroom cap. He had fairer skin than Miss Hilda and I, and wore a T-shirt, shorts and flip flops. The village boys wore only khaki pants, and ran around shirtless with no shoes.

Another day, he arrived alone on his fancy bicycle. I was sitting in the sand in front of the house, drawing a picture of SakiWinki with my finger. He braked in front of me, spun the wheels a few times which stirred up the sand and made it fly into my eyes, then got off and parked it. I looked at him suspiciously. Maybe he wanted to fight and I wasn't big enough to fight.

He pointed to his lips, "My name is MJ."

I gave him a cut-eye.

"Yoo, I said my name is MJ." He spoke so slowly, that for a minute I thought he was dumb and was only now learning to speak like me.

I understood what he said from reading his lips, but I ignored him and continued to add details to SakiWinki's face. He went to the *gamma gum* tree and broke off a small branch which he split into pencil size pieces and stripped off the bark with his teeth. He passed one to me, which I took reluctantly, and then he squatted in the sand.

"Look." He stuck both of his index fingers close to his eyes, then to mine. With the pencil stick, he made shapes in the sand then pointed to me and the pencil I held, "you."

I copied him. This was nothing new to me as Ma had held my hand and taught me to make lines and circles. MJ joined the lines to make a square and filled it with circles. For every line and circle he made, he pointed to me and after a while, I just knew it was my turn. When he spoke, I looked only at his lips to understand his words. His voice reached my ears but not clearly, even though I strained to listen.

It was nice to have a friend. I wished Ma didn't come to get me for my afternoon nap.

I loved Ma's voice as it was clearer than other people's, though it reached me from far away. She sensed this as she often went down on her knees so that she was facing me and signed with her hands and mouthed the words. The nicest thing she did to me, and only me, was that she would place her hands under my chin, her palms touching each other as if she was cupping my face, and lifted my head up so that I was looking at her. She would then smile her broadest smile, before her thumbs rubbed my lips, her index finger touched my nose, then circle my eyes and, lastly, my ears. She would massage around my ears with small gentle circles over and over. "These are your five senses." Her hands and fingers were not soft, but when she moved them along my face, I felt special. She would sign and speak slowly so I could read her lips. "You are a special boy. One day all the gods will help you to say words. You will say words in many languages. It will be a miracle." She was my favorite person.

I had covered a whole area with squares and circles when MJ returned the next day, ringing his bell loudly and spinning

his wheels. Early that morning, Ma helped me make stick pen-
cils and I was busy designing in the sand. "Yoo." He greeted
me after he parked his bicycle and squatted beside me to
inspect. "Nice," he said.

He brought me a treat, sliced green mango covered with
pieces of hot pepper. It burnt my mouth and I jumped around
like SakiWinki. He gave me some sugar cane strips and I had
to suck on them until the burning went away. Before long,
he started to make his designs of squares and circles and
something new. Inside of the square, he made two lines
that touched at the top and halfway up his design, he made
another line that joined them together, "A" he said at least five
times. I made a whole square of A's that day. When I went to
bed, I mouthed it over and over, stretching my lips across my
face, baring my teeth which caused my nose to squinch up
and push my eyes into their sockets. It finally came out.

I heard it. I repeated it just to be sure that the correct
sounds were reaching my left ear.

'Eh.'

I question-marked it.

'Eh?'

I rejoiced. I jumped up and down on the straw mattress
until the seams broke and the straw flew over SakiWinki's face

On his next visit, MJ brought me a bunch of *genips* that
looked like grapes. I had already begun the design work in the
sand by making an image of his bicycle which I wanted to touch.
As we pulled the *genips* from the vine and sucked the thin layer
of flesh until the pit was bare, he showed me how to make the
letter B. It was simple. One straight line, with two small circles
on the side. I was getting pretty bored and wanted to go inside.
So he showed me something new. He made only a big circle,
and then he tricked me. He wiped off half of the circle, and drew
a coconut beside it. C, he mouthed. I made the half circles but
they were not as nice as MJ's.

When I looked through the ABC book, I observed that
all the large letters can be made with lines and circles and
some with the addition of fishhooks. The smaller letters were

another story. Within a week, I was able to design all of the large letters from A to Z. My letter S was the best. No matter how hard I tried, it always looked like this . . . $.

The following day, MJ brought a backpack with a ghetto blaster and showed it to me. I could 'see, but don't touch.' Carefully, he placed a tape with a picture of a man whose hair was in the same style as his. He pressed a button and the ribbon tape started to spin. It was the first time I heard the sounds of music.

MJ started to sing and dance to the music. He twisted and turned, spun around and lifted his feet as if he had fire under them. He pushed and re-pushed the buttons so many times that I started to understand the words he sang, and I could hear them as he sang out loud and made letters in the sand, snapping his fingers.

"A-B-C. 1-2-3. You and me."

I started to follow him, copying his moves, mouthing out the words. By the time he left, I was humming, but only in my head. That night, Ma caught me humming in bed. She had a surprised look on her face. She took my finger and traced it over all the small letters of the alphabet, sounding out the name for each one over and over.

MJ went missing for a few days. He was very sad when he made an appearance a week later. He had no treat, no ghetto blaster, and no bicycle. One thing he had was a lot of tears. He said his grandma had punished him. I wanted to make him laugh. I started to dance and move my lips to say the words, the way he did. I ran around in circles, stomped my feet and tried to walk on my toes and on my heel.

"You can't dance for shit," he signed and laughed. He had a laugh that was so loud Ma ran out of the house thinking something was wrong.

He was happy when he returned the following day with all his toys. He invited me to look at his bicycle and, surprisingly, for a bike ride. I sat on the handlebars as he pedaled around and around the *koker*, which was a concrete bridge over a small, muddy stream. Sometimes. I felt like I was going to fall off, but then MJ would shout in my ear, "Tilt to the right," or "Tilt to the left," or "Lift, you *batty*." The most exciting part was, "Hold on. Big spinaroo coming up."

Later, he turned on the ghetto blaster to the highest volume. He began to dance. With no slippers on, he kicked up dust and I followed him. It was so much fun. Other kids, boys and girls and their mothers and fathers who didn't work came in a hurry to watch. Soon, everyone joined. Even SakiWinki started to monkey dance on my shoulder, until he got so excited I had to stop. My ears buzzed from all the movement. I sat down and watched the bodies move around, feeling dizzy.

A very old lady arrived and sat down next to me. She placed a basket filled with bunches of genips beside me. She smiled and all I saw were her gums. I reached over for a bunch and started to eat. She got up and shouted and I could hear some of her words.

"Oh me lawd, the deaf boy thief me genips." All movement stopped. MJ turned off the music. Too many words flew back and forth. Some I heard, some I understood, the rest were just off the wall. The lady took off after Ma gave her some money.

MJ was not happy his show had to stop. When the crowd moved on, we sat cross-legged in the sand. He tut-tut-ed, and made a sign of the cross.

"Oligue. That woman is an Oligue."

I looked at his lips to lip-read this word.

"Oligue suck your blood like vampire. Very dangerous. Worse than Jumbie Man. Jumbie Man is ghost. Only scare you."

My mouth fell open.

"You is deaf," he shook his head. "Deaf. Deaf. Deaf."

Distantly, I heard the vroom-vroom of a car. When it arrived and parked by the koker, MJ jumped up excitedly and ran to meet the man who opened the passenger door. "Uncle. Uncle. Uncle."

The man patted MJ's head affectionately. "Michael Jackson Rafiq. Are you still trying to sing and dance like the real Michael Jackson?"

24 Uncle the Drunk

Draft of *The Deaf Boy in the Mirror*

Alone in the sand, I watched as Nani and Ma, with Jalebi in her arms, greeted this Uncle. He was dressed in jeans and a T-shirt with the letters, XM RUM. He wore glasses on his nose. Well, they sort of rested on his nose, and he often pushed them over his eyes when he spoke. He was of medium height with a mustache that curled at the corners, which he twirled with his pinky finger. Around his waist, he wore a fanny pack. He pulled and tugged a very large suitcase.

Sometime later, when Ma realized she had another child besides Jalebi, she walked over and lifted me up to rest on her hip.

"Uncle." She pointed to the man. He came closer with an outstretched arm. I clambered down from Ma's hip to hide behind her skirt and half-peeped at him.

"Shake Uncle's hand," Ma encouraged in sign language.

"You deaf?" His arm was still out as he waited.

Even though I could not hear well, *deaf* is the one word I can lip read and understand. It had to do with the way the person who said 'deaf' looked at me, the same way this Uncle did.

Before he came, I slept with Ma and Jalebi on a straw mattress on the floor. Now, I had to sleep with him. I took to following him around as he was the only man in the house. Very often, he turned away from me and took a swig from the mickey he carried in the fanny pack. He had some preparation habits before bedtime, I observed. First he went by the fence, broke off a small sized branch from a black sage tree, chewed on it until it looked like a brush and cleaned his teeth, very fiercely. Afterwards, he went to the latrine with some newspapers, a bottle of water and the mickey hidden in his pants pocket. I waited outside with SakiWinki, who swatted the mosquitoes that buzzed around with his tail. When Uncle came out, he walked funny. Sometimes, he missed his steps, but he always took my hand.

Uncle showed me the hummingbirds' nest, the bees' nest and the cavern of sly mongoose who sometimes grabbed a meal from Nani's chicken pen in the nights. He climbed the mango tree and picked the ripest ones for me. He taught me how to bite the bottom end of a mango to make a small hole, squeeze gently with my front teeth so the juice flowed and then suck it out before it dripped down my arms. It was like drinking from the juice boxes in Montreal, but without straws.

Some weeks later, Uncle took MJ and me for a swimming lesson to a place where there was a bigger koker over a long trench with flowing green water. He carried two clothes beaters made out of greenheart wood. He tied the beaters around our waists and pushed us into the water. MJ and I held on to the boards for our dear lives, squealing and kicking, as he stood by the sidelines, a cigarette hanging from his lip, and SakiWinki perched on his shoulder. 'Kick. Kick.' He shouted out, indicating to us with his legs. That was my first swimming lesson. I didn't need more as I took to the water like a fish and, before the week was over, I could swim faster and longer distances than MJ and Uncle.

We had duties while we swam. We had to be on the watchout for the police. Uncle was great at multitasking. He boiled his bush rum in a little dried-up trench full of river rocks and, in between, threw his castnet in a nearby pond for *hassar* fish, which had scales that looked like iron. The first task was an illegal act, which he paid 'lil attention to because it was a 'lil crime. He was never pleased because his bush rum was cloudy. He had an idea one day. He used my white T-shirt and strained the entire pot through it. That night he was real happy, he filled up the mickey twice.

"Good night," he said.

My mouth rounded and stretched out to form the words "good night" silently.

Ω   Ω   Ω

Ma started to cry from the time she woke up until she left with Jalebi in the vroom-vroom car. She hugged me so tightly and said things to Uncle, who shook his head. I only understood that she wasn't coming back when I went to bed and she didn't come to tuck me in. Uncle signed to me that she went back to Canada. I remembered it as the first time I cried and Uncle took me out into the night to watch the stars in the sky. I wanted to count, but there were too many and I can only count to ten.

As a special treat, he took me out the next day on the donkey cart to the savannah where horses and cows grazed next to the cane fields. He showed me the macaw with bright blue feathers on its wings, a green belly and a red head. It was the most beautiful bird I had ever seen.

Uncle spoke to the macaw. I strained my ears. The macaw can say words? And he's smaller than me? When Uncle went to take a pee in a clump of bushes, I mouthed out "good nite" to it. I said it as many times as I could. I turned around to see if Uncle had finished and almost jumped out of my skin when the macaw shrieked, "goo night, goo night."

He showed me the snakes also, but I don't want to talk about them, because they scare me. Uncle did warn me that there are more snakes dressed up in human clothes and I should be on the lookout for them all the time, as they can be very, very dangerous.

MJ returned to school and he visited only on weekends. I was busy in the meantime, drawing pictures in the sand, mouthing out words and saying them to the macaw, who repeated them.

I accidentally responded to Uncle as he wished me a good night when I was almost asleep one night.

"You hear me?" he signed.

I stared at him blankly.

"You hear me?" This time he pointed to both my ears.

"Goo nite." I said.

He shot up in bed, reached for the flashlight and switched it on.

"You not deaf and you not dumb? Open your eyes."

I did.

"Lemme see your ears?" He spoke into one ear and then the other. "I see the problem. Left ear good. Right ear no good. You need a fix up."

The next day, he got dressed in jeans and the XM RUM shirt and left for important business in the vroom-vroom car. I was sad all day. On each occasion that the car came to the koker, someone was leaving and then I never saw them again. First, it was Pa and Biig Baba, then Ma and Jalebi, and now, Uncle. Late in the evening, when it returned with Uncle, I ran out and hugged his leg. He lifted me up high in the air and gave me a big juicy sapodilla.

That night, he drank so much from the mickey that he staggered into the room and lay sprawled on the mattress. Sometimes, he crawled to puke into the posey. When he finally fell asleep, I found the flashlight and sought out his suitcase in the closet. I snapped open the lock and saw several white shirts, pants, and a hat with the ABC word, 'Captain,' which I tried on. There was also a photo album. On the inside cover was a picture of Uncle dressed in the white clothes and wearing the captain hat. He stood at the stern of a ship. There was also a newspaper cutting with a headline in ABC words: DRUNK CAPTAIN RUNS SUGAR BOAT AGROUND.

I heard Uncle stir and quickly tucked myself under the sheet. He reached across and tapped me. I jumped into a sitting position, rubbing my eyes.

"You are Kaman." He fell back on the mattress. "And I am 'Uncle the Drunk.' That's me. 'Uncle the Drunk.'"

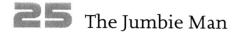 The Jumbie Man

Draft of *The Deaf Boy in the Mirror*

I didn't know if it was good or bad luck but, in the span of ten days, three incidents made me the center of attention. I did not understand any of them, as two were related to a church and the third involved grown men trying to find their marbles. In all cases, I was caught by a person or thing, called the Jumbie Man.

The first incident took place on a bright sunny Sunday.

That morning, Uncle the Drunk didn't take his early morning tonic from the mickey. He couldn't find it and that put him in a bad mood. When SakiWinki came for his usual visit and monkeyed around on the mattress, he shooed him out with a hiss. To make matters worse, he said, "There will be no swimming today because we are going to Ring the Bell church."

I had to dress up in my going-out clothes with socks and shoes which felt heavy on my feet. Uncle and Nani held my hands as we walked to a temple. Miss Hilda and MJ waited for us by the gates. At the doorway, everyone had to take off their shoes.

Panditji, the man who greeted us, was dressed in white, had a big red dot on his forehead with a string of marigolds around his neck. His pants were different. They looked like he took a sheet and folded it loosely over and around his legs. He held a bell in one hand that he continuously jingled. In the other hand, he held a book that had no letters of the alphabet from the ABC book. It was impossible to read as everything looked like symbols that were over-lined rather than under-lined with many squiggles.

He led Nani, Uncle and me to a dais at the front, ringing the bell as he walked slowly. Here, he placed us to sit across from him on a flour-bag sheet that covered the floor, with me in the center spot. He reached over and made a dot on my forehead with his pinky finger and hung a garland of white flowers around my neck. I stole a look around. There was a statue in gold color of a man with the face of a monkey and another of a beautiful lady like Ma, who sat in a lotus flower. She had four arms, that is two arms just too many.

I watched as Panditji arranged wood chips in a small, square mud-baked box that sat on the floor between us. With a mango leaf, he dropped ghee from a brass cup on the wood chips and then scratched a match to light a small fire. I breathed in the smell of incense as he fed the fire with ghee while he rang the bell. Stretching over, he grasped my jaw with one hand and with his other, he dipped a mango leaf into a glass and flicked drops of milk on my face. He then started to chant a special prayer as he turned my jaw from side-to side and flicked more milk, first into my left ear and then into my right ear.

I closed my eyes and drifted away.

Clouds swept me up and lifted me into the sky like a magic carpet. A rainbow with seven beautiful colors appeared. At both ends there was a gold bar. Beside each bar was a big G, the 7th letter of the alphabet in the ABC book. The clouds disappeared and I tumbled from the sky into a blue sea with the most beautiful colors of fish. The rainbow was still there. It was dancing and chanting to me. I started to count. For seven times, my ear picked up the chant of Om before it came to an end.

I opened my eyes to see the smoke curling into a cloud. Something caught my attention.I blinked. The gold statue of the man with the monkey face came alive. He was winking at me, sticking out his tongue at me and doing all kinds of funny faces. Then he started to blow out bubbles, which circled around my head and turned into gold bars.

I started to laugh. I laughed so loudly that heads moved to peep over shoulders for a better look. Something popped in my ears.

For the first time, I can hear my laughter.

I blinked as I heard the strange words Panditji chanted. "Oh Hanuman, destroyer-of-evil-forces. Take-away-the-demons-from-this boy. Oh Lakshmi, give-him-dharma-kāma-artha-and moksha."

I tried to stop, but the laughter would not cease. My body shook with it. Everyone got up from their sit down positions to look at me. Still laughing, I stood up and ran out the Ring the Bell church. From behind me, I heard MJ sing.

"Bambalaytee bambam. Jumbieman catch you"

Ω   Ω   Ω

The second incident happened on a dark, moonless Sunday night, a week after the Jumbieman caught me. Since this incident, I had noticed something strange with the other kids. They ran away when they saw me. Very often, my left ear picked up, "Jumbieboy." Not that I cared, because I can say some new words that MJ taught me, like *rass* and *batty* and *kakahole*, which I understood were related to my backside. Of course, I can only say them to myself.

The mosquitoes buzzed around and the fireflies flickered in the darkness. Uncle was still in a bad mood. It'd been a week to the day since I hid the mickey and he hadn't found it. He announced, "There would be no dominoes game tonight because we are going to the Clap Hand church."

Once again, I am dressed up in my Sunday best, held hands with Nani and Uncle who led the way with a flashlight. We walked until I complained about how much my feet hurt. They took off my shoes and socks and I felt much better, until I stepped into a big cake of fresh cow dung. Uncle did a suck-teeth because he had to wash me up by a trench.

Miss Hilda and MJ met us when we arrived at a big tent. Two oil drums close to the entrance blazed with smoke curling upwards. Inside, kerosene lamps hung from the walls and, as my eyes grew accustomed to the dimness, I saw the silhouettes seated on long benches. There was a podium at the front. A man dressed in a suit, tie and hat stood greeting people who called him Pastor John. Once again, Uncle sucked his teeth, saying to Nani that the Pastor was a fraud who travels from village to village, only to take poor people's money. He left.

I was sleepy when I finally met Pastor John. He smiled nicely as he bent down to shake my hand. I noticed he had gaps between his teeth. He held a brown book in his hands with letters from the ABC book which I can read.

HOLY BIBLE.

Once everyone was seated and quiet, Pastor John started to speak. I felt important sitting right up front. Not that it was the best place as, when he spoke, he sprayed me with a spit-shower. I dozed off. Nani nudged me awake. Something special was about to happen. MJ stood in the front with his arms in the air. I turned around and saw that everyone had stood up. Pastor John stepped down, lifted me up and placed me to stand on a chair beside him. He gave me a candle to hold and placed the Bible book on my head, saying words I could not hear clearly. Then, he would stop, turn away from me, and MJ would raise his hands in the air and all the people in the tent would shout, "Hallelujah," which bounced around in my head.

After the third time, I turned my left ear to his voice and heard his words a bit more clearly. "Lawd, hear me." Pastor John clapped. The crowd joined in, clap, clap, clap. I saw Nani clapping. I clapped too. MJ started to sing and mouths fell open. I looked at Nani, her mouth was open. I opened my mouth so wide that I heard my jaw click. The crowd said, "Hallelujah" again. I said it as loud as everyone around me. I heard myself saying it.

"Let us pray," Pastor said. Everyone bowed.

"Oh father, who art in paradise." I guess Pastor John could not hold his gas in because he chose that moment to let it out. Or maybe he made a mistake and thought the word "art" had something to do with fart – whatever. I *heard* him let it out. It came out in spurts and smelled disgustingly bad.

I started to laugh. I can hear the sounds coming out of my mouth and reaching my ears. I laughed as hard as Macaw shrieked, and as SakiWinki did his oh-oh, aw-aw. I cannot stop. Everyone stopped in mid-prayer to gape at me.

"Let the demons leave this child." Pastor John shouted. I got up and ran out of the church into the darkness. Everyone ran out after me, screaming, "Lawd, let the demons leave this child." I ran with the candle lighting my way, jumped over the cow dung cakes, past the trench where I had washed, past the koker dam right into Uncle the Drunk's legs. I was still laughing.

"What happened? Jumbieman catch you?"

Ω   Ω   Ω

"I am writing a letter," Uncle said as I peeked at the lined, white sheet of paper.

He sat down at the kitchen table and had been scratching ABC letters since his return from his day trip in the vroom-vroom car. I became very curious as he didn't speak. He would look up to the ceiling, think, and then write. It was impossible to read as all the letters were scrawled and joined together. I saw his problem immediately. He wrote with his left hand. His right hand was busy as he needed it to take a drink from the mickey. I had to return it after the eighth day, as he didn't have interest in doing anything. Because of this, I had to stay in the hammock with SakiWinki all day long, doing nothing. I kept the clothes beater close-by, hoping he would get the hint. Of all the things we did together, I missed swimming the most.

When he took a latrine break, I sneaked a peek at his papers laid out on the table. There were more pictures of him dressed in his white clothes and the captain hat. The pictures were taken at the helm where he stood steering The Demerara Sugar Boat loaded with bags of sugar. There was also a map on which he had inked an arrow and circled a country. I mouthed out the letters, *CUBA*.

He had been writing this letter for days. When it was over, he stretched out his tongue, licked a stamp and pasted it on an envelope. He held my hand as we walked to the red mail box and he dropped it inside. Life returned to normal, as the next day he took me swimming at a long stretch of sandy beach by the ocean where I could see a huge boat docked in the deeper water not far away. A rubber dinghy filled with men was lowered from the side. I watched as it circled around before the crew anchored it and waded to the beach.

Uncle greeted them with handshakes and helped them with their equipment. They were all dressed alike: one-piece black overalls with a green crest and the letters B and P in yellow on the chest pocket, except for one man who wore khaki pants, a shirt and a big hat. I think he was the headman as he spoke into a walkie-talkie. They walked along the beach with funny binoculars attached to their heads in search of something. I soon found out what they were looking for. The headman showed some samples to Uncle – little marble-sized black tar balls. I followed them, digging my feet in the sand to make a trail.

I wanted to leave my footprints behind on this beautiful beach.

After a while, I was tired of walking behind men who had lost their marbles and couldn't find them. I signed to Uncle that I would like to go swimming. He had brought along the wood beater, and now tied it around my waist. He warned me not to go past a certain area where the color of the water was a shade darker which meant that it was deeper.

"Jumbieman there. You hear me. Jumbieman in deep waters." He looked at me with a certain awe. "You not scared?"

"I am not." I boldly signed.

"If you run into trouble, flap the beater in the water." He raised his arms up and showed me how to do this before he rejoined the beachcombers.

When he wasn't looking, I untied the beater, dug a hole in the sand and hid them. I splashed around in the cool refreshing water, sprinkled it over my face and body. I threw handfuls at a shoal of four-eyed fish and chased away the hungry birds that dived with food on their minds. I ran back to the beach and then cannoned into the water. I floated atop, and wondered what lies below. Since no one paid heed to me, I dived and made an accidental discovery. It was indeed dark when I half peeped. I saw them. Little black balls floated around me and grabbed hold of my body. They felt sticky. Was this the Jumbieman? I turned around, closed my eyes and swam for my life toward the beach.

When my hands and feet touched sand, I stood up and opened my eyes. My body is covered in sticky black balls.

The entire crew surrounded me. The headman touched the Jumbieman that had taken over my body, rubbed it around his fingers then spoke into the walkie-talkie. "Captain, we have located oil."

I looked for my footprints in the sand.

They had disappeared.

$$\Omega \quad \Omega \quad \Omega$$

Three weeks after my last encounter with the Jumbieman, the postman arrived, ringing his bell nonstop. I made it to the front gate before Uncle and Nani. I was very excited, maybe another letter from Ma and Pa. I could tell from the envelope when they wrote. It had a stamp with the red maple leaf. Uncle always sat on the stoop with me in his lap and signed as he read them out loud.

The envelope I received had five stamps with dinosaurs on each one. I read the name that appeared on each stamp. *Cuba.* Uncle sat alone on the stoop as he read the letter. I sat in the sand, still trying to improve on my letter S.

When he finished, he walked over and lifted me above his head. "We are going to Cuba to fix your one side deaf ear. Now, we gotta get busy and make bush rum. The doctor wants a whole demijohn in payment."

26 Trust

THE JOY of hearing my first spoken word, "Eh," oh, yeah. I so remember how astounded and dumbfounded I was at that time. It means nothing to people who are not deaf, or who are not hard of hearing, or who are not hearing impaired but, to a deaf guy, it's like ecstasy, with a high that's higher than the designer drug. I rejoiced again just to rejoice, perhaps at the absurdity and serendipity. It was only fitting this should be my first word. After all, I am a Canadian boy. Yes, a Canuck through and through. And, screw anyone who thinks "Canuck" is a slang word.

I moonwalked with the wireless keyboard as I wrote about meeting MJ Rafiq. In later years, he told me his parents had chosen his first and middle name as a tribute to the famous American rock star Michael Jackson. Uncle the Drunk owns some rundown fishing boats that transport precious metals from the interiors of Guyana to neighboring Venezuela and Brazil, and occasionally, to the Caribbean islands. He still makes bush rum as a pleasure business.

As for the Jumbie Man, the last time I saw him was four years ago, when I overdosed on Uncle the Drunk's home-made brew on a visit to Guyana. That same night, I found out the reason Ma left me behind. She had heart surgery and was in the hospital for months. So, us kids were separated with Jalebi going to stay with Nonna in Italy, BB staying in Canada to go to school, and me being looked after by Uncle the Drunk.

Chewy was a great companion. He ate and slept when I did, and sat beside me when I worked. Every morning and evening, I took him for a long walk along the beach. It was refreshing, as we enjoyed the spray of waves against our bodies. He had moments of complaints where he would chew on his bed and other stuff he had a taste for. To keep him occupied, I let him watch television. His favorite show was *Lassie*.

Vibe had become an excellent tool in my routine. BB's message to 'check out the audio' popped up often on the watch's face, frustrating as I couldn't find the control button for it. While I was in jail I had worked out some of her capabilities. She had a proximity sensor, a chronograph that measured the moon phase and an unidirectional rotating bezel with cool functions, some of which I still couldn't figure out. I have to admit that she was nice, but she would never replace Om-7. He was a part of me and he was gone. I missed him in a way I cannot describe.

Dr. O, or her tech geek, had integrated an easy link that made sure her daily e-mail messages popped up on the screen. It all translated to the same, 'send me sample chapters.' The latest, written in capital fonts had a hint of aggression. I felt she was screaming at me. I sent an e-mail, requesting the return of Om-7 and received no answer.

I started to edit and found I was actually dragging my ass, as it turned out to be more tiresome than writing.

Today was day eleven of working on the memoir. I had become a bit of a recluse in this time, except for Carlos's visits to snorkel. I had set up my writing schedule so that, for every five chapters I finished, I celebrated with a fine dinner for Chewy and myself. So far, I was able to live comfortably off a mix of fresh and packaged food which most homes in The Cayman Islands kept as emergency grub in case of hurricanes and other natural disasters. Early this morning, I caught a good-sized fish and a conch washed up by my feet as I walked home. I made a conch ceviche from scratch and barbequed the fish on the complex's grill.

I had just finished turning off the communal barbeque when Bernie and Greg, a retired Caymanian couple returned from tending their hobby garden and handed me a basketful of fresh vegetables and fruits. They offered me the remnants of their fridge as they were leaving on a three-month trip. They knew about my shattered love life and that I had been in prison and conveyed their belief that India would come to her senses and return to me, and the cops were most likely dirty cops. They asked if I could pick up their mail and water their garden in their absence.

That night, I served Chewy his meal on a dinner plate. We had very intelligent conversations – more of a monologue, with me doing the talking and him pretending to listen. When he was bored, he turned his back to me, which I knew was a cue for me to shut up.

Ω   Ω   Ω

I had not heard from Rafiq, which was very unusual. From past visits to the island, he had a habit of dropping in on me with some cold beer and shoot the shit. I decided to visit him the next morning. It was going to be a hot day so I left Chewy home.

I walked to Georgetown, stopped in at the Tortuga Cake Shop to say a hello to Kara and stuffed my face with samples which she obligingly passed to me. We had a nice discussion in sign language about puddings. She was terrible at signing but, to me, she could do no wrong as I will forever hold her dear to my heart for what she did on the day I met her. She boasted that her mother made the best Yorkshire pudding. I asked her for the recipe now that I'm into cooking. She snuck me a take-home package of baby Tortuga Cakes.

As I walked to Da Roti Shaq I thought of Sparky and his whisperings to me about the gold being a billionaire's game. On an impulse, I stopped in at Books & Books in Camana Bay and found a poetry book by Robert Burns. I re-tracked to the post office and mailed it to Sparky at the Cayman prison's address with a little note.

I then headed over to The Nexx Complex. Hesitantly, I knocked on Engine's door. There was no answer. I walked away, swamped with regret at my insensitivity. For the hundredth time, I reproached myself. Friends don't do this kind of stuff to their best friends. Engine had trusted me and what did I do? I walked out on him like I was Mr. Moral sent by omnipresent God to judge people.

I trudged along, visited Carlos and found him alone and playing with himself, that is, he played two different video games at the same time. I invited him to Da Roti Shaq for a sandwich. My ulterior motive was to discreetly question him about India. He was so happy at this invitation that he reached up and gave me a smacking kiss on my cheek with, "Chico, you're the best HOH dude in town."

Kill two birds with one stone was how I saw this happening, but it wasn't to be. A new manager, a guy I had not met before, said Rafiq had left a week ago and he was uncertain of his date of return. I gave him my name and asked if he had left anything for me. After looking around, he found a package. On opening it, I found a cell phone with a pay-as-you-go card.

Had he cashed Dr. O's check and taken off? We borrowed from each other often enough over the years. I paid back on time, but lately, Rafiq was always over-extending himself on his trading deals. The last time I gave him a loan, he had taken three months before he paid me back. I would never forgive him if he pulled this shit one more time, knowing my situation.

When we returned to Carlos's condo, all my questions were answered with, "I don't know," or "I haven't heard from her." But when he went to the toilet, "you got mail" showed up on the corner of his screen. It was from India.

I opened it and read, 'Hey, Cuddles, I can't wait to meet you.' There was a photo attachment, which I clicked on. I stared in shock at an image of India and Engine. He had an arm around her shoulder and another around her waist. They were both smiling into each other's eyes. The slimebag! His coming out and all that crap about being gay was just a ploy to sidetrack me.

As I clicked on the properties to enlarge, I saw she wore the pashmina shawl with the heart pin I had given her. She too, had no shame, smiling up into the slimebucket's eyes, as if they were two peas in a pod. How long was this going on? "No way. No way," I muttered. There was more, but I heard the toilet flush and tried to close the screen. It froze. The washroom door banged. Carlos' footsteps sounded on the floorboards. I clicked and clicked on the frozen image that taunted me. How could India, who had made promises, shamelessly forget about me and erase me as if I had never been? And how could Carlos tell lies so easily? For heaven's sake, I had just befriended him. And Engine, hustling my ex-girlfriend?

I left Carlos's condo with a good excuse and saw that Dr. O's door was slightly ajar. I knocked. A brown-suited delivery man came to the door. He held several DVDs with racy photos on the cover. I peeked past him and saw the living room was filled with opened boxes. He answered a call on his cell and walked to the window. I entered and quickly did a sneak peek through the lot. All porn movies. I left immediately and. as I walked down the corridor, I saw Mamushi and Mr. Yoshio at the other end. Quickly changing directions, I headed for the back stair and hid. I saw them enter Dr. O's condo.

By the time I returned to my home base, I was beginning to lose trust in mankind, womankind and teenagerkind.

Ω   Ω   Ω

When I took Chewy out for our nightly walk on the beach, there seemed to be more people coming out for late night fishing and diving around the reef. Some were venturing closer to the cache. Too wired up to write, I started to spy on their activities with the powerful night binoculars.

Sleep didn't come easily the following morning. It had been hot and humid, the usual trade winds missing. The air conditioner's hum was driving me nuts. I shut it off. Still, I tossed and turned.

"Hiss." The sound awakened me. I rolled to my side, kicked off the covers and opened my eyes. I stared at the erect head with orange, beady eyes, tongue flicking in and out, inches away from my face. My body froze as if I had been dunked into a tank of cold water.

A snake!

"Run. Run," Uncle the Drunk shouted to me. But my feet were in chains.

The head of the snake whirled around and when it faced me, it became a man. His two arms reached around my neck. With all my strength, I pulled both arms away. They are covered with snake tattoos.

"Faster. Run. The Jumbieman will catch you," Uncle the Drunk shouted again.

I woke up to my own half cries. Beads of sweat covered my body. Chewy is licking my face.

Ω Ω Ω

That evening, as I picked up the mail for Bernie and Greg, there was a bundle of newspapers with a "Recycle" note attached. I took it home and undid the twine. In the Reuters section of the first copy I picked up, there was an article about the body of a woman that had been washed ashore in Cuba. This followed the discovery a week earlier of another woman who had been washed ashore in Jamaica. Both women were of European origin and both were bitten by snakes. The Caribbean Intel Agency was assigned to the case. I wanted to read the entire pile but when I looked at my schedule, I had to start on the next chapter of the memoir.

I forced myself to write. I thought of Engine, the sleazeball, and India, who didn't bat an eye to hook up with him.

They were good people when I met them so many moons ago.

27 Ten-squat-a-way

Draft of *The Deaf Boy in the Mirror*

The half-day kindergarten school is in the basement of a church, two blocks from my house. *Maternelle*, it is called, in French.

The lady teacher rang a bell and directed us to our seats, which were attached to the desks. I quickly counted there were eighteen girls and two boys, which included me. The other boy was older and much taller than me. We had front row seats.

"My name is Miss Elizabeth Victoria Edwards." The voice that reached my ear was soft.

"Is that like the Queen of England?"

I turned around to see who the voice belonged to. A girl with black, curly hair so big on her head it looked like a bird's nest, waited for Miss Edwards to answer. There were rubber bands attached to some braids that fell to her shoulder.

"Yes, my dear. It is. You can call me Miss Elizabeth." She smiled as she thumbed through a box. "I will give each one of you a name tag to wear every day in class. What is your name, dear?" she asked the girl.

"Indi Weinberger."

"You mean India. India Weinberger?" Miss Elizabeth pulled out a name tag. The girl nodded, the braids moved and I could not take my eyes off her golden eyes.

"That's a country," another girl said in a squeaky voice.

"That's right," India Weinberger said. "It has more than half a billion people."

"Can I have a name tag too?" asked the boy who sat next to me.

"Ladies first," Miss Elizabeth replied.

"But there are no ladies here," he answered back.

"Girls are ladies. Boys will be last."

Each person had to stand up and say his or her name to receive a name tag. Eighteen girls took a long time. I let the other boy go first.

"I am Ten-squat-a-way Rarahkwenhá:wi Montour. I am Mohawk."

"You have all those names?" India Weinberger asked. The whole class turned around to look at her.

"Yes, what's wrong with that?"

"It's wa-a-ay too much names to say."

"Here, children, let's move on." Miss Elizabeth led Ten-squat-a-way to his seat.

"India Weinberger has a big mouth," He whispered to me. When it was my turn, I froze. My name couldn't come out past my lips. I could hear my Ma's voice drumming in my ears. *"Say your words, Kaman."*

"Ka-ar," I said quietly. I felt the zinging in my ears and the urge to run out of the class.

"I can't hear you." I looked at the nest on India Weinberger's head and wondered if a bird would fly out and go tweet-tweet.

"I really can't hear you," she said again, but not rudely. It sounded nice to my ears and to Om-7.

"Kaman," I said, barely hearing my voice.

"I still can't hear you."

"Kaman Colioni." For the first time, I shouted out my name.

"Oh, my," Miss Elizabeth said. "You boys have real tongue-twisters."

At dinner time, Ma and Pa always asked Biig Baba end-less questions about his day at school. I felt important now as I waited my turn.

"Do you like your teacher?" Ma started off.

"We all have to call her Miss Elizabeth."

"Miss Lizbeth? Well that's a nice name," Ma said in her funny English.

"Do you like her?" Pa repeated Ma's question.

"Yes. She says she is like the Queen of England."

"Are the kids nice to you?" he wanted to know.

"Yes. There is only one boy. He lives at the end of our street. And there are eighteen girls."

"Lucky for you, my son. So many fish to catch." Pa patted me on the shoulder as if congratulations were in order for such an ordeal.

The next day, before class started, India Weinberger led the question period with, "What's that thing you're wearing on your ear?"

"It's funny looking," another girl said.

I couldn't answer. I didn't know how to explain that it helped me hear sounds. I told Ma about this after school. The

next morning she went to my school very early to see Miss
Elizabeth with cookies for the whole class.

At the beginning of class the following day, Miss Elizabeth
pointed to the blackboard and said, "Children, today we learn
about the senses." And there, up on the board, was a picture of
a girl with glasses, and a boy with a hearing aid.

I wasn't paying attention. I was looking at the new girl
in the class who wore very thick glasses. Miss Elizabeth had
pinned a name tag that read Æsa. I never saw the letter Æ in
the ABC book. She was cute with shiny, blond hair and spoke
neither English nor French.

I tuned out as Miss Elizabeth spoke about senses. Ten-
sqúat-a-way had brought a worm in a bottle to class. He
twisted and turned the bottle upside down under the desk.
I watched it curl up, straightening itself and then roll into a ball.

"Æsa and Kaman, can you come up front"

I stood by Miss Elizabeth's desk next to the new girl. She
smiled shyly at me.

'Æsa cannot see well, so she wears spectacles to help her
see things more clearly. Kaman cannot hear well, so his hearing device is to make him hear sounds better. Æsa, do you
want to tell the class about your spectacles?"

I peeked at Æsa. Her face was apple red. She was a very
quiet girl. She shook her head to indicate, "No."

"How about you Kaman, do you want to tell the class about
your device?"

"Yes," I paused. "I can hear things other people can't hear."

In the first week, there was show and tell. The girls brought
in Barbie and Ken, My Little Pony and other girlie things. Biig
Baba lent me his mighty sword from the He-Man TV show and
practiced with me to say the lines. Ten-sqúat-a-way brought in
two grocery bags.

Each one had to stand next to Miss Elizabeth's desk, and
show and then tell the class about the article, and why it was
their favorite thing. When my turn came, I froze again in front
of the class. All the practice from the night before with Biig

Baba was now useless as the words would just not come. I felt
something in my ears. It was a small movement, picked up from
a distance. I heard India Weinberger make an irritable sound
and as I looked at her, she blew out a puff of air. The rattling in
my ears started. I touched Om-7 in confusion and mumbled.

"I can't hear," one of the girls complained.

"Me too, I can't hear," another one joined.

Ten-squat-a-way came forward, took the sword from me,
lifted it into the air, and, in a very clear voice, said the words I
could not say.

"I am The Man, Prince of Caughnawaga with a gray skull
that has secret powers. When I raise my mighty sword, the
sorceress Teena comes running with her pussycat to play
with me. We do battle together with my mighty sword and
her pussy cat. It is the most powerful thing that can happen.
I become her Master and The Man, the most powerful man in
the universe."

Everyone clapped. Ten-squat-a-way bowed.

When it was his turn, he faced the wall, pulling out stuff
from the grocery bags. He walked to the front of the class
dressed in leather pants that swept the floor. On his head, he
wore a colorful feather headdress that kept tilting to one side,
and his face was painted. Around his waist, he wore a purple
belt with white squares and a tree in the center. What caught
my eyes was the bow and arrow slung over one shoulder and
the plastic tomahawk he held.

"Is that your Halloween costume?" India Weinberger
asked.

"Can you shoot those arrows?" another asked

"Go on Ten-squat-a-way. Tell the class about your costume," urged Miss Elizabeth.

"This headdress is made from eagle feathers. It belonged
to my grandfather who was a Mohawk Chief." He paused to fix
the headdress. "Only the chief can wear it and only on special
occasions, like when he is having a pow-wow or fighting off
bad cowboys."

"Show us how the bow and arrow works." I didn't have to turn around to know it was India Weinberger.

"I can't show you how it works, but I'll show how it fits together." Ten-sqúat-a-way took off the headdress and placed it on the desk. He set about arranging the arrow into the bow.

'Shoot it," someone shouted.

"No, you don't," Miss Elizabeth said, stepping behind Ten-sqúat-a-way. She reached out quickly to stop him and accidentally pulled back his arm. We all watched as the arrow zipped high over our heads toward the back wall. It settled in the center of the red maple leaf on the flag of Canada.

"That's a real bow and arrow! Ten-sqúat-a-way, where did you get that?" Miss Elizabeth seemed a bit worried now.

"My Uncle Flynt gave it to me. He lives in Caughnawaga. He said it has been in our family for seven generations. Only the men can have it, and I am the next man in line."

That same afternoon, Ten-sqúat-a-way rang our doorbell and asked if I could come out and play. I was so excited that someone wanted to be my friend. Ma invited him in. At first she couldn't say his name. She tried with ten-squats-away and he corrected her several times, yet she couldn't get it. She made him write his full name on a scrap pad. Her lips moved silently as she read it.

"How do you say your last name?"

"Montour."

"That's French," Ma said conversationally. "Where do your parents come from?" she asked.

"My mom is from Caughnawaga and my dad is from Montreal. My dad is half English and half French and my mom is Mohawk. If my dad was French alone, then I would be a Métis. Since my dad is half and half, I can choose who I want to be."

"What is Métis?" Biig Baba asked, not wanting to miss out on anything.

"Half-breeds. Half Native Indian and half French," Ten-sqúat-a-way answered. "But since I come from Mohawk

Chiefs, I choose to be a Mohawk Indian. One day, I am going to be a Mohawk Chief."

"Oh, you're Ingin?" To my ears, it sounded like Engine, because Ma didn't speak English so well, not like Miss Elizabeth or the neighbors, or the people on television. Words always sounded different when she said them. From that day on, no one in our house called Ten-squat-a-way by his name. He became Engine. Because he loved cars, he loved the name Engine. The funny thing is, he told his parents and they too, at times, addressed him as Engine.

He rang our doorbell the next day with a basket of fried bread. His mother had sent it over for us. Jalebi was jealous as she had no one to play with. She asked Ma if she could have a friend over who lived six houses away at the far end of the street. She met her at the playground. When the doorbell rang, I peeped out of the living room window. All I could see was a big bird's nest sitting on the friend's head.

India Weinberger waved to me.

For the next few days after show and tell, parents came in to see Miss Elizabeth with complaints. I heard India's father shouting, "Why doesn't he go back to the rez with his bow and arrow and then he can target practice and shoot all the drunks there."

The bow and arrow became big news. First it was on the télé news in French, then it was on Channel 12 in English. A newspaperman came in to school and made a picture of Ten-squat-a-way and the whole class. It made the front page of the English and French newspapers. Ma cut out the articles and scotch-taped them to the fridge door.

I made the news too, but not in a way I liked.

When the television crew came to film, Miss Elizabeth lined the class by the fence with Ten-squat-a-way at the front dressed in his Mohawk costume. The cameras were so big they didn't see me taking a pee by the fence, and so I was in the television piece that was broadcasted on the Canadian National News. For weeks after, when we were alone, Biig Baba teased me. He placed both hands on his pants over his privates and made the "pssssing" sounds and laughed hysterically.

The fight between the parents and the system went on for some weeks. The Montours disappeared. Miss Elizabeth told Ma there had been death threats to the family. I was sad and missed him in the schoolyard as there were no other boys to play with.

Pa explained to us kids what happened. It was complicated. Engine's mother was Mohawk and his father Canadian. Because of this intermarriage, and a Bill C-31, she lost her rights to live on the Mohawk reservation, and this is why they lived in Chouguay. I did not understand all this nonsense. All I wanted was for my only friend to come back to school. The newspapers ran updates every day. Many questions were asked and many opinions were expressed. I asked Ma to read it to me but she wouldn't. She said, instead, "I don't see why all the fuss. They should go investigate how many politicians are taking bribes."

Every night after lights out, Ma and Pa sat in the den, with the volume of the television on low, and had conversations which I could hear if I turned Om-7 toward the sounds. They spoke about Ten-squat-a-way and how sad it was that he was seven years old and still in kindergarten because of laws. They talked about how the indigenous peoples were not getting a fair deal and how much whisky India's foster father drank and how he wasn't even an indigenous person. They discussed how satisfying it was that I didn't have to go to the school for the deaf, even though the doctors recommended it.

After all the hoopla, which took a month, Engine finally returned to Maternelle, only when someone named The Minister of Education got involved.

I was so happy, I hugged him.

28 India

Draft of *The Deaf Boy in the Mirror*

Our house in Chouguay was a small, three-bedroom bungalow on a pie-shaped lot, with big trees, mostly maples. In the summer, they were tall and green and, on a windy day, the leaves danced. I taught everyone, except Jalebi – as she was too small – how to climb trees, as Uncle the Drunk taught me in Guyana. India was the best, as she climbed much higher than all of us on the first day.

That year, I understood why there is a season called *fall*. It's because all of the leaves would turn different shades of red and orange and yellow before they *fall* off the trees leaving behind bare limbs and branches.

In the middle of October, Engine and India would come over on the weekends and, together with Biig Baba and Jalebi, we piled the leaves in heaps. It was a race to see who would make the biggest mountain. Biig Baba was learning about mountains in school and he gave them names. We jumped and tossed and rolled around until Mont Tremblant, Mont St. Sauver, and Mont Royal became flat. This fun lasted for hours until the smell of Ma's baking reached us and we rushed inside, exhausted and hungry.

Our moms became friendly and invitations were extended to visit each other's house for lunch after school. The first was to India's house. In the living room, there was a cabinet with a padlock on the door. Inside, was a collection of guns – real guns. In her parent's bedroom, there were bottles with pills on the night table, and a bottle of Canadian Club whisky, which India's mom quickly put into a drawer. Over the bed was a big cross on a chain.

Mr. Connolly was a mechanic and Mrs. Connolly a

housewife who loved to watch the soaps on TV. The driveway and yard were filled with old cars. At the back of the house was a special garage with work tables. Tools, nails and screws were scattered on the floor.

Mrs. Connolly made a quiche and a casserole that she served with coffee. She looked frightened all the time, peeping through the window and becoming very uncomfortable when she heard her husband's truck pull into the driveway. I became scared just looking at her.

She told Ma that India was a foster child who they had taken in because her real parents could not take care of her. This is why India's last name was different from theirs. They loved her so much that it will be difficult when she leaves to go back to her parents. James, her husband, especially, loved India. She had become the apple of his eye.

When Ma told Pa about the cabinet with weapons, The Gun Control Act was passed without the process of a debate. We were not allowed to go to the Connolly's house "as of this moment," said Pa who emphasized this statement as if he were the Prime Minister. India was allowed to come to ours any time, he said.

The visit to Engine's home was very short because his mother worked. Behind his house was a stream and a bridge we crossed over before, without Ma and Pa's knowledge, to Caughnawaga, where his grandparents lived. Only his family can use this bridge. Mr. Montour was a lawyer and Mrs. Montour a gemologist who worked with stones. Her workroom was filled with different sizes, shapes and colors of stones. In one corner of the room, she was carving a rock man. She also carved miniature canoes out of wood, and dream weavers and wampum belts in beadwork patterns. Mrs. Montour spoke to Engine in her native Mohawk language.

Not all of Pa's warnings stopped us from going to India's house. One day, we were playing tag in the front yard when we saw her father zip down the street in his big wheel truck, the engines revved up as he turned the corner. Quickly, we went over to find India. She sat on the front stairs, a big bruise on her arm and the saddest look on her face. Her mother came out to see who had arrived. She held an ice pack on her face. Her clothes were torn and had blood stains on them as if she had been in a fight.

She allowed India to come over to my house to play. Soon, she was no longer sad as she ran around in a tag game. Jalebi went in the house and brought us some pop Ma bought on sale, but none of the caps would open.

"I can make two holes," India offered.

She searched the backyard until she found a certain size rock. We sat on the back porch and watched as she took a nail out of her pocket and banged two perfect size holes into the metal cap until the pop spurted out in a hiss.

The bruises on India didn't seem to go away. And there seemed to be more. I heard Ma and Pa discussing them and decided to ask her about it.

"I fall out of bed all the time," she said.

Ω   Ω   Ω

My dream to go on the school bus came true as Miss Elizabeth organized a school trip to a *cabane a sucre,* or the sugar shack, that was attached to an apple orchard. Parents were invited so Ma had volunteered and asked if she could bring Jalebi along. Miss Elizabeth seated me next to India. I saw fresh bruises on her neck. She was not very happy. She spoke very little. When we arrived at the farm, everyone was excited as a horse and buggy would take us from the bus to the apple orchard and then to see the maple trees with taps where the syrup dripped into buckets. India refused to leave the bus.

It was only when Ma, in her funny English, coerced her that she got up, held her hands and climbed into the buggy. When we arrived at the apple orchard, she climbed the first tree and, with a vengeance, picked apples and threw them at everyone who was around her. Tears streamed down her face. She then found a forked branch and sat down. Miss Elizabeth tried to get her down, but she would not budge. The farmer tried, too, but she turned her back to them.

Ma did the most surprising thing I ever saw her do. She kicked off her shoes, held on to the trunk and climbed the tree. Minutes passed before India came down, with Ma right behind.

She didn't speak all the way back home. She didn't speak for days. Her mom brought her over to play with Jalebi. They played pretend house with GI Joe as the father and Barbie as the mother and My Little Pony as the child. In her play, GI Joe was always swatting Barbie and My Little Pony. Her play would have a surprise turn. My Little Pony would grab GI Joe's gun, shoot him in the chest and head. Then, when he fell down on the floor, Barbie would jump on to My Little Pony's back and trot off into the sky.

 ## The Colors of Christmas

Draft of *The Deaf Boy in the Mirror*

This was my first Christmas in Montreal since Uncle the Drunk brought me back from Cuba with my 'new ear' which is a hearing aid with an antenna. I now spoke well enough that my use of sign language had decreased. With so much improvement, Ma and Pa said I could choose the toys that Santa Claus may bring me for Christmas, but there was another clause attached, "You'd better be good for goodness sake."

In case you haven't met Santa Claus, he's a big guy with a white beard, a bit on the heavy side and wears a red suit. I met him for the first time some weeks ago at the mall. I sat on his lap. He smelled of sweat and had a booger in his nose, but I did stay long enough to tell him I wanted the entire collection of Teenage Mutant Ninja Turtles, specifically, the ones who lived in the sewers of New York. I gave him the page I tore out from the Sears catalogue.

On the first Sunday of December, which was a very cold day, the entire family dressed up in winter clothes and went outside to decorate the house for the holidays. India and Engine came by too, and helped. We all held the Christmas lights as Pa wound them around the pine trees, hung icicles in scalloped patterns along the roof and lined the window frames and the front door. He had chosen multi-colored lights in green, white and red. He said the lights were special and were for Ma, because her name, Diwali, meant "festival of lights" in the Hindu culture. They were the most beautiful blinking lights and could be seen no matter which end of the street you were on.

The next weekend, he retrieved the Christmas tree from storage under the stairs and this was the fun part. The tree, an artificial pine, was as tall as Pa, and it almost touched the ceiling of the living room. Each person had a job to unwrap the decorations and place them on a white bed sheet on the floor. We all talked excitedly about what Santa Claus would bring us for Christmas when he came down the chimney. And we were very good, because we wanted to have that toy we had seen advertised so many times on television.

Jalebi chattered on and on about how pretty it would be if it snowed on Christmas Day. She took the quiet India by the hand and went to the windows from room to room to see who would be the first to spot snowflakes, in between playing with Barbie and Ken. They stood together, held hands and begged for snow. It was the only time India spoke.

On Christmas Eve, Pa prepared a seven fish dinner passed down from his Neapolitan tradition. In the morning, he woke us up early and we drove to the fish store in Jean Talon Market. All the fish were dead and lying on ice. I remembered the first time I ate fish. Uncle the Drunk caught them while MJ and I swam. We watched as he slit the head off, cook them over an open fire and, fifteen minutes later, we ate fish on bread with hot pepper.

At the market, Pa allowed us to choose the octopus, shrimp, calamari, baccalà, eel, smelt and sardines. At home, Biig Baba and I got to hold the octopus, scare each other, and

Jalebi. It took Pa all day to clean and prepare the meal. We became his slaves in the kitchen: taking his orders to find this pan, wash this dish, bring a dishcloth, and throw that in the garbage. Ma made some eggnog. I saw her pour in some rum and told BB about it. We were so tired we all had to have a nap before dinner. The cool thing was we got to eat the seven-fish dinner in our pajamas.

There was no snow when we went to bed, much to our disappointment. BB had a plan that, if all of us kneeled down and prayed, maybe snow would come. After Ma and Pa sat down for their nightly tête-à-tête in the den, we sneaked over to Jalebi's room and BB talked us through prayers which began with, 'Let it snow, let it snow,' and ended with, 'Please Santa, can you bring me Super Mario and Donkey Kong.'

After lights out, BB led us to the kitchen on tippy toes. He made us taste the eggnog from the fridge. Jalebi and I ran to the sink and spit it out as it tasted awful. Not BB, he had a whole glass. Then he brought out the chocolate chip cookies and some for Santa under the Christmas tree. He thought the poor guy would be thirsty after eating the cookies, so he poured a glass of milk then added some white stuff from a blue bottle that was stashed in the medicine cabinet that we were not supposed to touch. I read the letters carefully on the label – LAXATIVE.

Back in bed, I kept watch. I wanted to be the first to announce snow. I thought of how lucky I was to have a nice family, and how much fun it was to have a brother and sister. I especially liked Ma and her voice when she read and messed up words. And I loved Pa when he brought pizza home from the pizza parlor, where he worked as a chef.

This year was not like other years. I can speak, not perfectly, but I can speak. I can hear, too, very clearly, and sometimes I can hear things that I shouldn't hear. For example, I can hear things Ma and Pa were doing in their room after lights out if I turned Om-7 in that direction.

When I felt my eyes getting droopy, I took one last peep

through the window. Mr. Snow was a no show. Still, it didn't sadden me. I had a family. I loved my family and my family loved me. I was so happy for all these things. I went down on my knees and said some prayers to omnipresent God, thanking him for his kindness to me and, as a favor, please send some snow for Christmas.

Snow covered half of the window when I woke up. Biig Baba wouldn't wake up. I tried pulling his ear, his nose, his hands and his feet. He turned on his side, pulled the covers up and went back to sleep. I dutch-ovened him and he still wouldn't budge. I pulled down the covers and pulled his wiener, and he almost knocked me out with a Bruce Lee high kick. When he missed, he jumped out of his bed, yelling, "I am going to break all your Christmas presents."

"Look outside," I said excitedly. He forgot that he was mad at being woken up and jumped all around which, in turn, had Jalebi rushing over to our room. Together, we made so much noise that Ma and Pa finally woke up.

Santa was good to me. I received a sewer rat and . . . and . . . my most favorite Ninja Turtles – Mikey, Raph, Donnie and Leo. I hugged all of them close to me and gave Mikey a kiss because he was funny and he loved my most favorite food, pizza.

Jalebi was excited with her little ponies and Barbie doll. BB shouted out, "My prayers worked," when he opened his present to find it was Super Mario. Santa brought Ma a little red pocket dictionary for her handbag and Pa received videocassettes of *The Godfather Part 1 & 2*.

It wasn't long before Engine rang the doorbell. Santa brought him the whole collection of Transformers toys. How cool was that! His father made him a big sled and his mother gave him a special belt that was purple and white. He wore it around his head like a Ninja Turtle and pretended he was one, too. We were so noisy that Ma made us all, except Jalebi, get dressed and go out to play.

It was a Christmas card picture. The yard, the trees, the

rooftops were all white, and, oh boy, it was so beautiful. We
built a fort that had a front and back entrance and we crawled
in and out, throwing snowballs at each other. Engine ran back
to his house and brought his sled over. It was amazing as it
had special wheels and we took turns riding it around the cul-
de-sac. India must have seen us from her window for she came
out to have a look at how it worked. Engine offered to take her
for a spin, but she wasn't interested. She wanted to play inside
with Jalebi. I went in with her to get my new turtle buddies for
a ride. Santa had forgotten her house, but her mom had given
her a doll in the morning. When she took off her coat and her
sweater pulled up, I saw black and blue bruises on her tummy.
Quite a few.

Ma called us in for a brunch, another eat fest. The table
was covered with food as she tried to outdo Pa in the amount
of dishes she prepared. Engine and India joined us. There was
duck curry, dhal puri, chow mein, pepperpot, turkey stuff-
ing, and spaghetti with meatballs and sausage. We all stood
around Pa as he made funnies when he carved the turkey.
Three cultures, from three continents, on one table, Ma said
proudly. Canadian. Guyanese and Italian. And, then there was
the book lesson: "Who knows which continents?"

"Europe, North America and South America," Biig Baba
piped up. He ran to the fridge door to show where they were
on the map of the world.

"You guys are so lucky to be experiencing the best of three
worlds," Pa said.

Our bellies filled and our hearts contented, we were
shooed down to the basement to continue our Ninja Turtles
versus Transformers fight.

The doorbell rang. We all rushed to see if Santa Claus had
returned.

India's mom, Mrs. Connolly, stood shivering in the cold
with house slippers, pajamas and no coat. Her face was blue
and red with bruises. Ma covered her with a blanket and put
the kettle on. As soon as it started to whistle, the doorbell
rang again. From the window, I saw Mr. Connolly's truck.

When Ma opened the door, he pushed her aside, entered and pulled Mrs. Connolly to her feet, shouting out to India to get out of the immigrant's house. India cowered in a corner, her lips shook and her body trembled. I saw fear in her eyes. He grabbed her and pulled her so that she cried out. He then turned to Engine and scornfully told him to go back to the rez.

Pa woke up from his nap, came out and ordered Mr. Connolly to get out the house and threatened to call the police. He retreated, still pushing and pulling his wife and India toward the door. The insults were still coming as he opened the truck's door and shoved them inside.

"Dirty wop," he sneered.

I have never, ever, seen my Pa so angry. He ran out the door without coat and boots and shoved Mr. Connolly so hard that he fell heavily into the snow. "Woman beater," Pa shouted at him. Ma and all of us kids, Engine too, had run out, with boots only, and just as Pa was about to swing his fists, we held on to his arms, his feet, and whichever part of his body we could reach. All of us were afraid because Pa was much bigger than Mr. Connolly and could easily crush him to pulp. Pa looked at all of us, and I think he must have seen the fear in our eyes. Slowly, his arms dropped to his sides.

Once he was back in the truck, Mr. Connolly, still shouted out insults as he revved up the motor. He accelerated and reversed into our fort as many times as it took to make it flat before he raced off, leaving Engine's sled in pieces.

That Christmas night, Ma and Pa tucked us in early. Tuckered out, they, too, went to bed. I awoke to a feeble ringing of the doorbell. I peeked through the window and saw fresh footsteps in the snow. Scared, I woke up Pa who went to the window. What he saw made him shake Ma awake before he ran to open the door, with me behind him.

India stood there, her winter coat unbuttoned, the laces of her boots undone. She was covered in blood and shivering so much she couldn't speak. In her hands, she held a little doll. Pa quickly got dressed, went over to the Connolly's house and returned to say that no one had answered the door. He called the police. Ma had, in the meantime, run a hot bath and put India in it to soak. She still wouldn't speak, her body shook with the sounds that would not get past her lips.

I picked up the coat to hang it in the coat closet and something fell out. It was an empty pharmacist's pill bottle. The childproof plastic cap had two penny-size holes in the center.

When the police arrived, they found that India's mom had been beaten to death, and that India's dad had overdosed on a concoction of whisky and sleeping pills.

That night India slept at our house sharing Jalebi's room. I heard Ma and Pa talking late into the night. First, they spoke about how sad it was, and about where India would stay. They both agreed she could live with us. I turned and twisted in bed as I thought about this. I decided that even though she was a girl, and I didn't like girls, it wouldn't be that bad having her around.

Ma, with tears running down her face, would later explain what happened when two police women came early the next morning to take India away. They have to find her real parents, but in the meantime, she had to go and stay with some people in a place called Social Services.

The colored Christmas lights blinked in the white snow as the police car with India drove off. I watched from my bedroom window until I couldn't see it any more.

30 The Meltdown

THAT CHRISTMAS will stay with me forever. I still see the fight that Pa walked away from that day and India shivering in our doorway that night.

It was day eighteen of working on the draft, and it was not progressing as I had planned. Seeing the photo of India and Engine had thrown me off. Added to this was the task of writing about India as a child. There were missing gaps in her life which she herself did not know. I began to understand the inner conflict she had not knowing her biological parents. Engine also had a tough run as a Native Indian – trying to reclaim an identity that was crushed over the centuries under the banner of kings, queens, presidents and other madmen.

This did not mean that I forgave them for their deceit.

For a change of pace, I did the dirty. I reconnected to the world of social media. Purposefully, I had disallowed myself to be part of the estimated two billion of the world's population who engaged in this activity. I looked for communication from India. There was none. When we parted, she said she would be in touch. I didn't believe her then, but I still hoped that absence would make her heart grow fonder. It was more like out of sight, out of mind. She couldn't wait to cozy up with my best friend.

Now I know that love is just a four-letter word for her. Same as "fuck" is a meaningless four-letter word to more than half of the English speaking world.

As I surfed the net and familiarized myself with the outside world, another e-mail arrived from Dr. O, requesting chapters of the book. It was such a harassment, especially since I had written freestyle and still needed to edit. I also did not like the harshness of the last three chapters. I thought of changing the names of my friends and family, as people who read novels like characters with names that are easy on the tongue.

I checked out my blog. Prior to my arrival in the Grand Cayman Island, I blogged weekly and had a fan base. There were a lot of questions now from my followers. Are you sick? We miss you. How can you dump us? Did you find a job finally? Of all my followers, the most faithful was a man who used the name "Zingaro," which suggested he was a gypsy of Italian origin. He didn't post a picture so I had no idea what he looked like. When I announced I had finally graduated from university, he asked me to send my curriculum vitae, in the event that he ran into someone who had no qualms about employing a deaf person. When I complained about not even having an interview, he had graciously sent me a ticket to the Cayman Islands with a note saying there was a job there. I just had to look hard enough and use my common sense.

Zingaro often sent links of different things and places. In fact, on the day I arrived in the Cayman Islands, I had opened a link he sent that same morning, which was a video of baby octopuses leaving their egg casings and swimming toward the water surface. I recognized the reef and the three rocks that jutted above the water close to Ghost Mountain, not far from Paradise Beach. I was so captivated by the video I replayed it several times as I stood by the Tortuga Cake Shop and shoved the freebie sampling of Tortuga rum cakes into my mouth. It was just then that I got rolled and met Kara, who will forever be my friend for what she did and said.

Now, as I browsed through my blog, I opened the most recent link Zingaro had sent. It was of a place called Paraiba in Northeast Brazil. Of no interest to me, I closed it.

There were e-mails from Æsa and Lex Xi with endless complaints about each other. Ma and Pa sent pictures. They were now cruising in the Baltic Sea.

Ω   Ω   Ω

All attempts to write that night yielded zero results. I had reached a complete dead end which was not good. The next morning, I decided to walk down to The Nexx Complex and clear my head with people watching and looking up my old and new friends.

I knocked on Engine's door in case he had returned. I was lusting for a fight, a heated argument – something, anything – to settle matters. Through the peephole on the door, I saw eyes and heard a movement. He took a long time to open the door. When he did, he looked at me with such disgust. "I refuse to speak to you, on the grounds that I don't want a friend who is not there for me." He slammed the door in my face.

Dispirited at not being able to get a word in and no fight to talk about later, I knocked on Carlos and Ernesto's door. No one

answered. I went down to Da Roti Shaq and the manager said
Rafiq was still away on an overseas trip. Discouraged and feeling alone, I set out on a walkathon toward Hell. There's always
people in Hell. Today, it was filled to capacity. They came from
all over the world. Their interest was to see the short, black lime-
stone formations that were deposited over twenty-four million
years ago. I looked for Satan. So far, no one has seen him. Like
them, I was out of luck.

When I arrived home, it was late and Chewy had had a major
accident. The pungent smell of dog's urine and feces hit my nostrils the moment I opened the door. He had peed and crapped all
over his sleeping area. To top it off, he had ripped apart his bed
and chewed all the hundred dollar bills to shreds. I tacked it up to
separation issues with me being gone all day.

As I quickly checked my inbox, I found twenty-two e-mails
from Dr. O. She had programmed the same e-mail to be sent out
to me every half hour. As I pondered a response and a course of
action, another e-mail zipped in. "If I don't receive anything by
the end of day, you are evicted." It was a threat.

I looked at Vibe for some help. He indicated that it was 23.23,
which meant I had a bit more than half an hour to shape up or
ship out. Within ten minutes, the complex manager, pissed off
at being awakened was at the door. He had been instructed to
change the locks, take the dog and get rid of me by tomorrow
morning.

As if he sensed separation again, Chewy started to act
strangely, readying himself in a squat position. I grabbed his
collar. "No. No. No. Stop! You deaf and dumb dog. I have had
enough shit for one day," I screamed. "Out. Let's go," I said and
pointed to the door.

The moon was a big, round globe hanging over the sea.
Something I should appreciate, but the sight of Netts and
Rooslahn, sitting together in deep discussion on the pier, added
to my sense of being wronged. Vibe reminded me it was midnight. I threw her in the water. She didn't react kindly to my

angst and started to flash her colors. The lights spiked upwards and appeared as fireworks from the sea. Through the lights I saw Netts and Rooslahn, pointing in a direction, which alerted me they were getting closer to their goal of finding the gold.

It seemed every person or thing I had tried to make contact with, or come in contact with today, was against me.

Ideas, not all good, materialized in my head and attached themselves to each other. Quickly, they bypassed the toddler, adolescent, teenage years and matured to adulthood. They multiplied and fused themselves together so they became one big mass of "just do it."

I swooshed it out.

The piercing sounds came out in gasps. They bounced back into my eardrum. It was primal and joyful. I cannot remember the last time I had indulged in a good screaming session; mostly because it made Om-7 irritable, which in turn was transmitted to my brain in an offensive manner and forced me to stop. In his absence, I screamed to my heart's delight.

Netts and Rooslahn rushed over, but kept their distance. I continued to scream. I lay down in the sand and set the sounds free from my lungs. I rolled down the sandy incline to the water's edge, knelt in the waves, faced the skies, brought my hands to the side of my head, and released the frustration.

It felt good.

The meltdown had its rewards as the two gold diggers were right beside me now as I refilled my lungs in gasps.

"I think he has gone completely insane. He's singing looney tunes. Should we take him to the mental house?" the Russian asked Netts.

I didn't want to disappoint them about my condition so I did an encore. It was even better than my initial performance.

"There are no asylums on the island. The crazies are sent to Jamaica. Besides, it makes me crazy just seeing all those disturbed people. I say we just walk away from this."

The Russian seemed a bit concerned. "What if the idiot drowns?"

"That idiot can swim better than any Olympic champion."

"Maybe I should use him to find the gold. So far, you have come up with nothing. In Russian, that's *niette*."

"I told you there's no yellow gold, but you seem to think it's there. I have explored everywhere inside the reef and, may I mention, I have been trapping real lobsters here since I was a child. I know below these waters like the back of my hand. There's no gold here."

"There is. Find it. I will raise the bounty."

I watched their retreating figures until they were out of sight.

Completely exhausted from my one-man show, I found the most comfortable chaise lounge at the far end of the beach, and lay down. It was time to face reality. I was fed up. My relationship problems didn't help. Getting dumped by the woman who claimed she loved me is not easy, I had to admit. Hooking up with my best friend was the worst blow I've ever had.

Then there was the garbled text message and the sad face with an emoji. Was she playing head games with me? Was it a game of Truth or Dare?

I thought of India and Dr. O, two women who were related to each other, not by blood, but by some strange family bond. Were they both mind-fucking me?

I made up my mind. I will cross that bridge of Truth or Dare when I get to it.

It was a perfect moonlit night to sleep on the beach, but I went in after a while. I edited the first five chapters and sent them out to Dr. O. There was good to this, as the read-through of the chapters stimulated me and, before long, I started to tap away on the keyboard.

31 Quirkland

Draft of *The Deaf Boy in the Mirror*

"We are moving." Pa announced in the mid-summer of 1990.

He opened a folder and showed us pictures of the new house with a magazine article written about the Town of Quirkland in the West Island. Ma, in her funny English, called it "Waste Island." It had been voted as one of the best towns to live in Canada.

The summer had been a hectic one for residents of Chouguay and surrounding areas who had to take the Mercier Bridge to and from Montreal. It started with a land dispute between the Mohawks of Kanestake and The Town of Oka. In a stand of brotherhood, The Mohawks of Kahnawake joined in the protest. They built a barricade that blocked the side of the Mercier Bridge where it passed through their territory. It soon became a crisis that involved the Quebec Government, The Canadian Government, The Royal Canadian Mounted Police, Van Doos, gun battles, tear gas and the Mohawk Warriors. The media called it "The Oka Crisis" and every day there were news updates in the newspapers and on television. Pa explained that God was not making land any more so it was bound to happen that the people who had originally stolen land from the Native Indians wanted to steal more of their land.

It shouldn't have affected our lives, except Engine's mother was attacked at the supermarket in Chouguay, and the Montour family were forced to leave for safety. Now with both Engine and India gone, we had no friends. It sucked.

On moving day, the rabbit that we fed carrots to ran in front of Pa's rented truck as he backed out of the driveway. One minute he hopped around entertaining us, and the next, he lay still on the street. Ma scooped him up and placed him on the kitchen counter. She said she wanted to dispose of him in a fitting manner.

We were sent to our rooms to throw out and organize stuff she had taken out from our hiding places under the bed. Each one of us had a special box with our names in big bold letters. I found two things that I had forgotten about: the pill bottle with the penny-sized holes that had fallen out of India's coat and the purple and white belt that belonged to Engine that India had made into a headband.

The Mercier Bridge, which had been blocked for months because of the Oka Crisis, was clear when we crossed over it that Sunday afternoon in late September. There were two fishing trawlers below us in the St. Lawrence Seaway. The steeple of the Catholic church rose to the clear blue sky in Kahnawake. The train we had watched so often with Engine moved slowly on the tracks alongside the bridge. BB, Jalebi and I turned around to look at it until we reached the Whisky Trench and it disappeared from our view.

The cottage was a brand new model in the middle of a cul-de-sac in a new housing development. I ran from window to window in my own room and all I could see were lines of electric wires. There was a park nearby with a bicycle path, a soccer field and a baseball field. Except for the park, everything appeared brown and beige. If God had not painted this picture with blue skies scattered with white clouds, it would have been boring.

Ma served us chicken that evening. It tasted different. Jalebi whispered that she had seen Pa skin the rabbit and Ma cooking it. I almost puked at the thought of eating Bugs Bunny. I couldn't sleep that first night as I was used to having a conversation with BB and, now that we had separate rooms, I missed him. I tossed and turned as I thought about starting École Française, French School the next day.

Madame Reveille, my teacher was very sweet and nice. She spoke only French, which I had difficulty understanding, and she was very interested in my ear device. She made me stand

in front of the class and gently touched Om-7 as she explained
his function. Then, she accidentally moved him, which inter-
fered with the sounds that reached my ears. The movement
of the device placed it at such an angle that I heard two boys
giggling and their voices reached me.

"*Patate brulé* est deaf." I didn't have to put two and two
together to know what they said. "Burnt potato is deaf."

At break time, I found BB and we started to discuss. Before
the week was over, he had taken things into his hands. One
boy was tripped over and the other ran into a fence in a tag
game and ended up with a bloody nose. When we proudly told
Ma about it, she absolutely banned us from being involved in
acts of violence.

There were times in my life when I loved my brother more
than anyone in the world. Not only did he look out for me, but
he taught me words that were cool. The only problem is he
liked the word "like" so much that every sentence had at least
two "likes" from beginning to end.

"See," he said to me after the first week at École Française,
"It's like this. We have to deal with the kids as if they are assholes with diarrhea, just spurting out shit. When they are in
groups, they shit more but, when they are alone, it's like their
assholes tighten up and no shit comes out. That's when we
strike, just like that," he snapped his fingers. "This is our school
too, whether they like it or not."

For me, that meant 'fight,' and I was afraid to hurt Om-7.
Then I would not hear as well. Besides, Ma said she cannot
afford to go to Cuba and find the Russian scientist who fixed
me up the first time.

As part of the school curriculum, we had swimming lessons
every week at a pool at a recreation center. I had to take Om-7
off and give him to Madame Reveille for safekeeping. It didn't
matter that I could swim already, I still had to participate. An
area was blocked off for beginners. I got bored with the shallow water after the second lesson. When the instructor was not
looking, I dove in to the deep end and swam all the way to the
shallow end. I stayed underwater for as long as I could hold my

breath. When I surfaced, the instructor was by my side trying to grab me. I dodged and went back to the deep end, I could swim faster than him. I did this several times, loving the feel and freedom of gliding through the water. I got out when I was satisfied and saw that Madame Reveille had thrown an orange ring into the water. All the kids were at the side of the pool, their mouths and eyes wide open, staring at me.

Pa said we had perimeters, which meant we could only go one block from the house and could not go past the *Arrét* stop sign. After a week of being housebound, BB and I jumped on our bicycles after school to investigate the neighborhood and to find friends. There were many kids of different ages, but we were the new kids on the block and we couldn't make friends that easily. We tried for days. No luck. BB blamed it on me. He said it was because of my handicap. He didn't want to bike with me any more.

Ω Ω Ω

In the third week, BB got lucky and befriended a girl who lived by the *Arrét* stop sign. Her name was Lex Xi Ping. She was a mix of Japanese, Korean and Chinese, and she was delicate looking like the doll that danced on the wind-up music box that Jalebi kept her treasures in. After school, she went to karate classes and practiced on her front lawn. Her parents, Mr. and Mrs. Ping came over to welcome us to the neighborhood. They brought some cookies that had strips of paper with messages tucked inside. Lex Xi soon became a regular at our house and showed us her martial arts moves. Each time she finished a move, she screeched out her last name, 'Ping' which sounded like a golf ball in motion.

Lex Xi had lived in Quirkland for a year and she knew the comings and goings in the neighborhood. She told us that the red-headed family, who lived across from her, had a superficial disease called Ginger Vitus. It wasn't bad, as people who had this condition were fortunate as they are able to make Vitamin D in their skin and do not need sun. I had never seen a red-headed family before so perfect in their fit: The dad, the mom and the two boys all had red hair with brown dots on their faces which Lex Xi said was God's way of messing around with people's purity. In the same voice, she told me I was very lucky, as I had the most beautiful shade of brown skin that does not look like cheap hamburger meat when I stay in the sun for long.

The Ginger Vitus family was the only family on the street who spoke English as their first language. They had a Maple Leaf Flag on their lawn. The first day I saw them, I was watching Lex Xi practice karate moves and they were coming home from church. We waved to them as they came out of their car, but they all pretended to look the other way. The younger boy who was about my age, however, turned around, smiled and waved back to us. He was behind his mother. Later that day, I saw him alone playing in his driveway. I walked over and started a conversation with him. His name was Peter and he was quite friendly. I found out he went to English school and was a boy scout. Lex Xi joined me. He asked her to show him karate moves. The mother appeared just then, and called him into the house. This happened a few times, but Peter wanted to play with us and so he would sneak out. Before long, his mother would appear and order him back home. Once, I heard her say that Quirkland just wasn't what she thought it would be.

 Yaacov

Draft of *The Deaf Boy in the Mirror*

A few weeks later, I rode past the *Arrét* stop sign and noticed a family moving in to a big white house. I got excited when I saw another boy who was about my age. He was blond and blue-eyed. I was about to wave to him when I remembered what BB said to me. Not everyone wants to be friends with some-one who has a handicap. I rode back home, found a bag of chocolate chip cookies. I took it to my room, made a space in the closet and ate all the brown chips out of the cookies and thought about how delicious they were.

Some days later, and I remembered it being a Sunday as the street was quiet and most of the families had gone to church, I biked over to the park and there was the blond kid on his bicycle. I tried not to look at him. I didn't care if I was alone now that BB was playing with Lex Xi all the time and Jalebi was too young to come outside and play. I would still go out and ride and who's gonna stop me? Om-7 agreed.

The kid zipped past me, circled, did a wild turn, stopped close to me and shouted "boo" into my face. I stopped, got off the bike path and watched his antics. He was smaller than me, but he could do crazy twists and turns with his bicycle.

"Bet you can't do that." he challenged me after his fifth run.

I started to ride away, thinking about being handicapped.

"That's it. You can't do it. Chicken," he shouted to my back.

I turned around slowly, then pedaled like I was in the Tour de France. I built up speed and then I showed him. I rode hands free and did a few spinaroos, braked and did a mad-ass jump over the circles on the baseball field.

He followed me and clapped. Then the kid tried to do a spinaroo. I watched dumbstruck as he and his bike went flying. When he landed, he hit his head on the bicycle bar. He was bleeding something fierce and I got scared. I pedaled home quickly and got Ma. She took him to our house, tended to the bleeding, bandaged him up and gave us some treats.

His name was Yaacov Ben-Tzion.

He said he lived with his grandparents while his parents were away. Ma dropped him at his house, and I met his Bubby and Zayda. That evening, they came by our house with some homemade, hard, brown donuts with a circle in the center they called 'bagels.' They explained that if they are toasted, they are super tasty. Bubby, the grandmother, wore a chain with two triangles that interlocked, and looked like a star that she played with as she spoke. Zayda, the granddad, wore a kippah. They spoke English, a bit differently, but not as messed up as Ma.

The temperature dropped quickly in the month of October and, since there were no trees in our 'hood, play was in the park. Yaacov came by whenever he could to get me for bike rides. He had also made friends with the Ginger Vitus boys. As we biked together one day after school, Yaacov rang the doorbell and asked the mom, "Can Peter and Paul come out and play with me and Kaman?" I stayed in the street and waited. I had that feeling that . . . I cannot explain, but it was an odd feeling.

"It's cold out there, Yaacov. Why don't you come in and play with them."

I knew I was not invited in as she did a hand movement that indicated I should go. It reminded me of Uncle the Drunk chasing SakiWinki from the bedroom. I pretended it didn't matter, but I didn't go home and sulk. I went to the park and watched the teenager who delivered the newspaper making out with his girlfriend behind the chalet.

Yaacov, however, was not an indoor kid. He was born for the outdoors and soon he was back in the park, trying to outdo me in bicycle maneuvers. He couldn't get the art of spinaroo at first. I had to make him understand that it was all in 'the moves.' When he did get it, he actually outdid me in our 'let's see who can do this better without falling on our butts,' contests.

Some weeks later, Yaacov's mother Alizia returned. She came over to meet our family. Like Yaacov, she was blond and blue-eyed. Yaacov called his mom *Ima* and explained her absence this way: she had been away to a country called Israel where there is another little country called Kibbutz, so she could give birth to his baby sister the natural way. His dad Avrom still lived there.

Ashira, the baby, was four months old and very cute. I got to hold her. The minute she was in my arms, she did some smelly business that ran right through the diaper onto my clothes and she cooed and smiled all the while. But she was my favorite baby because, when she saw me, she had the biggest pink gummy smile and pulled my hair.

Yaacov went to a private school. We saw each other mostly on weekends, but we played in each other's houses some days after school. They spoke a different language, which Yaacov said was Hebrew. On Fridays, before sundown, they had a traditional *Shabbat* meal and lit candles.

Ma said it was courteous to ask people of different traditions what name they preferred to be addressed by. Bubby said her name was Batya and Zayda said his name was Solomon. Since I had started visiting their house, I had taken to calling them 'Bubby Batya' and 'Zayda Solomon.' I could tell they liked this because they smiled.

I was invited to join the family for a Shabbat meal one Friday evening. I was so excited, as it was the first time I had been invited to someone's house for a meal. Ma made me shower and put on my dress-up clothes. She bought flowers and chocolates for the family and a little teddy bear for Ashira, which I took earlier in the day as the family could not receive gifts at Shabbat.

I arrived an hour early. There was a note on the door in Yaacov's handwriting, "DO NOT RING BELL. BABY SLEEPING. DOOR IS OPEN." As I entered into the huge hallway, I saw my reflection in the floor-to-ceiling mirrors. I pirouetted and admired myself. I felt good. I was about to call out, "Hello, I'm here," when I heard the voices of Yaacov's mother and grandparents in the kitchen. The tone of their voices and the Hebrew language they spoke had caught Om-7's interest. Maybe I should go back home, I thought. Then I heard Yaacov's voice as he spoke to his grandfather in English.

"Zayda, what is Ima talking about? You were in a camp called Auschwitz in a country called Poland when you were my age. That's so exciting." He sounded incredulous.

"Exciting," Zayda Solomon scoffed. "Never say that outside the house, or to anyone who has been there. They will spit in your face."

"Why Zayda? Last year, when I went to the Jewish summer camp in St. Sauveur, I had the best time ever."

"This wasn't like that camp, Yaacov. I will tell you this story in Hebrew so you will remember it, always," Zayda Solomon said.

"You must remember this story Yaacov." Bubby Batya added,

I listened and heard words I didn't understand as Zayda Solomon spoke. At times, Bubby Batya joined in. Sometimes, they both stopped mid-sentence, their voices shook and I could hear them as they blew their noses. Then they would continue and Yaacov would ask a question in English and they would answer in Hebrew.

"That is so cruel," I heard Yaacov say. He sounded as if he were crying.

I really wished they had told this story in English, then I would always remember it as the first story I heard from living people and not one that I read in a story book.

I moved my head again. Om-7 is alert. I thanked God for delivering this gift of a fake ear so I can hear clearly, even though what I heard, so far, was told in a language I didn't understand. I made the sign of the cross and then remembered that I was in Yaacov's house and his cross had six points, so I made up a six point sign in respect for his family. God must have heard my thank-you-s, as I heard even more clearly the next lesson that Yaacov's Ima gave to him in a language I understood.

"Yaacov, you understand what I am saying?" Alizia said in her soft voice. "Your Bubby and Zayda were imprisoned by wicked people because of who they are. So, when Mrs. Johns says she didn't want her sons to play with a colored kid – that is wrong. What is more wrong is that Mrs. Johns told you that you shouldn't play with the colored boy either if you want to be friends with her boys. That is not right in my books. I cannot allow you to discriminate against a colored boy when your own Bubby and Zayda were imprisoned because they are Jewish. I will not bring you up that way."

There was total silence, broken by Ashira awakening from her nap.

I looked in the mirror, questioned the reflection that stared me in the eyes. I am colored? I must be, as the white-colored kids didn't want to play with me because of this.

I didn't walk home. I ran home with 'I am sick' excuse ready for Ma and Pa.

That night in bed, as Om-7 remembered the evening, I thought of Ma's favorite saying, *you learn something new every day.*

Today, I did learn something new. That I was a colored kid, and a white-colored-mother did not want her white-colored-kids-with-brown-dotted-faces-and-red-hair to play with me. It was confusing and senseless as when I look at people around me, I saw they all have colors of their own, whether they are white, or black or brown or yellow or green, like aliens.

Quirkland, the best town to live in Canada as voted by magazines, sure had some quirks.

33   The Beach Bum

DR. O CALMED DOWN AFTER I sent her two more chapters of the memoir. She wrote that she liked the way my voice came through, but asked, 'When was the good stuff coming?' I wrote back that I didn't understand. The next e-mail was no surprise.

"You and India. Your teenage years?"

"I am working on it," I replied, to which she answered, "Speed it up."

Once again, I asked for the return of Om-7 and didn't receive a reply. I had expected more e-mails. Either she was very busy or just slacking off. Something was wrong at her end.

I thought of India too. What can I say . . . I had fallen in love with the first girl who straddled me.

It was a good time for me to take a break and recharge the batteries.

Ω   Ω   Ω

I became a beach bum, of sorts. The land and sea became my supermarket. I nourished my body with lobsters, fish, eggs, fruits and nuts from the trees in the National Park. There were more chickens than people in West Bay. They wandered around and would have made an easy meal, but the leader of this flock, a colorful rooster clucked when he saw Chewy and he responded by lowering his head and blinking a few times. I took a wild guess they knew each other from his stray-dog days. To balance things off, I picked salads and greens from Bernie and Greg's hobby garden. Chewy, bless his soul, ate whatever scraps I gave him. No one starves on an island. All it takes is patience.

This virtue proved to be commonsensical as I observed Rooslahn's daily habits. He left his unit at 17:00 on his scooter and returned at 22:00. He was quite military about his departure and arrival – never early and never late. This gave me an opportunity to snorkel periodically in the reef to check out the booty. So far, so good. It was safe. It's all fun and games to keep my sanity. It was the only thing that amused me because, really, I am deaf, but I am not dumb. I know that anyone who tried to unload twelve million dollars of gold in the Cayman Islands would immediately attract attention.

Ω Ω Ω

Daily, I jogged barefoot along the beach in Barkers Park and watched the kite surfers sail away with the wind. At the far end, I admired the Jet Packers taking off. This new sport was fun to watch with the pedaling in the water before the takeoff skywards. It looked crazy appealing to me and my high testosterone levels.

There were some difficult days when I would over-think about the India-Engine affair and sleep eluded me. I am certainly disgruntled with being broke. Who isn't? On one of these 'off' days, I climbed a coconut tree in the park, picked some green ones and, as I threw them down, someone shouted up to me, "Hey, you up there! Can you knock down some for us?"

It was a man's voice, with a Texas drawl, which I have to really listen to, with or without my hearing device. I peeped through the branches and saw he was accompanied by an attractive street vendor who worked the port and was known for her great service to tourists on day visits from the cruise ships. Earlier, I had seen them naked as they indulged in sexual commerce inside the greenery of the park.

I looked at him blankly and pointed to my ear. He repeated and signed. When I descended, I opened the nuts and showed them how to sip the water and scoop out the jelly. The woman, cooled off from her hot spell, oohed and aahed and, as they were leaving, the man gave me a ten, but the lady smiled at me with a wink while she caressed his butt.

"Honey, this poor man, he's deaf, give him some more."

He searched his wallet and handed me a fifty.

Now, if every man who just got laid, or who engaged in the sport of paying for sex, gave me a fifty, I would never have to work another day for the rest of my life. This was my thought, as I walked back to the condo, whistling.

I was, suddenly, not completely broke.

Ω   Ω   Ω

"Money. Money. Money." I started to sing when I listened to Rafiq's voice on my phone. He had left a hurried message that he was back on island and a man by the name of Jacob with a high-end racer's bicycle had dropped in at Da Roti Shaq and was making enquiries about my whereabouts. This Jacob guy said he was a friend and would return in the evening.

There was no answer when I returned Rafiq's call. I couldn't place a face to the name Jacob. I figured if he showed up at Da Roti Shaq, it meant that he knew me.

That evening, I walked to the restaurant. The manager said Rafiq would be in at 9:00 p.m. I settled into a corner booth with a printout of the last chapter. It was a good time to edit.

Someone tapped me on my shoulder. I rose and returned Yaacov's man hug.

Yaacov had become a professional cyclist. He had perfected
the art of Spinaroo and made it his gimmick when he reached
the finish line. The crazy twists and turns amused sportscasters
and fans alike. Within the cycling world, he was a poster boy and
fondly dubbed, 'Mr. Spinaroo.'

"When did you change your name to Jacob?"

"I corrected your friend Rafiq several times. He couldn't say
Yaacov."

He sat down opposite me. He had changed since the last
time I saw him. He wore his hair shoulder length and had a small
tattoo of the Star of David on his wrist.

"What are you doing on the island?"

"Slow down. Let me eat first. All I have been eating is sushi,
seaweed and udon noodles. I want to have something different.
What do you recommend?"

"I'm having a roti sandwich with ackee and salt fish filling."
I went through the process of explaining to him that ackee is a
fruit and when it is cooked, it looks like scrambled eggs and salt
fish was cod fish imported from Canada.

"I thought you were diving with Kwame in Curaçao?" Kwame
was another friend from our younger days who also liked diving.

"I was, but then Kwame left for Montreal. I stayed behind for
a few more days. Big mistake. Things started to roller-coast and
here I am in the Cayman Islands."

"What happened? You missed me?" I joked.

"Funny. If you were of the opposite sex, I probably would.
I ran into Toussaint and BB in Curaçao. They said they were on
a job. Didn't go into the details. I suspect they were investigating
the gold heist. BB sent me here and said Rafiq would know where
to find you. I checked out Engine, and the kid who lived next
door told me he was off island. Amazing how everyone knows
everyone's business on this island." He stopped for a minute as
he noticed I was staring at his lips as he spoke. "Where's your
hearing device?"

"I lost it."

"How are you managing without it?"

"Ah, you know. I lipread well."

"I can sign if you want."

"You suck at sign language."

"Hey, I am not deaf. You're actually the only deaf person I know. I learnt the basics of sign language because you're my friend and I wanted to communicate with you. So now, I am here because I heard you're down in the dumps."

I am going to punch my big brother in his big mouth, I thought. I reassured him I wasn't. "Who told you this anyways?"

"Jalebi texted me." *I am gonna have to find a way to deal with my big mouth little sister, too.*

We had some reminiscing conversations about life in general as we ate our meal. He knew that India and I had 'gone in different directions,' as he nicely put it, and was sorry to hear about it.

"Come outside, I want to show you my new racer. Rafiq is an okay guy. He didn't know me but he let me lock it up in the shed because I was of friend of yours."

"Wow. Some toy." It was hard not to admire the new model lightweight bicycle. "How is it that you're in possession of such a beauty?"

"It's a coincidence. I rubbed shoulders with a Japanese billionaire who found out I was a pro cyclist and offered me a nice sum of money to cycle and dive with his wife in the Grand Cayman Island for a week. Turns out he owns a bicycle factory amongst other factories. In the week's work package was this beauty."

"Now, that's a lazy man's job. It takes less than a day to cycle around this island and that includes pit stops," I said, and realized that he, at least, had a job, whereas, I couldn't even land an interview.

"You think. You haven't met the billionaire's wife. She is one crazy gymnast. She has stamina is all I can say."

I was on my second beer, Yaacov still on his Guava juice when the cow bell on the front door chimed, announcing new customers, who I could see in the round reflecting mirror by the cash register. Yaacov ducked into his seat and placed a finger over his lips for silence. He wrote on a napkin and passed it to me.

My employer, Mr. Yoshio, and his wife, Shizu.
I pointed to my lips and signed.
The third person?
Henchman. Mamushi. He signed back.
Big story to tell you, Yaacov wrote on another napkin.

When they left, I turned to have a look and recognized them from previous sightings. Yaacov couldn't wait to tell me the big story.

Mr. Yoshio, arrived on his wife's yacht *The Orchid* in Curaçao on the day that Kwame left. Yaacov and some other divers were doing a night dive when Mr. Yoshio and his entourage showed up at the site. He was a friendly guy and invited Yaacov and the other divers for drinks on the yacht. Here, Yaacov met Mr. Yoshio's much younger mistress, Pavla, who was watched over intently by Mamushi.

Mr. Yoshio was a nighttime diving fanatic so their paths crossed at another site the following night. The next day, Yaacov was at the bank in Willemstad where he saw Mr. Yoshio, Pavla and Mamushi with the bank manager. Pavla looked very unhappy. Outside the bank, Yaacov was about to ride off on his bicycle when he was hailed down by Mr. Yoshio. He came over and was openly admiring his bicycle.

That evening, Yaacov went to the Mikvé Israel-Emanuel Synagogue and saw Pavla alone, sightseeing. She was Czech, in her mid-twenties, a very beautiful woman who loved the feel of the sand floor in the house of prayer. It got dark very quickly and he offered to accompany her back. Once again, Mr. Yoshio invited him to dine on board the yacht. That's when things started to get hot. His wife, Shizu arrived on a surprise visit. Mr. Yoshio is now faced with two problems – a much younger mistress, and his older wife. Both angry.

"So Mr. Yoshio pulled me aside and asked if I could pretend I was Pavla's boyfriend. He offered me a grand for each night I stayed," Yaacov sighed.

"Shit, you're lucky," I said as he took a break to sip some juice.

"I thought so too. Wait till you hear the rest."

Pavla, high on cocktails and pissed at the wife's appearance, opened up to Yaacov. She showed him something that almost made his eyeballs pop out. Aboard the yacht, below deck was a movie set – a porn studio. She started to cry then and told him how Mr. Yoshio had promised her five million dollars if she did a porn movie. When they went to the bank, he only gave her one million.

Pavla then led him to another room. Inside, were wall-to-wall cages filled with snakes. Each cage was well identified with labels and a chart showing how much venom each snake was capable of ejecting in a single bite.

"I had never seen so many deadly snakes in one place. I took pictures"

My stomach got woozy at the mention of snakes as Yaacov continued with the story.

Pavla was so upset, he brought her on the upper deck for some fresh air. She said she was cold and needed a blanket. Yaacov left to find one and as he took the stairs to go below deck, he saw Mamushi in the glass elevator going up. Mamushi was in the company of an older man who was carrying a clear plastic box. Inside was a snake. When Yaacov returned to the upper deck, Pavla was missing. He thought she went to bed, so he went to his room. Early the next morning, the sirens went off. Pavla was missing.

Later that day, her body washed up on the other side of the island. The doctor who performed the post mortem said Pavla had been bitten by a poisonous snake.

"The next day, Mr. Yoshio offered me this job to ride and dive with Shizu. I think I am being drawn into something. I was the last person who saw Pavla alive."

"You're worrying too much." I said. I felt like I was going to throw up.

He brought up his phone. "Here, I'll send you the pictures of the snakes."

He pressed send before I said, "No, don't!"

Ω   Ω   Ω

Rafiq arrived sharply at 9:00 p.m. One of his best qualities is he
is always punctual. His worst is he does not know how to deliver
bad news to soften the blow.

"Yoo," he said to me. "The Lady Doc's check bounced. That
means no bread for you and no bread for me. This is worth less
than toilet paper." He pulled out the check from his wallet and
gave it to me. Across was stamped: Not Sufficient Funds.

I looked at Rafiq's angry face and shrugged my shoulders.
"No worries."

"Yoo, you're the only bro I know who never complains. You
just keep it all inside. Me, I would find that Doctor Lady and give
her a piece of my mind. She took advantage of you."

I know he wasn't angry because of the money. He was angry
that someone had taken advantage of me, his friend, because of
my handicap. He had thrown a few punches to defend me in my
younger days. I tried to diffuse his anger now. "What's with no
bread, no bread. You and me, we know how to make pizza and
roti. And that's two kinds of bread."

"And," he continued in the same tone, pointing his finger in
my face, "Better to tear up dem pages you bin busy writing."

I was in full agreement with Rafiq until, out of habit, I sat
down in front of the computer to check out my In box. There
still had been no response from Dr. O. I let her know her
check bounced. Ma and Pa sent a short video of themselves in
St. Petersburg, Russia. A cute little puppy was following them
around. There was a little note attached, '*Doesn't this remind you
of Lady?*'

34 The Immigrant School

Draft of *The Deaf Boy in the Mirror*

"Why do we have to change schools again?" I asked for the tenth time. I was tired of having to make new friends and even more so of explaining the purpose of Om-7.

When I think back, Pa's explanation was not fit for someone who was just a grade-school kid.

I had just celebrated my eighth birthday. All I wanted to do was play, like all the other boys who lived in the bedroom community of Quirkland. I didn't have a problem with being deaf. I had figured how to get by with my handicap and with the excellent cooperation of Om-7. I read many books in English and French. I loved reading. It was my hobby and, after lights out, I sneaked a flashlight from the garage and read with the dim light. At the end of the school year in French School, I had an excellent report card with mostly A's, more than BB and Jalebi. Ma said I was very smart for my age.

I forgot that Pa could go on and on. I didn't think that my question would incite a long-winded response. There were too many big words and too much waste of my time. Since I was the chief instigator, I had no choice but to listen, and it was painful.

"To answer your question, Kaman, we live in Quebec, which is the French side of Canada. It is demographically divided into two groups, Anglophones who are English background and Francophones who are French background. There are other groups who are considered minorities."

"Are we minorities?" Jalebi interrupted.

"No, we are a special group, baby. We are multicultural. We are a distinct society. Quiet now, wait till I am finished," Pa said as he reached over and smoothed back her hair, before turning to Biig Baba. "Go bring the map from the fridge, BB."

I watched BB untape the map. The edges were curled. Different countries had been highlighted over time, which showed we had met someone with origins from that part of the world.

Oh, no, I thought wearily, here comes another geography or history lesson.

My mind wandered to the stray dog with newborn pups Yaacov and I had discovered yesterday on the only farm that remained in Quirkland. We had made plans to ride out this morning and check up on the puppies and bring some food for the mother.

"As I said," Pa continued, "there are other minorities. Italians, Jews, Africans, Chinese, Hispanics, South Asian Indians, and Native Indians who are the original peoples of Canada."

Some things did not make sense to me and so I questioned him. "Why are the original peoples of Canada considered minorities when they were here before the Anglophones and Francophones?"

Pa seemed surprised by this question. He turned to Ma. "Honey, this one's for you."

"I don't know," she answered, her brows furrowed. "The French think it is about some war they had won centuries ago and the English think they had taken away all the Indians' lands and so . . ." she paused, "Sheesh, I have no answer to this."

"Anyways," Pa continued, "we are all classified by the first language we speak. Anglophones have linked themselves to Queen and country, while the Francophones have linked themselves to the court of France. The atmosphere changed when the French took over the government, and many English moved out west. Guess what happened?" He paused and cracked a walnut with his bare teeth.

"What happened?" BB asked. I kicked him under the table.

Couldn't he just shut up and let Pa speak. That way, this boring conversation could be over and done with.

"There were less people to collect taxes from and that's a problem," Pa laughed as if he had told a funny story.

I couldn't get the puppies out my mind. They were so cute and cuddly.

"So, more immigrants were allowed in. Anyone with a quarter-million dollars could buy their way in. Then, there are the refugees seeking political asylum from madmen who ruled their third-world countries. There is also the brain drain. A points system allowed those with a good trade background, or a doctorate in some specific research an easy entry. The door is wide open to enter Quebec, La Belle Province."

Pa stopped and pointed to the map to show where the immigrants were coming from.

I thought about the puppies. Were their eyes fully opened this morning?

"Are you all listening?"

We all nodded.

"Through this door entered an influx of different nationalities which changed the face of Montreal. A famous law with the title Bill 101 was passed in Quebec to ensure that the *nouveaux arrivés,* or the newcomers, must learn to speak French and, if they have children, their children must be schooled within the French system." Another pause as Pa sipped some water.

"You forgot to mention the Allophones. They don't speak French or English," said Ma as she thumbed through the little red dictionary she carried in her handbag. "Would you believe it? That word doesn't exist in this dictionary."

"Your mother is right. This is why you all have to go to The Immigrant School with the *nouveaux arrivés,* or the new arrivals, despite the fact you were all born in Montreal."

I am back with the puppies. As soon as their eyes are open, and they can walk, I will sneak one home.

Yup, I decided. I am going to bring one of those puppies home. And I did.

We named her *Lady* after the beautiful dog in the movie,

"Lady and the Tramp." She had a brown body with tan colored paws and ears. Ma started to sneeze the minute we let
the puppy in the house. I think she faked it. Lady slept on a
pillow in my room at first, but then she took a liking to Pa and
sometimes would wander into my parents' bedroom. I think
Pa may have lifted her into the bed. I am not sure about this,
but I woke up to Ma sneezing and screaming. "Get that tramp
out. The only bitch who sleeps in this bed is me!"

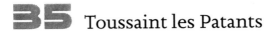 Toussaint les Patants

Draft of *The Deaf Boy in the Mirror*

The French Primary school to accommodate the new immigrants' children under the age of twelve was a special school
quickly put together in West Island. It used to be an English
high school that had closed its doors. My class was a mixed-
age-group with more boys than girls and, yippee-ki-yay, I was
not the only kid who had an unusual name. But I was the only
kid who was deaf.

There were two boys, however, who were strikingly
different.

One was named Toussaint les Patants and the other
Dara Singh.

Toussaint was totally Canadian, but one half of his body
was Francophone and the other half Anglophone. I could
not tell which of the two halves were attributed to his French
father or English mother. He only attended the Immigrant
School because he lived a block away. He told the class that his
parents had moved that summer from Rougemont where his
grandparents had an apple orchard that made the finest apple
juice. If I should use the phone-system categorization in effect,
he would be an "Otherphone."

He was the only Caucasian kid in the class. In the first week
of school, Om-7 picked up murmurings of how 'white' he was.

The other boys stayed away from him. In the school yard, he watched from the sidelines when we played soccer and tag; he was never invited to join in. He spoke three languages fluently – English, French and Québécois, which he said used to be called *Joual* – while most of us struggled with two. I was fortunate. I struggled with two-and-a-half, because Pa spoke to us in Italian, we watched English TV, and Ma spoke to us in half Creole and half English, which is also called Patwah in the Caribbean. If you have never heard this language, the next time you meet a Jamaican man, ask him this question: "Hey bumba rass, you got some ganja?" Don't blame me if he gives you a cuss down.

Toussaint had the smarts. After two weeks of not making friends, he decided to divide and conquer. I noticed when he watched the soccer game on a Monday lunch break, he cheered me on enthusiastically. The same day, he followed me to *la toilette*, peed at the urinal beside me, and then washed his hands in the sink next to me.

"Kaman," he said, "You're good in soccer. You'll be even better in hockey." He must have seen how my eyes lit up.

"You think so?"

"I am thinking of starting a hockey team. I need players." He smiled at me in the mirror.

"I don't have hockey things."

"*Pas de problem*," he said in French and then continued in English. "No problem. We can start off with floor hockey in the corridor. I have miniature sticks of all the teams. I will bring them tomorrow. We can play after lunch. You in?"

"For sure." It was my dream to play hockey since I first saw the game on TV.

He introduced me to floor hockey with miniature sticks made out of paper towel rolls and pucks made out of wads of toilet paper held together with rubber bands. He was the goalie and I was a superstar like Wayne Gretzky because he let most of my shots in. It was so much fun that other boys dropped soccer and tag to cheer us on. Within the week, most of the boys in the class had signed up, except Dara Singh.

Toussaint brought in a fold-up goalie's net and asked Mr. Toulousse, our gym teacher, if we could set up a mock hockey ring in the gym. He was reluctant at first until we all got down on our knees and begged him. As a trade-off, he wanted each one of us, on a different day, to bring him an apple. There were no rules, except we had to play with our socks on. All we had to do was shoot the puck at Toussaint. It was hard to beat him as he stopped all of them. I quickly lost my superstar title as Toussaint upped his game.

Dara Singh was the first to bring an apple for Mr. Toulousse even though he didn't play hockey. He brought a caramelized curried apple topped with chillies in a container, with some chapatis on the side. The next week, Toussaint brought a whole bushel of Rougemont apples.

Biig Baba sneaked into my room one night and asked if he could play with us. I couldn't believe it. BB asking me a favor! It was nice to have one up on him. Toussaint organized scrimmages of our class against all the boys in his class. Biig Baba was the goalie. All the offensive players loved to shoot on him because he couldn't stop a puck if his life depended on it.

Mr. Toulousse was very encouraging of this sport. He told us once that he coached hockey at a private boys' school. He sent out letters to parents asking for a contribution to buy hockey equipment and received thirty three dollars, which would buy approximately three and one-third hockey sticks. He was disappointed. He then wrote to all the NHL teams and asked if they could donate their used equipment. Soon, so many packages arrived; not only sticks, but brand new jerseys, goalie nets, helmets, water bottles, knee and elbow pads and pucks. There were enough jerseys and equipment to outfit every boy and girl in the school and a whole room of leftovers.

Not that it went to waste. Dara Singh's father made a bid for all the leftovers and started his own sporting goods outlet.

Mr. Singh Senior called his store Punjabi NHL.

We became regulars at the park in the 'hood. Most of the kids were Anglophones who went to English schools. The interesting thing was that they all wore 'Canadiens' jerseys. They were nice kids as they didn't make too much fuss when we asked to join them, but then Pa was there, so I think they didn't have much choice. Also, they needed a second goalie and Biig Baba was the only one with goalie equipment. They loved him too after the first game because each player could score off him.

Toussaint found out that we were scrimmaging in the park and he showed up in his Rangers jersey and skates. He asked if he could play with us.

"He can't play here," a big kid, who wore a captain's jersey said. He really was a nice kid who had showed me how to deke out the defenseman and get a shot on goal.

"Why?" Both Biig Baba and I wanted to know.

"Well, he's French, for one, and second, we have a full team, and third, he's wearing the wrong jersey."

"We could use a spare." Biig Baba tried.

"No spares. The team is made."

I watched Toussaint walk away, so disappointed.

"He plays goalie too." I said. "And he's my friend from school. And by tomorrow, he's going to have a Canadiens jersey."

"He's French and his kind wants to separate Canada."

"How do you know he's French?"

"Can't you hear his Quebec accent dude?"

I never noticed it, I have to say. But what I could not understand is why something as stupid as an accent became a problem. Such a fuss, really. When we told Pa about this incident, he was beyond angry.

"Plus ça change, plus c'est la même chose. The more things change, the more they stay the same. When I was growing up in St. Leonard, the same thing happened. Then, it was the French kids not wanting to play with the Italian kids. Now it's the English kids not wanting to play with the French kids. Enough! Tomorrow, Toussaint will scrimmage with those kids. I will fix that."

He did.

That night, Om-7 picked up Ma and Pa's discussion. They unanimously voted that the Province of Quebec needed another referendum to decide this issue about accents.

 Dara Singh

Draft of *The Deaf Boy in the Mirror*

Dara Singh was the other boy who stood out in the class. He was the most distinguished in his dress costume as he wore a turban, a *kirpan* that looked like a small sword on his belt, and all of this over his school uniform. His father, Mr. Singh Sr. was Sikh and his mother was from England. His parents were software engineers who worked with a major global video games developer. Dara was born in California, USA, where he spent his first three years. Before he came to Montreal, he had lived in England. He was two years older than I, much taller and more handsome, according to Jalebi. He always brought curry and chapatis in his lunchbox and called his dessert 'pudding.'

On the Monday after Canadian Thanksgiving, the class had a school trip to Ottawa, the capital of Canada, where the prime minister governed the country. As we entered the House of Commons, Dara Singh thought we had to sit down. He rushed over to the speaker's chair and struck a pose. A journalist invited a few of us to stand beside him as he snapped away with his camera. The next day, a photo was on the front page of the newspapers. The story was all about Dara Singh's turban and kirpan and whether this should be allowed in a school system. It started a debate that lasted for years.

Ω   Ω   Ω

BB explained to me that the word *Franglais* took one half of the French word, *Français* and the last syllable from another French word *Anglais*. *Franglais* was a mixture of French and English words in one sentence. It was a mixed-up business like my family. It became the most spoken language in the school-yard thanks to Toussaint and hockey.

Toussaint finally convinced Dara Singh to join the hockey team. This is how he did it.

"Dara, *mon ami,* my friend. Hockey, is fun. Hockey *est* big fun."

"*Oui.* Yes, I know." Dara replied.

"*Viens ici.* Come here. My friend. Let's play some puck."

"Toussaint, you mean *shoot-ez le puck?*"

A week later, while shooting pucks just for fun, Dara Singh fell down on his kirpan and gashed his hand, which would not stop bleeding. I was the only witness to this incident.

I rushed over to get Mr. Toulousse who said in Franglais, "*Vite, go bring le first aid kit. It's in my sac by my desk.*"

The sight of blood had thrown me off. I didn't quite understand what he said. He repeated in English, "Quickly, go bring the first aid kit. It's in my bag by my desk."

Hastily, I searched through Mr. Toulousse's bag which had several compartments while I worried about Dara Singh bleeding to death. A folder with the word "Hockey" written in big letters fell to the floor and the contents scattered at my feet. As I retrieved it, a photograph of boys – all Caucasians – caught my attention. At the bottom were two captions.

"HELP THESE BOYS LIVE THEIR DREAM OF PLAYING HOCKEY. DONATE YOUR USED EQUIPMENT. I also read, "TEN-TWELVE YEAR-OLDS FROM THE SCHOOL FOR AUTISM."

On the next page was a list of all NHL teams and against each one, Mr. Toulousse made notes of the amounts he received. There was a total at the bottom, $17,335.00.

Dara Singh cornered me at the urinal the next day. I forgot to mention the washroom, which all the kids now referred to as "la toilette," was the meeting place for the boys in my class.

Here, we heard good jokes, bad news and the latest of who was sent to the Dragon's Den where Mrs. Scott, the headmistress, reigned supreme.

"Thank you Kaman," he said.

"What for?"

"For not squealing to Mr. Toulousse that my turban fell over my eyes and the *kirpan* gashed me. I will never forget," he said, a worried look on his face.

"It was not my place to tell," I mumbled.

"Then, please, can you remember this. If the school knows, then I can't wear the turban and the *kirpan*, and my dad will be cross." He looked worried.

"Why do you wear the turban? Why can't you take it off?"

"It's my religion. It's same as people wearing a cross. I see no harm. As for why I can't take it off, it's a code of conduct, a religious belief. I have no problem wearing it."

"Don't worry, I won't tell," I assured him.

"And Kaman, from this day on, I will watch your back. And if ever you are in trouble, remember, I'll be there for you."

Ω   Ω   Ω

In the last week of school, before the summer holidays, Mr. Toulousse passed out brochures of sports being offered in parks around the West Island. He coached soccer and, if anyone was interested, he would help them fill out the necessary forms.

Dara Singh was the only one who lived close to the soccer field where Mr. Toulousse coached. Mr. Singh Sr. was very happy and enrolled his son. On the first day that Dara Singh showed up for a scheduled game, the referee approached Mr. Toulousse and told him that the player with the turban could not play. There was evidently a ban on turbans for safety reasons put in place by the Quebec Soccer Association.

Mr. Toulousse was so ticked off by the incident, as Dara Singh was a good player. He thought he should verify this with the Canadian Soccer Association. Before you knew it, Dara Singh's picture was in the newspapers again. What a controversial episode this became. The Sikh community was told that if a kid wanted to play soccer with a turban, he or she can play in his or her backyard. The media had a news frenzy while the matter was being straightened out far away in Zurich, Switzerland by The Fédération Internationale de Football Association.

When it was over, BB and I went to watch Dara Singh play in his first soccer game. He complained about the paparazzi. "Couldn't go to the loo and make a poo without them up me ass. Such poppycocking. All I want to do is play footy."

37 CSI

IT WAS DAY TWENTY-TWO of my non-writing career. I still had not heard from Dr. O. I thought of giving up writing altogether, but there's something Pa often preached which stuck between my head and keeps bouncing back to me, "If you start something and can't finish it, then you don't have balls."

Last time I checked, I had some sturdy boys down there.

In my humble opinion, my writing had improved as words flowed easily. I was enjoying re-telling the stories. I was pleased with the overall results when I re-read the three chapters I had written in the last two days. I was now ahead of my schedule. It felt good, and, I'm keeping an eye on the gold.

Dara Singh had moved back to California, USA, in his early twenties and later settled in Miami, Florida. He had landed his dream job as a Special Forces pilot. We communicated often. India and I spent a month with him after graduation while we job hunted. On Sunday mornings, when he was off duty, he attended a new age congregation called United and Unified, which was a denomination of the Church for Society's Improvement, with its headquarters in Delaware, USA. It often made headlines for its involvement in the global non-profit organization, Food Bank International, which donates food to the hungry in impoverished countries. Dara Singh didn't mind that, as a member, he had to contribute twenty five percent of his annual income for the good of the human race.

He loved both: his job as a Special Forces Pilot and being a member of United and Unified for the sole reason that neither asked him to remove his turban. Dara Singh looked like a Bollywood movie star in his turban. He was so handsome that he often had marriage proposals from around the world just from his social media profile.

United and Unified used two logos in the beginning, U&U and U2, until an Irish rock band told them to bugger off, leave the latter alone and get original. The Church for Society's Improvement had a single logo CSI, and was headed by a well-spoken gentleman by the name of Mr. Jeremy Richard, who hosted a television infomercial promoting the vision of the organization.

In his last e-mail, Dara Singh wanted to know when and where the annual commemorative bonfire for Wes would be held. I forwarded it to Jalebi who was still in Africa. Jalebi called me an asshole in her e-mail for thinking that Engine and India had hooked up. My own sister taking other people's sides!

There had been no communication from my exes, that is, ex-girlfriend India and ex-best buddy Engine. Yaacov dropped a line that he arrived safely in Montreal.

Money was tight, but Mother Earth was kind. I roamed Barkers National Park and found an edible food supply. I wished I had the stomach for blood as there were many little animals and birds that would have satisfied my yearning for meat. Call me a wuss, but I just didn't have it in me to kill a helpless creature. Seafood had little blood, and so I stuck with it. I forgot to water Bernie and Greg's garden and, as a result, it dried up which meant one less food source for me.

Ω   Ω   Ω

There was a neatly folded flyer tucked into the handle of the front door. As I walked around the complex, I saw there was one in every door. It announced the grand opening of the recently built Cayman Branch of CSI with the guest appearance of its founder, Minister Jeremy Richard. Half of the page had his bio. He had excellent credentials: pioneer in the e-commerce business, CEO of ACS, the American Canine Society, which was a subsidiary of the CCS, the Cayman Canine Society, touted as the largest animal welfare charity in the world. He sat on the board of a long list of blue chip companies and non-profit organizations. Recently, he had been appointed to another non-profit organization, Stop Hatred in Time, which I'm glad the marketing people didn't try to logolize, as it would read SHIT.

I am not big into churches since I already had a connection with God. He knows I am here and I know He is everywhere. What caught my attention was the bottom line on the flyer. *A buffet lunch will be served after the services.* Oh, yeah.

Decked out in my dress-up clothes, I allowed myself ample time to walk to the church. Halfway there, it came to me I had heard the name Jeremy Richard before; but that Jeremy Richard was associated with a man who wore a black cowboy hat and boots. Was he living a double life?

I arrived in good time to find a seat in the back row and close to the buffet table set up in the hallway. An added advantage was it gave me a view of who came in and who left. The church was over-packed with tourists and Caymanians. When the sermon began, Mr. Yoshio and his wife Shizu went directly to the front row where seats had been kept for them. Soon after, Kara, my new friend from the Tortuga Cake Shop, arrived in the company of an older woman. They sat a few pews away.

Rafiq entered and took a seat in the center row. He was a church-going person, but the congregation he attended was in North Sound. Sometimes, he was asked to sing in the choirs of other churches, which he liked, as long as he didn't have to contribute to the bread basket that was passed around.

Mr. Richard, dressed in the regalia of a minister, took the

podium. He was a very charismatic speaker, a man of wise words who commanded the congregation to listen and touched them on an emotional level. I was impressed with his vision as he preached about the changing world, the effects of war, world hunger, and his passion – dogs without homes. As he spoke, a slideshow on a big screen showed work accomplished by the various organizations. He ended with how each individual in the congregation could help with their donation. It was not a snooze-fest as I had expected and, when he terminated his speech, the applause was thunderous.

This was followed by the congregation standing up and singing songs. I became aware of the off-tuned voice behind me and turned to have a look. Toussaint les Patants winked and slightly moved his head to indicate a pew across from me where Dr. O stood with her hands clasped. Beside her were the two plain clothes cops who had been involved in my imprisonment.

Now, that's a surprise. I had missed their entrance.

I knew sooner or later she would make an appearance. I don't think she saw me, as her concentration was focused totally on Mr. Richard, who invited one and all to the buffet.

I was first in line. My mouth salivated at the sight of jerk chicken, pork chops, BBQ ribs and trays of cassava and bread pudding. I had brought along a plastic container in my backpack to sneak some food for Chewy. As I filled it, a heavy hand landed on my shoulder.

Guilt-ridden, I turned around and had a good look at the bear paw and at the big Kahuna himself, Mr. Jeremy Richard.

"Son. I hope this is for your sick grandmother." He smiled into my face.

"Yes, it is. She is doing poorly." I blinked several times in an effort to come up with something to cover my lie, as both my Nonna and Nani had passed on moons ago. "And for my dog. I adopted him from the CCS." I added.

I closed my eyes, sucked in a breath and told myself I had to stop telling fibs.

"Son," Mr. Richard said, "You're holding back tears, aren't you?" The bear paw patted my shoulder. "You are doing a wonderful thing. You exemplify the beliefs of CSI. You practice what I preach. Pure goodness." He then reached under the buffet table and passed me some Styrofoam containers.

"Thank you, you are very kind." I signed and mouthed.

"Oh, you're deaf. Son, pack a few extra containers for the rest of the week. And please call me Dick. Everyone does," he said.

I noticed that Toussaint stood by the doorway with a smirk on his face.

My hunger for meat and sweet satisfied, I mingled outside where there was a big tent and benches set out. I wanted to say hello and goodbye to Rafiq and Toussaint, but couldn't find them. I saw Shizu leave in a limo with her snake-tattooed bodyguard, Mamushi. As I left the church, I peeked into the choir room. Dr. O, Mr. Yoshio and Mr. Richard were in a deep conversation. It appeared that Dr. O, her face red, was not getting the best of whatever it was they were discussing.

I whistled as I walked home with the heavy pack, thinking of Mr. Richard's kind-heartedness. This could not be the same man I saw at the Ritz wearing a black cowboy hat, but then, he was in the company of Mr. Yoshio and Dr. O. Was this a three-way tryst? I counted the irregularities on my fingers:

1. Some shady characters under one roof.

2. Rafiq would never go to a congregation where he has to give 25 percent of his earnings.

3. Toussaint is an atheist. No involvement in any religion. Never sets foot in a church.

4. One person in common known to all parties – Dr. O. And, from Engine's account, she's barely making ends meet.

I concluded these irregularities were not worries for a deaf guy. For the hundredth time, I wish Om-7 was stuck to my ears to help me balance things out in my head.

Ω   Ω   Ω

Expecting a visit from Dr. O, I grabbed the vacuum from the broom closet and passed it through the condo. I had just finished when the doorbell rang. I replaced the vacuum and a bunch of keys fell to the floor. I made a mental note not to forget this detail.

Toussaint stood at the front door. "Where's all that food you brought home? I am hungry."

"Do you know I spent the last half hour cleaning and vacuuming like crazy thinking Dr. O will pay me a surprise visit? Where is she?"

"She jumped into a limousine with Mr. Richard and Mr. Yoshio."

"Why didn't you eat at the church?"

"I don't like churches. Besides, I saw the act you just put up. I wanted to puke. Your grandmother?"

He ate half of my meal plan for the week. Licking his fingers, he looked at me with squinting eyes. "You're holding back on me."

"What do you mean?"

"You know what I'm speaking about." He had a cocky look.

"You found out about me writing a memoir?"

"What does you writing a memoir have to do with a scam artist who uses the Church for Society's Improvement as a front for gambling and porn sites? All registered in Curaçao. *Merde*, shit, I told you too much."

"Tell me more."

"I can't. I thought you would know, as there seems to be some kind of connection with Dr. O'Ligue."

"Wish I could help you."

"You know what's happening tonight? The Canadiens are playing their first game. You and I have to go and make some noise for our home team."

Hockey! The word itself lifted me up to another level. "I'll be there for you." I started to sing and dance until I remembered my financial situation.

"Sorry man, I am low on cash. Can't afford an outing."

"My treat. Hey, if you're broke, I can give you a loaner."

I accepted the outing and passed up on the loaner. There is always the worry of my never being able to pay back.

Ω   Ω   Ω

"Hey, look over there," Toussaint whispered to me as we sat at a Tiki Bar overlooking the water later that night. "A cute redhead is waving to you. She was at church today with her mother."

"That's Kara." I waved back. "She's sweet. She works at the Tortuga Cake Shop. She has a heart of gold. Wanna meet her?"

"Too late. The mother just joined her. Isn't that the governor?"

"I don't know. Kara is the daughter of the governor?"

"*Collice.*" Toussaint swore in Québécois French. "You gotta start reading the news. You're way behind on what's happening in the world."

On our way home, Toussaint asked if I had heard from Engine.

'No," I replied with emphasis.

"Last time I heard from him, he was in England helping India with some problems. Do you know what he's helping her with?"

"How would I know, Toussaint? She and I are over. I really don't care what she, he, or both of them are doing."

"Attitude."

"What do you mean by that?"

He laughed. "You should see your jealous face right now."

Ω   Ω   Ω

Late that night, I'm still pondering about the two sides of Mr. Jeremy Richard. I wrote an e-mail to Dara Singh enquiring about Mr. Richard and the CSI. He responded with links to the CSI and other related associations. Each one I opened had praise for the man who was in charge of the CSI and his work.

Mr. Jeremy Richard was as clean as a whistle.

I sent a thank you out to Dara Singh, or so I thought. Within minutes, I got a response from Zingaro that read '*Check your blog.*' I had accidentally sent him the e-mail meant for Dara Singh with all the threads. "Damn," I swore.

I ignored Zingaro's response and moved on to the next chapter of the memoir.

▄▄ 38 The Dragon's Den

Draft of *The Deaf Boy in the Mirror*

On the first day of the third year at The Immigrant School, the bus had a flat tire, which delayed meeting up with my old friends and checking out the new students in the school-yard. I was late for class, which made me unhappy. As soon as I opened the classroom's door, I noticed the familiar bird's nest and the yellow gold eyes of the girl who sat in the front row.

India Weinberger had two fingers in her mouth which she sucked vigorously.

She withdrew them when she saw me, smiled and waved. I smiled back, just a small one. She was seated beside two boys, who, like her, were newbies. I no longer was pissed off at the driver for taking so long to fix the tire when I also discovered that Mademoiselle Cointreau, the hot babe from Paris, was to be my teacher. This would make BB so-o-o envious.

Each newbie had to stand up in front of the class with a name card for all to see and tell the basics of name, country of birth and first language spoken. This was written on the blackboard in French with blank lines to guide. India went first.

"Mon nom est India Weinberger. Je viens de Montreal, Quebec, Canada. Je parle Anglais."

"Mon nom est Khalil Kaleb Kwame. Je viens de Tennessee, United States of America. Je parle Arabic, Spanish et American." The next newbie, a boy with a mischievous smile, took a chalk and underlined his last name. "I only answer to the name Kwame." he started to sing. "I was born in The USA."

Madame Cointreau had to lead the second boy who was very shy to the front of the class. He reluctantly held up his name card for all to see.

"M-m-on nom est E-e-rnesto Gu-gu-vera I-i-ibáñez." It took a long time for the words to come out.

She helped him by mouthing the words of the second line. "Je viens de Brazil."

"J-je, j-je, je." He could not get the words out. I remembered being in Ernesto's place in kindergarten and couldn't say my words. My head felt funny with an indescribable sensation.

"Do something." Om-7 zinged.

I shoved all my books so they clattered noisily to the floor. I then moved my chair so it scraped loudly on the wood. Ernesto ran out of the class and hid in the toilette. Mademoiselle Cointreau had to coerce him back to the classroom.

That night, Ma's usual first-day-of-school interrogation started out with, "What's your teacher's name, Kaman?"

"Miss Cointreau." I said slowly, because Ma really had trouble saying French words, much more than she had with English. I knew this because last week, when we waited for the city bus, one passed by with a sign that read *hors service,* which meant "out of service," in English.

She asked BB to read it and then made him repeat. Her face scrunched up with a disgusted look. "Whore service? They have a bus for them?"

I watched now as the name registered and she blinked a few times. "Miz Cun-trow? What kind of name is that?"

"She's from Paris, France, Ma."

"Those Parisians sure have strange names."

I told her about India, Kwame and Ernesto, the boy who had difficulty getting his words out.

Ω   Ω   Ω

India had become a total stranger since I last saw her. She outright rebuffed Jalebi's attempt to be friends again. She didn't play with other kids. During the lunch breaks, she sat on the fence, which was not allowed, sucked her finger and watched us play pick-up hockey. At half-time, I walked over and sat in the grass close by.

"You don't like this school?" I asked, in what I thought was a friendly voice.

"I hate this school. Too many immigrants. My new parents said that as soon as they get the right documents, I will go to an English school." I am happy she had found her voice.

"Who are your new parents?"

"They're hippies and Jewish. I am going to be Jewish, too. When I grow up, I am going to have a big sweet sixteen party."

"What do your parents do?"

"They are lawyers. My new dad is from Israel and my new mom is from New York. They met in India, in a place called Goa where many hippies go to grow up. They said they liked Goa because they can smoke pot whenever they like."

"They told you that?" I don't know what pot is, but I know if you are a parent and you smoke, you try to avoid telling your kids about it.

"Yes. And next summer, we are going to Israel, to a kibbutz. Bet you don't know what that is?"

I remembered Yaacov's family had left last summer to live in a place called Kibbutz. "Of course, I know what a kibbutz is. It's a place where Jewish people go."

"I want to play hockey," she said, changing the subject.

"It's a boy's game." I said very nicely.

"Says who?" She looked at me, as if I were crazy.

"Well, look, there are only boys on the team."

"I guess I will be the only girl, then. It's time things change," she said indignantly. "Besides, look at you, you're deaf and you play with a hearing device. I have all my senses so what's to stop me, deaf boy?"

I felt my heartbeat accelerate, my ears thumped, my head

pounded, my nostrils widened and my eyes squinted to slits. Om-7 buzzed his annoyance. I stood up and pushed her off the fence. She fell on her backside. Quickly, she got up and gave me a punch in my stomach. I fell back in the grass, on my ass. She stood above me, her body rigid awaiting my next move. I tripped her. This time she fell beside me, flat on her butt.

In a jiffy, she was on top of me, her legs pinned mine down into the grass. The bird's nest had come apart so that her hair fell over my face as she grappled with my arms above my head. I shook my head from side to side to get it out of my eyes, and dislodged Om-7 in the process. I looked up at her and saw the tiger eyes were a blazing, golden fire.

I had seen that look before on the night her foster parents had been found dead and she arrived at our front door with her clothes bloody and her body bleeding. I slackened my hold. I saw kids running in our direction and shouting, their voices barely reaching me from a distance.

"Oh, my God, I think I broke your hearing piece." The fire had gone from her eyes. She moved Om-7 who was dangling from the side of my head and replaced him on my right ear. Her eyes had changed to a warm yellow glow. Concerned, she whispered into my left ear, "Can you hear me?"

I nodded.

"Fight," I heard Kwame's voice clearly now, followed by six others, each in a different language.

Biig Baba pulled me up, just before Mademoiselle Cointreau arrived and marched us to Headmistress Scott's office, also known as the Dragon's Den. I had been told you were in deep shit once you entered and you left with detention assignments such as scrubbing all desk tops in the classroom and picking out chewing gum and boogers from the under-side. The worst fear was to be suspended or expelled. The best was you earned respect if you managed to walk out smiling. So far, no one had earned this respect.

Inside the Dragon's Den, a sofa and two chairs faced each other across a coffee table, with several notepads arranged on it. From the corner of her eye, India watched me. I ignored her, worried about the Dragon who lived in this den, the outcome of this unplanned rendezvous and, mostly, the extra punishment Ma and Pa would dole out.

I heard the click-click of high heels and turned to see Mrs. Scott coming through the doorway, *"Bonjour mes amis.* Hello, my friends." She greeted in French and English. She dropped her opened handbag on the table and headed for the toilette. A bottle of pills rolled out. India picked up the bottle and was about to open the cap.

"Put it back," I whispered.

"Okay," she pouted. Her eyes widened in an instant. "Oh my God," she said and passed the bottle to me, pointing to the label. I didn't know much about pills, only that you take them when you are sick. "So?" I said.

India pointed again to the name on top. "Dr. Olga O'Ligue."

"And?" I questioned in a whisper.

"Dr. Olga O'Ligue is my adopted aunt. She's a psychologist, a shrink." With her index fingers, India made circular motions on both sides of her head. "She treats disturbed people."

India quickly replaced the bottle of pills when we heard the toilette flush.

"Mes amis, my friends." Mrs. Scott sat down on the edge of her desk and got straight to the point. "Who started the fight?"

India began to explain that she had stumbled and fallen. I saw her and ran over to help. I was giving her a hand up and fell down as well. It was not a fight. "Kaman was really trying to help me to get back on my feet," she said.

I left the Dragon's Den smiling from ear to ear. Om-7 cooed happily.

On the bus ride home, I was the star victim as my friends teased me.

"Who was on top?" one bantered.

"India Weinberger," the rest chorused.

"Who got beaten up by a girl?"

"Kaman Colioni," the chorus sang.

"Did she kiss you, when she was on top of you?"

"Smack – smack – smack," The chorus teased.

"Did she whisper in your ear?"

I smiled. She had whispered in my ear.

Usually, when Jalebi returned from school, she would drop her schoolbag and run to the toilet. Today, as we entered the house, she tattled to Ma and Pa about the fight.

"Did you get suspended?" Ma had a worried look on her face.

"Did you get expelled?" Pa asked in his coarse voice.

"India was on top of him, straddling him." Jalebi shouted from the toilet.

"It wasn't a fight." I repeated the story India had told Mrs. Scott.

I grabbed three gulab jamuns, two cannolis, a cup of chai and ran upstairs to my room. I sure had lots of things to think about.

Ma had another favorite saying these days, "live and learn," which she repeated often enough, explaining that it's a lesson in life. Today, I had seen the light of that lesson as I learnt to say the word, "fight," in seven languages.

But my biggest lesson was, girls weren't all that bad and I liked India Weinberger – a lot.

Ω   Ω   Ω

The following week, another girl joined our class. She was lighter in complexion than Toussaint, with hair as blond as Jalebi's doll, and she wore very thick glasses. When she wrote her name on the board, the first two letters hugged each other, and the last had an "o" with a baby "x" on top.

Æsa Hleið was taller than everyone in the class and spoke neither English nor French. For that matter, she hardly spoke at all. When she did, she spoke a language that made Om-7 perk up to attention, when he first heard it.

During the first week, Æsa stayed by herself, during the recess and lunch hours.

Toussaint said she was a Viking, a *nouveau arrivé*, a new arrival from somewhere in Europe. I checked out 'Viking' in the Encyclopedia. Everything was written in the past tense so I assumed they were all dead. I was puzzled. I took the world map from the fridge door and, with sign language, showed Æsa where my parents came from. She became very excited. She had lived with her parents in Surinam, another little country in South America and a neighboring country to Guyana where my Ma was born. Then she showed me a place called Denmark where her mother was born. She also showed me where her father originated from, a country named Finland. I presumed everyone from her father's country had fins and, so I kept looking for hers, 'cos she sure was cute like a mermaid.

We communicated through a different kind of language. She brought a series of pictures and showed me what she wanted to talk about. After my visit to the Dragon's Den, she brought in a newspaper cut-out of the kindergarten class in Chouguay with the story about Engine's bow and arrow. Æsa stood beside me in the picture. We were both overly excited that we knew each other. She pulled out a little book from her bag. It was an ABC book in sign language. She wanted me to teach her sign language. Aw, shucks, my heart melted.

The next day, I had forgotten my shoes in the gym. When I returned to get them, I saw Æsa on her knees, searching the floor for her glasses. I saw them immediately. The lens had separated from the frames. I passed the pieces to her and watched as she tried to re-assemble them, but the plastic lens kept falling off. Tears ran down her face. I had an idea. I placed the frames in her hands, squeezed her fingers around to just the right tightness while I tried to snap the lens into the frames. After several attempts, the first one snapped in. The second one took a bit more work, but it finally gave in to our combined efforts. When I peeked through, they were as thick as a magnifying glass. I wiped the fingerprints with my shirt before handing them back to her. She stopped crying and managed a smile. To my surprise, she leaned over and kissed me on the lips.

I ran outside to meet up with my friends, my thoughts befuddled. *I kissed a girl, or a girl had kissed me.* It wasn't yuck. It was nice. Vikings sure have a strange way of saying thank you.

I hope India Weinberger saw that kiss.

39 Splendor in the Sand

THE DRAGON'S DEN brought back memories of India.

In the wee hours of the morning, when my brain refused to work and writing became difficult, I took Chewy for a breeze-off on the beach. I found the most comfortable chaise lounge and, before long, I felt myself dozing off and succumbed to the sweetness of it. I froze when I felt the warm body beside me and the scent of a woman taking over my space.

India.

"Kaman, wake up," she whispered, with a nudge in my ribcage. I blinked several times not believing my eyes.

She moved over me before I caught my breath to answer.

My body immediately weakened to her touch and melted completely when her lips touched mine and her tongue invaded my mouth. When the kiss was over, she rose, took my hands in hers and led me to the edge of the water. Some floating seaweeds entwined my ankles and felt like chains as they tightened with the advancing and receding tide.

She became the leader, and I, the follower. I made a note to myself, for future reference, that I would definitely repeat what happened, when she beckoned me with open arms into the sand and the aftermath filled with the added splendor of waves crashing against our naked bodies.

I had been nurturing severe thoughts, over the past months of how I would put her in her place and send her packing if she ever returned. Who was I kidding? I didn't stand a chance from the moment she touched me.

I read somewhere about different tribes and their mating rituals. Some engaged in lengthy profanities, some in passionate flowery language. Others opened the Kama Sutra and did a step-by-step until they fell over on their faces. I belong to the gentleman tribe. I don't kiss and tell.

But damn, just on this one occasion, I will temporarily renounce my tribal ties as I need to share this. It was hot . . . wild . . . tantric at its best . . . with a record-breaking oxytocin level.

Much later, our bodies sated, we sat by the water's edge and watched the expanse of sea in front of us. The light in the skies indicated the sun would be coming out before long. I knew India speaks only when she wants to and there was so much more that had to be discussed to make our relationship right. For now, I was content to just be together – no discussion of the past, the present or the future.

Just us welcoming a new day on Paradise Beach.

Ω   Ω   Ω

India and I woke up to Vibe's alarm which I had pre-set for 05.00 a.m. daily to take Chewy out for our morning jog. I rose quickly, looking around.

"Chewy has gone astray." I said.

India looked at me with sleepy eyes. "No, he hasn't. When I arrived and found master and dog missing, I came out to the beach. You were so dead to the world and Chewy was so excited at seeing me that I took him back in, fed him and put him to bed. You know what else I saw?"

"What?"

"Netts and the Russian next door came out at 3:00 a.m. and checked up on you. Did you hear them?"

"Really? I was that dead?"

"After they left, several dinghy type vessels with divers and high-tech lighting equipment were scouring the reef. I couldn't pick up who they were even with the binoculars."

I think, *this is not good news. As soon as she is asleep, I am going to check out the booty.*

"Why didn't you wake me up?"

"You looked so peaceful."

"Let's go in. I want to sleep the entire day through, with you, of course. You do know I am writing a memoir?" I looked at her quizzically.

"To be honest, I read the chapters you sent my aunt while I was in York. When I first arrived, I checked what you were up to and your computer lights were blinking. She requested more material. So I became your beta reader, approved two chapters and sent them out."

"That's strange. She's been out of touch."

"She's traveling," India said quietly.

"You sent her two chapters? They weren't even edited."

"I edited them before sending out." She paused and nuzzled up to my chin. "I loved the stories. Did I really have a bird's nest?"

"Not all the time. Sometimes, it looked like a beehive."

"Which one did you like better?" she smiled that special smile she kept only for me.

"The bird's nest. It reminded me of when we were in kindergarten and the only thing we had to worry about was which toys and games to play with."

"For you, Kaman. For me, it was a hellhole, especially in Chouguay when I lived with the Connolly's. I was afraid to close my eyes at night."

I hugged her tightly and asked, "Do you want to talk about it?"

"No," she replied.

"I'll wait till you're ready. I want only to remember the India who whispered into my ear, then told Mrs. Scott, the Dragon that I had helped her, so I wouldn't get in trouble."

"Do you realize something, Kaman?"

"What?"

"You hear everything I say. I spoke to you without signing and you understood what I said. And, you weren't even looking at me to lipread."

Instinctively, my hand moved to my right ear. I stared at her intently as I thought about people who claim they lost their senses when they are in love. Such nonsense. Not my case at all. Alas, I couldn't find the words to tell India her voice was the only one that didn't bounce around in my head.

"I miss Om-7," I said. "Let's go back to the condo."

$$\Omega \quad \Omega \quad \Omega$$

There were all signs that India was in residence as she and I entered the condo. Clothes were scattered around her suitcase on the living room floor. Her laptop and camera were on the table surrounded by an empty coffee cup and a half-eaten slice of toast. Her handbag lay open on the kitchen counter, from which protruded a passport and a cell phone. Om-7 lay apart from the mess. My face broadened into a smile as I picked him up, turned him over gently and checked to see if he was still in one piece. "How did you find him?"

"With the help of Ten-squat-a-way."

"Engine? How's that?" A wave of guilt overtook me as I thought of how I had been suspicious of him and her.

"You have to remember that Engine prefers his real name "Ten-squat-a-way." And we have to respect this. He made contact with me through Carlos. We met up in York, England. I don't know how Carlos found me, but he did. Before Dr. O and I left the Cayman Islands, she accidentally dropped a bomb. She and my adopted mother lived in York before they crossed the pond to the Americas. This, I didn't know."

"India, are you sure you want to talk about this?"

"Yes. No." She sighed, "Yes, because I love you and I owe you that much. And no because it hurts."

I changed the conversation. "How did you get back to the island?"

"I overheard my aunt making plans to return to the Cayman Islands for a short visit. It had something to do with the opening of the Church for Society's Improvement. I wanted to come along with her. She made me promise I would stay in York until she returned and then she would tell me everything about my adoption. It's all too confusing. It's like she wanted to tell me, but was afraid. She said she wanted to protect me. I didn't trust her, so I asked Ten-squat-a-way for help. He orchestrated it with Æsa. I actually flew directly from London to Cayman in Æsa's husband's private jet." She yawned loudly, "Sorry, jet lag."

Sensing her need to sleep, I led her upstairs.

Ω   Ω   Ω

I got dumped by a dog. Chewy would not leave India's side from the time she woke up in the late afternoon. The three of us sat on the balcony overlooking the courtyard and I had to play second fiddle, sit back and watch as he hunkered down by India's feet with his face on her crossed ankles.

"I can't keep this charade in. I have to tell you. I found my mother," India blurted out.

"Who?"

"My mother."

"What?"

"My mother," She repeated.

"Where?" I said, looking daftly at her. "You went all the way to Asia? To the ashram where she secluded herself to eat, pray and find love?"

"That's my adopted mother, Shoshanna Weinberger, the lawyer. I found out who my real mother is. Her name and other details.

Now she had my attention. "When?"

"That was the purpose of our separation."

"And your father? Did you find anything on him?"

"No. That was a dead end."

"Tell me more."

"My real mother suffered from mental illness after my birth. She couldn't care for me. She was Caymanian, you know. I think that's why I have always felt drawn to this island. According to Dr. O, she died some years back. The Weinbergers, who were newly married, adopted me, in York, England. I was a newborn baby when they moved to New York. A year later, they visited my aunt, Dr. O, who at the time lived in Montreal. They loved the city and decided to stay. Two years later, their marriage fell apart and they arranged foster care for me. That's how I ended up with the Connolly's. After their deaths, the Weinbergers reconciled and reclaimed me." She took a deep breath. "That's my life – adopted, foster care, adopted again and now, no parent to claim me."

"How did you discover all of this?"

"I had it out with Dr. O. She's turned into an alcoholic. When she drinks, her tongue gets loose and she spills out secrets. Yet, she would not tell me who my father is. She got scared when we touched on this subject. On one occasion, she told me that I am a murderer and was responsible for Mr. Connolly's death."

"What?" I bolted upright in the chair.

Tears rolled down her face. "I can't remember," she sobbed. "All I remember is dragging my body through the snow that night. All the houses looked the same. I kept repeating to myself, 'Look for the house with the blinking Diwali-Christmas lights.' I could barely reach the doorbell when I got there. Then, I saw the curtains move and you were there." She blew her nose noisily. "Look at me. I am a crybaby."

"I love you, crybaby." I held her in my arms and kissed the moisture from her eyes.

When she was calmer, I asked, "Will you tell me who your mother is? If you don't want to talk about it, it's okay." I waited in the silence.

She closed her eyes tightly and sucked in several breaths. "I'm not ready."

Minutes passed before she picked up the conversation with, "I had lots of help from Carlos Santana to find you. He sent me a picture. You had just come back from snorkeling."

"Carlos Santana? I call him the ketchup kid."

"Ketchup kid?"

"He loves ketchup. How come you didn't meet him? He lived next door to Dr. O."

"They, Carlos, and his brother Ernesto, moved in two days before I left the Cayman Islands. I should tell you about . . ."

I interrupted quickly with my best puppy dog eyes "India. Just us for today. Please?"

"If you promise me that tomorrow, you will continue writing the memoir." India agreed amicably. I had forgotten that India liked bossing me around . . . and that I liked it.

Ω   Ω   Ω

Late that night, I finally checked out the many links Zingaro sent on my blog. Either he was going weird on me, or I am confused.

Some engineers at an American University were working on a prototype battery that used manganese and lithium, which can be recharged to ninety percent in just two minutes. They had received millions in donations from an unknown source who was big into scientific research. Another link was about the re-opening of a manganese plant in the interiors of Guyana that was being financed by the Russian billionaire, Roman Romanov. Good for Uncle the Drunk; he would be busy with his fleet of rundown vessels, as he was the only local who knew and liked to travel those murky waters filled with alligators and anacondas.

I moved on to another link. It showed the price of gold – pretty good these days. This was an attachment to a recent news article that covered a gold heist in the Caribbean, which I knew about. A picture of the vessel and the captain was included. I zoomed in, enlarged it and stared at a photo of Uncle the Drunk, a cigarette hanging from the corner of his mouth. Another link on this page was about a find in Brazil of the largest Paraiba tourmaline that had disappeared soon after. Now, this is new news. New, as I never heard or read about this metal, and news because the next link showed the second largest of this rare gem had been auctioned off in Montreal last July. The buyer was the Russian billionaire Roman Romanov.

I left the blog and continued to write.

40 Khalil Kaleb Kwame

Draft of *The Deaf Boy in the Mirror*

Khalil Kaleb Kwame sat next to India in class. Their friendship developed quickly because she had visited Tennessee with her parents, the Weinbergers. Om-7 discreetly picked up their conversations about country music, Elvis Presley and Graceland. By the end of the third week, they had become best friends. "Special K," she fondly called him.

After the fight, I avoided being in the same place where she hung out until Toussaint said, "Kwame is moving in on India." Dara Singh agreed. I disagreed with them at first and then I got a first-hand look at what a smooth operator he was. He sat in the grass where her feet dangled off the fence and looked up at her with puppy-dog eyes as they watched the different sport activities in the schoolyard. My daily involvement in sports soon had a link to the location on the fence where India sat and disgustingly enjoyed her fingers, with Kwame at her feet.

Kwame was the most diminutive in the class picture. He didn't take the school bus; his parents took turns at being his chauffeur. In the first week, his mom, who was half-Cuban and half-American, drove up in a Jaguar, parked it by the fence and walked him to the classroom. She was, wow, like a fashion model. All the sixth graders stopped whatever they were doing to have a good look.

The second week, his dad drove him to school in a Porsche. He was a tall, dark-complexioned man who constantly glanced at his gold watch. Kwame said he was from a country called Uganda, in Africa, that once had a terrible dictator named Idi Amin. He was a diplomat who worked for the United Nations and wanted Kwame to mix with children of other cultures, which was the reason they enrolled him in The Immigrant School.

Kwame was diabetic and had to eat snacks and use a special needle at odd times of the day. A screen was placed in the classroom for this purpose. He sang as he squirted the liquid from the needle before he injected himself, which made everyone think it was a fun thing. The entire class had looked and weren't bothered by the needle, except for me. I had to run to the toilette when I finally worked up the courage to have a peep.

He was the only boy in our class who was not involved in sports. He didn't like tag or soccer, had no interest in hockey, and was excused from gym because it coincided with his prescribed drug habit. He emphasized he was born in the USA, and he only wanted to play ball in Montreal like Jackie Robinson, the famous baseball player. Kwame had a sense of humor and told jokes that had the entire class in stitches.

After a week of close scrutiny of how he was moving in on India, and, of course, having Toussaint and Dara Singh rubbing it in, I decided to play interference. I organized a tag game where each one had to throw in five cents – the funds to go toward the start up of a baseball team for Kwame. Then, I invited Kwame.

"You kidding? Me? Play tag? That's a kid's game. Look at my size." He lifted his thin arms up, flexing them. "See these muscles, they're better than Andre the Giant."

"C'mon. Pretend you can kick Andre the Giant's ass and have fun."

It took three days to persuade him that tag was like baseball and, because of his size, he could dodge better than all of us. And, because he spoke Arabic, which was the most

common language in the whole school after Franglais, he
could convert the tag team to baseball. Within the month
there was a baseball team with Kwame as captain. It helped
that his parents provided all the equipment and that his mom
often visited to check on the team which most of the sixth
graders had joined. Om-7 picked up whispers of a secret name
they had for her – MILK – which meant Mother I'd Like to Kiss.

Kwame started something that puzzled me, the whole
school population and Mrs. Scott, the first time we witnessed it.

It was the Monday of the last week in September. When
Kwame's father drove him to school in a Mercedes Benz con-
vertible, (BB told me it cost more than $100,000), he carried
a woven mat. After lunch, as soon as he had eaten and punc-
tured his stomach with the needle, he tucked the mat under
his arm and headed outside. Curious, I followed him, with the
baseball team tagging behind.

Kwame walked toward the fence, away from where India
sat. He took out a compass from his pocket, whispering as
he pointed with his index finger, "North, South, West, East."
Satisfied, he laid out the mat, faced east, bent his knees and
went down on all fours. Then he lined up his hands with his
knees, closed his eyes and lowered his head as he started to
pray. The soccer team joined as spectators and, before long,
the hockey team, an inquisitive, rowdy bunch, arrived, pushed
each other to have a better look at Kwame as he raised and
lowered his head.

The next day, some older boys headed out toward the fence
with Kwame, spread their mats in the grass and crouched
down in prayer. From the Dragon's Den, Mrs. Scott opened
her eyes in amazement at this occurrence in her schoolyard.
Within minutes, she marched out, stood beside me to watch
thirteen boys, butts up in the air, heads down to the ground,
facing east in deep prayer.

By the fence, I recognized the local newspaper photographer who was always on the prowl with her camera. She
was the one who had written the story about Dara Singh and

the soccer federation. She was snapping away at this scene that everyone was now staring at. What she captured with her camera appeared some days later on the front page of the newspaper. She took the photo from behind the boys in such a way that thirteen butts in sweatpants were visible, with Mrs. Scott standing in front, her arms and legs askew, surrounded by boys and girls, different ages, different colors and different sizes. And there I was, standing right beside her.

Ma said it was the most popular story in Waste Island. She heard customers talking about it in the supermarket and discussions on the call-in radio talk shows. People were questioning whether this kind of prayer should be allowed in schoolyards. Some said it was comparable to the boy who wore a kirpan and a turban.

Ω   Ω   Ω

At the end of October, the leaves had completely fallen from the trees and the temperature dropped. India finally got off the fence thanks to a soccer ball and Ernesto Guevara Ibáñez, who Mademoiselle Cointreau nicknamed, "Che." He spoke Spanish, Portuguese, some English and very little French. He played tag for a while, then gave up, because he couldn't understand Franglais, which became the most popular spoken language in the schoolyard. He chewed paper for a pastime.

Kids made fun of him because he stuttered. He shied away from being jeered to a corner of the schoolyard where he dribbled a soccer ball, controlling it like a pro – lifting it up to his knees, kneeing it onto his head, and letting the ball fall into the sickly green grass. He would then finish with some pretty fancy foot work.

Che's antics caught India's eye. She jumped off the fence, playfully grabbed the ball and tried to copy his maneuvers. Her movements were so bad that Che took the ball away and slowly showed her how to control it. I was happy she had gotten off the fence and did not spend her time with her fingers in her mouth, but I had a niggling thought that, maybe, just maybe, she liked this Che character, now that her best friend, Special K, had turned to prayers.

Ω   Ω   Ω

Mr. Toulousse announced there was going to be indoor soccer in the gym as an after school activity on Mondays if he could find parents as volunteers to coach and drivers for the kids who needed a lift home. Mr. Ibáñez, Che's father, was the first to volunteer. BB and I tried to convince Pa he should help, as Mondays were his day off from work. He was reluctant at first, but quickly changed his mind when we told him the other volunteer was Mr. Ibáñez, who was from Argentina originally, and lived in Brazil before settling in Mexico. Being Italian, he took the sport of soccer seriously and felt a South American – an Argentinean/Brazilian combo – would make for terrible coaching techniques.

There were so many kids registered for soccer that Pa and Mr. Ibáñez each had their own team. As no coach was found for the girls, the teams were coed. There were times when I saw Pa ecstatic; however, when he won the first scrimmage against Mr. Ibáñez's team, well, it was indescribable. We heard him repeat it all week. The only person unhappy about all this was BB, as he was on Mr. Ibáñez's team.

Ma volunteered to drive kids home after the games. When India caught sight of her, she ran and hugged her very tightly. She was even bold enough to ask, "Mrs. Colioni, can you please, please drive me home after soccer today?"

I saw where India lived. It was a huge mansion, in another part of West Island called DeeDeeOh, and I met Mr. and Mrs. Weinberger. They invited us in when they found out that India had known us when she lived with her foster parents in Chouguay. Once again, India and Jalebi became best friends.

Ω   Ω   Ω

In December, the darkest month of the year, the first snow-storm blasted Montreal early on a Monday morning and continued throughout the day. Normally, school was cancelled on high snow days, but the weatherman had predicted this snow-storm to start late afternoon. No one was allowed to go out during the recess and lunch breaks.

"Oh, I wish I could go out and pray," Kwame said wistfully as he looked through the classroom window. "I have never seen snow like this in Tennessee."

"No pray outside today, Kwame," Mademoiselle Cointreau said. She was a good sport and indulged us by sometimes speaking English.

When the bell rang at three thirty, the snow had blown and blocked the fence. Pa arrived late and asked me to make sure the team stretched and got in position while he changed. I did a headcount, only to discover Kwame missing. I asked Amin, another boy who prayed daily, if he had seen him. He said Kwame had gone outside alone to pray in the snow.

"I am going to look for him." I was worried as was the whole team.

Dara Singh volunteered to come with me and, once we were dressed, we rushed out the front door. Outside, visibility was hampered as the snow blew furiously into our faces.

"He usually prays over there," Dara Singh said. We turned in the direction he suggested. Snow had blown and built up so much it looked like mountains with deep valleys. Very pretty to look at and very scary as we ventured forward. I had to walk sideways to avoid snowflakes blowing into Om-7. We struggled to climb over the snow banks, our feet sinking deep as we dragged ourselves forward. I was covered up to my butt and Dara Singh to his knees. We stopped often, looked around, and shouted out Kwame's name. No answer.

"Tell you what," Dara Singh said. "You stay here and I will go down by the fence to see if he's there. It's only two snow banks away."

I had to turn my back against the gusts of wind blowing

the snow around. When it momentarily died down, I caught a glimpse of Kwame's mat and hat in the snow. I shouted out to Dara Singh, as I fought to climb over a snow bank, and made it to the mat. I barely saw Kwame. He was lying still between two snow banks. When I reached him, and brushed the snow from his face, he rolled his eyes. Not in a mocking way but in the way that people rolled their eyes just before they die in the movies. I started to panic in a big way.

"Kwame, Kwame! Get up. Let's go." I pulled at his arms.

"Insulin," his lips trembled as he spoke.

"What?" I crouched closer to him, my heart racing.

"Insulin. In my jacket pocket," he mumbled.

I searched his pockets, found the pen and placed it in his gloved hands. He was so cold that his hands shook when he took it.

"You have to do it," he said in a weak voice. The sight of the pen gave me the heebie-jeebbies. I turned in all directions and called out to Dara Singh. No answer.

"Kaman, help me," Kwame's rolling eyes begged.

The last time I had dared to sneak a peek behind the screen where he self-injected, I had to run to the toilette. When I returned, India had slipped a note on my desk. "WIMP" was written in big bold letters. Now, as I undid the pen cover and saw the needle, my stomach lurched. I threw up yellow Jamaican Patty into the white snow.

"I can't do it, Kwame."

"Yes, you can," he whispered.

The wind started to howl. Diffused sounds reached Om-7. Nothing seemed clear. What if Kwame dies? What if . . . Om-7 started to have behavioral issues.

"WIMP," I heard India Weinberger's voice mocking me.

"No, you're not," the wind sang in response.

"Close your eyes and count," Ma's voice reached out to me.

"All the way to ten," the wind sang again.

"When you gonna shoot, shoot!" The ugly guy in *The Good, The Bad and The Ugly* smirked.

Once again, I shouted out to Dara Singh. Snow had blown into Om-7's receptors, which worsened his behavior. It made me dazed and confused. The pen fell and sank into the snow. "Christo Mio!" I swore in Italian, as Pa did when something didn't go the way he wanted it. I went down on my knees and searched until I found it.

"Come on, let's get this over and done with," Pa's commanding voice reached me.

I moved Kwame's jacket and sweater to his chest, located a spot on his stomach, closed my eyes tightly and jabbed the pen into his flesh. I counted to ten. When I reopened my eyes, he was asleep. I pulled down his sweater and jacket, grabbed his legs, tugged and pulled him until we were over the first snow bank.

I heard Dara Singh call out my name.

"I got him," I shouted back.

"Keep talking, so I can follow your voice."

When he arrived and checked Kwame out, his next words scared me even more. "He's frozen. Let's cover him up."

Not stopping to think, he removed his turban and wrapped it around Kwame's head and face.

"I thought you never took off your turban Dara?"

"For a friend in need, I do."

Together, we pulled Kwame until we were over the last snow bank. Dara Singh carried him piggyback to the gym. It seemed like forever before an ambulance arrived and took Kwame away. He was still breathing, but would not open his eyes.

That night in bed, I prayed like Kwame did. My butt up, my head down, my lips moved to say, "Please God, don't let Kwame die, because I was a wimp and took too long to inject him. I will never ask another favor, God, not even for my ears to stop playing tricks on me."

God was on duty that night as Kwame returned to school with new jokes a week later. I never understood his medical condition, but Kwame's parents took Dara Singh's family

and mine out for dinner at a fancy restaurant, in downtown
Montreal. They picked us up in a stretch limo.

Pa rarely gave compliments but when we arrived home, he
said he was so proud of me. He said I had been 'quick on my
feet' when I gave Kwame his insulin shot.

41 X-Rated

DR. O HAS not been in contact, but I don't care. I just wanted
to finish writing the memoir. India had visible signs of jet lag,
yawning and dozing off in the middle of conversations. She apologized and went to bed. Her return definitely had a positive effect
on me and, with renewed energy, I tapped away on the keyboard
to finish another chapter in one night. Or maybe, it was just
having Om-7 back in my life to balance things in my head. It is
day twenty five and I am back on schedule.

I also had been thinking about the activity by the reef that
India mentioned.

Last night, as soon as she fell asleep, I timed my underwater outing to coincide with Rooslahn's departure on his scooter.
Many of the baby octopuses had grown and moved on. Still, there
were hundreds of them feeding and playing around by the rocks,
some lazing in the sand below.

The booty was still in place, undisturbed.

$$\Omega \quad \Omega \quad \Omega$$

In my world of deaf-hood, to soliloquize is a discipline in talk therapy that helps me to hear my voice, argue with myself and be my
own critic. It's best done in front of a mirror, so mistakes, body
movements and hand movements can be corrected. Incidentally,
it was my mother's idea and I now remember this, as Dr. O

had placed a large mirror behind the computer screen. I usually engage in this practice when I am alone, as I am now, checking out my blog. And no, I am not having a bout of depression.

Zingaro, my generous and deaf fan who had sent me the ticket to The Cayman Islands forwarded several new links. One was a video posted by two underwater photographers who had encountered a frisky male bottlenose in West Bay. The dolphin, nicknamed Harry, had alternatively pinned the two men to the seabed floor and tried to hump them. As they tried to ward him off, he had become aggressive and charged at them. At close look, the dolphin's genitals could be seen.

UUUgh-ugly.

I closed the video.

I clicked on another one titled, "Lone Dolphin," that was two minutes in duration. It was fuzzy, but there was the bottlenose again. At about fifty-five seconds, the video was clearer. The dolphin, seemingly in stasis, was surrounded by a v-shaped streak of orange, blue and green fish.

Glow fishies. Oh, yes, I must take India to see this. She will be wowed at this sighting.

As I concluded this thought, the green glow fish moved closer to the dolphin, surrounding its rubbery looking male parts.

Wow, look at that. Fully loaded.

No, no, no. There is no way India is going anywhere near to you, Dirty Harry.

At one minute and fifty seconds, the screen changes to show a background of the three rocks that jutted above the sea.

Now, this is strange.

I checked the properties of the video. It had been tampered with, as it showed the current date and time.

Zingaro, what the hell are you up to?

Ω   Ω   Ω

India was in good spirits the next morning. She announced she would surprise Carlos with a visit while I continued to write. She was excited at this first meeting with him. She would also drop by and see Ten-sqúat-a-way.

India didn't have to work at the moment because her mother, who was now on a spiritual journey in Nepal, had given her a generous allowance until she found a job. She returned earlier than I expected with news that Ten-sqúat-a-way was away. And, her visit with Carlos had not gone as she anticipated. She was shocked at what he was involved in. He had broken in and decoded a porn site, showing off his smarts to her. The base of the business was in Curaçao, then pipelined from Los Angeles to screens around the world. He showed her how all the sites were interconnected.

She fanned herself with her hands. "I am amazed at how smart and intelligent he is. I just can't believe the porn sites stuff," she said. "He is only fourteen, for heaven's sakes."

Boy, was she cranky! If only she knew the statistics of how many teenagers visit porn sites. I'm not going to be the one to tell her.

To get her mind off it, I told her about the gold as we ate the crab soup with cassava, yams and plantains cooked in a coconut milk broth. She didn't believe me. She outright said that I had become over-imaginative and was certain that it was related to me reading too many thrillers.

Through the window, I saw Rooslahn leave his unit with his diving gear and walk toward the pier. It was too early for his habitual outing. What was he up to?

"You know what you need? A good workout." I suggested. "How about we go diving? It will be a good time to test out the new binoculars and underwater camera you brought back."

Her face lit up.

As we checked out the equipment, I was hoping Dirty Harry had departed to Seven Mile Beach where there would be more offerings of half-dressed ladies and gents. India decided she would handle the camera and do some underwater photography. I was glad, as she had a better eye for details. She wanted to test Vibe, so I strapped him on her sleeve.

It was a warm night, with a half-moon in the sky when we arrived on the pier. Testing the new binoculars, I saw a single small yacht moored close to Ghost Mountain. As we submerged ourselves in the water, India turned to me and signed with a smile, "Thank you for this."

We descended to fifteen feet, not far from the three jutting rocks when the school of glow fish made their appearance and, automatically, Vibe's beam of light shut off. India's reaction was priceless. We had a special underwater language from our many diving trips. She now signed, "Look below."

The floor was covered with octopuses. Some lay asleep in the sand, their eight arms spread out like petals. Others had awakened, sensing an intrusion into their world and walked in the sand. A group, attracted by the light of the glow fish surrounded India. She playfully touched them, her face animated as they moved away, then returned. "Cute little buggers," she signed.

With the light of the glow fish, we circled to the back of the rocks and descended until we were at a depth of twenty feet. Her eyes widened when I scraped off the sand to expose a crate. Minutes later, her brows furrowed as Vibe started to vibrate. She signed, "We have company." Quickly, we covered the crate and shoved octopuses above them.

She pointed to her ears now, which meant I should listen.

"I'm deaf," I signed.

"Oops, I forgot," she signed back. "There's someone out there."

"Let's get outta here." I gave her a little push upwards, the glow fish following her.

I sensed movement. It was eerie in the ink black water with no light. I felt in the darkness along the rock edges, turned the corner and tried to locate India so we can abort the dive. She was five feet above me with the camera light on and frolicking with the octopuses around her. Heading her way was Dirty Harry.

I ascended just in time to grab India by the wrist and pull her lower. Accidentally, I activated Vibe which set off a firework display and sent the school in another direction. When I looked up through the spikes of light, I saw Harry had found another target, a huge man who was fighting back with hand blows. Not getting the better of it, Harry turned around, dived lower and pinned me against the wall. In my subconsciousness, I remembered there is a drop of 6,000 feet and I did not have enough nitrox in my tank to sustain such a depth, which meant, goodbye, mother earth. The diver followed, angrily grabbed Harry by the tail and swirled him around a few times. With a grunt, Harry swam off.

Shaken up, I reached for India again and, as we made our ascent. I noticed the glow fish were back and two divers were moving away speedily toward Ghost Mountain. One was a slim-bodied woman; the other a big man. I recognized them as they turned around to look at me. Shizu and Mamushi.

When we surfaced, there were now two fishing yachts docked, at different angles close to Ghost Mountain.

"Oh Whew. Now, we know for sure the proximity sensor on Vibe works. The guy who swirled Harry around is the Russian next door." India said with a laugh. I couldn't believe she found the whole incident funny, as I worried whether Shizu, Mamushi and Rooslahn had seen me when I exposed the crate.

Ω   Ω   Ω

Kwame notified India he was coming to the island for a job interview and asked if he could spend the night with us. Over the years, he had worked extensively in social services, and recently completed his Ph.D. in psychology. It was no surprise to me he was interviewing in the Cayman Islands. He always wanted to work in a small tropical paradise.

Kwame was small-framed with light brown coloring and was just over five feet in height. His welcoming wide smile in a round face made up for any physical shortcomings he had. He arrived at dinnertime. Tired out from the interview, he fell asleep on the sofa and woke up at midnight. When he realized India was asleep, he whispered to me, "I need to discuss something with you. Let's go out to the beach."

Once we were comfortably seated, Kwame opened the conversation with, "I know you're writing a memoir."

"Who told you?"

"Come on. There's no secret amongst us friends. We help each other out. We watch out for each other. Give that little push when it's needed. Most of us have attained our goals – except you. And so, I want to put some thoughts into your head."

"Yeah, I know. I am just a loser."

"You're not." He did the spiel I had heard before – how smart I am, how I made it through university even though I am deaf, and there's a job out there for me. I just have to be patient. I tuned it all out.

"There's a personal incident I want to talk about. I've never shared this with anyone. I feel the need to tell you. It has to do with Dr. O'Ligue." I tuned right back in and listened attentively to his story.

When Kwame was in his early teens, he had a problem. All of his friends had stretched and shot up inches. At sixteen, he was still "short," as he put it. His parents were worried and sought out consultations with the best in the medical field. Each one had a different diagnosis. First, it was thyroid. Another thought it was the insulin. One was sure that it was genetics. That's when his parents told him the truth. He was an adopted child and his mother was a crack whore and his father an alcoholic.

"It started to play with my head in a strange way. At that time, I wanted to run away and live in a tribal village in Africa. I can relate to India wanting to know her parentage."

"Kwame, you have the most loving and caring parents."

"I know that. But when you're a confused teenager, in a selfish way, you only see your problems, and each one is magnified one hundred times."

"I hear you. How does Dr. O come into this?"

Kwame's parents arranged for sessions with Dr. O'Ligue, who was the big name in psychology. At that time, there were stories circulating about molestations of youths by people around them. There were all kinds of ad campaigns in the media emphasizing if you are uncomfortable with the way certain people touch you, then you should report it.

"The media was pounding this information into our heads. Don't you remember? I'm not saying it doesn't happen. You know Dr. O'Ligue is a very friendly woman. She does that touchy-feely thing – touching your head, your back, your arms. I misunderstood it for what the ad campaigns were shouting out to us. I told my parents that I was being molested. What's worse is they didn't question it. My father approached Dr. O'Ligue and threatened her. She didn't hold it against me. She's helped me a lot over the years toward achieving my goals. With her contacts and references, she opened doors that made it easier for me with my career choice."

"What are you saying Kwame? Did she or did she not molest you?"

"She didn't."

I thought a lot about Kwame's story after we said goodnight. Was I brainwashed into thinking what happened? I had fallen asleep on her sofa and when I woke up, she was asleep on the other side. It had been nothing really, yet I had been suspicious it might be a prelude to a come-on.

It took me a long time before I could get back into the next chapter of the memoir.

42 Montreal Pizza

Draft of *The Deaf Boy in the Mirror*

The same year that my parents became the owners of a pizza restaurant, we were having lessons in school about how French sailors travelled more than 375 years ago to find a route to China and India. When they made their way through the *St. Laurent*

River, they thought they arrived in China, so they gave the land the French name, *La Chine.* On their initial encounter with the First Peoples of Canada, they called them 'Indians,' a misnomer used by other Europeans in this period of exploration of the New World. When they tried to convert these so-called 'Indians' to Christianity and they rebelled, they renamed them *sauvages* or savages. From the black-and-white photos on the restaurant's walls, La Chine had changed its face over the years and became a one-word name, *Lachine.* Visible also in the photos is Caughnawaga, which also had been renamed to *Kahnawake* where Ten-squat-a-way's grandparents live.

Pa worked for many years as the chef in the pizza restaurant that belonged to Mr. Silenzio. It was in a two-story, run-down building on St. Joseph Street by the man-made Lachine Canal that ran parallel to The St. Lawrence Seaway. Day or night, a flow of vessels could be seen going to and from Montreal to the Great Lakes. The most prominent sight from the restaurant's windows was the cross that loomed over the waterways from atop the St. Francis-Xavier Catholic Church in Kahnawake.

Pa's friend who worked at city hall told him about available subsidies to refurbish the run-down properties and revamp St. Joseph Street. There were also plans for a bicycle path, a green space for picnics, ice cream trucks, and a poutine stand. With this knowledge, Pa seized the opportunity, and made Mr. Silenzio an offer. He traded the house in Quirkland for a block of run-down buildings, including the pizza restaurant, and we moved to a Chinese town, that China did not know existed, but which most Montrealers knew as *Lachine.*

When Pa made the announcement to us kids, he explained that, in the purchase agreement with Mr. Silenzio, he had to make a weekly payment for a year. There was no extra money to pay for help in the restaurant so, "you kids have to give a helping hand until the restaurant belongs legally to the Colioni family."

"It's only for a short time," Ma added. "We will live upstairs. And, if we pull together, this will be a success."

The only good part was we could still attend The Immigrant School.

The bad part was there was only one bedroom upstairs which Ma and Pa claimed. Us kids had to share a king-sized mattress on the floor close to a vent that sent out spurts of heat and made noises that Om-7 did not like. He reacted by making zing-zing sounds, which irritated me. A piece of work he was, for he became extremely quiet when he picked up sounds late in the night coming from the bedroom where my parents were supposed to be sleeping.

Ma and Pa decided that the restaurant needed a make-over and a new name. They asked each of us kids to think about possible names, write them down on pieces of paper and drop them into BB's smelly Canadiens' hat. There was only one name choice per day. This process continued for five days while we tore down wallpaper, scraped glue and prepped the walls inside and out before applying a fresh coat of paint. I chose the name "Michelangelo" after my favorite pizza-loving Ninja Turtle and dropped two pieces of paper in the hat, daily. It paid off, or I got lucky, as Pa pulled out one of the ten pieces I had neatly folded; but he said there was another restaurant with that name. As a compromise, there will be a Machiavelli pizza on the menu as he liked the way my thought processes worked.

Ma was the winner. She chose a name with a lot of senti-ment attached, *Montreal Pizza*. As a Montrealer, she felt it was a nice way to pay homage to the city where she had fallen in love and had her children. It made sense, as there was Montreal Smoke Meat, Montreal Steak Spice and Montreal Bacon – all of which can be found in menus and grocery stores across Canada and the United States.

Ω   Ω   Ω

The second floor of the pizza restaurant quickly became our home. BB, Jalebi and I became child laborers. We had to do nasty, unpaid work like rolling out pizza dough, chopping up vegetables, squishing hamburger meat to make meatballs, slicing pepperoni and greasy Italian sausages, cleaning the sinks, scrubbing the floor and taking out the garbage. We were no different from the kids in third-world countries who worked in factories to make sports shoes and knit carpets. At least *they* got paid. *We* didn't. When we mentioned this to Pa, he had a curt response.

"You have a roof over your heads, clothes on your backs, food in your stomachs." He had a look on his face I can only describe as a mix of hurt and guilt.

Pa must have thought about it, as a family meeting was called for the following Monday evening at the round table he had built for the family's use. We all grumbled, as Monday nights were quiet in the restaurant and us kids were allowed to watch taped TV shows with chips and popcorn. I wanted to laugh at Steve Erkel's jokes on "Family Matters." And Lex Xi had passed on back-to-back shows of "Full House." Besides, it had been a tough day watching India and Che. Something was definitely going on between them.

Once we were seated, Ma gave each of us a pen with Montreal Pizza, the restaurant's telephone number and address emblazoned below the *Tricolore,* the Italian Flag.

"What is this for?" we all asked at the same time.

"Marketing and advertising," she replied. "C'mon, let's get on with the agenda." She passed a stack of coupons to each of us. Each had Montreal Pizza written on the top with *Escompte/* Discount of 10% in the center on one side. The other side bore the flags of all the countries on the map of the world.

Without advance notice, we now had added the responsibilities of passing out pens and coupons to classmates and teachers at a convenient time, which was morning break for pens, afternoon break for the coupons. We had coaching lessons on how to make it a game. Each time we gave out a coupon, we asked the kid to find the flag of his native country with a free slice of pizza as a reward.

"What's the logic behind that?" BB asked.

"Well, if they don't know, they might ask their parents. And maybe, the parents might feel they have to bring their kids to Montreal Pizza."

"This is stupid." I complained, since giving up both of my breaks was not good for my social life. "Pa, this is working in school." I groaned.

"*Mia famiglia,*" Pa said in Italian. His voice had that proud tone to it, as he placed his hand on his chest, over his heart, then pointed to each one of us in turn, "*Vostra famiglia.*" He then circled the entire table to include us all, "*Nostra famiglia.*" His voice dipped. "The success of this family depends on each of you. All we have is each other, and so we have to work together to make the restaurant a success." He wiped a tear from the corner of his eye.

Pa, emotional? This was a side of him that was rare. Come to think of it, the last time I had seen him so shaken up was the day I said my first words. He took a sip of wine, then passed the glass to Ma.

"Second item on agenda. Kaman, you read it out," Ma said.

"Wages," I read.

"What this means, is," Ma paused, "each child is entitled to a paycheck." She reached into her apron pocket and passed an envelope around to each one of us. I forgot about the twins and their overcrowded house.

I tore mine open like a maniac. In Ma's neat handwriting was my name on one line, ten dollars on another line. It was the first time I heard Om-7 whistle.

There were still three more items on the list. If everyone hurried up, we still could watch "Full House" with the Olsen twins. I loved that show because I always could tell which twin was in each scene. It was easy, one was left-handed and the other was right-handed.

The doorbell chimed to announce the evening's only customers so far, the Weinbergers. To be honest, India had been the source of my discontent of late and so, I made a quick exit upstairs.

Ω   Ω   Ω

In the past month, India and Che were getting too close for my comfort. I saw this affair with my own eyes. She would bring him food, which her housekeeper packed into her lunch box. They had a secret thing going on that went down like this: As soon as the lunch bell rang and all the kids scampered out of the classroom, they stayed behind. That's when she would give Che half of her lunch and, together, they made their way to the lunchroom. They sat next to each other and I watched him wolf down the food like he had not eaten in days.

Now, as I listened through the vent, I heard India excitedly tell Jalebi about the family vacation they were taking to an exotic place called The Cayman Islands, which, to me, sounded like paradise. She showed pictures of the beach condo that was co-owned by her adopted mother and her aunt.

My heart cheered with this news because I wouldn't have to watch Che feeding off her and teaching her Spanish. And she, enunciating words slowly in French and English, which he had trouble repeating. Some kids made fun of him, and India had been in a few scraps in the schoolyard for defending him. She also held the honor of being the student with the most visits to the Dragon's Den. Jalebi told me India had been sent to see the school counsellor because she was hyperactive. Her parents had to take her to a doctor who prescribed her something called Ritalin.

On the day after India left, Che was absent from the lunchroom. Madame Le Blanc, the lunch monitor, found him alone, in the toilette. He said he was not hungry. This happened for two more days. Since there was no Che to make fun of, and no India to defend him, the kids turned to just misbehaving, throwing paper planes and paper balls at each other, myself included. The rowdiness was uncontrollable.

On the fourth day, I got caught throwing paper balls at Toussaint and Dara Singh. My punishment was to go to the toilette and find Che. "Don't come back without him," Madame Le Blanc warned. I found Che locked up in the cubicle of the toilette. I begged him to come out in Spanglish, Franglais, English and French. The kid ignored me. Maybe I was going too fast. I placed my mouth close to the keyhole and repeated slowly, in each language.

"Che, *Por Favor* come out." I started out in *Spanglish* and listened. No answer.

"*S'il-vous-plâit*, get your butt out of *la toilette*." I tried *Franglais*. Silence.

"Che, no one takes a crap that long." I tried to reason with him in English. Nothing.

"*Arrêtez. On fait pas caca si long. Sortez toute de suite.*" I shouted to him in *Français*. Still, not a peep from Che.

"Big soccer game on. Brazil and England. Brazil needs you." I tried soccer and heard a tiny movement.

"No," came his answer from behind the door.

Now that I got his attention, I racked my brains to think of a way to lure him out of his pretend crap. Food, the kid was a born glutton.

"I have an extra sandwich. I will give it to you," I coaxed him. I didn't, but he opened the door."

As we made our way back to the lunchroom, we ran into Dara Singh. He always had more *chapattis* than he could eat, but no one wanted them because his mom added hot chili peppers. He often dumped the extras in the toilette's garbage can, so as not to upset his mother. He willingly gave me his lunchbox contents when I explained the situation to him. Everyone cheered when we returned. I bowed and took the seat where India usually sat and sipped my juice. Che devoured the chapattis stuffed with channa and hot aubergine curry, then he looked at my drink with such hungry eyes that I just gave it to him.

"Gr-Gra-Gracias, Kaman."

"Why no lunch?" I whispered.

"Mi-mi padre, no work. Mi-mi madre, sick."

"Where do you live?"

"I-i-in, in a place."

"When was the last time you ate?"

It took a long time for him to get the words out to say the following: yesterday, when Dara Singh put his chapattis in the garbage. I took them home for my little brother. But we have ketchup from McDonalds. My brother likes ketchup with bread."

I became a thief overnight. I stole the bottle of Heinz ketchup, a loaf of bread, and added the left over pizza slices I found in the fridge. I slipped them to Che in the toilette at lunchtime. Dara Singh also brought some extra food. Che ate some and packed the rest into his bag. "For *mi Madre*," he said.

I finally got it out of him. He lived with his family in a van.

Ω   Ω   Ω

"Hide the English menus. The Language Police are at the laundromat next door," Pa shouted as he and Ma entered through the backdoor into the kitchen, their arms loaded with boxes of groceries.

It was a weeknight and us kids sat at the round table, our heads buried in our books. We had to finish homework as soon as we possibly could then help in the kitchen Half of the restaurant was reserved by twenty English-speaking ex-Montrealers who had moved to Toronto and chose Montreal Pizza for their annual reunion. They wanted to make a video of their special occasion. Ma set the tables with flowers in vases and placed English menus on each plate. They promised us kids any tips would be divided equally among us.

At Pa's announcement, we quickly dropped homework and moved into action. We were prepared for this inspection, which many businesses complained was harassment. Pa explained, if the restaurant is fined for not meeting the French language requirements, it gets into the newspapers and becomes negative news. "We might as well shut the doors," he said sadly.

The organizer of the group, a big, burly man, videotaped each guest's arrival. His bulky camera had a small tag that read CNN News, which was the logo for the Canadian National News. Pa, dressed in his chef's hat and uniform, served them his homemade wine and appetizers on the house. Business for him was to give the best customer service to each person who came into his restaurant. He knew how to chat up the guests. Since the restaurant's opening, there had been three good reviews in the newspapers, which brought in more pizza lovers and repeat customers.

By the time the Language Police, a man in his mid-forties, arrived at the door, we were in the kitchen, very nervously chopping up vegetables. We watched as Ma greeted him and gave him a menu. He asked for a seat in a far corner and ordered a pizza before he beckoned Pa over to grill him about the French menu. His index finger moved from one item to the next. His eyes squinted as if he were looking through a microscope.

He found it.

The word pizza was not in French. That triggered a nerve in Pa – the one that takes pride in everything Italian. He asked the man to translate pizza into French. Instead, he received a fine which sent him into a tirade of speaking Italian mixed with French, mixed with English, his voice raised, which made the Language Policeman irate. He slapped down noisily another fine on the table, "for not receiving service in French." This got the attention of the reunion group. Displeased with what they thought was a *faux pas*, which spoiled their *joie de vivre* for the evening, they gibed him until he got up and left. One lady threw the fines behind him. The whole affair was filmed by the guy with the CNN video camera.

Pa went back into the kitchen and did what he does best. Make pizzas. The cameraman followed, and asked if could get some shots of him as he worked. Though he wasn't in a good mood, he still smiled as he threw the dough in the air, caught it and stretched it out into the pizza pan.

That night, Om-7 picked up the fight between Ma and Pa. She accused him of being a hot-headed Italian, just when the business was turning itself around. The argument went on and on. The last thing said was they will definitely have to shut down the restaurant. I didn't sleep that night.

The next evening, an excited Mr. Ping called up Pa and

told him to turn on CNN. Montreal Pizza was in the news. Pa in turn shouted this out to Ma, who, in her excitement, shouted back, "CNN is American, we don't have cable." Us kids, doing our homework, heard this back and forth. Exasperated, we all shouted out, "Canadian National News."

It was a short video of the incident as it happened the night before. The newscaster mentioned over and over it was the best pizza he had ever tasted. Later on that evening, other television networks, Canadian and American, showed the same video. The newspapers picked it up the next day with 'Pizzagate' as the heading.

That weekend, there was a line outside of Montreal Pizza that went around the block.

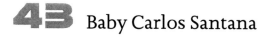 Baby Carlos Santana

Draft of *The Deaf Boy in the Mirror*

'The Biz,' as Pa and Ma now referred to Montreal Pizza, took over their lives. They had to step down as volunteers for the after-school soccer program. Mr. Ibáñez, Che's father, took over both teams, much to Pa's consternation. He voiced the same grievance. The kids would learn to play South American style soccer instead of European style. I think it was his Italian pride taken to another level, as it was obvious he secretly disliked the South American teams because they were very competitive in the World Cup and gave Italy a good run for the esteemed title.

Mr. Ibáñez was a very likeable man. He spoke Spanish and Portuguese fluently, and conversational Franglais. Surprisingly, he knew many Arabic words which made half of the team, who were from the Middle East, very happy. He told us he worked the midnight shift in waste management and his early evenings were always free and there was nothing better he liked to do than coach soccer. BB and I agreed he made soccer so much more fun than Pa did, as he was less competitive; but, of course, we couldn't tell Pa for fear of being labelled traitors.

India returned from the Cayman Islands with seashells for the entire class and a big conch shell for Mademoiselle Cointreau. When she found out I had taken over her sneak job of looking after Che, she gave me a high five. My debut into the world of mischief was rewarded by her secret smiles.

I graduated from stealing food to stealing cold cash.

Pa did not believe in a cashless society so The Biz accepted only cash, which he stashed in a secret belt under his shirt. Once Ma and Pa closed up for the night and came upstairs, they sat on the bed together and counted the money. Through the peephole in the wall, I saw that they placed the cash in an envelope and hid it in the closet before they took a shower together.

On my first heist, I tiptoed into the room and took a five dollar bill.

I was caught red-handed by Jalebi the second time. I had just taken out the wad of bills, when she sneaked up behind me and said "gotcha" in my ears. When she saw me with the bundle of cash, she went ape shit.

"You're stealing? I am telling." She was on the ready to shout out, but then BB heard the little commotion, and he, too, joined the lynching party.

I explained about Che's family and where the money was going. With the fear of the punishment that lay ahead, I looked down at my feet and felt the tears rolling down my face and meeting up with the snots from my nose. When I did look up again, I saw the tears in Jalebi's eyes, for, as much as she would rant at me, she was a softie. BB's eyes also showed concern, for he was just a kind and caring person right down to the bottom of his heart. Without hesitation, they wanted to help and decided they, too, would contribute five stolen dollars every week.

India was exhilarated when she heard the news. We were becoming thick as thieves helping Che's family. We used the code name 'guerilla' for this operation. For three weeks, we pulled it off before the shit hit the fan.

Us kids were doing homework when Mr. Silenzio, a very quiet man, arrived with his bodyguards who looked more like thugs. Previously, they came in weekly. Mr. Silenzio collected the sealed envelope from Pa and left, without a word. On this occasion, the thugs requested a sit-down with Pa and Ma. We were shooed upstairs.

We had our ears glued to the vent. Mr. Silenzio accused Pa of short-paying him – there was fifteen dollars missing from the envelope for the last three weeks and five dollars for two weeks before that.

"That couldn't be." Pa shook his head at this news.

"We both counted the money," Ma added.

More conversation followed sotte voce that we didn't hear clearly. I felt my heart beating heavily, saw the fear in Jalebi's eyes. BB said the f-word. We were frightened.

As soon as they left, we ran downstairs. Through the window, we saw Ma and Pa walking back and forth in the alleyway, deep in discussion. Their faces, eyes and body language told another story – that of being weary, tired and in total disbelief.

When they re-entered through the backdoor, we were seated at the round table, our heads buried in our books. Ma plunked herself down in her chair. Pa pulled out his chair and very slowly sat down. His silence was scary. Usually, when he joined us as we did homework, he brought a glass of ice cubes, which he cracked noisily with his teeth. The cracking sound irritated Ma and she'd tell him off. He, in turn, would touch her cheeks and call her, 'mia amore,' or he would pinch her chin and call her 'my Caribbean Queen.' With a pout and a smile, she would dodge the caresses before she reached over and gave him a loud smacking kiss. "Kids present," we reminded them on those occasions.

Now, he ignored us completely and turned to Ma.

"Is all the family here?"

"All of them that I gave birth to and that you fathered." Ma replied.

None of us said a word. Ma sucked her teeth finally, one of

her bad habits from the old country. "Get to the point, *caro*. We have to make a plan."

Silence is golden, supposedly, but Pa had gone quiet and a quiet Pa was a 'danger warning.' When he finally spoke, I was relieved. Om-7 was ready to fly off the handle with the pressure build-up in my ears.

"Which one of you in this family is stealing?" Pa's glaring eyes bore into us kids, from one to the other. Jalebi and BB looked away. I kept his gaze, until he shook his head and looked at Ma. I held my breath and waited for the blow-up that would make the building foundation shake.

We were saved by the bell. The telephone rang and Ma hurriedly answered the cordless phone she carried around in her apron.

It turned out to be Mrs. Montour. After the Oka crisis, Engine's mother was allowed to move back to the Mohawk community with her family. She wanted to know if we could deliver eighteen large pizzas for a Long House meeting as they didn't have power at Kahnawake and there was a council meeting. And could we do some fried bread and salads. "Sure, sure," I heard Ma answering, barely trying to control her excitement. Once she hung up the phone, she turned to Pa.

"God is watching over us. It is the biggest order for delivery we ever had."

"This discussion is on hold for the moment. By tomorrow night, I want to know which one of you is stealing from the family coffers. Now, all of you, put on your aprons and get busy."

Homework was forgotten as we chopped vegetables, cut and rolled out pizza dough, smeared tomato sauce and decorated the top with pepperoni, green and red peppers, olives and mushrooms. Pa checked the special orders: three with Italian sausage, five with double cheese, and four with anchovies – all ready to go into the oven.

The doorbell chimed in the middle of this as customers filled up all the tables. Pa was in panic as there weren't enough ingredients, and there wasn't enough money to buy the ingredients.

"We won't make it," Pa voiced his worry.

"Yes, we can." Ma said.

"This is how we do it." While she worked, she threw out options, finally throwing up her hands in the air. "We need help. Who can we call?"

"Ghostbusters." BB shouted out.

The backdoor opened and Mr. Ibáñez entered, wiping snow off his boots. He took out an envelope from his pocket. "*Buenas tardes*. Good evening Mr. Colioni. I wanted to talk to you."

"Sorry, I can't speak about soccer tonight, Mr. Ibáñez." Pa slid three pans of pizza into the oven.

"It wasn't that. It's about this." He held out an envelope to Pa. I can see my handwriting scrawled across it. A dead giveaway.

Us kids froze as we looked at him, our eyes silently begged him not to do what he was about to.

Thankfully, the doorbell rang again, announcing the arrival of more guests.

"Mr. Ibáñez, please, my husband can't talk about anything right now." She went on to tell him about the big order and the customers and the shortage of ingredients, and no time to spare, all in between making fried bread.

"Let me help, please. I can drive for the ingredients. I have money." Once again, the envelope was raised above our heads.

Us kids held our breath.

Ma made him a list. When he came back, he offered to help with the oven. There is something to be said for "many hands make light work." He was as fast as Pa rolling out dough and boxing the pizzas when they were removed from the oven.

Right on time, the order called in by Mrs. Montour was ready. Ma threw in some of her famous cakes and cookies as extras. Pa brought me along on the delivery run.

Engine was happy with the special pizza that Ma had made

him with his name *Ten-squat-a-way* spelled out in pepperoni.
It took up three lines and it was the first time Ma spelled his
name correctly.

I had never seen a hundred dollar bill until that night. That
was the tip that the Chief of Kahnawake, handed to Pa.

As we drove into the parking lot, I noticed Mr. Ibáñez's van
was still running. The windows were half frosted up. I went
over to look and saw Che inside. He pretended not to see me,
but I knew that he did. His mother lay on the back seat with
her hands on a very large stomach which she rubbed in gentle
circles.

The following evening, we thought the meeting at the
round table was cancelled, as all of the restaurant tables had
been reserved. This was not to be, as Pa called out to us the
moment we returned from school.

"Who has something to tell me?" He asked as soon as were
seated.

We all looked into our cups of chai.

"Well, have you all lost your voices?" His voice was getting
scarier. Pa was never one to spank us for wrongdoing. His bark
was always worse than his bite. Tonight, however, he had the
big three-foot paddle spoon which he used to stir the tomato
sauce beside him. As I had the seat closest to him, all I could
see was the size of it. I was afraid.

Jalebi was the first to raise her hand. "I did."

I looked over at BB. He raised his hand the same time I did.

"Three thieves in *nostra famiglia*." He turned to Ma. "We are
raising crooks."

"Why are you looking at me?" Ma had her eyebrows raised.
"It must be the Italian in them."

"I will make you pay later." Pa wagged a finger at her.

He often said that to her when they had small disagree-
ments, but I never questioned how she paid, nor when was
later, but I can truthfully say that I did not bear witness to this
punishment. Perhaps I was asleep when it was administered.

"Each one of you has one minute to tell why." Even Ma
had a chilly, demanding tone. We all became like Mr. Silenzio,

quiet. I had to break the silence. I coughed, covered my mouth and when I moved my hands away, I knocked the paddle spoon onto the floor and, as a safe-guard, pushed it under the table with my foot.

Jalebi, as usual, could not hold up. She spilled out the entire story. Both Pa and Ma's expressions changed from wanting to punish us to that of concern for the family. I added that they live in a van and I think Mrs. Ibáñez is having a baby.

"*Dio Mio*, no one lives in a car. Not in Canada, said Pa

Ma started to ask questions. Where do they park their van? How do they shower? Do they have a change of clothes?"

"It is going to be a really cold night tonight. They will freeze," Ma said, her voice heavy with worry.

"India knows where they sleep," Jalebi piped in. "I can call her."

Once Pa had a possible location, he was dressed and out the door in no time at all.

When he returned with the family, we cheered. A shame-faced Che looked down at his feet. It was only when Ma placed a plateful of food in front of him that he looked up. Afterward, she led them upstairs. Mrs. Ibáñez was so pregnant she had trouble climbing the stairs. There, they enjoyed their first shower in a month.

That night, I heard a sad story. A story that my eleven-year-old mind questioned and answered: This should never happen in a First World country.

Ω   Ω   Ω

Last summer, the Ibáñez family, who had moved from Brazil to Mexico, came with a special workforce to pick tomatoes in the farmlands of Quebec. Once the work contract terminated, Mrs. Ibáñez, who was pregnant at the time, became ill and they had to stay in Montreal. She was turned away at the hospitals because she didn't have the required coverage for medical care, nor the money to pay for it. It turned out Mr. Ibáñez was indeed into waste management. Unemployed, and with no excess money, he had to forage into garbage cans in the shopping malls to feed his family. During the day, Mr. Ibáñez moved his wife from one shopping mall to another for warmth.

Che did not have a little brother. He imagined the unborn baby to be a little brother. His mother, because she could not get proper care for her pregnancy, or because she couldn't stomach food, ate only ketchup with bread. Whatever money they had saved from working as tomato pickers was used to pay for gas.

That night, the family slept in the bedroom and my parents slept with us on the mattress. It was a tight squeeze. We were all awakened to the sounds of Mrs. Ibáñez's moans, which sounded as if she was in great pain. Ma rushed into the room, came out and whispered to Pa, "It's that time. Go fire up the stove and boil water." Che joined us on the mattress. It lasted only half an-hour before we heard a baby crying.

"*Es un niño.* It's a boy." Mr. Ibáñez rushed out the room to announce. He was half crying, half laughing.

"What will you call him?" Pa asked.

He held his head to one side, deep in thought. "I want to name him after the great musician, Carlos Santana."

Later in the week, as the family settled down, Pa asked Mr. Ibáñez about the baby's name.

"See," he explained, "I named my first born after a man who fought for equality but was misunderstood, the great Ernesto Che Guevara. For my second born, I chose someone who is still fighting for equality, but is making good music, too."

I held the baby one day and, when he started crying, I sang a song that Ma and Pa sang to us kids, when we were very little. Che joined in. It was the only time he didn't stutter.

44 Wrestle Mania

ANOTHER USELESS writing day – my nadir, I concluded, as I stared at the blank screen. My stars are not lined up. Maybe this writing dream of mine was an unattainable zenith, same as that of a homeless person dreaming of a mansion. With India's return and the change from night-time to day-time writing, I was experiencing a case of disrupted circadian rhythm. My body clock was not adjusting well. The last chapters I wrote were drafted before her arrival.

I did all the right things, I think. I started the day with a satisfactory breakfast, jogged along the beach with Chewy to get the adrenalin flowing, showered, planted myself in front of the monitor, and stared into space. Today, like yesterday, words do not form themselves into coherent sentences, and sentences do not flow into paragraphs that fill up pages. Without pages, there are no chapters.

It was not India's fault. She had changed, mind you, and she had a lot on her mind. She didn't want to talk, and insisted I finish the memoir. The book had become an invisible wall between us.

Also, Kwame's visit threw me off with what he had to say about Dr. O'Ligue, which made me less suspicious of her and our time together in therapy.

Fishing was always a good break, as it took so little brainwork.

Moving along different sections of the pier, I kept baiting and throwing in line after line. An hour later and still no bites. I moved along the shore and went into the water waist deep and, finally, I felt the push and pull on the bait. It was pretty heavy when I pulled it up. I whistled when I saw the size of the curved body. The darn fish was fighting, really fighting. It took all my concentration to keep him on line.

"Colioni, you deaf and dumb?" The voice caught me off guard. I turned around slowly.

Engine was dressed in Bermudas and a cut-off T-shirt.

"I called out to you three times," he shouted against the waves. As I was not expecting him, I let the line drop and heard it go down with a plop.

"Come out here," he called. It had tones of aggression and challenge, none of which I liked.

"No, you come out here," I answered in the same tone.

"If I come out there, I will bust your ass."

I shrugged my shoulders. At least, we were now on semi-speaking terms. I returned to the fish and line. The fish had won. The line was bare. Interested to see how this would work out, I walked toward him, my shoulders square, all alpha male, ready for the confrontation.

He waited.

As soon as my feet touched the sand, he charged and drove his head into my abdomen. We both fell into the sand. I figured out his game quickly. Wrestling was his passion and he had a whole lot more experience than I did. When we were teenagers, he trained at the Kahnawake Survival School and was their champion for several years running. He had been trained by Tatanka, a famous Native American Indian wrestler and so he had the strength and moves to take down his opponent very easily.

He rolled and I rolled with him, feeling the gritty bits of coral digging into my arms. He got up and I did a "rolling thunder," but it didn't quite work out for me as, when I sprang into the air, he let out his Mohawk call of the wild and I was back in the sand, not quite prepared for the "big splash," just feeling the weight of two hundred and twenty pounds of solid muscle. There was no referee to count so it seemed forever before he moved and wrapped his legs around me, crossed his ankles and tightened his grip by squeezing them together. He reached up to get hold of my arms, but I grabbed his head. He managed to get out of this and held on to mine. The "cobra" was his favorite finish and I was ready. I counted slowly, let him feel comfortable and then I twisted, stood up and steadied myself. He was fast on his feet, and I didn't have a second to contemplate his next move, nor dodge it. He "bear-hugged" me.

Under the strain, I looked up at him and saw the laughter in his eyes, yet his hold didn't slacken.

"So, are you gonna kiss me now?" I croaked at him.

He released me then. "You just not my type. Too much man."

"You know I just dropped the biggest catch I have had in a while. That was my supper. You just have to reciprocate in a big way and buy me dinner."

"Are you inviting a gay guy out to dinner? That's just so damn suggestive."

I felt gratified and, despite the stress of writer's block these past few days, I rejoiced, knowing that Engine was a bigger man than me. I touched Om-7 to see if he was all right. I had not been in a tussle where he was a participant in a long time. He was fine, firmly hugging my ear and doing his tap dance sequence – an indication that he was happy.

Engine asked about India, and I explained her outing with Carlos.

"Actually, Carlos is the reason I am here. My first assignment turns out to be the complex case of a minor left in the care of his older brother and two families I have known for a long time. What are the chances of this happening?"

"Geez, Engine, you sound like a high-profile lawyer," I joked.

"Screw you," he responded. "Let's go for a pizza."

I left a note for India, while Engine returned his calls.

Ω Ω Ω

"Nothing like your Pa's pizza," Engine commented as we chomped into slices of pizza.

"Yup, my Pa's pizza will always be the best in my books."

We eventually returned to his first assignment.

"Remember, I said I knew Ernesto from someplace when we met him that first time?"

I shook my head.

"Turns out we both know him."

Engine told me a story that pieced together The Ibáñez family's life.

Mrs. Ibáñez' health worsened after she gave birth to the baby. Since the family didn't have legal papers to stay in Canada, Pa asked Engine's father, Mr. Montour, for legal advice. He didn't have this kind of experience, but he referred a top-notch immigration lawyer, Mrs. Shoshana Weinberger, who happened to be India's adopted mother.

Mrs. Montour, seeing the woman so ill, took the Ibáñez family to Kahnawake where she was nursed by the healers and bush medicine. When she was well enough to travel, Mrs. Weinberger and Mrs. Montour made arrangements for the family to travel to Miami, Florida, crossing the US-Canadian border through Mohawk land.

In Florida, the Ibáñez family eventually settled in a little town called Hollywood, where many Montrealers spent the winter months. Mr. Ibáñez saw a good opportunity and opened a Montreal Pizza in a hole-in-the-wall place, with money contributed by an unknown source. When the Montrealers saw something that reminded them of home, Mr. Ibáñez's business grew and expanded. He opened a Montreal Smoked Meat in another place called Boca Raton, where more snow-birds from Canada vacationed. He also started to make Montreal-style bagels. Soon, he started to package these items for sale through local stores.

Mr. Ibáñez didn't stop there. Where there was a dollar to be made, he put in the time and worked hard. Good luck came his way when a cruise ship line contracted him to supply frozen pizzas and bagels. His hard work paid off. He became a millionaire, invested wisely and stashed the leftovers in investments handled by the law firm Maple & Maple in the Cayman Islands.

"That's some story," I remarked.

"It gets better," he said.

"The only people in Montreal he kept in touch with were

Mrs. Weinberger and your parents. A year ago, Mr. and Mrs. Ibáñez sold all their assets in Florida and returned to Brazil for a visit, leaving their two sons behind. Sadly, while there, they were killed in a car accident. Ernesto brought Carlos to Cayman Island while he waited for the will to be finalized. There are notes in the file that indicate the condo in The Nexx Complex, where they now live, was sold to them by Dr. O'Ligue's deceased husband and, get this, so was the condo where you are currently staying and several others around the Caribbean. The papers have disappeared, or were never finalized and, since it was a cash transaction, it will take twice the time to get through the paper trail."

"Wow," I was actually getting goose bumps.

"There's more. The Ibáñez's will has some stipulations. Ernesto cannot touch the money until he's twenty-five, which he will be in four months' time. Two families, Mr. and Mrs. Weinberger, and Mr. and Mrs. Colioni, are named executors, or, in their absence, any of their children who attain the age of twenty-five. And, since they are absent, this means India or you, or your brother, for that matter, can execute on the estate. Then, it becomes disturbing, as Mr. Ibáñez modified the will just before he left for Brazil. It had the same stipulations and added Dr. Olga O'Ligue as the next person to be an executor of the estate in the event that the two families previously named are unable to commit."

As Engine told this part of the story, I remembered the hungry Ernesto, who we all knew as Che at the Immigrant School, eating Dara Singh's leftover chapattis from the garbage can in the toilette.

"Another thing, Mr. Ibáñez had hoped to retire in this paradise, so he started investing here. He owns four restaurants so far, including the one where Ernesto now works."

"Don't you remember Ernesto stuttering in school?" I asked.

"I didn't go to The Immigrant School. I am a Native Canadian by seven generations," Engine reminded me.

"Well then, how do you know him?"

"You're not listening. They stayed in Kahnawake when the mother was sick. It was your parents who drove them to our house before my mother took charge. And yes, I remembered Ernesto stuttering. He started to sing this song which he said you taught him and it helped him to overcome his speech impediment."

'So, what happens now?"

"Well, either you, your brother, or India has to step up and help them out until Ernesto is of age or Dr. Oligue gets the job. If I could, I would do all that can be done to stop her involvement in this. She's already up to her neck with her deceased husband's estate." Engine looked at me questioningly. "You seem hesitant. It's not a hard job. They are really struggling as the estate is frozen until someone commits. It's only four months."

"Does India know?" I asked.

"No. She doesn't. Neither does your brother."

"So, why did you honor me with the privilege of being the first to know?"

"Because I felt like seeing you and wrestle an apology out of you. Just for fun. That night I came out, it was the only time in my entire life that I needed a friend. When I found out from Dara Singh that you were down and out in the Caymans, I fast-forwarded the job interview so I could be here for you."

"I . . . I." Once again I am stilted for words. Om-7 zinged. I blew out air. "Sorry, bro. I have been . . ." I trailed off again.

"An asshole? With sausage fears to boot. We have had too much mileage as friends. You, me, India. Just can't let me being gay fuck up a friendship."

I nodded like the dumb ass I was.

He changed conversations. "So, how's the memoir coming along?"

I told him about the difficulty of writing. His advice was, "when you start something, finish it, and make sure you tell the story you wish to tell."

He was beginning to sound like my Pa. Eerie.

I heard familiar laughter. Om-7 cooed at the infectiousness. Engine and I turned around. We chuckled quietly as India came through the door. She was followed by Jalebi, who had finally made it out of Africa.

Ω Ω Ω

That night, I took Engine's and my Pa's advice to heart. Finish what I started. I will have to find this in my inner me, I realized, if I am going to tell the story about the next year of my life. My feelings are mixed – that of being a prepubescent boy and that of being a man. It doesn't matter how you slice it, the man you become is always linked, in some way, to the experience of the boy you were.

45 Wes

Draft of *The Deaf Boy in the Mirror*

BB was responsible for my life spiraling downward in the year before I was set to go to high school. It would be my last year at the Immigrant School and I was looking forward to the schoolyard, the teachers, the friends I had not seen during the summer, and India. She had sent a postcard to me from Haifa in Israel where she spent the summer at a Kibbutz with her family. There were xoxo's at the bottom where she had written her name.

At about the same time, Lex Xi and her mother, Mrs. Ping, visited us unexpectedly at the Biz with the worst of bad news. Mr. Ping was diagnosed with terminal cancer. He was Stage 4 and the doctors told them that he would die if he didn't take care of the disease. He was very weak and had to fight daily for his survival.

Even though I was not sick like Mr. Ping, my life took a

nasty turn in stages where I realized that I, too, had to fight daily for my survival.

Stage 1 was when BB started Bickeringsfeld High School, the most reputable English secondary school in West Island. Stage 2 was to be blamed solely on my parents. They finally sorted out the necessary paperwork that exempted us kids from mandatory French school. We now had a new status which allowed us to attend English School. Stage 3 was the cause and effect of Stage 1 and 2.

Bickeringsfeld High School was named after the town where it was located. There was no school bus service from Lachine, which meant BB would have to use public transportation – a two-hour commute. Ma and Pa agreed this was a problem and quickly found a solution. They decided to move to the town of Bickeringsfeld. Jalebi and I would attend an English Primary School within walking distance of our house. Ma would take some time off from Montreal Pizza until we were settled in.

Another town, another house, another school, was too tedious a job for me. I complained about how unfair it was. It didn't matter that Lex Xi moved the previous year and lived close by, went to the same school and would be in the same grade. I told Ma and Pa that, in general, people think Bickeringsfeld to be the utmost in snobbery among all the other towns in Waste Island. As a compromise, they said Jalebi and I could have a sleepover with our old friends from the Immigrant School.

Stage 4 started as a skin itch on my first day at English school.

The entire grade six students were lined up in the corridor with Miss Louise, the teacher at the front. I was last in line. Lex Xi stood next to me. This was her second year at the English school and she hated it.

I noticed something right off the bat. I was different. Ma always said I was lucky, as God had kissed me with a full-time suntan. Today, I questioned His thought processes. I didn't much like the style in which He did stuff, as He sure messed up the world playing around with who could be what – and He got way too personal with my family and, more so, with me.

For starters, He had his people write and preach how mankind should love each other and how they should go forth and spread their seed. Pa had literally followed this to the T. Falling in love with Ma and spreading his seed. Except the seedlings, us kids, fell into a non-linear spectrum. He didn't tie things up nicely, this God fella, He shortchanged my brother BB and that's why he is off-white. My sister Jalebi received enough kisses that she was like chai with just the right amount of milk. And me, He kissed way too much that I was almost a burnt-bronzed brown.

Lex Xi kicked me gently on my shin. I looked at her with annoyance, as any kick from her was dangerous. She had rights to attend the English school because her parents were from British Columbia where the Rocky Mountains are. She was a mountain girl and not to be trusted. She can kick like a mountain goat. She had a title to prove it. She was currently Canada's girls-under-twelve karate champion.

I realized that I stood to be corrected. Lex Xi was also different.

My thoughts strayed from how different Lex Xi and I were, as Miss Louise explained that there were two grade six classes and she would point us to the respective classroom.

"I hope I don't get her. She's mean," Lex Xi mouthed.

"Who? Miss Louise? She seems nice," I whispered. Lex Xi rolled her eyes.

From her list, Miss Louise barked out a name. No one responded. I hesitated when she called out "Kaman" next, before I stepped forward.

"Oh, so you're Kaman," her head moving up and down as she inspected me. "It rhymes with Cayman – like Cayman Island." She seemed to think it was funny, because she laughed and this made some, not all, of the kids laugh. I decided, then and there, that I didn't like her.

As she continued to call out names, a tall, skinny kid ran through the corridor, dragging his schoolbag. He took a place in line next to me. He was different as well. He was a whole head taller than me and everyone else waiting in line.

"Wes Beier. You will not be late this year. Understand?" Miss Louise snarled at him.

The gangly kid apologized and explained it was his brother's Justin's first day of school and he had had to take him to his classroom. She gave him a stern look and a second warning.

When she returned to her list, Wes whispered to me, "I hate this b-" I knew what he was going to say. I turned to look at him and he smiled at me. He wore braces over his buckteeth.

"Ssshhh, she can hear you," Lex Xi kicked Wes on his ankle. Her name was called next and she was directed to the other grade six. Wes and I ended up with Miss Louise. The classroom was nicer than those in the Immigrant School. Above the blackboard, a poster proclaimed the school's motto in bold, capital letters, "VIOLENCE IS PROHIBITED."

School wasn't too bad that day as most of my classes were in English, which was cool because it was our spoken language at home. I had two French classes, but since I already had completed five years of French school, my written and spoken French was quite good. I got bored, and I have to explain that anyone can doze off if they have to listen to Miss Louise's monotone voice, as she mispronounced French words. I began to correct her, not that I was a show-off or anything, but if someone does something improperly, then it calls for correction.

After school, very pleased with my superior performance in the French class, I met up with Jalebi and Lex Xi at the school gate. They were both bitter. Lex Xi said Kent Whitemore, a boy in her class, stretched his eyes toward his ears and mouthed a nasty word to her. Jalebi had tears in her eyes. Two girls asked her why her skin was so dirty colored. This made me so angry. I didn't like it that ignorant kids were making fun of my little sister and my friend because, when they did that, they were also making fun of me. I made a silent vow that I would take care of them, as no one messes with my family and friends and gets away with it. We walked Lex Xi to her house and, as we turned the corner from her street, I heard my name being called. It was Wes Beier. He held his brother's hand as he hurried toward us.

It turned out that he lived a street away from our house. He showed us a shortcut through a vacant lot adjoined to our backyard. The smell of chocolate cake reached me, and I knew it was coming from our kitchen. I ran up the back porch, right into Ma's apron.

"Didn't I tell you to hold your sister's hand all the way home? And why are you walking through the bush? There are two dogs always quarreling at the back."

Wes piped up then. "Hello, madam. I am Wes, and this is Justin, my brother." He flashed his buckteeth-with-braces smile.

"Oh, hello." Ma sized him up. Not shy at all, he walked up the porch and shook her hand.

"You all look tired. Here, sit on the porch and have some chai with brownies."

Wes became my best friend. He came by our house every day and loved Ma's cooking, especially her duck curry. He, in turn, invited me to his house to meet his parents. The next day I asked what they thought about me. I was a bit unsure, as Mr. and Mrs. Beier were second-generation Canadians, pink-skinned and spoke only English. Most of my friends' parents from the Immigrant School were multi-ethnic and multi-lingual with pigmentation that ranged from number 5 to number 11 on the Skin and Hair Color Palette that Ma had taped on the fridge door.

"They liked you. They think you are a decent hybrid."

"What's a hybrid?" I asked him.

"Half-breed. Mixture of two or more kinds. My dad is Austrian and my mom is German. On the map these are two countries. That makes me a hybrid, too."

I am noticeably a mixture with a distinct color, but who

would think Wes, so fair in complexion, with blond hair and blue eyes, would be a half-breed. I mentioned this to him.

"Mixed cultures are like the hybrid cars that inventors are talking about. I saw a program on TV last night." He went on to tell me a fascinating story about cars that functioned on gasoline and diesel. He knew a lot of stuff because he was allowed to watch a lot of television. His parents had a black box that was not quite legal, which picked up many channels on the American network.

"Did you know the British Royal family are hybrids too? They are German and English bloodlines."

"You mean, like, if you mix an Aston Martin and a Porsche?"

46 Lex Xi

Draft of *The Deaf Boy in the Mirror*

Mrs. Ping came to see Ma and Pa at the Biz. She had a dilemma. She would like to take Mr. Ping to China for a special treatment. They had rare magic mushrooms full of antioxidants that could kill cancer cells. The mushrooms were only available illegally in Montreal. She had obtained some on the black market and she found it to be better than the chemo treatment Mr. Ping received at the hospital. She complained that the doctors who treated her husband were arrogant and spoke down to her as if she were stupid. Her predicament was that Lex Xi was in a series of martial arts competitions and they didn't want her to miss them.

Ma and Pa quickly offered to take care of Lex Xi. Jalebi was happy when she moved in, as she now had another best friend. I became her main opponent as she practiced her strikes, blocks and kicks each day. They hurt. A look of absolute bliss shone in her eyes when she flipped me and I lay on the floor in pain. Sometimes, I faked it just to make her happy. I soon learned her moves and could defend myself, but I begrudgingly had to admit that she could really kick ass.

Ma returned to work at the Biz, and we became latchkey kids until she returned to oversee dinner and homework. BB was supposed to babysit us, but he had a girlfriend and spent most of his time making out with her behind the *Dépanneur,* which was the convenience store at the end of the street. He liked high school and spoke often about the *Ninjas,* a group who befriended him when they heard that Lex Xi, who they adored, lived with us.

My first infraction happened because of Om-7. He picked up Kent Whitemore shouting a nasty name at me. Kent's family lived for generations in Bickeringsfeld and his father was a city councillor. He was the most popular sixth grader, and he had a posse of wannabees. No one touched him because he was the nephew of Miss Phillips, the principal. I called Kent something similar and he pounced on me, punching me in the nose. I saw red, reacted, and threw him to the ground. His posse stood around egging him on. Wes quickly intervened and pulled me off.

My life changed dramatically and drastically soon after that. It became an ugly pattern. I hated school. I hated the names that I was called. Every time I looked in the mirror, I saw fresh cuts and bruises – visible marks that I had been in a fight. It never happened on a one-on-one basis, either, as Kent was like a pompous duke, who traveled with an entourage. BB asked me about it and I lied. Ma and Pa noticed and I lied to them, too. Jalebi, for once, didn't tattle. She was scared. Lex Xi said she would take care of Kent once she finished the competitions.

On one occasion, Kent's second-in-command ran behind me and pulled Om-7 off my ear and threw him up in the air. I watched in horror as he fell with a heavy thud. He wasn't broken, but he didn't communicate with me for days after. He was depressed, dejected and disoriented. I could tell someone had crossed the lines. He had been victimized and there was nothing he could do about it. Violence was no longer prohibited.

Lex Xi suddenly became ill – pretend ill – and didn't want to go to school. Jalebi told me the truth.

Kent often made fun of Melissa Mahoney, a sweet-faced, plump girl who was a friend of Lex Xi and a so-so friend of Harper, one of Kent's lower-level minions. Harper was beginning to have guilt feelings about Kent's next move, which was to attack Lex Xi and break her leg before the competitions. He told Melissa about it because he didn't think it was right.

It was frightening. I wanted to tell Ma and Pa, and decided against it, as I would then have to tell the truth about the black eye I had. I had to come up with a plan. But as much as I tried, I couldn't think of one.

Engine came for a sleepover that weekend. When I told him about it, he was outraged. I thought I could trust him, but before the day was over, he had told BB, who then told Wes.

Ω   Ω   Ω

As the date of Lex Xi's competition drew closer, it appeared that Kent had changed his mind. Wes and I kept a close watch over her.

It happened when we least expected it.

Lex Xi and Jalebi were supposed to wait for me outside my class. Instead, a worried Melissa Mahoney met me with news they had decided to walk home through the shortcut and Kent and his posse were following with no good intentions. Wes and I grabbed our coats and ran out. Halfway home, we met up with a breathless Jalebi who told us what was happening.

We heard the ping sounds of Lex Xi as we approached the pathway to the bushes.

Kent stood on the sidelines giving orders. Lex Xi was surrounded by the posse. She kicked and fought, dropped two boys to the ground. She was poised now, in a *mae geri*, a front kick that brought down her opponents in competition. I saw

Kent from the corner of my eye with the iron bar. He had it raised, advancing, and on the ready to strike Lex Xi. I ran into the melee, pushed her to the ground, turned around and rammed Kent in his abdomen. I saw Wes pull Lex Xi up and run toward our house. They had a field day with me alone against them. I couldn't count how many licks and kicks I received until BB arrived with the ninjas.

The buzz in school was how Kent and his posse received a kick-ass from a high school gang of ninjas. That kept him quiet for a while. Within a month, though, his big mouth was once more going strong.

Ma added another newspaper cut-out to the fridge door. It was a half-page write-up about Lex Xi. She had retained her title.

47 The Meaning of Bullying

Draft of *The Deaf Boy in the Mirror*

Good news and bad news arrived on the same day.

The good news came by snail mail from China, more than 10,000 kilometers away. Mrs. Ping wrote to Ma that the magic mushrooms worked on Mr. Ping's cancer. The bad news came from the English school, less than one kilometer away. I would not graduate to high school.

It was the end of the third semester. Time flies and I wasn't even having fun. When I received my report card, there were notes from Miss Louise that I would have to repeat grade six and would not graduate to high school. Ma decided that she and I would have a visit with Miss Phillips, the principal. I sat in the office, wishing to be anywhere else but there, and stared at 'Violence is prohibited" on the wall.

"Mrs. Colioni, did you know that your son has had four

fist fights to date? I have notes that his class teacher sent to you. In the last one, she asked that you acknowledge receipt." Miss Phillips sternly stated as she set the meeting in motion and passed the notes. I saw the confused look on Ma's face, her nostrils flared, as she read them.

"I do apologize. I'm here to address this problem. I'm beginning to question the way your school is handling the course content because I have his old school report cards from grades one to five." She reached into her handbag and unfolded documents. "This one, for example, all the notes are excellent: very good, super work. Here have a look." She passed the report cards to Miss Phillips. "What amazes me is that he barely passed French, and yet, his teacher asked him to stay late, on several occasions, to help the other students with their French homework."

As Miss Phillips thumbed through the report cards, I stole a look at Ma. She was quite controlled now, her nostrils back to their normal size. I was really proud of her and, I have to admit, I loved her for what she was doing. I sank deeper into the chair, ashamed of myself.

"I think if Kaman fails grade six after passing all of his previous grades in other schools, then it can only mean that there is something wrong with the teaching style at this school."

"We've received no complaints from parents about the teaching style in this school. What I have had are complaints about Kaman's fighting. He has been busy in the school yard," Miss Phillips said, her cheeks growing rosier.

"Well, Kaman," Ma turned to look at me. "Why don't you to tell Miss Phillips why you were involved in fights in her school yard."

I wanted to hide, but I looked at Ma and her determined face and how she was indirectly taking my side. Om-7 encouraged me with a tweet. I took a deep breath. "They called me and my sister ugly names, and they said nasty things about my family. So, I called them bad names back, and then they tried to wrestle me down and I gave them the smackdown."

I saw that neither Ma nor Miss Phillips understood the word 'smackdown.'

"I see," Miss Phillips said. "But two wrongs don't make a right, Kaman. If you fight every time someone calls you a name, then you are going to have many fights in your life."

"The issue is not how many fights Kaman will have in his future life, Ma'am, but that there are kids who initiated these fights. Did their parents receive notes?" Ma spoke quietly, and I know from experience, this could be dangerous.

"They have."

"Can I see them?"

"School policy prohibits this," Miss Phillips said sternly.

Ma walked to the motto and pointed to it. "There's a lot of prohibitions in your school, Ma'am, and it's not even the Prohibition Era." She looked tired and beaten up, and her brows wrinkled in deep thought. "Did you know about the name-calling my children have had to endure?"

Miss Phillips creased her brows, before she answered. "Kids do sometimes get into this name calling in the school yard. They are kids. They get over it. It's no big deal."

"It is a big deal. It's called 'bullying.' Do you know the meaning of 'bullying?'" Ma pulled out the red dictionary from her handbag, opened it to a dog-eared page and shoved it with a smack right under Miss Phillips' face. I slunk deeper into the chair, embarrassed as I looked at the dictionary. There were spatters of curry sauce and bits of dried pizza dough on the opened page.

Miss Phillips pushed the dictionary away with, "I don't need to look at this. I have been a headmistress for twenty-five years. I know the meaning of bullying."

"It doesn't look like you do or you would do something about it. I know that Wes Beier reported one incident to you. Maybe, we can call him and find out the real story. We can also ask Melissa Mahoney."

Miss Phillips, her face now apple-red, thought about it, before answering, "Wes did mention that incident to me and it was addressed. The situation is Kaman walked into the fight. Isn't that so, Kaman?" I sank deeper into my seat.

"No," Ma interjected. "What you're saying to me, Miss Phillips, is that my son has to turn his back to all this name calling and brutality, and the kids who are doing this, walk free. It's sounding to me like you're one of those people who believe that if someone slaps you in one cheek, you turn the other cheek. But you see, I am from another belief, the one that will not encourage my child to turn his other cheek. It's plain foolish and stoo-pid."

I moved my feet around, wishing it would end, I know how Ma can go on and on when she gets going. It's this unique part of her that us kids love and hate at the same time.

"Since you are aware of the problem, and we have witnesses, and I feel that it has not been handled adequately, I have no other choice but to take this matter to the school board and the police." Ma sucked her teeth and I was more embarrassed than I was before at this annoying habit she had.

"I see no reason why we should take this case that far," Miss Phillips said quickly. "I will personally speak to all the kids involved and, as a matter of fact, I will speak to all classrooms about this name calling."

"Please do." Ma stood up. I could see how tired she was. "I'll be writing a letter to you about our meeting, just so we have it on record. And, if Kaman does not pass grade six, then I will definitely go to the school board and all other boards until I feel satisfied." Ma picked up the dictionary, tucked it inside her handbag and walked out. Meekly, I followed.

At home, after Ma closed the door and dropped her handbag on the floor, she turned to me. "You want to be a dunce-fied goat? What you wanna be – deaf and dunce for the rest of your life?" She lifted her hand. I flinched and moved my head quickly to one side. Her hand froze in mid-air. For some reason, she didn't engage. She must have seen the tears welling up in my eyes.

"Oh, God. I wish you had told me. They hurt you, didn't

they?" The hand unfroze, wrapped around my neck and pulled me close. "Oh baby, why, why, didn't you tell me?" She cried too.

I had a quarrel with Wes that day, as he had no business tattling to my Ma.

"But I can't lie," he said. That was true, but I was still mad with him for a whole week. As punishment for not passing along the school's notes, Ma and Pa gave me a series of curfews which wasn't too bad. What was worse was being banned from watching the hockey play-offs. I also had to do double-time homework every weeknight during my last semester. Fortunately, Wes and BB helped me with the homework package and taped the hockey games for me to watch on weekends.

I missed another event I would have given my eye teeth to witness. It happened on the last day of school, outside the school yard, by the front gates. Melissa Mahoney socked Kent Whitemore one on the kisser. His posse didn't lift a finger to help him after he fell, so she straddled him and punched him as if he were a bean bag while everyone cheered her on. It just goes to show there is always a bigger bully.

The reason I missed this grand finale was that I opened the envelope with my report card and saw that I passed grade six. I ran all the way home, tears streaming down my face.

I had made it to high school.

PART 3

Some men see things as they are, and say, 'Why?'
I dream things that never were, and say, 'Why not?' "

George Bernard Shaw

48 The Gov's House

GOVERNOR WEDGEWOOD sank back on a lilo and floated away from the beach. Once she had reached some distance, she took a sip from the water bottle that held her drink, a *Mudslide*. Her face screwed up at the taste and, as she looked at the contents through the clear plastic bottle, she muttered, "This is my life, bloody muddy." She was not one who started and never finished anything, so she sucked on the straw until the bottle was empty. "That's how you deal with a mudslide, take control," she said angrily to the empty container.

Using her hands as a paddle, she slapped the water vigorously and steered the lilo in the direction of the port. It was hard to miss the two super yachts, *The Orchid* and *The Gypsy*, rocking gently in the four o'clock sun. Several super yachts had dropped anchor in the last weeks, stayed a few nights and moved on, except for these two. She remembered then that Shizu Katsu, The Orchid's owner was here because of the casino project. And Roman Romanov, owner of The Gypsy, what was he up to?

Governor Wedgewood took a deep breath and did a root cause analysis of her problems. It all boiled down to one source: MI7 – trying to program her with what and what not to do! How can she perform her duties as a ROBOT when she was expected to act like a robot? Seriously, they were taking their own word linkage too far.

What brought her to this state of vexation was MI7's

insistence on installing security cameras everywhere, from the
bedroom to the bathroom, from the grounds to the garage and
inside the kitchen. Bloody hell, there's no end to the invasion of
her privacy. If that wasn't enough, she was given a work list to
follow. It was at this stage that Governor Wedgewood realized
she had to put her foot down or become MI7's puppet.

Her schedule in the last two weeks had been tight. On week-
days, she followed MI7's agenda of meetings with government
departments and did write-ups of each one, followed with her
own personal in-depth analysis. She was beginning to dislike the
word "analyze."

In the evenings, she made three public appearances and met
people of interest. The first was the opening of a drug rehabilita-
tion center set up by United and Unified. The second was the
opening of a new seniors' home sponsored by The Church for
Society's Improvement. The third was a charity dinner organized by Æsa Hleið, the gorgeous model who was a spokes-
person for breast cancer. Here, she met, for the first time, the
Russian billionaire Roman Romanov who flirted outrageously
with her. Shizu Katsu had been in attendance and made a generous donation.

On her to-do list, she had decided on a smaller, but similar
fountain as the model in Camana Bay and found a landscaping
company owned by a retired Trinidadian agronomist who came
highly recommended. She hadn't gotten around to buying cotton
panties, but she found costumes for herself and Kara for the
upcoming Pirates Week Ball. The casino project was still up in
the air and the mental facility, her personal project so dear to her
heart, had not taken off as she hoped. Letters requesting donations came back with small offerings. The most generous so far
had been from Roman Romanov with an offer to match whatever she collected. Æsa Hleið telephoned with an exclusive offer.
She can do a fashion show, just let her know when. Shizu Katsu
dropped by her office with the promise of a very big donation if,
she, Governor Wedgewood, would help her to convince the locals
that a casino would boost employment on the island.

The only good news came in a small package. She had interviewed a Dr. Khalil Kaleb Kwame, who was willing to work for a small salary. She hired him on the spot at her own expense.

Governor Wedgewood bared her teeth and whispered, "I will not give up on this project." With renewed determination, she scrawled notes on her notepad:

1. Be aggressive. Send e-mails instead of letters.

2. Find a tech geek who's willing to work long hours.

She scratched off the first item and quickly texted a message to Carlos: *Can you meet me behind the Gov's House ASAP? Just had a brilliant idea. Need your help.*

She received a response immediately: *For sure, Señora Governor.*

Before coming out to the beach, she had met with the renovations' foreman and saw the progress firsthand. As soon as the alarm system and the security cameras were wired in, they would paint, then move to the grounds. She explained it had to be ready because the governor always hosted a Pirates Ball on the lawns. He gave his word the landscaping crew would work day and night to have everything in place.

She shifted to the conversation she had with Kara this morning as they sat having breakfast on the balcony. Kara waved to a man sitting on a balcony in the opposite block.

"That's Ten-squat-a-way. My Mohawk friend. I had lunch with him yesterday in town. He works a block from the Tortuga Cake Shop."

Emma squinted her eyes. "My, he's handsome."

"He is. I met a French fella yesterday. A friend of Ten-squat-a-way's. Later on, two female friends joined them. They had names that made me laugh. One is named India and the other, Jalebi."

"Did you say India and Jalebi?"

"Yes. I know what you're thinking. Jalebi is a dessert from India. Scrummy, love it." Kara smacked her lips. "Remember Kaman, the deaf man I befriended who was in jail. Well, India is his girlfriend and Jalebi is his sister. He has a brother named

Biig Baba, whom I haven't met. Do you know who stopped by? The model Æsa Hleið and Lex Xi Ping. Lex Xi is the world's top female karate champ. There's eleven friends and they get together every year for a bonfire for one of their friends who was murdered. I still haven't met them all, but I know their names. One has a bible name, Jacob and the other one is Khalil who is a doctor. And there's Dara Singh." Kara jabbered on as she drank tea from the dainty china cup.

Her mood changed as she put the cup down with a clatter. "They have all been friends since they met in primary school. They told funny stories about each other when they were young. I envy them. I don't even have a friend from college," Kara said sadly.

"You're making friends, Kara, and that's an upswing. You must not give up hope, darling. You will get better. I know you will," Emma-the-mother consoled, her heart breaking at the same time.

"Does anyone ever get better from mental illness, mother? I'd rather not think about it."

Emma changed conversations. "So, tell me. Is the French guy from Paris?"

"No, he's French Canadian. Half English, half French with the most unusual name – Toussaint les Patants. I didn't know they had such a big French-speaking population in Canada."

Emma thought of telling her daughter about the Seven Years War between the French and English, known as the French and Indian War in American History. She let it ride. Kara was so fragile. Wars upset her.

"Mother, did you know the Heights of Abraham, not far from York, was supposedly named after a battle between the English and French on the Plains of Abraham in Quebec, Canada?"

A surprised Emma turned to Kara. "Well, how do you know this?"

"There is a plaque in the visitor's room at the Heights of Abraham." Kara lay back in the lounge chair, closed her eyes and, just like that, shut her mother out.

As Emma thought about that morning, she wished she had a

crystal ball that would make her understand how her daughter can be so brilliant in some things and just messed up in others.

She heard water swishing and turned to look. The new diving instructor had just arrived on a beach tricycle and was organizing the diving gear for the lesson she would take later in the day. When she advertised for a personal certified diving instructor, she didn't think a professional cyclist, a very fit one, would apply for the job. She waved to Yaacov Ben Tzion.

She saw Carlos arriving with his backpack. "Hola, Señora Governor," Carlos shouted out to her from the pathway close to the house. "I'm here."

That same night, Governor Wedgewood checked out Kara's new friends on social media. They all had excellent profiles. She was quite surprised to see Yaacov Ben Tzion and Dr. Khalil Kaleb Kwame were also friends of Kara's other new friends. She was worried for nothing.

49 The Runaway

"I LOVE THE HEART YOU put into the stories of when we were kids. It takes me back to that place and time. The Immigrant School was just the best. So much laughter, so much fun, and all the different cultures under one roof. The smell of exotic food in the cafeteria was just out of this world. Do you realize most of our friends are from this period of our lives?" India said as we watched a heron dive from the pier into the water for its morning feed. She had offered to edit the finished chapters. From the look on her face, she was amused.

"You like?" I asked, a bit nervously.

"You have to continue. There's more stuff when we were teenagers."

"What will you do?"

"I will continue to edit," she said quietly. "Seriously, I want you to write about me. Don't hold back."

I spent that day thinking of how to write about India, a defenseless little girl who had no say as she was shuffled from adoption to foster home and back to adoption, her life manipulated by a system. Since her return in the last week, she had shared snippets of her teenage years with me in a disjointed manner. I realized then she had blocked out these memories and opening up to me was her way of cleansing herself. She finally told me about that time she ran away and ended up in the United States.

It was a harsh period of her life, and, at times, very ugly.

Ω   Ω   Ω

India and Jalebi had remained best friends throughout my family's move from one town to another. She often slept over on weekends when we settled in Bickeringsfeld. Every so often, she stared at nothing, her face a mask and her eyes blank. She didn't seem to like many things in life except swimming. Adult authority brought out the worst in her, except for Ma, with whom she had a special bond.

She hated the private high school she attended, and started on a rebellious route in her early teenage years. It peaked when she turned sixteen. Her parents gave her a sweet sixteen birthday party at a prestigious golf clubhouse to which I was invited. She wore a black dress that flowed to the floor with gold trimmings and a revealing slit on the skirt that showed her legs as she moved. Tiny gold flowers around the neckline brought out the color of her eyes. The bird's nest had been coiffed into ringlets. She was dazzling. All my friends who were there said she was 'hot.'

It was a non-alcoholic event that was supposed to end at midnight under the strict eyes of the manager. India had made other plans. She invited some of her older guy friends who were of legal drinking age and who brought their own bottles. They arrived tipsy and were soon embroiled in a petty dispute that quickly became an all-out brawl. The underage kids saw an opportunity, seized the bottles of booze, discarded in favor of fight, and indulged in the forbidden. When the cops arrived, they were smart enough to run, myself included.

She was grounded by her parents and cut off from all contact with friends. After two weeks of being a prisoner, she stole a wad of money from her parents' safe and ran away. The Weinbergers hired a private detective who had no luck finding her. The stress caused them to split up. Mrs. Weinberger stayed in Montreal and her husband went overseas.

Months later, India showed up at our house. She was very ill, emotionally and physically, with an addiction. She had replaced Ritalin with other prescription drugs.

Mrs. Weinberger begged Ma to convince India to return home. India wouldn't hear of it. Finally, the two mothers agreed she could stay with us. Our home life changed as Ma was now coming home earlier to take care of her ward. I once asked her why, and she replied, "That child has had so much sadness in her life. It just isn't fair."

The India I knew, who was so filled with energy, and who gave anyone and everyone who dared to cross her path a good mouthful, was now a glassy-eyed phantom who lived in sweat clothes and slept all day. All of our common friends came by to cheer her up. The only time she seemed content was when she cuddled with Lady, our pet dog who she carried around like a baby.

Being in the same house and so close to India played on my mind. I began to have feelings for her that were beyond friendship. It had always been there, but now it surfaced in different ways.

Mrs. Weinberger sought help from her sister, Dr. Olga O'Ligue, who, at that time, hosted a radio and television show. I noticed that India cringed from the very first visit. It was obvious she didn't like her aunt. I returned home early from school one day and found her alone, sucking her fingers and crying. She didn't remove them when I sat down next to her on the sofa.

"I have to go back home or go live with my aunt, Dr. O'Ligue." Her body rocked back and forth as she sobbed. I moved closer to comfort her and she slumped on my shoulders.

"Why?"

"Because I am not yet eighteen. The other choice is to go into foster care again."

India agreed, in the end, to live with Dr. O.

It didn't work out. India ran away again at the beginning of summer. She lived in the streets of Vieux Montreal. Here, she met Kayla, a visiting street artist from San Francisco who wanted to learn French, enjoy the jazz and comedy Festival, and eat poutine while she sketched tourists on the go for a living. In her mid-twenties, she, herself, had run away as a teenager. She took India under her wing. They soon formed a partnership. India would show Kayla the places and things she wanted to see and, in return, Kayla gave her a place to stay. At the end of that summer, they boarded the cross-border bus to San Francisco.

Kayla, street smart and experienced in living alone, took charge once they arrived. She showed India where to sleep, where to get food, how to hide and who to avoid in case there was trouble. The best thing India learned from her was how to draw, how to use colors and light, how to hold her brush at certain angles to paint the sea lions that frolicked in the Bay, and where to frame and sell her sketches. Kayla was a kind sort who hung out with a bad sort. The not-so-good thing was she introduced India to cocaine.

With fluency in four languages, India soon found a part-time job as a tour guide. Meeting people from around the world made her realize there was more to life than being a drug addict. By her seventeenth birthday, she had cleaned up and was slowly getting back on her feet. Her whole world shattered, however, when she returned to the apartment after work one evening to find that Kayla had been stabbed to death in a coke deal gone wrong. Quickly, she packed her bags and left, reporting the crime from a public phone booth.

Devastated, India fell off the wagon. San Francisco, a beautiful city by a port with two big bridges, reminded her of Montreal; but it was expensive. Not even the extra income she earned selling her sketches of the Golden Gate Bridge and Twin Peaks provided the money she required for her living expenses and drug habit. She soon found a way.

India often ate in Chinatown, revered as the best in North America. She became aware of a thriving market for 'snow.' She began hanging out there daily and found out that 'white dragon,' 'Yao sugar boogers' and 'devil's dandruff' were other names that floated around for cocaine.

Limousines stopped and passengers attracted by her exotic looks and curvy figure propositioned her for sex, but that wasn't her thing. India preferred to trade in coke rather than her body, and she was doing extremely well. One of her regular customers, a director of a television series, purchased coke for his entire cast and crew and that, alone, paid her rent.

On one of her trading days, someone called out her name. She stopped in her tracks as she recognized the voice and slowly turned around to greet Lex Xi who introduced her to Tommy Lee, a cousin from New York. Tommy invited her to join them for dim sum. During the meal, she found out that Lex Xi was in town for a martial arts competition that would last a week, and she insisted on seeing more of India. India was worried her whereabouts would become known back home. She confronted Lex Xi, who answered, "Who are you? I never met you before."

India attended all the events, along with Tommy. A handsome mix of Chinese and Irish-American, in his mid-thirties, she found him to be intelligent and worldly. He told her he was a business-man with clients in Silicon Valley and would be in town for an indefinite stay. When Lex Xi won the title, he took them both out to the most expensive restaurant to celebrate. After Lex Xi returned to Montreal, she saw more of him, not by choice, but more accidentally as he remained a constant presence in Chinatown during her trading hours.

She was hesitant when he asked her out on a date, not want-ing to get involved, but he was persistent. It had been a long time since she felt so comfortable in the company of an older man and soon confided passages of her life, though not all. He didn't mind she was only seventeen, a runaway, and addicted to cocaine. He was, himself, a small-time user. He fed her coke habit, and her ego with shopping trips to expensive boutiques where he dropped money on designer clothes and accessories. On the weekends, he took her out in his Maserati to nice restaurants, trips to the vineyards in the Sonoma and Napa Valleys. She thought he was a real gentleman because he didn't make sexual advances toward her.

A month after wining and dining her, Tommy started to ask India a lot of questions. Did she have a valid passport? Could she travel to Europe? Would there be problems if she returned to Montreal? He had heard so much about her hometown from Lex Xi and would like to visit. Some days later, he propositioned her with an all-expenses-paid trip to Europe. They travelled separately and met up in Paris, where they spent a week eating baguette sandwiches and drinking wine in outdoor cafes along The Champs-Élysées. He knew she liked art and took her to the museums. India was in seventh heaven. Her love for the arts increased, and she knew this is what she wanted to do for the rest of her life.

The next stop was Amsterdam. Tommy gave her a separate ticket and met up with her a day later. On the third night, he announced he had to return to New York, but he needed her to do him a favor. Could she go to Montreal and drop off some packages for him? He would meet her there in a week. India started to get suspicious and questioned him about the packages. He was evasive. By this time, she figured out that he was using her as a mule. She confronted him and demanded a payoff. She kept thinking of how Kayla had been slashed up for coke and she was starting to feel a need to clean up and be somebody, not a junkie. She knew she had the skill set to be a linguist or an artist. She promised herself this would be the last 'worst' thing she ever did.

If she made it, she would go to the rehab mountain retreats scattered in Quebec. She didn't want to think about the consequences if she got caught. The night before the trip, she had definite plans for her future – make the drop and get Tommy out of her life. She knew the street value of cocaine and, when she demanded five thousand dollars upfront and another five after delivery, he didn't fuss. In the taxi to the airport, he handed her a quilted jacket heavy with the goods, which she had to wear throughout the trip, and a cell phone. Someone would contact her once she arrived in Montreal.

India started to sweat the moment she entered Schiphol Airport. When she saw the restaurant with the blue and white teacup and teapot display with matching chairs, she stopped to recollect her thoughts and remembered we had met there two years ago. We were both headed to England – she on a trip to meet up with *Æsa* and I to meet up with Dara Singh. It had been a very memorable afternoon. She snapped a picture and sent it to me.

I texted back: *Where are you?*

Ω   Ω   Ω

The India who walked toward me at the airport was now a woman dressed so elegantly I did a double take. She wore a black jacket over a pretty beige sweater with skinny jeans tucked into leather boots.

She was surprised when I called out her name and she recognized me. I opened my arms and saw her eyes well up in tears. As I held her, I knew right then she had fallen off the tracks. I found out she had no home to go to as her mother had moved to Nepal. Ma said it was all right for her to come stay with us.

The next day, I noticed how often her cell phone vibrated, but she didn't respond. I checked it out when she was taking a shower. It was a private number. I stole the phone and took it to Engine who had friends with the smarts to decipher and track phone numbers. It was the listing of a restaurant in Chinatown. I confronted India. She broke down and told me about Amsterdam and Tommy Lee. Jalebi and BB were there. We all agreed it was way above our heads. It was time to go to Pa.

Pa knew the restaurant's owner very well. He took the jacket and returned with five thousand dollars in cash but didn't give it to India. He wanted her to go to rehab and if she came out clean, he promised he would pay for any schooling she wanted.

That was early September, 2001. Soon, television screens everywhere carried endless scenes of the 9/11 attack on the Twin Towers in New York. Later Lex Xi found out Tommy Lee was on the 95th floor of the World Trade Center's north tower. Nine days later, we lost our friend, Wes, in a familicide.

We all went into shock as we heard the news that Wes was no longer with us. I think India and I turned to each other as we knew the pain of losing a close friend. She never went to rehab. She asked my parents if she could stay with us until she sorted herself out, and they agreed. She kept her word and moved out a year later.

'We' didn't happen overnight. As soon as she settled in her apartment, she invited me over for dinner and a movie. Dinner was awful. The movie *Jungle Fever* was awesome. I don't remember much of what it was about. I was busy.

Om-7 took notes that night. Whenever he hears the name *Spike Lee*, he taps into my head with, 'He's the director of movie. The one you didn't watch when you pulled an all-nighter. Remember that time you and she went at it from 7:00 p.m. to 7:00 a.m."

Except for the few weeks when she went off to find herself, she has been my girl.

5️⃣0️⃣ The Gambler

"CHICO, I know, me and you, we had something. From the first time I saw ya, I feel it here." Carlos fisted his hand over his heart. He was clowning around now that we were alone. "I wish India was here too."

"India has an online interview. I'm here."

"Chico, ya always thinking. Too much serious. Ya not fun like India. She is nice to look at too."

Jalebi had organized this reacquaintance lunch at Camana Bay with the Ibáñez boys when she found out that BB was on a work visit for two days. She cried when she met Ernesto and Carlos, and sniffled throughout the meal. Ernesto was at first shy until BB told a joke, which I had heard at least ten times before. Carlos made us repeat the story of that night he was born. After lunch, Ernesto invited Jalebi and BB to his unit. As soon as they left, Carlos moved over to sit beside me with his new laptop that Ten-squat-a-way had given him as a thank-you gift for picking up his mail while he had been away.

"Much faster, more power, camera. It's my baby. It's better than my old one as I can find scenes I want to watch and move it to a side box. Like this." He showed off by bringing up a live view. "See, this is the water fountain. I move it like this, and over there are tourists having coffee."

He stopped, looked at me and then typed: *SSHHH. People watching u. Don't look.*

I still looked around cautiously and saw no one. "Where?"

He typed again: *I'm serious. Pick up yur phone & pretend ya speaking to someone.*

Maybe he was playing out one of his spy games. To entertain him, I opened my cell and pretended to dial a number, engaging in a conversation with a non-existent person.

Don't look. Sitting @ table @ 11 o'clock.

He was a fast, three-finger typist. He snapped a picture of the tourists, a man and a woman, dressed in bikers' outfits with sunglasses that covered half their faces as they sipped iced coffee and browsed through tourist brochures. Helmets rested on the table. Another screen change and Carlos was in a video game.

"Do you know them?" I asked my make-believe friend on the phone as Carlos typed:

No, I find out who they r.

I got dizzy just looking at his fingers moving upwards, downwards, sideways and backwards on the keys. Weird configurations appeared on the screen, as photos rolled, until a match was found. Her name was Shizu Katsu. His name was Mamushi Takeshi.

Om-7 zinged and my interest piqued. I recognized the names

and faces then and paid full attention when Carlos passed the laptop to me to read their bios.

Shizu Katsu, age forty-five, was born in Australia to a Japanese father and a Korean mother. She was the only child of self-made billionaire Fuji Katsu. At her father's death on her thirtieth birthday, she had inherited his billions, which she had quadrupled, to become the only woman in the top ten of the world's billionaires. She was married to Mr. Izanagi Yoshio, a titled sumo wrestler who had given up his career to help her with her business. The Yoshios have a penthouse on Seven Mile Beach, a mansion in Lichtenstein, and a yacht named *The Orchid*.

Mamushi Takeshi, age thirty-five, was born to a Japanese mother and a British father. He emigrated to Australia in his early twenties. He was listed as a private bodyguard. There were several pages of images of his snake-covered, buffed body. He was a bushman on a short-lived television show called "The Snake Handler."

"How are you able to get into those files?" I whispered as I returned the laptop.

"You mean the SS files? Chico, I've been playing with computers since before I started school. Any small-time hacker can get access to the SS."

"You know you can get in trouble for doing what you're doing."

"I built a block so no one can find me."

"Be careful. The Mafia Boy was smart too. He got caught."

"Chico, he was good, but I'm better than him." He brought up another video game and showed me his scores. He played under the name "Tango," and was the highest scorer. A small square in the corner of the screen showed the movements of Shizu and Mamushi.

"Player No. 2 and 3 are not too far behind, so is player No. 4. They will kick your butt soon."

"That's because I am No. 2 and 3 under pseudonyms. Player No. 4 is close because I give her a break. She's a street kid who plays from an internet café in Detroit."

I didn't get a chance to get over this surprise when he typed on the screen.

They r leaving.

Shizu and Mamushi, empty cups in hand, walked to the bin beside us. Carlos maneuvered an accident that saw my cup fall and, as I turned to pick it up, I am face-to-face with Mamushi. I thought a snake would creep out of his body and serpent its way to me. I flinched and he smiled. I sat down thinking I had to get these snake thoughts out of my mind or I would go mad. As they walked past us, they hesitated for a minute and looked at the screen. Carlos had on display a game of snakes and ladders. They walked to their scooters parked near the bicycle rack, revved up the engines and rode off.

$$\Omega \quad \Omega \quad \Omega$$

On her return from Africa, Jalebi had left a briefcase with India at the beach condo for safe-keeping. When I came home from fishing at evening time, I found her in the living room, trying to pry open the lock.

"You need help?" I asked.

"Sure. I just broke a damn nail."

I took the screwdriver from her and, at my first try, the lock opened and papers spilled out. "Wo-wo-wo. Where did you get all this from?"

"It's all job-related. I have no idea what they are, but once they are sorted, I will understand better. Don't just sit here, help me. I'll make dinner."

Since I had nothing better to do and India was visiting with Carlos, the offer of a dinner that I didn't cook was too good to pass up. We heard the door open and quickly re-stuffed the briefcase and hid it. Jalebi and I looked at each other in puzzlement. Om-7 picked up sounds of the visitor sitting on the bottom stair, removing socks and shoes before padding up the stairs.

"Is there any lock you can't decode?" Jalebi walked over to help Biig Baba with the bags of food he carried.

"I thought I would be a good big brother and surprise my little brother and sister with dinner. You both have no appreciation of my kindness."

It's been awhile since us kids were alone. As we ate Caribbean lobster, the topic, of course, was the memoir with threats outlined of what my punishment will be if anything minutely related to them appears in the stories.

"As siblings, you are so boring I wouldn't dream of that." I assured them.

BB was naturally interested when he heard about the briefcase. Seated on the floor, we emptied and arranged the papers into three piles, which we sorted into stacks by names, all of which I had seen before: The Food Bank International, United and Unified, Church for Society's Improvement, American Canine Society, Cayman Canine Society, The Canadian Canine Society and Stop Hatred in Time.

"This is serious stuff. How did you get your hands on this?" BB wanted to know.

"I'll tell you what happened." She passed some tamarind balls candy before she told the story of the briefcase.

The FBI had sent Jalebi to Congo as a French translator with a group of U&U scientists who were setting up a mini hospital to study native diseases under the auspices of the CSI. The project was taking off nicely until one of the native volunteers was diagnosed with ebola. Mr. Jeremy Richard, the head of CSI, quickly sent his personal plane to evacuate all the workers and volunteers and close down the hospital.

In the group of evacuees was a Congolese man Wonplago Kimbamba. No one wanted to sit next to him because they were wary he may be contaminated. Jalebi invited him to sit next to her. He was a friendly guy, loved that she spoke French, and they chatted non-stop. She noticed he kept a tight hold of the briefcase throughout. After three days of airports, and no country to welcome them, the pilot finally announced he was given the go-ahead to land in the Grand Cayman Islands. Hearing this good news, Wonplago said he would take a nap and stuck the brief-case under his seat. Some hours later, he woke up and clutched Jalebi's arm, his eyes rolling and his body jerking in a strange way. He was having a heart attack. He asked her to take care of the briefcase and made her promise she would never let anyone get hold of it and can she make sure it gets into the hands of his friend, the governor of the Grand Cayman Islands. He died soon after. As she was leaving the plane, she stuck the briefcase into her suitcase.

Mr. Jeremy Richard came to meet them before they all went into quarantine. He asked if anyone had seen the briefcase.

"I didn't give it over. I made a promise to a dying man. Did I do the right thing?"

"Absolutely," BB said as we tackled the mess on the floor.

When it was sorted out, it was not what we expected as we perused spreadsheets, income statements and printouts of bank accounts from almost all the tax havens around the world, the most being in the Caribbean, with the Cayman Islands holding the Number One spot.

"This is a bit too complicated for me. Needs someone older, wiser and more experienced to analyze this," BB said, shaking his head.

"I thought you're a PI and CSIS hired you because you were smart?" I said.

"Me too." Jalebi agreed.

"Look at all this stuff. Companies handling pornography with an amalgam of websites offering live video chats, gambling and gaming, cyber money processing. That pile over there with the names Blue Gold and Green Gold are investment corporations buying up land around the world under the guise of water pres-ervation and saving trees for future generations. Then there is a third set of companies, the do-gooders which are the FBI, U&U, CSI, ACS and CCS. This is way over my head."

"Glad I'm working for the good guys." Jalebi crossed her hands over her chest in relief.

"What should we do with it?" I asked.

"Pass it on to the CIA, the Caribbean guys," BB responded.

"No. I must keep my promise to a dying man. It must go to the governor. We have to find a way."

Ω   Ω   Ω

It was nice of Ernesto to invite me for dinner at Da Roti Shaq when India was visiting with Carlos. Rafiq was once again on a business trip. I knew he was on CIA business and was meeting up with BB and Toussaint in Saba Island, close to St. Maarten.

Ernesto thanked me for teaching Carlos to snorkel. "You're a good guy," he said. "You always were kindhearted. So are your parents. My dad told me that your parents gave him the start-up money for his first business venture in Florida. That first day at the Immigrant School when I stuttered in front of the class, I saw you shove your books down to the floor. You know, an apple doesn't fall far from the tree."

Not used to compliments, I managed, "That was so long ago and you don't stutter any more."

"I do. It took a lot of speech therapy to overcome it. Like now, I don't have trouble with my words. I am comfortable in your company. Meeting people for the first time throws me off, but I sing and it helps. In these last years, I didn't stutter at all. It's back now, but not as bad as it was before. The loss of my parents, the stress of handling my parents' will and looking after a teenager who is hurting, certainly had something to do with it."

"You and Carlos will be all right once everything is settled," I said like a wise old man.

"I hope so. I have a bigger problem. Kaman. I need your help."

"Tell me," I invited, feeling important.

"I went to the bank this morning and there's a big, I mean, a huge sum of money deposited in my account. I called up Ten-squat-a-way right away. He checks it and found it was transferred from a gambling site. Ten-squat-a-way knows a lot about gambling sites as many are registered with the Kahnawake

Gaming Commission. This one wasn't. It was registered in Antigua. As he dug deeper, someone was gambling and winning with my identification."

"That's identity theft. This is serious."

"Very serious. Especially when the thief is Carlos."

"How did he do that? I thought you guys were sort of low on cash." I was in shock.

"He registered with my ID on several online gambling sites. He took the money that Ten-sqúat-a-way transferred for our living expenses and bought something called bitcoins which I think is digital currency, cyber money or something like that. Then he finds a way to beat the odds on the gaming sites and wins. And he wins big. He then cashes out and transfers the money into my account. So now I have all this money that a 14-year-old who is not of age to gamble, has won. Can you speak to him? He has to stop."

That kid needs someone to keep an eye on him 24/7, I think. I don't know if I can keep up with him. With as much doubt as I felt, I asked Ernesto, "You think he will listen to me?"

"You're big in his books. He talks a lot about you. You've become an important part of his life. Please Kaman, you have to help me."

"I'll give it a try," I promised.

In truth, I was worried about Carlos, having recently seen his happy fingers on the go and where it went. He was defensive when I confronted him the next morning. "I did it to help my brother. He works too hard. It's not fair. Besides, ya make me out to be a cyber terrorist. Us hackers wear different hats. White hats are good guys. Black hats are bad guys. Grey hats can't make up their minds. Me, I am a hacker-cracker. I just wanna outsmart bad guys and take their money and give to people who need it."

"Carlos, what does wearing hats have to do with this conversation?"

He shook his head from side to side. "I know, it sounds like Spanish to ya. One day, I teach ya Spanish."

51 Ocean 11

WHEN JALEBI professes she will do something, she doesn't beat around the bush. She had colluded with India and Æsa to organize the annual commemorative bonfire for Wes at Paradise Beach.

Biig Baba was the first to arrive that night. As always, he brought the beer. Engine came next with Æsa in tow and some of his no name whiskey. Toussaint arrived later with Lex Xi. Jalebi had picked up Yaacov and Kwame from the airport. Dara Singh sent his apologies. He was on duty and unable to get a leave of absence. India was having an e-interview when I left the condo.

BB and I gathered wood, dug a hole in the sand and started the fire. As we fanned the flames, we watched the twigs light up and the smoke curl to the sky. There was a twinkle in his eyes. I knew he was thinking about the time I caught him smoking his first joint. He had quickly thrown it, accidentally into the fire wood stacked by the garage which burnt down to the ground. I had never squealed on him though there were occasions when I was tempted to. He reached across now, palmed my hand and squeezed them. Brotherly love, I thought, was such a nice thing. The next instant I was lying flat on my butt, as he took advantage and pushed me into the sand. "I got you again!"

"Stupid fool," I said, as he offered me a hand up.

India arrived with a big smile on her face and whispered to me, "I got the job." I was happy for her. "So are they on speaking terms?" she asked as she plopped herself beside me.

"Who?"

"Æsa and Lex Xi."

"No. It's strange to see them sitting so far apart."

We sat around the fire in a tight circle. Æsa started the dialogue.

"Guys, we've been doing this every year since we were on the cusp of becoming men and women. There are more reasons to get together this year. We all made it through University, now that Kaman and India have "finally," graduated. I say, finally, because they took five, long years. Most important is, they finished. But I think there is more to our lives now. Interviews and jobs."

Yay, for all you guys, I think. Wish I had one to talk about.

"I want everyone to know that..." Æsa never finished, as Dara Singh made an appearance, decked out in his Army uniform.

"What's this? Ocean 11 without me?" Everyone rose to greet and hug him. The ladies shed a few joyous tears. He started to undress, revealing shorts and a T-shirt under his uniform.

"What did I miss so far?" He sat between Lex Xi and Toussaint. Jalebi suggested that we play catch-up, which meant that each person had to tell how their last year had been. BB put his hand up as a signal that he will be the first.

"Oh no." Kwame groaned. "Hope you're not going to do the same long-winded spiel as all the other years."

"I am." He stood up. "I remember the first time we did this. Wes was the guy who introduced us to this divine pastime. So, I say we raise our bottles in salute of Wes."

My thoughts moved back to that summer when Wes suggested a bonfire at the park close to his house. Twelve of us had gathered then. We sat in a circle, under the stars while he strummed his guitar and everyone took turns requesting songs. We were all teenagers then, and I was the youngest of the boys. Now, there were eleven of us. There was an empty spot for Wes with an unopened bottle of beer.

I am light-headed as I looked around the circle. After Wes's funeral, we were all emotionally wilted. It had been such a devastating period of our lives. Each one of us present remembered some kindness he had extended, some joke he had shared that got us all in stitches, or some nonsensical thing he did that pissed us off.

I thought about the last day I spent with him. Wes had chosen to become a musician, and he was studying classical music at a

Cegep, which was a prerequisite to Universities in Quebec. I was studying marketing at a sister school. We met up for some jamming in my room and we took turns playing pieces on his guitar. He had asked me to write the notes while he practiced a piece he was trying to fine tune. Om-7 had a strange zinging that day and I took him off for a rest period.

"Do you think better without your hearing device?" Wes asked out of the blue.

"Why do you ask?"

"Just wondering what it's like to be deaf. You always take off your device and think and then you write."

"I do think better."

"That's your extra sense at work."

"Wes, you're just trying to make me feel good about being deaf. I have come to terms with my deafness and that my life is limited."

"Beethoven was almost deaf. Yet he wrote some beautiful symphonies. You can write music."

"That's your dream, Wes. You'll be superbly good at it too, because it's in you. I want to become a novelist. This is my dream."

"A novelist?" he echoed. I peeped from behind the music sheets to see his reaction. He moved over to the mirror, the frame decorated with tiny flags of the world. At the top, was a purple and white flag of the Iroquois Confederacy done in beads, a gift from Engine's mother.

"You're talking about *The Man in the Mirror*," he sang.

"Stop, right there. You're messing up a No. 1 bestseller."

"Well here's one for you. This one is called 'The Deaf Boy in the Mirror.'" He strummed his guitar and scrawled notes until he was satisfied.

"Thanks." I looked at the music sheets musingly.

"And get your ass writing. No point in talking and not doing." He pointed his index finger at me. "Anyways, what makes you think you can be a good writer?"

I showed him several humorous pieces I wrote about being

deaf. He smiled as he read the pages. "So this is what you've been writing. It's damn good and funny. Although I think you're gonna piss off deaf people."

His dad picked him up that day from our house. I saw him the next day driving down our street with his dad. He waved to me and tipped his baseball hat in a funny salute. I didn't hear from him for a few days. When I did hear about him, it was a breaking news story on the radio. His dad had shot the entire family, then himself. Later, it was linked to mental illness.

I developed the pieces into short stories and started a blog after graduating. No one who followed it was pissed off. Many people within the deaf culture contributed stories. It became a hit within the deaf community.

Om-7's zinging brought me back to the circle. Æsa and Lex Xi had reconciled which erupted into a lot of "yays." When they hugged, the noise was deafening. Whew, I breathed a sigh a relief.

"Well, let's move on. Next." Yaacov broke the silence.

Jalebi stood up. "I want to talk about Food Bank International and how your donations can save lives."

"The FBI? How much money do you want to hit us for?" Toussaint asked.

"A cool million will do." Jalebi answered without a blink.

"Get real Jalebi. Everyone here is trying to get their hands on a million," Ten-sqúat-a-way added, with a laugh.

Yaacov stood up. "Good news on my side. I qualified to race with Team Canada." Cheering, followed by questions. "Training in mountains of Utah in spring. Can use a million easily," I heard distantly. "Your turn, Kwame."

"I have just been recruited by the governor to set up a center for mental illness on the island. It is her pet project funded with her money in a community center. Small pay and hard work as it's a no-frills facility. I am hoping you, my friends can help me to get more funding to open up a real facility. I can use a million."

"Good stuff man," Ten-sqúat-a-way chimed in.

"How about you Engine? What's up your way?" BB asked.

"After my two-year legal stint on island, I have made definite plans. I want to work with the Coalition of The First Peoples of Canada to oversee that all First Nation kids are educated. And please note that my name is Ten-squat-a-way. Engine is officially retired. I need your help here guys."

"Here's to you my friend, Ten-squat-a-way, and to another good cause." Kwame cheered.

"How about you, India?" Lex Xi asked.

India was brimming with excitement. "I have just landed an amazing job, in England, of all places. Something I always dreamt of doing. Translation of childrens' books and designing book covers." She squeezed my hand. "It's all electronic. I can live just about anywhere and still work." She added happily.

"Here's to you, Miss India," Dara Singh saluted with his bottle of Caybrew.

BB and Toussaint stood up. "Private investigators," they said together.

"Spies." Kwame joked.

"Special agents," Yaacov corrected.

"We all know you two are investigating the gold heist in Curaçao. So boring. If you find the gold, then that's something to talk about," Dara Singh added with a laugh.

"I agree," Æsa said. "I don't need the money, but for you guys, it'll be something."

"I'm with you, Dara," Jalebi said.

"I agree, too," Lex Xi added.

I heard Yaacov and Kwame adding, "I agree."

"Enough about fantasy, guys. Kaman, your turn. Hurry up, please. I gotta go pee." Lex Xi's voice cut into me, feeling sorry for myself.

I looked around at each face in the circle. Everyone had a job, had something to tell, all success stories. I, the deaf guy, had nothing to tell. Loser, loser, reverberates in my head.

"No. You're not." Om-7 tweeted.

"I am."

"Tell about the booty."

"I found the gold." I spurted out.

"Ok, Kaman, we all believe you." Lex- Xi rolled her eyes. I watched the reaction around the circle closely. The disbelief was written on most of their faces.

Except Dara Singh. He had an odd smile. "You did, huh."

"Dara, don't get Kaman going. You know he's good at telling small fibs." Lex Xi dismissed.

"Hey, I was joking guys." I felt India squeeze my hand. I looked at Ten-squat-a-way. He had a questionable look on his face. So did BB. There were some who didn't disbelieve me.

"What's shaping up at your end, my sweet Army pilot?" Lex Xi patted Dara Singh's arm indulgently.

"Why are you asking? You all know I am dressed to kill. Most of you make fun of me. One of you recently asked, 'How many people have you killed today?' Well guess what? I don't kill. I am only a drone trigger-holder. The drone does the killing. And if you think it's easy to go home and sleep after that, it isn't." We all stared at him, stunned.

"Easy, bro," Ten-squat-a-way tried to calm him down.

"Cyber warfare. That's what I do for a living. Gone is the thrill of flying between the clouds. I sit behind a screen for twelve-hour shifts, manning unmanned aerial vehicles and spying on people with whom I have no connection. Well, last week, I drew the trigger on a wedding party. Seventeen innocent people, whose only crime was being in the wrong place, at the right time. I killed them all. Some were children." He covered his face with his hands.

No one expected this outburst. "Oh my God. Poor guy," India whispered to me.

I was the closest friend he had, or so I thought. I walked over to him. Nine others followed me. The circle of eleven with arms around each other's shoulders swayed to the turbulent song of the sea in unison. It was so tight that we could feel the heat of each other's breath.

No one sang Kumbaya.

Everyone cried.

52 The Inside Man

THE LADIES decided there would be a bonfire every night until the out-of-towners leave. Æsa was most generous, organizing sightseeing tours around the island and picked up the tab for all the meals. In the late afternoon, everyone returned to chill out and watch the sunset from the pier at Paradise Beach.

Dara Singh excused himself from the outings. He wanted only to snorkel, dive and see the underwater beauty of the reef. We all understood this and let him have his space. India offered to accompany him the first day. Having had rigorous training in the Army, he was a good swimmer and appeared to be enjoying himself in her company. On their return, they sat apart from the rest of us and were engaged in a deep hush-hush conversation which Om-7 could not pick up. Each day, he invited a different person to go out with him. He seemed relaxed and animated when he returned.

Ten-squat-a-way joined us in the evenings after work. He, too, had a turn with Dara Singh for a soak in the sea, as he called it.

I was the only person he had not invited out and it bothered me.

Dara announced his leave of absence was up and he seemed glum. "I feel for him," I said to India when we were in bed. "He's trying to come to grips with the casualties of a silent war."

Yesterday, India had signed off on the documents that made her Carlos' guardian, a commitment she took seriously. This morning, they had planned a snorkeling trip out to the reef, before joining Ernesto for lunch at Camana Bay. Æsa organized a day-long excursion to Stingray City. Meanwhile, I had nothing to do. I had no interest in writing, even though I had promised India I would spend the entire day on the computer.

Ω   Ω   Ω

The cell phone that Rafiq gave me had probably been rejected by the quality control department of the company that manufactured it. Or maybe it was just my luck I should have communication toys that malfunctioned. There was so much static, I had to speak very loudly when Dara Singh called and asked if I could meet him.

He was dressed in his Army uniform when I met up with him at the airport.

"Did you at least change your underwear?" I asked.

"You have no idea what power the military uniform commands, especially when you go through airports," He sounded world weary for a young guy.

Once he sorted out his flight details, we went to the sports bar where he chose a seat close to the big screen television. A live tennis match was playing on the muted screen. Dara asked the waitress to turn the volume up just a bit before he ordered a meal. I passed up on the lunch he offered and accepted a coffee.

We had always spoken to each other in a mixed dialogue, switching from English to French to Franglais. Now, as we indulged in small talk, he spoke more Franglais. I inquired about his family and he enquired about mine, but I sensed he wanted to talk about something other than the present conversation.

When his meal of conch fritters and cassava fries arrived, I reached over for one without asking.

"See how comfortable you are with me," he spoke with his mouth full of food, but had the decency to cover it. "Remember this as we speak. No matter what I say, do not look serious. And chew on fries so that your voice is distorted when you speak," he said as he scrolled on his cell and chewed on a conch fritter.

"I found something interesting from our younger days. Here, have a look. Do you remember this carpet?" He showed me a photo on his cell. "You saw my granddad weaving it at our house. He used a special tool to cut the threads, like this one." He scrolled and enlarged the image of a knife and then brought up a second image of a similar knife lying flat in sand. A long tubular pipe is half buried close to the knife. Corals and a rope floated around the pipe. "Want some more fries?" He passed his plate to me.

I declined. My mood had changed.

"Remember that time in the Immigrant School, when I promised you I would watch your back for a favor once done?"

"No, I don't." Who remembers anything when they are thrown off balance?

"Well, I am now. You know who I work for and you know that I have to reconnoiter what goes on globally. There's a rumor floating around about some yellow minerals dropped off close to where you are staying."

"Reconnoiter? Shit, Dara. You sure learn some big words in the Army. Is there a hint in what you just said that I might know about this stash of yellow minerals?" I asked with just the right amount of *je ne sais pas* attitude.

"I didn't say *stash. You* just said it." He gave me a questionable look. "Just saying that you gotta watch your back. It may be a rumor, but the global traders are watching closely. My radar has picked up that the minerals disappeared while the private carrier was docked at a port on one of the ABC Islands. The stolen goods were dropped off in the waters somewhere along Paradise Beach with a cache of Colombian white."

I had read about that heist. In a matter of minutes, twenty crates of gold had been stolen from a fishing boat in Curaçao by six men dressed as policemen. News agencies compared the heist to a movie plot. In the same article, there was a little map for geography dummies that showed the ABC islands – Aruba, Bonaire and Curaçao, three small little dots in the Caribbean Sea at the tip of South America.

He stuffed his mouth with more food. "I heard you go snorkeling at odd hours on the reef."

"I always liked snorkeling at odd hours. Nighttime has always been my preferred slot. You know this." Dara gave me a raised eyebrow, his head tilted to one side.

"Minerals?" I said unbelievingly. "You're sure?"

I started to get suspicious. What if he was testing me? After all, he worked for the US Army. I had read so many thrillers that Om-7 was going into overdrive. If I were writing a spy novel and put what I was hearing into perspective, I was actually the villain.

"Dara, what you have to ask, is, who's collecting yellow minerals?"

"Here's something interesting. While surfing the data bank, I came across a project labelled 'The Cayman Hustle.' When I saw the images collected of who's who in the hustle, I almost shat my pants. There you were among the most elite of hustlers – unrecognizable to most as the pictures were shoddy images and there was a shark blocking the face. I tell you, man, the guys down at the base are a having a great time expanding the size of your big Italian salami – the only thing that is clear in the pictures." For the first time since his arrival, he laughed.

"How do you know they were mine, Dara? It could belong to any Joe Blow."

I think, *there is no damn privacy any more with the presence of technology all around. Just imagine a guy can be ID'd by his family jewels.*

"Remember, we used to go swimming naked in the night way back when we were teenagers with Ten-sqúat-a-way in Kahnawake? The shark's intervention cut off the camera so what took place after is only for a sharp mind to put two and two together. Rumor has it there's a reward of a cool million to squeal on the hustler, and another million if the location is correctly identified. Easy money." He had his elbow on the table and his index finger on his lip.

A fly settled on the outer panel of the TV screen, moving slowly along the female tennis player's legs as she waited her turn to serve, then it moved upward to rest on her breast. Our eyes were glued to the TV screen.

"Lucky bastard. Wish I was where he is at the moment," Dara commented with a smile. "See, Kaman, the average Dick Tracy will seek the reward by squealing on the hustler. But there is more – much more fun to just . . ." he paused, searching for the right words. "Loot the loot. The challenge lies in bringing it up from sea to land and then knowing how to smartly dispose of it."

I brought the coffee mug to my lips. "What are you saying, Dara?"

"I said it, watch your back. Big Brothers are watching. They are electronically smart and can mess up your life to no end. They can steal your identity and lure you with wads of money. They can even use your very close friends or relatives. Can't trust anyone."

"Noted. But I am not into that kind of stuff." I said.

There was no sense and sensibility to Dara Singh's discourse, or was there, and I had missed it? I am a bit freaked. A minor detail I had overlooked suddenly became a major concern.

"Back to these minerals, who owns it?"

He looked at me cockeyed. "It's linked to a consortium of billionaires. These carpetbaggers all have umbrella companies hidden in tax havens around the world. No one is breaking the law. They basically own the banks around the world."

I think now that Dara had always been big into spills and thrills movies, as I was. What troubled me is that he's over thinking. Was this related to job stress? I could only listen and pay lip service when needed.

"Paradise Beach is a nice stretch of sand by the sea. It's perfectly located close to Barkers National Park. I see a big party there during Pirates Week when the island is overflowing with people in costumes. That's coming up soon. Jalebi is a great events planner. She can raise money for that foundation she is so ardent about. What's it called, FBI?" He turned his full attention to me now as the fly had flown off. "It's a total Caribbean theme – music, food, shows. Distraction from the air and on ground. Awesome. I see it happening." He looked at me quizzically. "Don't you?"

"On the night you arrived, Dara, you had a breakdown. After all this garble, I'm worried about you. You need a break from your job," I voiced my worry.

"True. Can't leave what I do. Not just yet. The Army looks after its soldiers suffering from PTSD," he shrugged. "It's very common in my field of work."

"What is PTSD?" I asked, as Dara was known for using big words and strange terms.

"Post-traumatic Stress Disorder." He wiped his lips with a napkin. "Because of what I do Kaman, there's always someone watching me."

"You mean someone is watching us right now?" Shit, he was worse off than I thought.

During the time he spurted out all this stuff, he was shimmying his head, something he never did before. To see someone I had known for the better part of my life like this, was distressful.

"Hey, do you see a lot of Engine, I mean Ten-squat-a-way?" He broke into my thoughts. He didn't wait for me to answer. "He's a great guy. You know what I like about him. He was always proud of his Mohawk culture. He handles multiphrenia with class."

"That's a new word. You just made it up?"

"No. Look it up dumdum," he shimmied. "Ten-squat-a-way carries a Mohawk passport. Some countries recognize it. He wasn't confused like us. Never knowing which culture to choose, our mother's, our father's, or the new one we grew up with in Canada. The greatest thing of all is that, through this multiculturalism, each of us can speak several languages, a very useful tool in the trading world. Ten-squat-a-way, as an example, works in the most reputable legal firm that trades all kinds of stuff. So, what do you think?"

"Dara, promise me you will get help." I looked earnestly into his eyes.

"I did." He pulled out a bottle of pills from his pocket. "See. Prescription. I have been assigned to a desk job. I handle data entry at the computer lab."

When his flight was announced. I walked with him to the customs check-in point. I am shaken up over his condition as we said our goodbyes.

"You're a great marketing guy, Kaman. You have the gift of gab. That's your job now. To convince the others. Remember, I am the inside man, if you need me. " We shook hands. "Your only worry is to figure out how to get India to keep a secret."

Suddenly, I am not amused about twelve million dollars of yellow gold. And everyone around me was a suspect.

53 Off the Deep End

I TOOK A TAXI FROM the airport with the intentions of meeting up with India and Carlos at Camana Bay. All the way, I kept looking back to see if I was being followed. I thought of what Dara Singh had said. None of my friends from the circle of friends could be implicated to this? My family? Not a chance. I didn't have time to finish this train of thought in full as my phone rang.

"Yoo, Kaman. I am back. Glad the phone is working. Uncle the Drunk sent you some money. Gotta go. Busy here at Da Roti Shaq." Rafiq hung up.

I had just replaced the phone into its jacket, when it rang again.

"Kaman. It's Rafiq again. I forgot to tell you. The Lady Doc was on the same flight with me last night. One more thing. I have a very important message for you. It's from Uncle the Drunk. Listen carefully now. He said, if you find it, you must keep the one with the number Brazil on it. Later." He hung up again without saying goodbye.

The number Brazil? Doesn't make sense. Was Rafiq going off the deep end?

As the taxi made its way to Camana Bay, I had a change of mind and re-directed the driver to the beach condo. India left a note that Carlos had not shown up for snorkeling and she was worried. I went straight up to the computer to see if I could track him down. The word WIRED filled the length and breadth of the screen. I pressed keys and The Hot Babes website appeared. I am worried. Did someone install a malware? I tapped keys and the featured Hot Babe, a full-bodied thirty-something brunette, dressed as a maid, pointed to a blackboard. On it was written, 'Ketchup Kid needs Chico's help.' The Hot Babe turned around and there is a message on her derrière, 'little room at Dr. O's.'

Strange. When I put the messages together, my heart jumpstarts. Carlos is in trouble.

I called India. No answer. I was about to text her when the pay-as-you-go card ran out. I cursed Rafiq for passing me a useless phone just to vent my frustration. And, as I had used up all of the fifty dollars that the pay-for-sex Texan had given me, I was left with zero funds. India had offered me some cash, but I had a rule. I look after my girl, not the other way round.

I heard a movement downstairs and took the stairs two at a time to find Chewy squirming in a corner. Nearby lay his rooster friend. Its neck was twisted.

I grabbed Chewy and his leash and made for the door.

Ω   Ω   Ω

As I was making my way out of the parking lot, a truck jammed with inmates drove by. They all waved and shouted out pleasantries to me. In the last week, the prisoners, mostly those who were in for petty crimes, had been involved in the clean-up of Barkers Park for the upcoming Pirates Week celebration. The truck turned around, and came to a halt in the parking lot. Mr. Rory, the prison-guard stepped out with a, "How are you, Kaman?"

I pulled him aside and asked if I could borrow his phone. Sensing my urgency, he passed his cell to me without hesitation. My hands trembled as I dialed Ten-squat-a-way's number. His voicemail kicked in immediately. I left a message and to emphasize my need for speed, added, '*Ókhsa*' in Mohawk and ended with, 'Hurry up' in English.

"You in a hurry? Can I can give you a lift somewhere?" Mr. Rory offered.

There was that feeling that I had to rush, my other sense kicking in. I accepted. I sat in the back with the guys. As we drove along, they whispered to me how good the new brand of lingo was, and now that Sparky was out of prison, no one knew the recipe. I felt sorry for them because what do you do in prison where there isn't much to do? I shared the filtering process. As a thank you, several cell phones were offered to me.

"Guys, you know you're not allowed to have these in prison." I feigned surprise. I knew Rafiq was their supplier.

"How else can we do business in the pen?" Loco quipped. During my time in incarceration, he had an important title in Sparky's business. He was the "in charge" guy of the lingo distribution. I took the phone he pushed into my hands.

I inquired about Sparky. Loco said that as he and the guys were being driven to their therapy jobs on the beach yesterday, they had seen him in Camana Bay, They heard through the grapevine that the restaurateurs complained about his presence as he hung out only in their vicinity and, as people left their tables, he grabbed the remnants on their plates.

When the truck arrived at The Nexx Complex and I said goodbye to the guys, Mr. Rory came out to shake hands once again. "Come by and visit. Tell some jokes. It brings the prisoners' morale up." He was a good-natured guy with an easy smile. "By the way, how's your friend, the one who set up the bail for you?"

This was news to me, as I always thought it was Dr. O who had put up my freedom money. He must have seen my confusion.

"Your Mohawk lawyer friend with the long name. He works for Maple & Maple."

Ω   Ω   Ω

It was busy at The Nexx Complex with buses unloading locals armed with picket signs. Recently, it had been announced in the Cayman newspapers that Shizu and Izanagi Yoshio had bought five condos in The Nexx Complex and moved in on the weekend. The locals brought their discontent in front of the Yoshio's condos located on the opposite side of the street from Dr. O's unit. Chewy was nervous and I had to keep a firm grip on his leash as he bumped into the picketers. I re-dialed Ten-squát-away's cell phone and, once again, his voicemail kicked in.

A distraught Ernesto opened the door when I knocked. Carlos had disappeared. He tried to tell me the sequence of events in Spanglish, his speech incomprehensible with his stuttering. I saw tears in his eyes and felt mine tearing up, too.

"We'll find him," I said and placed both my arms on his shoulders. "Let's start from the beginning. When was the last time you saw him?" I wished my stomach wasn't so tight with worry.

"L-last night. We had dinner together. When I woke up this morning, he had vanished."

"He was supposed to meet India for snorkeling. She left a note that he didn't show up," I told him.

"I-I saw India about an hour ago. She was going to see Dr. O'Ligue," Ernesto said.

"Did Carlos have his laptop?" I asked.

"N-no, it's on the kitchen table. That's the strange part. He always carries it around."

On opening the laptop, the screen was a live feed of the little room in Dr. O's condo that Carlos warned me about. As I zoomed in, blinded momentarily by the revolving lights, I saw Carlos. His arms and legs were tied to the four poster bed. A red cloth was stuffed in his mouth. At first, it appeared as if he was not breathing. Slowly, the door opened and he turned his head as Dr. O entered. I started to hyperventilate as I stared in horror at the screen. Ernesto's shrill voice brought me back to the now situation. He was calling the police. I took the phone away from him. "We have to deal with this ourselves or she might hurt Carlos."

"H-h-how?" he asked. His voice shook.

"I don't know yet, but can we go through your balcony up to her second floor?"

He didn't know. He would be of no help, I realized, as he was too worried. I had to take charge. I picked up the laptop, keeping an eye on the screen as I climbed over the balcony to Dr. O's unit. Chewy, once again, with separation issues, jumped and tugged at my pants. As I reached down to calm him, I dropped the laptop and watched it shatter on the sidewalk.

The latch of the sliding door didn't give easily as I tried to move it back. I broke it. When I entered the master bedroom, I was confronted by the interspersed reflections of myself in the mirror strips on the wall. It was not the best situation to see myself in so many slides as a criminal. Breaking and entering could land me in jail again.

A moment of uncertainty glided over me. I squeezed my eyes tightly shut as I tried to balance and counter-balance. Indecisive, I struggled with go or no-go. I could not leave Carlos to suffer through such trauma. Om-7 decided for me with his zzzz sounds which was his prompt that breaking bad was actually for a good cause.

Stealthily, I moved on until I reached the hallway. The door of the little room was closed. I tiptoed to the stairs and scanned the open area below. India was gagged and tied down in a chair. I signed, "Quiet. I'm going to get Carlos."

Slowly, I opened the door to the little room, my heart thumping away at a non-stoppable rate. I knew Dr. O was in there from the live feed. I listened for movements, heard none, then I entered. It took seconds before I became adjusted to the lights, and to Carlos strapped in the bed. Om-7 went into a frenzy on hearing Carlos' muffled sounds. I felt something cold against my neck.

"Turn around," Dr. O commanded, as she poked the gun into my back and propelled me farther into the room. She was breathing heavily, a bad sign.

I did, and looked into the beady eyes of my worst nightmare. Mamushi held a snake, its tongue flicking in and out, inches away from my face. He brought it closer and then pulled it back. He continued with this game and, each time, I flinched inwardly. I wanted to shout and scream. Instead, I bit my tongue and tasted blood. Finally, he pulled the snake away and held it at his side. He pushed Dr. O into a corner, grabbed the gun and jammed it in my head. It was so close to Om-7, and he, already in a state of despair, squeaked *Do something.*

"This piece of crap you wear makes you look stupid. I can get rid of it with," Mamushi jiggled the muzzle against Om-7, "one single bang."

Vibe started to vibrate to remind me that it was time to take Chewy for a walk. I pressed a button to make her stop as well as some other buttons in my confusion. She reacted in a way I did not know she could.

"Stupid. Stupid. Stupid. I am gonna give it to you." A voice sang.

"Just tell me where you wanna get it mofo." A second voice joined in.

This confused Mamushi fleetingly as he tried to localize it. I recognized it immediately as BB and Toussaint playing around with the audio feature on Vibe, which I had never been able to figure out. It gave me an opportunity to stand up, but Mamushi reacted quickly and stuck the gun deeper into my ear.

I closed my eyes and said my prayers in every language I knew. Om-7 zinged, *"We gonna die now?"*

54 Urban Lingo

SLOWLY, Mamushi moved the gun from my ear. I felt the blow on my head, stumbled and fell on the bed beside Carlos.

"You," he pointed the gun into Carlos' forehead. "You little shit. Breaking into my personal computer and gambling. Cheating. Winning. Then stealing the winnings. I had everything organized." He dragged the gun slowly across Carlos' face. "And you laugh at me with your hacker friends?"

"Please don't hurt them," Dr. O begged. "They're just kids."

Mamushi shoved the gun into Dr. O's face. "You'd better shut up and find me the tapes your husband has hidden."

"Not so fast, Mamushi. I want the gold. The mute knows about it. The tech guys found out that he was at the site on the night it was dropped off." We all turned toward the voice. Shizu stood in the doorway.

"Holy crap. There's a third player in this scene?" Om-7 tweeted.

"Shizu, get out of here. This is a man's job." Mamushi said.

"What? That's an insult. I show you how this woman can do a man's job better." She flew into the air, somersaulted, spun around and kicked Mamushi in the face, before landing squarely on her feet. He staggered toward the wall, dropped the gun, which went off, the bullet striking the lights. Glass shattered and scattered around us. Shizu came back with a second kick which Mamushi dodged. Laughing like a lunatic, he shook the snake in her face. She aimed and delivered another kick at his arm holding the snake. We all watched in horror as he threw the snake at her. It fell on the floor hissing. The reptile smelling freedom slithered its way toward Dr. O's bedroom and the open patio door.

From the corner of my eyes, I saw Chewy charge past Shizu and ram his bulky body into Mamushi's leg. Buckling, he fell to the floor. Chewy now stood, his body erect, baring his teeth at Shizu who stood motionless, her ear cocked toward the door. In the distance, I heard sirens. She flipped out of the room and into Dr. O's bedroom behind the snake.

The cell in my back pocket rang. It was Ten-squat-a-way. "Where are you?"

"Dr. O's condo. Need help. Where are you?"

"Downstairs in the parking lot." I pressed the camera feature on the phone and made some pictures. I meant to send them to Rafiq, but accidentally pressed Loco's directory. Clumsily, I took out the red cloth from Carlos's mouth and detached him from his bondage.

Mamushi didn't give up without a fight. He tussled with Chewy. When push comes to shove, a stray dog that had to fight daily for survival has the basic instincts to beat down the enemy. He had Mamushi on the floor with his full body weight over his face, his teeth bared close to his jugular vein.

Dr O, all shook up, made her way out of the room. A quiet Carlos helped me to clamp Mamushi's wrists and ankles to the four poster bed. I rushed downstairs to untie India as Dr. O opened the door to let in Ernesto and Ten-squat-a-way.

"How did Chewy get in?" I asked.

"There's a doggy door between the two condos. Dr. O'Ligue's husband had his office in our unit." Carlos finally found his voice, nursing a small cut from the glass lights on one leg.

India recounted the sequence of events. She was so fired up from the experience that she was all over the place in re-telling it.

The basics were that Mamushi grabbed Carlos as he was leaving for the scheduled snorkeling trip with India. Dr. O left a hurried voicemail on India's cell phone insisting she immediately come over to her condo. On India's arrival, Dr. O took her to the small room where she saw Carlos strapped to the bed. She moved to help Carlos, and that's when she saw Mamushi with a gun pointed at her. "How do you fight someone who's poking a gun into your head and dangling a snake in your face? The next thing I know, Mamushi tied up and gagged me." She stopped to catch her breath.

Ten-squat-a-way then took control.

"Kaman and India, you both get out of here. Less people, less questions to answer. As Ernesto's and Carlos' lawyer, it will be easier for me to deal with the law." It made sense. I grabbed Chewy and, with India, ran out into the street. We mingled into the crowd of picketers chanting, "No casino. No casino." India and I found a corner at an intersection with a few on-lookers and watched as the police cars arrived.

"What's happening?" I turned around and recognized Kara's mother, the governor.

"No clue," an old man answered.

India and I waited until Ten-squat-a-way, Ernesto, Carlos and the police came down from the condo with Mamushi in handcuffs. Following them was Dr. O in the company of the two dirty cops.

"Oh my God. Look." I turned around again. Governor Wedgewood's mouth was wide open, a finger pointing to a snake hanging off the balcony of Dr. O's unit. It fell into the crowd of picketers. Not wanting to be part of the mayhem, I took hold of India and Chewy and walked to Da Roti Shaq.

Ω   Ω   Ω

The bonfire was put on hold since it had been a very off-the-wall day. Everyone decided that it called for a good night's rest.

India fell asleep the moment her head touched the pillow. I tossed and turned with the events of the stormy day uppermost on my mind. Finally, I got dressed and took Chewy for a long walk. We were so tired, we both collapsed, I in a chair and Chewy in the sand beside me.

Two silhouettes on the pier caught my attention. It appeared that Rooslahn and Netts were still gold hunting.

I wondered how Dara Singh fared and if he had arrived safely. I am still perturbed at his instability. As soon as I can clear my name, I will visit and spend some time with him. As much as I wanted not to think about it, I couldn't put aside his nonsensical blabber.

A party on Paradise Beach? The more I thought about it, the more ridiculous it was. His parting words too were puzzling. Something about India keeping a secret. It clicked then as I put two and two together. It made absolute sense, and it was something that could make anyone laugh out loud. I couldn't of course. Dara had it all worked out. Bring up the gold in bright daylight when a party was in full swing.

"Dara, you are a hyperopic genius," I said to the stars in the sky.

The small light on the little skiff brought my attention to the present. Netts jumped into it and slowly made his way to the opening of the reef. Rooslahn watched him for a while, then turned around, whistling as he walked toward the beach. Chewy rose, his nose flaring as he sniffed and wearily sat down again.

Rooslahn made it to the water's edge and slowly dragged his feet in the sand. I heard the thundering noise of the approaching pack of wild horses as they headed in a straight line toward him. It happened so fast that, one minute, Rooslahn was standing in the sand, and the next, he was down on the ground. There was no way he could survive those hooves. Or so I thought, until

I flicked on Vibe and saw that he lay in a heap, painful sounds escaping his lips. On arrival, I saw that one of his legs was at a forty-five-degree angle and he bled on his head. I could have left him, but I ran back to the condo to get India, who called an ambulance.

Ω   Ω   Ω

It was a very glum bonfire that we sat down to two nights later. It had become big news when the video of a 14-year-old boy, held hostage by a villainous snake handler, hit the media. Within a day, it had gone viral, thanks to the spare time of the prisoners I had accidentally sent it to. The social networks took over, and this started an echo chamber.

The fire had not reached its full potential yet, as it had rained earlier, and the twigs and wood were wet. No one seemed to be in a hurry to leave for the night. I sat by Lex Xi, who seemed withdrawn. She touched my arm, looked around at the circle, before she whispered, "Did Dara tell you the crazy story about the party on the beach that he foresees happening in Pirates Week?"

"He told you that story?" I asked incredulously.

"I am just so worried about him. We have all come through so well despite the crap that really should have screwed us up as human beings. For me, it was always dealing with the xenophobia. You know, one person's fear of another person's culture. It's a sick culture by itself. Luckily, we had each other, a shoulder to lean on, when things got rough. But Dara just went off and became what he always wanted to be. I blame it on the *gwai-lo* movies. He watched *Top Gun* way too many times. He should have watched more *Jackie Chan* and *Jet Li* movies."

"What does "gwai lo" mean?"

"It's urban lingo. Cantonese for "white." Get with it, already."

Lex Xi had a point, I guess. Not that it mattered, Dara Singh *was messed up in a strange way.* And I am going to do something for him, as soon as I can figure out how. As I spoke to the others during the night, I learned that when Dara Singh had swum out to the reef, with his invited guest, which was one of us, he repeated the same story. I could only admire his brilliant mind.

It hit me later as I was about to fall asleep that there must be a certain boredom in humankind after they have achieved their primary goals, or the need for an adrenalin high, as it was with the circle of friends who earlier sat around the bonfire. It only took me the rest of the night to market Dara Singh's mad-ass project to them. At sun-up, overzealous to the point of uncontrollable, we were all planning a Pirates Week party on Paradise Beach that also happened to include a gold heist.

55 The Party

"HOW CAN YOU forget to water the plants? All you had to do was hook up the hose and spray." India was not happy as we looked at the dried-up garden. "Bernie and Greg were so proud of this garden. Do you know it was featured in The Cayman Daily with a full layout, section by section, as an example of how to grow your own organic garden?"

"You don't have to beat me up more than I've already done. I was busy writing."

"You have Post-It notes in every room and you forget? I still can't believe you forget such a simple task. We have to replant it."

"I . . ." I bit my tongue. Her stern, bossy voice was not sitting well with me this morning. I was about to say it was her fault as it happened after her return, except Om-7 tweeted in my ears. *"That's three forgets. She's gonna win this one. Better find a solution."*

"What's with you and threes?"

"Three is the first number that forms a geometrical figure, the triangle. Three is considered the number of harmony, wisdom and understanding. We are a threesome, you, her and me. And threes are spelled like trees. So you better plant some and save your butt."

I sneezed. He shut off.

"It would never re-grow before their return in three months. And how would we know what to plant?" I knew my tone was sharp and I didn't care, as gardening was not my thing. I sensed an argument coming up.

"That's easy. Find the article in the newspaper and follow the guidelines. We should do this as soon as possible while we have friends to help out. It's a golden opportunity."

"*Hm,*" Om-7 tweeted. "*Ding Dong.*"

"Did I say golden opportunity?" There was a sparkle in India's yellow-gold eyes as she looked at me. "Are you thinking what I'm thinking?"

"A golden opportunity is exactly what you said, babe. Let's go for a walk and a talk."

$$\Omega \quad \Omega \quad \Omega$$

It was an easy job according to Rafiq when I explained the plan. The base of the garden was there, just needed some digging up, a truckload of dirt and twenty bags of river rocks. He had a Trinidadian friend, an agronomist who owned a landscaping company that coincidentally was replanting the grounds and garden of the governor's house. Faced with a time constraint, Rafiq embarked on free trade negotiations. He made his friend an offer he couldn't refuse – three laborers free of charge to help finish the governor's garden, if he could borrow his equipment for one day only. The three laborers would work through the night to complete the job at the governor's place.

When our friends found out about the garden party, India and I did not have to ask for their help. They offered, and threw themselves wholeheartedly into the work schedule, pumped up to the limit. Ten-squat-a-way regretfully said he couldn't join us, then all of a sudden he was sick for work that day to give a helping hand. I was appointed PM, as in, Project Manager, which I took seriously as I walked around giving orders as my friends argued just for arguments' sake. We worked together so that three friends were always digging and re-planting a garden while another three were windsurfing in the vicinity of the three jutting rocks and keeping a watch over the general area where three others went diving from a rented fishing boat. India and I, alternatively, were in the diving team as we knew the area best.

Yaacov had the fun job with a beach tricycle that carried bags of rocks, dropped them off in the water and brought back crates that were loaded into a landscaper's truck driven by Toussaint and BB. Rooslahn, hopping around on stilts with Koshka in one arm, dropped by to check out the three bikini-clad ladies who were planting an herb patch. He only had one comment. "*Troika*, you work in threes. I like this plan."

It was a damn good job when we finished. On the morn of the Pirates Party, the well-tended plantings had shot up.

Ω   Ω   Ω

Jalebi's party on the Sunday afternoon to raise funds for The Food Bank International was a sight to see. The sun was yellow, the sea and sky were blue, the sand was white and every walking person on Paradise Beach was dressed in ensembles made up of whatever other colors existed. The only person who broke the dress code was someone wearing a white cassock and black mask. A holy man. It was at least ninety-six degrees under the shade of the palm trees, where Yaacov, Kwame and I were set up in a special tent with a lifeguard sign. We wore matching scuba outfits.

The Pirates theme had brought out the 'Who's Who' in the Cayman Islands, all dressed up and disguised in makeup and eye patches, and some wore masks that made it difficult to tell who was who. There were more photographers than necessary with a fashion show scheduled which Æsa had organized with some of her famous model friends. When word got around, tourists jumped in with a spectacular show of costumes and painted faces. There were several Jack Sparrows, Big Black Dicks and Blackbeards among the men. The women were more imaginative, showing off more legs and cleavage in get-ups that probably would have caused their enemies to surrender without a fight in the days of real piracy.

Ten-squat-a-way was the only Mohawk pirate. He wore a top-heavy headdress of feathers, which was clearly an amateur's job, as it took India, Æsa, Lex Xi and Jalebi all of their spare time to dye and sew the turkey feathers. His specific gig was to distract and oversee that a certain area near the replanted garden was out of bounds for partygoers. He was so into it that he could be heard no matter where you were on the beach, shouting out, "I, Ten-squat-a-way, have come to steal your booty." It was followed by his crazy call of the wild. Children loved him and soon they followed and imitated him.

Jalebi, with her helpers, were the designated meet-and-greet team, to the backdrop of a local steel band playing reggae, calypso and chutney tunes. When it changed to hip hop, some teenage pirate girls were demonstrating the moves for twerking; a low-cut dress resulting in one case of a titty bong. Carlos had been given a loudspeaker and his job was to encourage one and all to participate in the activities. He was having such a ball with the twerkers that I had to text India to remind him he was being paid and he had to work.

At one end of the beach, India gave free art lessons and did make-up on kids' faces. At the other end, Lex Xi demonstrated her skills as a karate champion, inviting spectators to participate. Rafiq had two Da Roti Shaq trucks parked at each end of the beach. He and Ernesto worked one and BB and Toussaint worked the other.

The fashion show started on time. Æsa's billionaire husband dropped a cool million, which kicked off a challenge to all the big shots who hid under umbrellas of hedge funds and trust companies, but received only one dollar in earnings annually. It brings to mind the cliché, "behind great wealth, there is always a crime."

I took a look at the fishing and diving boats docked by Ghost Mountain. They came out as I had expected.

Trios of qualified lifeguards, in two groups, had been organized to man similar smaller-sized catamarans like the one that

Yaacov, Kwame and I would use for our expedition. Their positions were set so their view would only be of the designated snorkeling area beside the reef. All three cats were anchored in the sand, not far off from the food truck where Rafiq and BB were serving up food. The music changed from chutney to rock 'n' roll, a cue the fashion show was about to end and we had to get to work. The trio of lifeguards would work the beach with invitations of free rides to snorkel and dive. They supplied the snorkels and fins for a small donation to the Food Bank International.

We had done practice runs in the last week on a regular basis with a single catamaran so *that we would be noticed*. When the two catamarans were filled with snorkelers and shoved off, we followed.

Overhead, kite-boarders and jet-packers took over the area above the reef. Rafiq had invited a friend to keep the sky filled with colorful kites. This drew spectators below, their eyes glued above, rather than to the area where we worked. No one seemed interested in the third catamaran that went in and out, except for the holy man. I noticed that his mask had built in binoculars and he was looking keenly at us.

Being the strongest underwater swimmer, I had the difficult job of going down and roping the bags. Yaacov and Kwame took turns pulling these up and repackaging them into the heavy duty bags that divers use for their equipment. Each time one of the other catamarans returned with its passengers, we had to be ready to leave. On the first and second run, we brought up 15 bags and I wanted to disregard the last five, but Kwame and Yaacov encouraged me on with their chant of, "Stop being so lazy."

The only tricky part was when I had to lift the last diver's oversized bag, heavy with its weight, into the truck. I was so tired, I dropped the bag into the sand. From behind me, two huge helping hands appeared and picked it up.

"This is heavy. What do you have in here? Gold?"

I recognized the voice behind the mask.

"Sparky, what are you doing here?"

"Oh, *mon ami,* my friend, I missed you so much when you left prison. *Merci beaucoup,* thank you for the poetry book. I have been trying to find you. I need to borrow some money," he whispered. "Just enough to get me back home."

I promised I would lend him some, if he stayed away from the food trucks. He went off in another direction, with a pirate's gait, and a bottle of lingo in his pockets.

56   The Green Flash

INDIA INSISTED we participate, at sunset, in the couples' competition for best costume. I changed into the Sir Francis Drake get-up she had picked out for me. The trousers were too tight. Tired to the bone, I replaced Om-7 in my ear and sat down in the sand with a cold beer a distance away from the festivities.

I couldn't locate my friends, or, more accurately, my partners in crime. They also had changed and were mingling with the crowd – all except BB and Toussaint, who were the designated truck drivers. I looked at Vibe. They had been gone for more than an hour. Did something go wrong? I searched for India and found her. She was dressed as the Irish pirate Anne Bonny and stood on a platform built on stilts, deep in conversation with the holy man.

A pirate dressed in the most dirty, raggedy costume imaginable walked backward in my direction and blocked my view. He peeped through binoculars focused in the vicinity of the three rocks. Not paying attention to where he was going, he stumbled over my feet and fell face down in the sand right in front of me. I reached over and gave him a helping hand to which he bowed a thank you. The idiot deserved the fall as he wore a mask with barely two eyeball sized slits. He continued on his way, stumbling on his own feet. Five minutes later, he retraced his steps past me and bowed another thank you.

"See anything interesting?" I asked.

"Yes. Right outside the fenced garden, a kick-ass pirate woman and her companion ambushed Da Roti Shaq's truck. She kicked out the two lifeguards and drove off."

"Dara, it's kind of you to turn up after the hard work is done."

"Aren't you worried?" I realized then that he had no clue about the garden party.

"Got it covered."

"There's obviously another plot. Tell me."

I told him how we brought up the gold and replaced it with bags of stones.

"So, where is the gold?"

"At Æsa's penthouse. Before that, it was buried in the fenced garden, the one you just went by. The next day, we moved it to the governor's garden. And, that very same night, we moved it again. We had to bust up her sprinkling system to unbury it. It was quite a job."

"That's moving the gold four times. You sure there are no sinkholes?"

"See, the governor's house and gardens were under renovations. Carlos tampered with the security cameras when we dug up the garden."

"Carlos? The teenager kid?"

"Yup."

"I think my plot was better," Dara Singh said.

"No, it wasn't. It was good. Mine's better. Look out there. See all those yachts. They're all hustling gold. The kamikaze lady you just saw, she's the owner of *The Orchid.*"

"Smooth," Dara Singh smiled. "First time you did something smart, Mr. Colioni."

"Gotta give it to you, Mr. Singh, I wudda never been able to mastermind such a plot."

Dara moved on to join the party. Toussaint and BB returned and were now speaking to Kwame and Yaacov. I wanted to capture the scene so it would stay with me for a long time. I stood up to have a better look. The holy man and India were still in a deep conversation. What if she was thinking of going to confession?

I put the thought aside. She was not religious. I saw Sparky haul-
ing his weight up the stairs to the platform. Dara Singh's warning
words . . . what were they?

"Your only worry is how to get India to keep a secret." Om-7
tweeted.

In the course of the day, when I checked my phone, she had
texted often, which, as the hours went by, became a sort of tex-
tual intercourse. Her last one had me rooted: *IWTBWY*.

I translated it a few times to be sure: *I want to be with you.*

I wrote back: *4EVER?*

She texted back: *Yes, Forever.*

The next line read: *And always.*

The sun, a big globe in the sky, was far west. I knew when it
touched the water it would be a big yellow-gold ball that dipped
into the sea, splashing an indescribable sparkle of colors that
masters of the art world tried, yet failed, to capture on canvas.
Stretching out before me the sea glistened with mysterious
shades of blue, cyan and azure. It was calm.

It came in a flash of light and travelled at the cosmic speed
limit that suddenly my vision is changed. I closed my eyes as
the light momentarily blinded me. When I reopened them, the
sunset was a green ring. I looked at my hands, my costume and
at my body. I was covered in green from head to toe. Once more,
I looked at the water, fearing if I missed just one second, it would
be too much time lost. Right before my eyes, ribbons of green
intermeshed and became a dazzling carpet. Was this a sign?

Om-7 zinged in annoyance. Vibe retreated at the competition. I looked for India. She, too, was covered in green. Her eyes
were riveted to the vista in front of her. I turned from the haze,
blinking as the carpet unmeshed and the ribbons disappeared.

I had read that The Green Flash miraculously sweeps over
everything near sunrise and sundown for seconds only and disappears just as quickly. It is a wondrous, amazing sight and feeling.
You're never the same once you have experienced it.

Om-7 cooed in agreement with the decision I made. Vibe had
no complaints. For once, they were attuned.

I walked over to Carlos and took the loudspeaker from him.

"India Weinberger," I called out. Pirate-dressed-people stopped in their tracks and stared at me. Sensing something unusual, they stepped aside to let me pass. I said her name again, and louder, as I walked toward her with a fixed determination.

Her lips parted as she looked up in total confusion.

"India Weinberger, will you marry me?"

"Theatrics needed here." Om-7 prompted.

I went down on one knee in the sand, and reached for her hands.

"Will you marry me?"

"A proposal," Sparky shouted out.

Pirates gathered around us, waiting for her response. I looked into her big tiger eyes, brimming over with tears.

"And yes, the salt tears blind her eyes," Sparky quoted Robert Burns. He had tears in his eyes, too.

"I promise to love, honor and, maybe, obey you," I said into the loudspeaker, and passed it to Sparky. I took India's hands and placed them over my heart. "And I promise your secret will be mine and mine yours. Never to tell."

"So what will it be my lovely lass?" Sparky roared into the mouthpiece.

The pirates picked it up and chanted along with Sparky.

She took her sweet time before she reached down and whispered into my left ear, and then into Om-7 on my right ear. "I will."

Om-7 had to have a word in. *"That means yes."*

I wasn't taking chances. "Are you sure?"

"Yes." She grabbed me and kissed me like a mad, wanton pirate woman.

The holy man stepped forward for this unplanned call of duty. "Who stands to give this fair lady away?" He had a strange voice.

"I, Ten-squat-a-way, Mohawk from Kahnawake, do so." He was on such a 'gold heist high," as were all the others who stepped forward with, "we all do."

"We need a ring," the holy man said.

"Here, take mine," Ten-sqúat-a-way offered.

The pirates cheered. The music blared. Pirate couples danced. I held on tightly to India. She reached into her brassiere and placed something in the palm of my hands.

It was an old Yankee dollar with a heart and two arrows crossed at the midpoint.

Ω   Ω   Ω

Æsa hosted a dinner for all of us at her penthouse on Seven Mile Beach. Since her husband was away in Dubai, we had enjoyed the luxury of her home in the last week. The ladies took it upon themselves to unpack the crates and spread out the booty on the living room floor. We all had a turn to walk on solid gold, except Dara Singh who did a Bollywood dance sequence and pulled us all in to join him. What a high!

Later, Rafiq and Ten-sqúat-a-way joined me in the search for the bar with the word Brazil. It was like looking for a needle in a haystack.

"This one has numbers." Ten-sqúat-a-way held up a bar double in size from the others. It was irregular in its molding and looked like it was soldered together.

"Lemme see that." Rafiq took it, squinted his eyes. "Can't read this. It's heavy. It's ugly. It is unreadable."

"Rafiq, you going blind. Give it to me."

"Here, take it Mr. Hard of Hearing. Let's see if you can read that."

I couldn't. The three of us had a second round at checking out each bar, and came up empty handed. We removed the irregularly shaped, odd-looking piece from the lot.

I started to feel a bit of guilt at this point. Maybe the crate I left behind for the governor contained the bar with the word, 'Brazil.' So far, no one had mentioned anything about a missing crate. I have to tell someone because, if it does come out there's a crate missing, then fingers will be pointing, not just at me, but at all of them. Going back to retrieve it is out of the question.

"Rafiq," I said cautiously. "Are there poisonous snakes in the Cayman Islands?"

"Yoo. Yuh kidding? Cayman snakes sense people and take off. Why yuh asking?"

"Well, that night we were at the governor's garden bringing up the gold, I thought I saw a snake. I freaked out. It just kept going round and round in circles, hissing. So I opened up the last crate, took out a gold bar and tried to smack it. Then you announced time out, so I left the crate there."

"Wimp." Rafiq laughed his head off. "Yoo. That was the coiled re-tractable black hose. It re-winds itself sometimes with a hissing sound."

Ten-squat-a-way joined in with, "Wuss, you mean there's still a crate of gold under the fountains in the governor's garden?"

I nodded my head.

"Oh Jesus, Mary and Joseph," Rafiq said and put his face in his hands. "That's why the Gov is complaining about the fountain. The crate is blocking the water flow on the plastic pipe. Every time the fountain goes on, there's a hissing sound as the trapped air is released. The Gov thinks it's a snake."

"Let's not worry about it. Who's to know anyway?" Ten-squat-a-way, the thinker, settled my worries. What I didn't tell them, is that Carlos had confided to me about the security cameras and that Señora Governor was short half-a-million dollars to build a much-needed mental facility on the island. So, I had left a crate of gold for her.

Rafiq suggested we should have a specialist validate that it is 24-karat gold. Ten-squat-a-way agreed and Rafiq took a single bar, along with the ugly, irregular bar, to his jeweler friend in town. He called me, hysterical with laughter, when he received the news.

"Yoo, Kaman, Uncle the Drunk said keep the one with the number Brazil. I repeat, number, not word. And that is 272945, which spells Brazil on the old keypad-type phones – exactly what is written on that misshaped bar. Here is the messed up news. My friend tried to melt it in his smelter. Only the surface melted off and that was real gold. The rest of it is a big stone piece with colors of the rainbow. Looks like a big paperweight. The chap said he's never seen one before. Thinks it's worth a few hundred dollars. The other bar is pure 24-karat."

I laughed too. I gave the paperweight to Ten-squat-a-way. I figured, as a lawyer, he can use it with all the paperwork that ends up on his desk. He said he will take it to his mother on his next visit so she can polish it up.

Ten-squat-a-way had set up the coordinates of a company in Malta. With the help of Carlos, he set up companies and e-mail addresses that had no links to him personally or Maples & Maples. Within a day, there were several buyers for the gold, which started a bidding contest. He suspected that the front men who contacted him were behind people with a shitload of money as they offered cash up front to be deposited in any bank account the seller wished.

He had a surprise visit in his office one day. A tourist walked in and outbid all the offers. He had half of the money in cash and within half an hour, the rest was transferred to the shell company's account.

When the sale was wrapped up, we all breathed a sigh of relief.

I had a one-on-one with Ten-squat-a-way that night. He was worried. How did the guy find him? He followed him after their meeting, but lost him in the throng of tourists by the port.

57   The Interview

THE CONFERENCE ROOM where I sat and waited was in a modern building in Georgetown. Floor-to-ceiling tinted glass windows on three sides allowed for an ample view of the port and the sleek yacht docked in the blue waters. Beyond, the sea stretched out and glistened with the reflection of rays of sunlight.

I didn't have to come to this interview ... well, since I had come into some money of late, I was not desperate to find a job, but I needed to tack at least one under my belt. I wanted to be the deaf guy who was hired because he can get the job done.

As this was my first-ever interview, I was nervous.

I rose as the door opened and my interviewer entered. He introduced himself with a smile and a handshake. His first name, Roman, registered but I missed the last one. He was in his sixties, average height, dressed casually in golf attire, which made me feel overdressed in the new suit I had splurged on. He gestured that I sit and he settled himself in a chair across from me.

Om-7 was respectfully quiet.

Roman opened a folder and I saw a headshot of myself. A security check had been done. No worries there as the drug charges against me had been dropped. Ten-squat-a-way had done the legal legwork. From a drawer at the side of the table, he retrieved a remote control, which he clicked. My attention was drawn to an area in the ceiling that slid apart. A screen slowly descended and purred to life.

Underwater images reeled out in a slideshow. The water is brightly lit, the colors changing from orange to blue and then to green with each image. I almost jumped out of my skin as the surround sound amplified the arrival of the tiger shark. The next screen was revealing in more ways than one; the camera shot was a frontal view of my confrontation with the shark in slow motion. My face is concealed but my boys are exposed and no doubt, photo shopped as they appeared twice the normal size.

I felt momentarily ashamed.

Roman smiled as the screen went static.

"Too bad Rooslahn slaughtered that shark for a small amount of cocaine that was used as bait. For a seasoned player, he sure can be erratic at times. Gotta tell you kid, you got balls the size of Montreal. Your last name should have been *Coglioni*. That's a pun on your name."

I took it as a compliment as I knew the Italian word *coglioni* meant courageous. Just the fact that he said the name of my favorite city made me like him without knowing him. "You've been to Montreal then?" I asked.

"Yes. I was there for Expo '67 and then again for the '76 Olympics. My most recent visit was last July for the Comedy Festival." He opened another folder and retrieved an envelope. "Beautiful city. The best poutine I have ever tasted.' He passed the envelope to me. "Open it," he encouraged.

I did and almost had a heart attack. There was a bank draft for a million dollars payable to Kaman Colioni. I re-checked that it was my name. It was.

I whistled inwardly and waited for Om-7 to do the same. Instead, he treated me to a string of zings and buzzes in my eardrums. I started to get nervous.

Roman spoke then. "Surprised?"

I nodded. My throat is dry.

"Aren't you going to ask why you are in receipt of this nice check and it's not your birthday or Christmas?"

"I was about to."

"I'll tell you about it. Have you ever heard of the billionaire's bounty?"

"Never," I answered. Om-7 did not buzz at this little fib.

"I will tell you about it. Would you like a coffee or something cold to drink?"

"Water would be nice, please, if it is no trouble." A million dollars can make any guy sickeningly over-polite.

He pressed a button and his secretary, a sweet-looking lady in her fifties, dressed in a flowery summer dress entered with bottles of water.

"I'll start with the Billionaire's Club. We are a bunch of guys with too much money and too little time to spend it. Well not all guys, this year, we had, for the first time, a woman. And she has balls. She was neck-to-neck with me until you moved the gold a second time. We are ten in total, from just about every continent and culture. Like the average person, we need a pastime. In the short time, when we do find some time to waste, we get together and organize games. Mostly, these are thinking games to see who could outdo the other. The idea is to keep our brains sharp. The name of the game is the Billionaire's Bounty. Every year, one member of the club has a turn to choose a recruit."

I noted there was 'we,' 'they' and 'our' in his monologue, which meant, he is inclusive.

I think . . . *so this is what a billionaire looks like . . . so ordinary.*

I recognized him then. Roman Romanov. There was no clear story on his background, although there were suggestions he was born in Rome of gypsy parents who settled in Odessa, Russia. He never confirmed or denied the rags-to-riches story the media splattered about his elusive lifestyle. Never married, he built a shipping empire second to none. His passion was technology, rare minerals and his yacht Gypsy, which I now recognized as the beauty I could see from the windows. His name had been linked to the mining of rare gems in Brazil.

If this is an interview, I am lost, never mind that it was certainly unorthodox.

"I must apologize. I'm not able to follow this game."

"The game plan was simple. Drop off twelve million in gold at an undisclosed location. Drop hints to all the hustlers. The word gets around and we stand back and watch."

I think, *he meant twelve million stolen gold.*

"Sounds like fun," I smiled.

"It is," he smiled back.

"You mentioned Rooslahn earlier. How is he involved?"

"He's an old timer. Retired now. He holds the title of the most wins since the competition's inception. I paid him to watch over you."

"It still doesn't explain . . ." I tapped the bank draft.

"We each throw in some pocket change and have a bet on how the game will end." Roman grinned in contentment.

This made sense. Gambling is open to one and all.

"How much is pocket change?" I asked.

"On this one, we each threw in five million, winner takes all. That makes fifty million. Best part is you made me a winner." He laughed. I guessed five million going down the drain can tickle a billionaire.

"How so?" I am confused.

"I bet on you. You were my recruit."

Now, I am super confused. "Why did you bet on me?"

"Because you're short on one sense, so you gotta hustle harder to compensate."

"Why would you take a chance on someone like me?"

"My other sense. It didn't fail me. Moving the gold to the octopuses' nesting ground was ingenious."

"How do you know this?"

The screen buzzed to life again. I am fully dressed in diving gear as I tied Chewy to one of the three rocks that jutted above the water lit by Vibe's beam of yellow light. Before submerging, I turned on my primary dive light. Underwater, I struggled to pull the rope that banded and attached five crates of gold together. This was my first of four trips to move the twenty crates of gold, I remembered. The screen changes and I am surrounded by octopuses' hatchings swimming upwards. As I looked at the screen, something is amiss. *Vibe had automatically shut off and I had turned off the dive light, wonder-struck at the beauty around me. Tiny octopuses' babies worming their way out of their sacs, lit up by orange, blue and green light. That source of lighting is nowhere to be seen in the images.*

"The glow fish are not in the picture." I scratched my head as the realization sets in.

"Yes." He nodded with a smile. "They are a string of hidden cameras. New technology. That sure fooled you. What was even better was moving the gold and planting it in your neighbor's garden and replacing it with bags of rocks. That sure fooled Madame Shizu." He laughed heartily and I wanted to laugh harder because me and my friends sure fooled him when we moved the *stolen* gold and buried it in the governor's garden.

I tapped Om-7. "Help me out here, buddy."

Om-7 woke up then. "*I don't like this guy. He gives me bad vibes.*"

I looked at the only billionaire I will probably ever meet in my lifetime. "I can't believe you're giving me a million dollars for a game."

"Why did you get involved, then?"

"It seemed like fun at the time."

"Take the money, kid. You won it fair and square." He walked to the window. "One question. If you had to look back on your life, what was the most influential factor that became your driving force to succeed?" He asked.

I had written this down a long time ago. I carried it in my wallet which had been stolen.

It was my animus that motivated me to prove wrong all the people who classified me as a mutt, a mute and a geek.

But I don't know this Roman guy, and I was done with psychoanalysis. I chose not to answer him.

"I see you are thinking about it. Let me help you along. Just off your head. What was the most important thing in your life?"

Om-7 is quiet. I think. *Love. India. My family. My friends who helped me to steal 12 million dollars' worth of your gold in your crazy ass game. My need to succeed as a deaf individual.*

"There are many," I managed.

"I will tell you what drove me along." He sat down and laced up his golf shoes. "It was always . . .," he stopped to check the laces before he stood up again and turned an ear to me. He pointed to the minuscule earpiece stuck into its orifice. He then turned around and lifted some hair behind his ear. The button was penny size and the same color as his hair. "Being deaf," he said.

I stared. The billionaire wore a cochlear implant.

"Russians have come a long way in this technology. You should consider a change. Your hearing device . . . it's a bit dated," he smiled at me amicably.

I heard Om-7 then. He was offensive in his quest to irritate me.

"Come over and see the difference," Roman invited. He walked to the mirror at the back of the door. I followed and stood beside him. His chitter-chatter is lost as I stared at myself. I saw only my reflection with Om-7 fitted snugly to my right ear.

I am *The Man in the Mirror.*

58 The Set-Up

ROMAN walked back to the table and, from the drawer, withdrew a clear plastic bag which he emptied on the glass surface. The contents were my hacky pack, my wallet, passport and my cell phone. He picked up the cell, activated it and palmed it toward me. India smiled sweetly from the screen, a rare moment when she didn't clown around for the camera. I snapped this on Mont Royal with a view of downtown Montreal in the background.

"She grew up beautiful." He looked at me with a smile that irked me.

"Past tense with a touch of familiarity." Om-7 tweeted

"You knew her as a child?"

"As a baby, I held her in my arms. I know she's looking for her father. I may be able to help her."

I am speechless.

"I need one thing in return from you."

I looked at him.

Om-7 zinged. *"It's going to be a bombshell."*

"I would like you to return the gold bar with the Paraiba tourmaline. It has numbers 272945. I placed it in the batch of gold myself. "

I am totally blank now. It is too much information I could not process.

"It's missing. The biggest tourmaline ever found. I stole it from the world's number-one billionaire who wanted it for the mantelpiece on his yacht. He stole it from the Native Indians in Brazil who found it. I, however, will auction it back to the same guy I stole it from. It's called Quomodocunquize, make money any way possible. He wants it back so badly, he's offering a billion dollars. It's a piss in the bucket for him to own something so rare. I know what you're thinking. No honor among thieves. Know what I will do with the billion dollars? I will give it to a

charity that supports a better life for gypsies. Or maybe I will buy
Antigua, or a part of Greece, or a part of Italy for that matter.
They're all going broke. You know what? Italy may be the better
one. I like pasta. The thing I have against them is they treat gypsies terribly."

WTF. This is one crazy dude. Dumbly, I stared at him.

"You don't recognize me?" He looked at me cross-eyed.

"No," I said.

"I am Zingaro from your blog. I set you up with all the links.
And I was the holy man who presided at your wedding."

I sat in the chair, felt my butt muscles tighten. The whole
thing was a set-up?

"Find it." He said.

My mind is in another area of the world. Yesterday, Ten-
squat-a-way left with the stone. He texted me this morning he
had arrived safely in Kahanawake.

His mother said the paperweight was a rare tourmaline stone.

Ω   Ω   Ω

India announced the following day that we had a meeting in
Georgetown with a Mr. Taye Wordsmith from a small publishing
house in Florida. He was on island and wanted to talk about the
draft chapters of *The Deaf Boy in the Mirror*. In confidence, she
told me he was actually a 'special' friend of Ten-squat-a-way and
I should leave my homophobia hat at home. I had to convince
her, in all the ways I can, that I was so over that phase of my life.

It was all a surprise to me. I asked India how he got hold of
the draft and, with a straight face, she said, "No idea."

Taye was in his early thirties, handsome and had lived in
Montreal before his family moved to Florida. His mother was a
Māori native of New Zealand, and his father was Canadian. We
immediately had a common ground. He had been a student at the
Immigrant School a year before me and two years before India.
I was hesitant to believe him until he touched on the Dragon's
Den and Mrs. Scott, which gave all three of us a good chuckle.

Taye was very excited with the chapters of the draft he had read. He would like to do an adaptation into something more marketable.

"What's interesting is that the cast of characters are all multi-ethnics and multicultural. Being one myself, I salute you for the effort of presenting what will become the next social phenomenon. It's already happening in Brazil. Within the next two decades, there will be more of us. When you look at the statistics in North America, the numbers have jumped to a twenty-five percent increase in mixed relationships which always result in half-breeds like us. The United States of America has the most famous multicultural person alive, President Barak Obama. It is just the beginning before you see more of us out there," he said and pointed to himself, then to India and then to me.

He had an easy, likable way about him as he picked up my cup and started to read the dregs in the bottom. "I see it as a coming-of-age multicultural novella. You're on your way, Kaman Colioni," he winked at India, then at me.

"What about your name? Do you want to change it or keep it?"

"I have always had that name. It is part of who I am." I answered. Ma and Pa would have been proud of me for sticking to a totally illogical name they had chosen for their middle child.

Taye smiled, "Good call."

"There's one thing I don't understand. How did you get the draft?' I asked.

"Dr. O'Ligue sent the first five chapters." Taye looked at India. "And yours truly here, sent me the rest."

I looked at India crossly and saw an emoji of a smiling face with heart-shaped eyes.

Ω Ω Ω

It's been a month since I became an unexpected millionaire. I had not heard from Roman Romanov since the day of the interview. He left the island on his yacht soon after. I decided not to tell India about his mention of knowing her father. Maybe at a later date, I will.

There is a small setback in being a millionaire. I can't splash it around as I fear it might draw attention. I did splurge on a high-end laptop and Carlos is teaching me Spanish. He now calls me 'Noob' instead of 'Chico.' In my spare time, I compile data, visit sites on the internet and spy on people. All my friends are lying low and taking it easy. The ladies took off for a shopping spree to Paris. The guys . . . we are still on island doing our own thing.

Kwame is busy setting up a makeshift mental facility and works closely with the governor. Yaacov is giving diving lessons, waiting out his time before he goes to his training camp. BB and Toussaint are now working with CSIS, The Canadian Security Intelligence Service. They convinced their boss that the Cayman Islands was the best place to be centered. Ten-squat-a-way still works for Maple & Maple. Dara Singh was placed on permanent medical leave from his job. He is now on island working in a five-star restaurant called *The Blue Cilantro.*

Rafiq talked me into a business deal. We are expanding Da Roti Shaq into a drive-through roti place. I invested in it as I saw it as a lucrative business. We are adding some interesting fare to the menu, pizza with seven toppings of curry sauce. We did a sample tasting at the port where the tenders from the cruise ships drop off their passengers. The feedback was excellent. When the marketing guys from Pizza Hut heard about it, they came begging for the recipes with a nice offer. We refused.

Ω   Ω   Ω

I was surprised at Dr. O's invitation for a meeting to discuss various topics of common interest. She was dressed down today in a simple white shirtdress and sandals as we met up in Camana Bay.

Earlier, I met up with Carlos for our daily Spanish lesson. He easily gets frustrated as I am a slow learner. I had to remind him that I am deaf and my brain absorbs information slower than someone who is not, to which he replied, "bullshit."

He greeted Dr. O on her arrival and then excused himself as he had another student to tutor. I saw him meet up with Kara and, together, they went inside the coffee shop and sat at a table close to the window. Today's lesson was, 'listening behind closed doors.' Kara and I use the same book, *Spanish for Beginners*. She is more advanced than I am.

"How are you?" I asked as Dr. O kissed me on both cheeks.

"I've had a decent week. Baron's estate has been settled finally to my benefit. Taye Wordsmith informed me your book has been picked up for publication. It's all good news. Except ..." She tailed off.

"I guess I should be thanking you?" I said matter-of-factly as I tried to gauge her mood.

"I only opened the door Kaman. You stepped right through and did it on your own. You're deaf, but that didn't stand in your way of making your dream come true."

I expected some recriminations about the manuscript not being sex enhanced. She didn't mention it, so I decided it was better to let sleeping dogs lie.

She's quiet. What was she up to?

"Kaman, I need your help." She took off her sunglasses. I see the desperation in her eyes. I must have a face that draws people with sob stories, because she starts spilling out her problems to me.

"Before Baron was killed, a freelance cameraman who worked for the CSI gave him a video that documented the murder of a porn star. I found the video after Baron's death and hid it. The cameraman was murdered. He was gay and his death was made to look like a hate crime."

"I thought Baron died in a boating accident."

"It was made to look that way. They killed him and made me watch. I couldn't squeal because they were holding me responsible for Baron's gambling debts. Soon everyone out there was hustling me. The CIA, the Caribbean guys, the CSI, MI7, who I had never heard about until a representative by the name of Nigel Moore approached me. They all knew there was a video and wanted it. The Yoshios wanted it as the incident was on their yacht and incriminated them. The worst was Mamushi with end-less threats. It coincided with the release of my new book and bad publicity affects sales. So I was forced to collaborate with the two undercover agents assigned by MI7. They had to look good and you happened to be there."

Just the mention of Mamushi's name and my blood boils.

"I am sorry you had to do time in Cayman prison." Her voice was full of regret and I noticed a tear forming at the corners of her eyes.

Ah, prison, I think, it was kinda fun. "To every bad, there's always some good. I met some nice guys."

"Still, I'm sorry."

I see the sincerity in her eyes and reached for her hands. "What can I do to help?"

"The tapes are in a special locker built in the floor under the alcove at the beach condo. I lost the keys," she sniffled.

I get a text message from Carlos: *Keep talking. We're onto you.*

I looked over at the window. My view of him and Kara inside the restaurant is obscured by tempered glass.

"I guess you want me to find the video. What do I do with it?"

"See that it gets into the right hands," Dr. O answered.

Carlos texted again: *That's mine.*

"Also, there are the legal documents for the Ibáñez's proper-ties. I had to hide them too. I feared they would find ways to get their hands on that or hurt the boys."

The text message from Carlos read: *Ya know what that means. I'm gonna be rich.*

"Yoshio and Mamushi were using my condo for pornography-related stuff. I have evidence of that too."

I promised Dr. O I would see the tapes get into the right hands. We chit-chatted for a while before she left for a book reading.

I was about to join Kara and Carlos inside when Kara texted: *2 suits just arrived. Sitting side-by-side in front of you. 4 tables away. One is dressed in white suit with shaggy hair. Looks like your idol Sir Richard Branson. I hear he's friendly. I dare you to go over and say hi.*

I typed back: *I'm thinking about it.*

Arranging Om-7 under my hat so he could pick up the new arrivals' conversation, I sneaked a peek and saw the two suits at a table positioned behind a rock garden with some tall shrubs.

"She knows too much. We have to kill her." Om-7 made a frightening sound. Neither of us recognized the voice of the speaker.

My heart starts to race. Kill her. Who is "her?"

Kara texted: *Have to abort Spanish lessons for now. My mother is by fountain. Heading this way. Looks angry. She thinks I'm working. Going to the loo.*

I typed a message to Carlos: *Any match?*

Carlos texted back: *Kara's on it. p.s. I am not matchmakers. com.*

Kara wrote: *1 is 60+. 2 is 30+.*

As I read it, I remembered that Kara had a small problem with numbers in a cute way. One suit was sixty-odd years and the other was thirty-something.

I refocused Om-7 on the conversation between the two suits.

"How?" Om-7 zinged as he recognized the voice. Mamushi? This can't be, I think. Mamushi was in prison. Did he escape? If he did, then they were going to kill Dr. O. She was in more trouble than I thought. I listened attentively, my heart racing double-time.

"She dives. Make it an accident." The voice said.

Now this confused me as Dr. O does not dive. She's scared of water.

"Where?" Mamushi asked.

"She's going to a site off Paradise Beach," the voice stated.

"When?" Mamushi questioned.

"At twilight," the voice answered.

"You come with me Father?" Mamushi asked.

"Yes. Son," the voice replied.

Carlos texted again: *Found match. Guy dressed up as Sir Richard Branson is Mamushi in disguise. Escaped jail this morning. Wait . . . found match for second guy. Nigel Moore omg.*

Within the last hour, the name Nigel Moore had popped up twice.

I texted: *Who is Nigel Moore, omg?*

Carlos texted back: *Nobo, ya too slow. Yesterday's lesson. Remember Nigel Moore is head of MI7 and omg is Oh My God.*

I read a message from Kara: *Nigel Moore is my mother's boss. Anyone seen her?*

Carlos texted: *Entering coffee shop. She's heading over to see me. Bye.*

Things started to click then. In yesterday's Spanish lesson, Carlos introduced me to the fascinating world of hacking. He hacked into a secret super computer nicknamed MI7. Its main function was to watch over newly appointed ROBOT's, which meant MI7 was spying on Her Excellency, Governor Emma Wedgewood.

This morning Yaacov told me he was taking the governor for a night dive by the three jutting rocks close to the reef off Paradise Beach to see the octopuses.

This is serious.

Nigel Moore and Mamushi rose and went into the cinema. Now, I dislike Mamushi more than ever especially since he's dressed up as my idol. I saw the governor leave the coffee shop. I tailed her until she was safely in her car, then returned to meet up with Kara and Carlos. My stomach grumbled as I smelled food. I ordered two double poutines.

59 MI7

SETTLING HERSELF comfortably in a lounge chair on the back patio, Governor Wedgewood admired the colorful ceramic planters overflowing with bougainvillea and hibiscus flowers. She inhaled the salty smell of the sea mixed with the perfume of roses and lifted her face skywards. "Heaven," she whispered to the sun that, this morning, was playing peekaboo behind the scattered grey-white clouds. There were no super yachts to admire by the port. Shizu and Izanagi Yoshio were the first to leave. The locals had spoken and the government listened. There would be no casino on the island. Roman Romanov left a week later. He had sent her a bouquet of red roses with a note, "I'll be back."

She picked up a mug scripted with 'GOVERNOR' in Kara's handwriting and sipped a local blend of tea. Watching Kara blossom and mature into an exotic flower was worth the move across the ocean. The new friendships with the Canadian clique certainly had changed her to a woman with a zest for life. Why, this morning, before leaving for work, Kara reached out with a hug and said, "I love you mommy. Later."

Emma-the-mother felt tears encircle her eyes. It's been years since Kara called her "mommy." She will remember this endearment until her dying moment, she was certain. This island was slowly healing her daughter's mental illness. She was certain of this too.

Kara's friendship with Carlos also opened a new world and brought out her confidence. Carlos was teaching her Spanish, and she, Kara, was glued to her laptop for endless hours. In more ways than one, she was glad that Carlos' name had been withheld because he was a minor – and the scandal involving him and Mamushi that had rocked the island.

Her personal cell phone beeped the latest Cayman news bulletin. She read the few lines and sat up with a start. "It can't be." Mamushi escaped prison by cutting through a zinc fence. This meant that someone from the outside helped him. "Terrible. Grotty. Another scandal. I must notify Nigel," she murmured. She checked her special mobile for communication from Nigel Moore. He had been out of touch for a few days now. There was none. She would just have to wait until he communicated.

Governor Wedgewood picked up a diving magazine and read about the site where she was scheduled to do a night dive. It seemed like an easy enough dive. "No worries," she said, dropping the magazine on the table. She picked up a pile of photographs of the gardens and looked through them. She was chuffed with the house and lawns. It had been an excellent coordination between the renovations and landscaping team. The landscapers, especially, had worked hard during the day and late into the night to have the lawns ready for the Pirates Ball.

There had been two small recurring glitches, one with the fountain and sprinkler system, and the other with the security cameras. Thanks to Carlos, the security cameras had a special back-up and were now running smoothly, something that baffled Nigel as he complained that MI7 was not receiving consistent feeds in real time. The fountain and sprinkler system on the front lawn were still problematic, going off at odd hours with a hissing sound.

She took another sip of tea, tasting the sweetness of the brown sugar, the sourness of the sorrel and the piquant flavor of the ginger. What a melange. Exactly how her professional life had been.

As was her nature, she began to analyze.

It started on the first night she moved into the house and found a briefcase with the contents spilled out on her bed, all neatly batched, categorized and clamped together. She was shocked as she read through the documents that showed Jeremy Richard and Izanagi Yoshio jointly headed corporations linked to the CSI, The Church for Society's Improvement. Most were involved in felonious affairs at an international level with the money filtered down to the Cayman Islands.

On the other side, there were some corporations under the CSI's cap that were too good to be true. The FBI has done so much in feeding hungry people around the world. U&U, the CCS and ACS were world-renowned for their humanitarian work and SHIT was all over the place these days, spreading like wildfire.

Perplexed, she spent hours on this quandary. The correct thing to do would be to pass it on to MI7 and watch two empires fall. Millions of people and animals would ultimately suffer. She couldn't face the guilt of being the one responsible for the fall of these acclaimed charitable associations.

What a dilemma.

Finally, she reached a conclusion. It was not a case for MI7. Too much damage was at stake. What did Jeremy Richard and Izanagi Yoshio do that others hadn't? As far as she was concerned, making money any which way you can without hurting people was fine in her books. So they filled their pockets too, but that was forgivable, as it takes good planning to achieve such a feat.

Governor Wedgewood smiled now as she remembered how she had planned and turned a disadvantage to her benefit. Her role as a watchdog had not changed, except that she had become a participative observer. It had taken some brain work, hers and Carlos, to pull this off.

She invited the suspects to the Pirates Ball on the lawn. As they socialized and drank bubbly, evidence of their iniquities were dumped into their personal cell phones. That was when she approached them. Thrown off balance, Jeremy Richard and Izanagi Yoshio didn't bat an eye to make donations for the mental facility, writing out checks on the spot. Shizu Yoshio who had nothing to do with the crimes, except she was the spouse of Izanagi Yoshio, gave a donation without being asked.

As soon as Shizu moved on, Roman Romanov approached her and asked how much she received in donations, kept his word and doubled the amount. Strange man, Governor Wedgewood blushed now as she remembered his invitation. "So, my sweet treacle. Are we ever going to have a dinner date?" He actually had a small book of Yorkshire quotes in his hands.

A hissing sound from the sprinklers brought Governor Wedgewood to the present. She hated that sound and so she rose from the chair. The sun had come out finally. She went inside and got dressed in her bathing suit, all the while puzzling about who had placed the briefcase on her bed.

Ω   Ω   Ω

An hour later, as Governor Wedgewood suntanned on the beach, her personal cell phone beeped with unusual sounds. She stared at the screen as information was uploaded at a speed that had her eyes rolling from side to side. Thinking it was a virus, she pressed the "end" and "power" buttons. There was no shutting it off. A short message appeared on the screen soon after.

For your eyes only.

Very funny MI7, she wrote as a response and quickly deleted it. MI7 sent messages only on her special mobile.

Reluctantly, she downloaded the two video links and viewed the contents.

The first was at sea. It was clear the powerful speedboat with the escaped convict Mamushi at the helm forced the lone man in a small fishing boat into the three huge rocks. Witnessing this horrific incident was the famous writer Dr. Olga O'Ligue, who was screaming in horror.

The second video opened with a masked man. He was joined by another man, laughing like a crazed madman, and together, they participated in a bizarre snake ritual. Governor Wedgewood covered her mouth as she recognized the unmasked man as Mamushi. His masked partner in crime danced around with the snake before he brought it to the screaming woman. Within minutes, the woman's body was limp. Mamushi then lifted the lifeless body and threw it overboard. The video ended with a picture of a room filled with snake cages and details of the toxicity of each snake's venom.

Governor Wedgewood stifled the nausea in her throat. These men were sick and dangerous. Who was Mamushi's masked partner?

She should do the right thing as a ROBOT and fulfill her role as an observer. This was another scandal waiting to happen. MI7 did not want another scandal. And she, as the governor, was faced once again with a dilemma – how to avoid a scandal. She cannot let this happen. She had fallen in love with the people, the food, the sea – everything that was the Cayman Islands. She stressed over this dilemma before she finally decided to forward the videos to Nigel's personal mobile. She didn't get an immediate response from him, which was very unusual.

Another puzzle was, who sent this information to her personal phone?

"That little scamp," she muttered as she drove over to the coffee shop in Camana Bay where she knew Carlos hung out. She found him inside, his head buried in his laptop. When she confronted him, he denied it with, "No, No. Señora Governor. It's not me. Maybe it's MI7."

"You little liar," Governor Wedgewood snapped. No one knew about MI7. They were the Motherland's best-kept secret. "How do you know about them?"

"It spies on the government, the politicians, the police, the billionaires, the millionaires, the super yachts and it spies on you. And I spy on it. "

"It?"

"*Si*, Señora Governor. MI7 is a super computer."

Governor Wedgewood felt her face turning red. How did she fall into this trap? She should be angry with Carlos, but what for? Carlos was just a teenager with a special gift and too much brains. Hadn't she used that brain to her benefit? He had only confirmed what she initially suspected.

As she walked back to her car, she had a strange intuition someone was following her. She turned around and saw Kara's friend, the deaf man crossing the street. She couldn't remember his name. Driving back to the house, she had time to analyze her current situation. Her conclusion was, "you're getting paranoid, Emma Wedgewood." Her stomach grumbled as she went through the front door. Craving carbs and sugar, she headed to the kitchen and stuffed herself with Yorkshire pudding and Bakewell tart.

60 The Gov's Garden

WITH TWO HOURS still on her hands before the scheduled dive, Governor Wedgewood opened a hidden closet in her bedroom that housed the monitors for the special security cameras she had installed for her personal use. What prompted her to do this was an uneasy feeling she had about MI7 and Nigel Moore.

She navigated to the first day when the cameras were activated. It was on that same day the landscapers worked late into the night to finish the sprinkler and fountain. At 11:20 a.m., three men wearing sunglasses, their faces covered with handkerchiefs and scarves tightly wound around their heads worked in unison to unload what looked like crates into a dug-out area marked for the fountain. Nothing unusual about this as all landscaping workers dress this way to protect themselves against the heat and dust. One stopped, shook his head and removed his sunglasses, then touched his ears. He rearranged his head scarf and gently removed a hearing device, blew dust off before replacing it. As she looked closer, she saw it was Kara's friend, the deaf man. Now, what was his name . . . she could not remember.

At least he's working, she thought. Many deaf people had trouble finding jobs.

They refilled the hole and left.

She moved on, diligently looking at screens of workers moving back and forth in the house until she saw a figure with a briefcase walking into her bedroom. "Kara?" she whispered into the hand that covered her mouth.

Gobsmacked, she perused several hours of activities for that day and saw nothing unusual or suspicious. Close to midnight, five landscapers, dressed in overalls, returned and commenced to re-dig the fountain area. They seemed to be looking for something as they had powerful flashlights concentrated into the hole as they dug up dirt. Two of them climbed out of the hole, dropped their shovels, and walked to the truck, returning with a tarp which they spread out at the tip of the hole. Maximizing the screen, Governor Wedgewood did a double take as she recognized the two men who she assumed were the truck drivers. Rafiq from Da Roti Shaq and Kara's Mohawk friend, Ten-squat-a-way. She zoomed in, and did another double take as she recognized the two men inside the hole from their social media profiles, and photos Kara had shown her – Toussaint les Patants and Biig Baba Colioni. They were lifting crates from the hole onto the tarp. Once they placed five crates on the tarp, they pulled it the short distance to the truck. It took them four trips and nineteen crates, she counted, before they closed the truck door and returned to pick up their shovels.

Governor Wedgewood rotated the image until she had a view of the interior of the hole. At the far end, she saw a lone landscaper dancing around with his shovel. She had no time for such tomfoolery, but then he quickly stopped and looked up, as if he knew he was on camera. He then pointed to his eyes as if he was trying to say "look." She peered at the screen and tried to remember the deaf man's name. She couldn't and gave up as she watched his movements.

Something must have spooked him as he quickly dropped the shovel, pulled out a knife from his pocket, bent down and ripped open the top of a crate. He then withdrew a brick from the crate, which he used to smack something that was not picked up in the image. The others started to shovel dirt on him and he stopped, held the brick out with both hands at arms' length with a gesture that indicated he was giving it to someone. He dropped it slowly and mouthed something. He then clasped his hand together and bowed.

She knew then that the deaf man had knowledge of the security cameras. She zoomed in closer to his face until she was able to lipread. She did this several times before she understood the three words he mouthed were, "For you, Gov."

Once more, she rotated the view and zoomed to the brick. It was way too shiny or her eyes were playing tricks with her. It couldn't be a gold bar? She zoomed the image to maximum. Yes, it was, and as she looked closer, she saw a whole crateful of gold bars being covered up with dirt in her garden.

She watched the screen as the truck slowly made its way out the driveway. At the turnoff to West Bay Road, it stopped, and two men dressed in security uniforms jumped into the back. She squinched her face as she recognized the two men who she had recently employed: Dr. Khalil Kaleb Kwame and Yaacov Ben-Tzion.

The reality of what she just saw hit her like a lightning bolt. These men, Kara's friends had stolen the 12 million in gold bars and hid it in her garden. Did Kara know about this?

Tired and worried, Governor Wedgewood closed the screen and went to Kara's room.

Kara's Spanish book lay opened on her bed with a colored printout beside it. Emma picked it up. Her brows furrowed as she stared at headshots of Nigel Moore and Mamushi, side by side. Below was written *Padre e Hijo* in Spanish and Father and Son in English. She paused to question if she had introduced Kara to Nigel. She hadn't, she was absolutely sure. What was Kara up to? Noting that it was time to leave for her dive, she quickly got dressed and made her way to meet up with Yaacov. She decided to first have a chat with Kara before she initiated any discussion about the gold.

Tonight, without fail, she and Kara would have to have a mother/daughter talk.

Ω   Ω   Ω

"Promise me you'll never go out diving alone in the night, Kaman," India said before she left for Paris. "I know you have done more than 100 dives in the reef. I'm serious. You should always go out with a buddy."

This warning followed after I told her about my encounter with the tiger shark. She showed me an article that explained how global warming was messing up the sea creatures' habits. As an example, she brought up some videos from the net to show me dolphin habits and pointed out that they feed in the same area habitually until the food source runs dry. "It's different with Harry. He's not hungry. He's lonely. His brain is remembering that he found possibilities of a playmate and pleasure by the reef at a certain time of day. So, he returns. If you look at the times on all the videos we have seen of Harry, he's always there around 7-to-10 o'clock in the night."

So far, I had kept this promise, but tonight was different. Two bad-to-the-bone scumbags had plans to kill my friend Kara's mother, the governor, while she was doing a night dive. I didn't have to do what I was about to do, but in my memory, was Kara at the Tortuga Cake Shop passing out samples to me on that first day of my arrival on the island. Soon after I got rolled, which she had witnessed, she said, "Oh my, you look hungry and beaten up. Here, take this." She held a twenty dollar in one hand and, with her other hand, she reached out for both my hands. As our hands touched, something in the sky caught her attention for she looked up, her eyes widening in wonder like a little girl. "Look." She pointed. "There's a rainbow in the sky. They say there's gold at the end." A soft smile broke out on her face as she looked back at me. "I think the end drops into the waters of the reef by Paradise Beach."

It must have been karma that I met Kara. The next day I passed on the twenty dollars to Carlos Santana. In my book, one hand washes the other, and now it's my turn to do something for her.

I also had my own personal reasons for this mission. One of those scumbags held a snake in my face, scaring the hell out of me. Furthermore, that same low-life pushed a gun into Om-7's private domain with a threat to shorten his life span with 'one single bang' which traumatized him to the extent that I can't even watch *The Big Bang Theory*. Just the word 'bang' gets him going off into a hissy fit. And I really like that show.

We are both pissed off.

Om-7 agreed we had to find a way to take these guys down.

How, was the question? And there were no clear answers. I couldn't call up BB, Ten-squat-a-way, Dara Singh, Kwame, and Toussaint – they were all diving in Little Cayman. When I discussed the bad guys' plan with Yaacov, he started to get nervous and suggested we go to the authorities. I called up Rafiq to brainstorm. He said going to the authorities was a mistake. He had heard from the 'street intel' they were looking into divers who frequently dive in the reef.

Carlos came up with a plan. He remembered Vibe had an audio feature that went off when Mamushi held him prisoner in Dr. O's little room. We all rushed back to his unit and watched as his flying fingers went to work. Following his orders, Kara and I were assigned to research dolphins and their mating calls. Carlos then transferred signature whistling sounds that mimicked frolicking dolphins into Vibe's audio feature. He then dunked Vibe into a sink full of water over and over to test the audio. It worked. As a finishing touch, he added a double-sided, waterproof tape.

"Are you sure you want to do this?" Kara and Carlos voiced their worry.

"Just watch me," I said like an action hero while my insides churned.

I was scared shitless when I dipped myself into the water off the pier and made my way toward the reef at twilight. I was dressed in my lucky blue wetsuit. I saw Yaacov and the governor below me on their descent. I now had Vibe strapped on one hand and another computer dive watch on the other. I hid behind the three jutting rocks until Vibe's proximity sensor picked up Mamushi and Nigel Moore.

The only unknown in the plans was whether a lone dolphin, separated from his pod would show up.

Ω   Ω   Ω

Twilight blanketed the sea with mysterious light shadows as Governor Wedgewood sank herself in the tepid water with Yaacov beside her. She should be distrustful of him from what she had seen earlier on her security cameras and, though she didn't condone their wrongdoing, she found it humorous they had pulled off such a caper. Reluctantly, she had to admit she had a lot of admiration for what he and his friends accomplished.

She turned on her primary dive light at four feet and followed the guidelines of her computer dive watch for the descent. Yaacov was, as always, attentive, checking her equipment and going over light handling and communication techniques underwater. She felt safe as she made her descent to ten feet, frog kicking around in exhilaration at the beauty of the corals and aquatic life in different shades of grey until Yaacov indicated it was time to move on.

She felt nervous and mentored herself with, "You can do this, Governor Wedgewood." She followed Yaacov's lead and flutter kicked. She aimed the light downwards, and saw baby octopuses swimming upwards, all around her. "You're doing it, Emma," she congratulated herself when she reached twenty feet.

She soon became aware of two divers dressed in short-sleeve, red wetsuits in the vicinity. Men, she determined from their physique. She waved to them and continued on her descent. Concentrating the light at different angles, she saw the sandy bottom below her, the wall that indicated there was a 6000 foot drop and the mass of the three rocks that she knew jutted above water level.

The unexpected blow on her butt stunned her so that she kicked out wildly with one arm flailing. The other arm, which had the dive light attached, dropped downwards. Thinking she lost the light, she looked down and saw a light beam. It encircled one of the divers dressed in a red wetsuit forcing Yaacov into the sand. The action caused a silt-out that immediately blocked visibility. From the silt-out, a red-suited diver emerged and was making his way toward her. He aimed his light straight into her face. She started to reverse kick.

Just then, another diver in a red wetsuit appeared in front of her. He also directed his light at her. She realized, then, she was being cornered. She brought up her light and alternately let it glare into the eyes of the two red-suited divers. Suddenly, a blue-suited diver emerged from behind the mass of rocks and tailed the diver in front of her. When he was close enough, he stuck something on the leg of the diver's red wetsuit, and then pushed himself downwards into the silt-out where she had last seen Yaacov. In front of her, the surprised red-suited diver did a helicopter turn, trying to see who touched his leg. This allowed her to concentrate her light downwards. Following the beam, she had enough time to notice the tattoos on both arms of the red-suited diver who was coming up. Mamushi. She was in danger, she assessed. She couldn't think. Her brain was numb. She closed her eyes.

Different sounds reached her ears. The synchronized whistling of dolphins quite close to her, she registered. This was followed, it seemed, by a single high-pitched response farther away. She opened her eyes and focused the light in the direction of the sounds and the approaching dolphin. Harry. She had read about him. He wasn't in the vicinity a minute before. *Eeh Bah Gum.* Was she seeing right? The dolphin's member was fully extended. He swam around in a state of excitement, whistling his high pitched 'eeeee' to another signature whistle. What she couldn't determine was where that signature whistling was coming from.

The others heard it too as Mamushi now joined his diving partner. Both men were doing helicopter turns trying to locate the signature whistle which seemed to be somewhere around them. Harry excitedly charged at Mamushi and his diving partner, pushing them closer to the wall. Swirling around, his powerful tail knocked off the partner's mask and breathing apparatus.

She recognized Nigel Moore; the surprise left him with his eyes and mouth wide open. Harry, seeing an opportunity and a chance at pleasure, had his rubbery distended genitals right over Nigel's mouth. In an attempt to avoid this abuse, Nigel kicked out and was over the wall. Governor Wedgewood had an 'Oh my God' moment. Short lived, as Mamushi appeared again, and now, was directly in her vision. Behind him, Harry charged at full speed, intent on finding a playmate. The impact of the dolphin's 500 pounds body mass sent Mamushi crashing on the ledge of the wall, and dislodged his tank. Emma watched as the tank and Mamushi rolled over the wall. There was no way either men could survive without their tanks.

"Steady, now," she cautioned herself as she gained control of her senses. Her breathing was irregular. Harry's crazy swirling and twirling and her continuous reverse kicks pushed her over the edge of the vertical wall. She grabbed at the edge and hung on until she managed to get her breathing back to normal. The dive light flickered and died. She moved her legs to lift herself upwards and both her fins fell off. She looked below and realized there's nothing to see in a dark hole, but darkness.

She didn't have the strength to hang on any more. She let go. She felt herself sinking slowly, lower and lower into the abyss.

Governor Wedgewood closed her eyes tightly and did what she was good at. Analyze. Her conclusion. *Death awaits me.*

She wondered, for a moment, what the process would be like. A quick one or a slow one? This shouldn't be happening now. Who would look after Kara? She thought of Kara's parting words that morning "I love you mommy. Later." She wished she had returned the sentiment. It had been there, at the tip of her tongue, she just couldn't get it out. Now, it was too late. The small part of her brain that was still thinking, admonished, "it is never too late."

For the first time that day, Emma-the-mother bypassed the need to analyze this and analyze that and went straight to a conclusion. *I have to live.*

In the darkness, she grabbed out randomly until she felt the wall, steadied herself, before she arched her body and sunk her feet into it. Slowly, she started to spider-climb the wall.

From behind, she felt hands under her armpits. The arms were lifting her upwards. She felt the roughness of the wall as she was bodily pulled over. The water had a different buoyancy as her bare feet grazed against fine sand. Finally, she opened her eyes and, through a beam of light, she recognized the deaf man. He was dressed in a blue wet suit. She was safe. She closed her eyes again. She still couldn't remember his name.

He held onto her arm all the way through the long and slow ascent. When they surfaced. Governor Wedgewood looked at her saviour. She remembered then that the deaf man's name was Kaman Colioni.

Ω   Ω   Ω

Emma had the mother-daughter talk with Kara that night. Kara had finally straightened out her numbers, adding her sixes and sevens to figure out that Nigel Moore was a farce, as was MI7. She kept watch on Nigel's activities and found he visited Mamushi in the Cayman prison. As she dug deeper, she found out Mamushi was Nigel's son born out of a relationship with a Japanese woman. Mamushi had opted to use his mother's surname.

Knackered out, Governor Wedgewood downed several *Jagerbombs* before she entered the bathroom. She didn't mention the gold to Kara. For now, it was her secret. She understood now that, although Kara was bipolar, she had an intelligence that was surprising and amazing. Kara wasn't the only person who suffered from this disorder. More than ever, she was determined to see the full fruition of a mental facility on the island she had fallen in love with.

"What a night," Governor Wedgewood murmured as she slipped out of her new cotton panties and admired her naked body in the long mirror on the bathroom door. She turned around to open the faucet, screamed, and ran out the front door into the spray of the fountains.

There was a snake in the shower.

EPILOGUE

I AM BACK IN the Cayman Prison. So are my friends, the guys only. We got caught red-handed.

I am sequestered in a one-person cell with a toilet and a sink because of my hearing impairment. Rafiq, Yaacov, Dara, Kwame, Toussaint and Biig Baba are holed up in a common room where prisoners are kept until charges have been laid. Ten-squat-a-way was here too. He was the big mouth who started blabbering and got us all in this pickle. He was released when Rafiq vouched that he had nothing to do with the incident.

I spent the night thinking about my time in the Cayman Islands. I am no longer bitter and lost. I used to think of myself as a milquetoast, but these days, I think of myself more of a cognoscente – a deaf man with a superior knowledge in the fine art of surviving with his disability. I also used to dream of being a novelist who wrote kick-ass thrillers and, well, you know, that didn't work out. I'm not beating myself up, because I like *The Deaf Boy in the Mirror*. It won't make me a millionaire, but I am that already. I look at the experience as nothing ventured, nothing gained. I think about the tourmaline that the billionaire desperately wants and I see an opportunity, not one to fall back on, but one to go forward with. As for love, India has shown me that a thousand words cannot describe the experience.

It was stupid how it happened, how we got caught and how we ended up in prison. We were all at the Café-del-Sol in Camana Bay celebrating Ten-squat-a-way's return and discussing Toussaint's proposal to build a hockey arena on the island. Om-7 was responsible for the incident. He was picking up conversation from a table where some senior Italian ladies were discussing what they would do with Giorgio Clooney if they had a night with him and laughing hysterically at the different suggestions and positions put forward. The amplified laughter was too much. I took Om-7 off.

Just then, a group of tourists led by a man holding a map stopped to ask me a question and I signed in response, my hands moving in all directions. The man grabbed my hands to make me stop signing and this made me overreact. I flipped out. Ten-squat-a-way got up and pushed him away, blabbering off insults at the same time. Others from the man's group came to his defense and attacked Ten-squat-a-way. Rafiq threw the first punch. All the guys at our table rose and, before I knew it, there was a fight around me. The police arrived, broke up the fight and brought us to prison.

The prison supervisor, after we told him the other party started the fight, said he would request a tape of the webcam from the management at Camana Bay. In the meantime, we have to spend the night in prison. Using my rights to 'one phone call,' I telephoned the one person who knew the webcam inside and out. When I explained our predicament to Carlos Santana, he said, "*Oye come va*. Listen, how it goes. Chico, the ketchup kid, promises ya'all be out tomorrow."

I don't blame the unknown man for what happened because there's a lot of people out there who don't know *that you should never, ever grab a deaf person's hands. This is like putting your hand over the mouth of someone with perfect hearing.*

Ω   Ω   Ω

AUTHOR'S NOTE

My inspiration for The Cayman Hustle

On a cold winter day in Montreal, a six-year-old boy rang my doorbell. His hands and fingers were moving in all directions. I tried to have a conversation with him and he continued with more hand movements, all the while smiling. I misinterpreted this unusual visitor as a rude child and so I waved him goodbye and closed the door. He returned five minutes later with his voice – his older brother who explained that they had just moved into the neighbourhood and his deaf brother was looking for friends. He wanted to play with my children. This deaf child was a constant visitor and an absolute joy to our household until his family moved away.

I never forget him nor that day I was so judgemental.

On a very hot summer day on a beach in The Cayman Islands, I met a twenty-five year old deaf college student whose field of study was Neuroscience. He, and his friends were having a reunion. For a week, I observed the camaraderie that they shared and how the friends were always looking out for the well- being of this deaf man.

And I think again of that deaf boy in Montreal. The Cayman Hustle was born on that beautiful beach. But it is my deaf sister who cannot function without a hearing aid in each ear who truly inspired me to write a novel with a deaf protagonist.

There are many deaf children in some parts of the world whose parents cannot afford hearing devices. Funds from the sale of this book will go toward foundations that fit deaf children with hearing devices in underdeveloped countries and make their world a better place.

ACKNOWLEDGEMENTS

Foremost, I would like to thank my husband Giuseppe for pushing me to the finish line and my children Robin, Nodin and Sonjali for their humorous stories at the dinner table, some of which have been fictionalized into this book.

I am very grateful to Dr. Karim Sorefan, Dr. Elizabeth Alvey, Dr. Fred Shiff, Devesh Persaud and Jorge Mendez for their help with the multi-cultural content.

To my dear friend Sirjirick Phillip Gibson, "He who carries the Sun," I am forever indebted to you for your help throughout with Mohawk history. My thanks to Jon Reisfeld for pulling the story out of me. Steve Eisner who believed in the voice, and the fantastic group of writers at When Words Count Retreat in Vermont who encouraged me on.

Also, Steve Bonspiel at the Eastern Door who opened doors for me in Kahnawake, The Kahnawake Cultural Center, Tsi Niionkwarihò:ten Tsitewaháhara'n Center, MCK Language and Culture Training Program and The Kahnawake Library – Niá:wen for sharing your knowledge and resources.

Thank you Bernadette Devlin and Greg Elcock for your help in the Cayman Islands, Michael Jackson for your beautiful music, and Devi Capey, my hearing impaired sister – you are and still is my first heroine, with fond memories.

CPSIA information can be obtained
at www.ICGtesting.com
Printed in the USA
LVOW12s1526281016

510723LV00001B/69/P

9 780995 322707